Praise for DESTROYER:

"This series has lost none of its vigor. *Destroyer* is an excellent adventure."
—*The Denver Post*

"Well-developed characters, fine style, and intense psychological realism. Cherryh's many readers should snap this one up."
—*Publishers Weekly*

"With every new "Foreigner" novel, Cherryh strengthens the saga's already imposing reputation as one of the foremost series exploring the complex and delicate relationships between human and alien cultures. Cherryh's Foreigner saga is cerebral science fiction at its very best—as entertaining as it is contemplative."
.   —*The Barnes & Noble Review*

and the "Foreigner" series:

"Cherryh's gift for conjuring believable alien cultures is in full force here, and her characters . . . are brought to life with a sure and convincing hand."
—*Publishers Weekly*

"A seriously probing, thoughtful, intelligent piece of work, with more insight in half a dozen pages than most authors manage in half a hundred."   —*Kirkus*

"Close-grained and carefully constructed . . . a book that will stick in the mind for a lot longer than the usual adventure romp."
—*Locus*

"A large new Cherryh novel is always welcome . . . a return to the anthropological science fiction in which she has made such a name is a double pleasure . . . superlatively drawn aliens and characterization."
—*Chicago Sun-Times*

DAW TITLES BY C. J. CHERRYH

THE FOREIGNER UNIVERSE

FOREIGNER	PRECURSOR
INVADER	DEFENDER
INHERITOR	EXPLORER

DESTROYER
PRETENDER*

THE ALLIANCE-UNION UNIVERSE

DOWNBELOW STATION
MERCHANTER'S LUCK
FORTY THOUSAND IN GEHENNA
SERPENT'S REACH
AT THE EDGE OF SPACE Omnibus:
Brothers of Earth | Hunter of Worlds
THE FADED SUN Omnibus:
Kesrith | Shon'jir | Kutath

THE CHANUR NOVELS

THE CHANUR SAGA Omnibus:
*The Pride of Chanur | Chanur's Venture |
The Kif Strike Back*
CHANUR'S HOMECOMING
CHANUR'S LEGACY

THE MORGAINE CYCLE

THE MORGAINE SAGA Omnibus:
Gate of Ivrel | Well of Shiuan | Fires of Azeroth
EXILE'S GATE

OTHER WORKS

THE DREAMING TREE OMNIBUS:
The Tree of Swords and Jewels | The Dreamstone
ALTERNATE REALITIES Omnibus:
Port Eternity | Wave Without a Shore | Voyager in Night
THE COLLECTED SHORT FICTION OF
C.J. CHERRYH
ANGEL WITH THE SWORD
CUCKOO'S EGG

*Coming next month in hardcover from DAW

C. J. CHERRYH

DESTROYER

DAW BOOKS, INC.
DONALD A. WOLLHEIM, FOUNDER
375 Hudson Street, New York, NY 10014

ELIZABETH R. WOLLHEIM
SHEILA E. GILBERT
PUBLISHERS
http://www.dawbooks.com

First Paperback Printing, February 2006

1   2   3   4   5   6   7   8   9   10

 DAW TRADEMARK REGISTERED
U.S. PAT. OFF. AND FOREIGN COUNTRIES
—MARCA REGISTRADA
HECHO EN U.S.A.

PRINTED IN THE U.S.A.

DESTROYER

1

Spider plants had taken over the cabin, cascading sheets of spider plants growing from pots improvised from sealed sections of plastic pipe arranged in racks around the ceiling of every wall. They made showers of green runners and gave out clouds of miniature pale-edged spider babies that swayed in the gusts from vents, in the opening of doors.

The plants were fortunate, *kabiu*, to atevi sensibilities. They were alive. They grew, they changed, masking steel walls that never changed, and in their increasingly abundant green, they reminded a voyager that ahead of them in the vast deep dark of space was a planet where atevi and humans shared natural breezes, enjoyed meadows and forests and the occasional wild mountain-bred storm, in an environment where, indeed, growth was lush and abundant.

"The planting is becoming extravagant, nandi," Narani had once suggested, that excellent gentleman, when the pipe-pots were only ten, and ran along only one wall. "Bindanda wishes to inquire if we should simply discard the excess at this point."

Bren Cameron's devoted staff had by now offered spider plants to every colonist in the deck above, and bestowed them on every crew cabin that would accept them, where he supposed they likewise proliferated to the limit of tolerance. He had consulted the ship's lab, to whom he had given the first offshoots, fearing the spread of his house plants might provide lifesupport a real problem . . . but lifesupport declared that, no, living biomass provided their systems no problem at all, except as they tied up water and nutrients. The ship had plenty of both, and the chief disruption to the closed loop of life aboard *Phoenix,* so they said, was simply that the plants made "an interesting intervention" in the daily oxygen/carbon dioxide cycle, the energy budget, humidity and climate control. "A catastrophic die-off would be a matter for concern," lifesupport told him, "but we would of course consume the biomass that might result. Slow changes, we accommodate quite well. We find this an interesting variance in the system. They balance humidity. And they clean the air."

So the plants grew, and showered out their runners with baby spiders unrestrained over the two years of their voyage, proceeding from one wall, to two, and now four, having found conditions very much to their liking—the plants especially liked their intervals in folded space, such as now, when plants thrived in crazy abundance and intelligent beings operated on minimal intellect. The spider plants cured dry air, static, and nosebleeds, that persistent malady aboard. They were, most of all, *alive,* and in the metal world of the ship, they were a bizarre sort of hobby.

Pity, Bren thought, that he hadn't brought along tomatoes instead of inedible house plants, preserved tomatoes having completely run out aboard, in the two-plus years of their voyage—tomato sauce depleted along with other commodities, like the highly favored sugar candies. The better part of three thousand souls aboard consumed a great deal of sugar and fruit, fruit being novel to a spacefaring population, the simplest flavors generally being favored over more complex tastes.

He, himself, was *not* from a spacefaring population, and he dreaded the day that their daily fare would get down to the yeasts and algaes that had been lonely Reunion Station's ordinary fare for the few centuries of its existence.

Reunion was now in other hands. Its population was aboard, headed for a refuge and a new life on a station orbiting what they understood to be an eden, a reservoir of fruit candies and other such delights.

They consumed stores at a higher rate than planned. Now tea was running short. Caffeine was about to run out altogether. *That* was a crisis.

Bren took his carefully cherished cup—he afforded himself one small pot a day and kept a careful eye on what remained in their stores, knowing that his atevi staff would sacrifice their own ration to provide for him till it ran out, if he did not insist they share.

This late evening as usual, after a very nice dinner, he seated himself at his writing-desk, which supported his computer along with the paper, pen, formal stationery and wax-jack of an atevi gentleman . . . not the only paper aboard, but close to it. He set his teacup down precisely at the proper spot, just so, opened the computer, and resumed his letters, a tapping of keys so rapid it made a sort of music; it had a rhythm, a living rhythm of his thoughts, like a conversation with himself.

He wore his lightest coat in the snug, pleasantly humidified warmth of his cabin, maintained only a minimum of lace at the cuffs—in the general diminution of intelligence and enterprise, no one stirred much during their transit of folded space, few people went visiting, and entertainments were mostly, during such times, television of the very lowest order. Staff gathered in the dining hall to watch dramas from the human archive . . . but there were no longer refreshments, under the general rationing, and the whole affair had begun to assume a worn, threadbare cheerfulness, which he usually left early.

He dressed, every day, wore the clothes of a gentleman, which his staff meticulously prepared and laid out daily . . . the lace now unstarched, that commodity having run short, too, but the shirts carefully ironed, the knee-length coats immaculate. He read in the afternoons. He was learning ancient Greek, long an ambition of his, and working on a kyo grammar—being a linguist, the translator, the paidhi, long before he became Lord of the Heavens. He had been charged with retrieving a few thousand inconvenient colonists and getting them back to safe territory, and in the process he had discovered a further need for his services. He had words. He could make a dictionary and a grammar. He reverted to his old scholarly duties to keep his mind sharp.

He likewise kept up his letters, daily, his evening ritual, along with the after-dinner tea. He had a cyclic record of the rise in the quality of his output during sojourns in normal space, when his brain formed connections, and, longer still, those intervals of folded space, when his prose suffered jumps of logic and grammar and other flaws. In the latter instance he learned that the ship's crew had a reason for rules and discipline and careful procedure. He found that strict schedule and meticulous procedure afforded his dimmer days a necessary structure, when it was oh so easy to grow slovenly in habit. Rules and formality were increasingly necessary for him and the staff, when getting out of bed these days took an act of moral fortitude.

But every day his staff dressed him completely and properly, no matter that he seldom called on the upstairs neighbors and received no guests. He was *their* necessary focus, as his letters and his dictionary had become the purpose of his interminable days—and he went through his meticulously ordered daily routine on this day as on over seven hundred days before this. The letters, the one to his brother Toby, and the other to Tabini, aiji of the *aishidi'tat*, the association of all atevi associations, each totaled above a thousand pages. In all reason, he doubted either his brother or the aiji who had commissioned him to this voyage would ever have the patience to read what amounted to a self-indulgent diary—well, they would read certain key sections he had flagged as significant, but that was not the point of creating it in such detail.

Sanity was. The ability to look up a given day and remember they had made progress.

Dear Toby, he began his day's account, *a peaceful night and a day as dull as yesterday, which, considering our adventures of time past, I still count as good.*

What have I done since yesterday?

I solved that puzzle I was working on. I learned a new Greek verb form. The aorist isn't as hard as advertised, compared to atevi grammar. I reviewed the latest race car design. Remember I had lunch with Gin and her staff last week, and we have that race in their hallway next week, Cajeiri's team, namely us, against Gin's engineers, with some of the crew betting on the outcome. I have to bet with my own staff. She has to bet with hers. I have second thoughts on the bet between us being in tea, of which Bindanda tells me I have one cannister remaining, and they are likely as short, by now. I think we should have kept it to sugar packets. We have more of those. Either of us losing will put us in truly desperate straits for caffeine. I think I should propose to Gin that we change the bet to sugar. And it's the theory of a bet that matters, isn't it?

Meanwhile Cajeiri's birthday is coming on apace. He just this morning proposed we turn the birthday party into a slumber party—God knows where he learned that term, but I have my suspicions he's seen one too many movies—and he's insisting on inviting his young acquaintances from upstairs. Cenedi has informed him that propriety wouldn't let Irene attend an all-night party with boys. Cajeiri absolutely insists on both Irene and Artur, and Gene, of course, and now he wants no chaperons at all. Atevi security is sensibly appalled . . .

He deleted that paragraph—not the first he'd set down and then, considering the reputation and future safety of the boy who someday would be aiji in Shejidan, erased from the record.

Too many movies, too much television, too much association with humans, the aiji-dowager said, and he by no means disagreed with that assessment of young Cajeiri's social consciousness and opinions. But what could they do? He was a growing boy, undergoing this stultifying trip through folded space during two critical, formative years when youngsters should be asking questions and poking into everything at hand. And Cajeiri couldn't. He couldn't open doors at will, couldn't explore everything he took into his head to do—he couldn't breathe without the dowager's bodyguards somewhere being aware of it. There were no other atevi children aboard. No one had considered that fact, Tabini-aiji having had the notion for his son to go on this voyage as an educational experience, as a way of making his heir acquainted with the new notions of space and distance and life in orbit. Argument to the contrary had not prevailed, and so what was there for a six-year-old's active mind on their year-long voyage out to Reunion Station? What had they to entertain a six-year-old?

The collected works of humanity in the ship's archive. Television. Movies. Books like *Treasure Island, Dinosaurs!* and *Riders of the Purple Sage.* The six-year-old had already become much too fluent in human language, and remained absolutely convinced dinosaurs were contemporaneous with human urban civilization, possibly even living on Mospheira, right across from the mainland. Hadn't he seen the movies? How could one get a picture of dinosaurs, he pointed out, without cameras being there?

And then—then they had picked up their human passengers from the collapse of Reunion, 4043 passengers, to be exact, now 4078 going on 4149 in the enthusiasm of people no longer restricted and licensed to have a precise number of children. On the return leg, there were 638 children aboard, an ungodly number of them under a year of age, and seven of them of Cajeiri's age, or thereabouts.

Children. Children let loose from a formerly regimented, restrictive environment. And just one deck below, a very lonely, very bored atevi youngster, heir to a continent-spanning power, who had rarely been restrained from his ambitions where they didn't compromise the ship's systems.

It was like holding magnets apart, these opposites of amazingly persistent and inventive attraction. Once they were aware of each other, they had to meet. The situation made everybody, atevi and human, more than anxious. Two sets of human parents had vehemently drawn their children back from all association with Cajeiri, fearing God knew what insubstantial harm. Or substantial harm, to be honest: Cajeiri, at seven years of age, had most of the height and strength of a grown human—he could hardly restrain the boy if he took a notion to rebel.

Cajeiri had hurt no one, physically. He was ever so careful with his fragile friends. He was not given to tantrums or temper outbursts, which, considering his parentage, was extremely remarkable restraint for a seven-year-old. He had, of the remaining five children, a small, close circle of human associates who dealt with him almost daily—a clutch of mostly awed human children who kept Cajeiri busy racing cars and playing space explorer and staying mostly out of trouble . . . if one discounted the fact that they had learned to slip about with considerable skill, using service doors and other facilities that were not off-limits in the atevi section of the ship.

That was one problem they had to cope with.

There was another, lately surfaced, but the first of all fears, namely that these young human associates *told* the boy things. Cautioned never to use the words love, or friendship, or aishi, or man'chi, and constantly admonished, particularly by the paidhi, they had found others he should have forbidden, had he halfway considered. Notably, the words *birthday party*. They had told him, and, worse, invited him to Artur's twelfth, an occasion of supreme revelation to an atevi youngster.

Refreshments. Presents. Parties. Highly sugared revels.

Four months ago, Cajeiri had served notice he wanted his own birthday celebration, his eighth being the imminent one, and the one he looked forward to celebrating with his—no, one still did not say *friends,* that word of extreme ill omen between atevi and humans. His *associates.* His co-conspirators.

No, had been the first word from Cajeiri's great-grandmother, early and firm: aside from all other considerations, the eighth was not an auspicious or fortunate year, in atevi tradition. The dowager refused, even cut Cajeiri off from his associates for a week, seeing trouble ahead. So Cajeiri's determined little band had attempted to corrupt the ship's communication system (Cajeiri's clever trick with the computers) to contact one another in spite of the ban.

Break them up and they fought the harder to reach one another. *Aishi. Association.* No question of it. Be it human or be it atevi, a bond had formed between Cajeiri and the particular four of that five who, inexperienced in the facts of human history, innocent of a war that had nearly devastated the atevi homeworld over interpersonal misinterpretations, secretly regarded Cajeiri as their *friend,* as he called them *aishidi,* that word which did not, emphatically not, mean *friends*—vocabulary which didn't match up emotionally or behaviorally, a circumstance of thwarted expectations which had historically had a devastatingly bad outcome in human-atevi history.

And here it was, like the planet's original sin, blossoming underfoot.

Dangerous passions. But how did one explain the hazard to a human child who was just learning what true friends were; or to an atevi boy who was trying to iron out what constituted trustable *aishiin,* that network of reliable alliances that would, in the case of a likely future ruler of the *aishidi'tat,* make all the difference between a long, peaceful rule or a series of assassinations and bloody retribution?

He wrote to Toby about their several-months-long problem, he confessed it to himself, because he had not the fortitude or the finesse to lay the whole situation out in detail for the boy's father in that other letter. And then he inevitably erased the paragraphs he wrote, saying to himself that humans had no need to know that detail about the future aiji's development—and saying, *I should let the dowager explain the boy's notions to Tabini.*

But after the computer incident, which had incidentally locked all the doors on five-deck and caused a minor security crisis, even Ilisidi had thrown up her hands. And, instead of laying down the law, as everyone expected, the dowager had seemed to acquiesce to the birthday. Locked in her cabin and grown unsocial in the long tedium of folded space, she undoubtedly knew hour to hour and exactly to date what was going on with preparations for this eighth, infelicitous birthday, and she had said, on that topic, as late as a week ago, "Let him learn what he will learn. He came here for that. Best he see for himself the problems in this association." And then she had added the most troubling information: "Puberty is coming. Then things will occur to him."

That posed very uncomfortable notions, to a human who had long passed that mark and who had found his own intimate accommodation with an ateva of his own bodyguard—an understanding which they neither one acknowledged by what passed for daylight. Much as humans knew about atevi, and an earlier puberty in certain high-ranking individuals was one of those items, there were items the outrageous dowager might mention, but that even his most intimate associate would not feel comfortable discussing in pillow talk. Puberty, it seemed, was one of those unmentionables. It was, and it was not, the point at which feelings of man'chi, of association, firmly took hold of a developing ateva. It was intimate. It was embarrassing. The dowager, armored in years and power, would mention such things with wicked frankness. Jago, with whom he shared his nights, would rather not.

Well, damn, he thought, embarrassed himself, and on increasingly difficult ground. It was so embarrassing, in fact, that Jago had turned her shoulder to him and gone off to sleep. Which left him staring at the ceiling and wondering if he had offended her.

The explanation had left him with more questions than answers, *and* an impending birthday.

That topic, his staff would discuss. Had discussed, in detail. Atevi birthdays tended to be celebrated *only* if the numbers were fortunate, which worked out, with rare exceptions, as the paidhi well knew, to every other year. The infelicitous numbers, those divisible by infelicitous two, were questionable even to acknowledge in passing, except as properly compensated with ameliorating numbers. There might permissively be quiet acknowledgement in the case of a very young child—a sort of family dinner, for instance, had become traditional in the worldly-wise capital, elders felicitating the young person and admonishing him to good behavior, mentioning only his next, more fortunate year, and pointedly not mentioning the current one.

But, God help them, Cajeiri had seen Artur enjoy his birthday presents and being the center of festivities and adoration.

Was it awakening man'chi? Was it that inner need to be part of a group? If it was, it damned sure shouldn't be satisfied by a human, however well-disposed.

We're having the long-awaited birthday party for Cajeiri. This is, inescapably, an event involving the whole staff. There will be Cajeiri's young guests, and I've given Bindanda recipes for authentic cake and ice cream, such as we can manage with synthetics and our own stores.

We're very careful about the ingredients, to be sure—no incidents, no alkaloids served to the human guests . . . no poisoning people's children at a birthday party.

And this being, of course, an eighth birthday, we mustn't mention it's the eighth. You know what that means.

So there's been ever such careful plotting on staff to figure how to do this gracefully. Narani suggested a beautiful patch on the situation, that we can celebrate not the oncoming eighth, but the felicity of the very fortunate seventh completely completed, so to say. And after that little dance around numerical infelicity, we have only to communicate to the parents of his human associates that they and their offspring must in no wise say 'eighth birthday' or 'eight years old', but rather say that he will be 'completely seven.' We seem to have finally persuaded the human parents that this semantical maneuvering is no joke. I tried to explain to the parents in that meeting yesterday, and they are the best of the best, who at least can conceptualize that passionate feelings other than human might exist in very non-human directions. Most of the Reunioners can't remotely imagine such a case. Especially they can't imagine it in folded space, where their brains aren't quite up to par. Universally it's a hard sell, in concept, to people who've always defined universal reality by their own feelings, and have never met anyone unlike themselves.

The humans they had rescued off Reunion Station were, to say the least, not acclimated to dealing with non-humans—they were incredibly provincial, for space-farers, and Artur's mother had even called the to-do over the attachment between the children that very dangerous word, silly.

The woman had meant, certainly, to reassure him that she didn't expect there would be any trouble. But that was precisely the point. She didn't remotely grasp the history of the problem, or its potential outcome. Any Mospheiran, and he was Mospheiran, from the on-

world island enclave of humans, found that mother's attitude of laissez-faire both sinister and very scary. This
was, he saw in that statement, a well-meaning human as
naïve in atevi culture as Mospheirans had been before
the Landing—before each side's ignorance and each
side's confidence they were completely understanding
one another had triggered the War of the Landing, the
cataclysm that nearly ruined the planet.

Out of that conflict, the one good that had come was
the paidhi's office—a human appointed as the atevi
aiji's own translator and mediator where it regarded the
mysterious thought processes of humans, the human appointed to execute the terms of the treaty that had
ended the War, turning over human technology to the
atevi conquerors at a pace that would not work such
grievous harm on atevi culture. He understood his predecessors' history, he knew what they'd been through,
what they'd learned painfully and sometimes bloodily,
over the elapsed centuries.

And trying to convey his Mospheiran-born experience to the Reunioners, it was like starting from the beginning—like *being* the first paidhi that had ever
existed. Reunioners, born in space, entirely unaccustomed to accepting other languages and other human
cultures, let alone non-human mental processes, had just
come within a hair's breadth of starting an interspecies
war in the district where they had come from.

Which was why humans elsewhere had had to send
Phoenix out to collect them and get them back to safety
in the first place. Humans who lived with atevi had
known the moment they heard of human encounters
with neighboring aliens that they were possibly in deep
trouble. And, oh, God, they had been in trouble—had
all but provoked another species into wiping them out
and hunting down the rest of humankind.

Had the Reunion refugees now learned from this experience? No. The majority of them chose not to regard
the near-war as in any sense their fault, were quite in-

dignant at any such suggestion, and had no ingrained appreciation what a serious business it was to trample on other species' sensitivities. Certainly they had not a care in their world that their Mospheiran cousins had, some hundreds of years in the past, fought a great war over such 'silliness' as humans insisting on fixed property lines and disregarding the fingernails-on-chalkboard effect of human numerical deafness, in their children's *considerate* attempts to learn the atevi language.

Infelicitous eighth?

The fact was, as every Mospheiran knew, and Reunion folk did not, atevi heard numbers in everything. Numerical sensitivity was embedded in the atevi language, very possibly even in their brain architecture, influencing their whole outlook on the universe. Bjorn, Irene, Artur and Gene, who had made rudimentary efforts at talking to Cajeiri in his own language, had seemingly grasped the facts of the situation faster than their parents, though their own human nerves were absolutely deaf to the mistakes that made atevi shudder: they were continually trying to figure out what made Cajeiri scowl at them as if he'd been insulted, and to add to the problem, they were not particularly good in math, which was so matter of course to Cajeiri he had trouble understanding their mistakes. Their back-and-forth computer correspondence, which protective atevi staff had hacked, were full of very long, very convolute explanations to each other as to what one had meant by "two of us," and, apologetically, how two wasn't really "two."

The youngsters' willingness to analyze their communication was at least encouraging, no matter that they were surely not destined for a career in mathematics and would never progress beyond the children's version of the language. Their being drawn to Cajeiri—in a bond that, for reasons he himself could not completely understand, atevi were reluctant to sever—was fraught with every imaginable difficulty.

But if they could somehow keep an even keel under the relationship, and avoid an emotional breach, who knew? The next generation necessarily extended into a scary dimension of time the paidhi couldn't control, couldn't even imagine, let alone predict. He only saw, uneasily, that the very circumstance of there being *four* young humans had seemingly undermined atevi resistance to the idea of their association: he knew that four was calamity unless combined with an apex fifth, a dominant fifth. These *four* under the peculiar circumstances of this voyage, constituted some kind of foreboding threat in certain minds. Joined to an atevi future ruler—they made a five of potential power—at least by what he could figure Ilisidi's reasoning to be.

Scary as hell, to a human trying to figure out a volatile situation that might undermine everything he'd struggled to preserve.

But today all he had to cope with was the debated slumber party, in which Cajeiri had not even remotely twigged to the impropriety of young people of various sexes spending the night in the same bed. Irene, Cajeiri said, wasn't a girl, she was Artur's sister. Translation: she was clan, she was family, she was part of his *aishid*. Which had to worry anyone in the context of oncoming changes in the boy.

Not to mention the understanding of human parents, who saw a boy as tall as a grown human proposing to sleep with their very underage daughter.

Three ticks of the keys windowed up an ebony face, a young face, though humans not used to atevi might not see how young . . . gold eyes that brimmed with questions, questions, questions. There was so much good in that young heart. So much enthusiasm and willingness.

And his parents' good looks, and his father's cunning and, when thwarted, his father's volatile temper. Which, fortunately, there was the aiji-dowager, his great-grandmother, to sit on, when needed.

Tantrums there might be, a last-ditch insistence on the slumber party.

We decided to offer a movie for the entertainment, he calmly wrote to Toby. *Since we haven't encouraged the boy in his movie-viewing out of the Archive lately, and since the dowager has loaded him with homework to fill his time, this should be a special treat.*

In several well-considered opinions, Cajeiri had gotten far too fond of those human-made movies. Prepubescent as the lad still was, most machimi plays, the classic and common literature of his own people, did sail right over his head, both intellectually and emotionally, and unfortunately that had combined with the boredom of a long voyage to make the human Archive all too attractive to a boy who should have been out riding the hills and conniving with other children—not that Cajeiri understood the nuances of the human dramas, either, but there was in the vast Archive a great store of the sort of movies he favored . . . notably those with abundant pyrotechnics, a great deal of sword-swinging, and most especially horses and dinosaurs.

Machimi were, in origin, stage-plays, largely filled with people talking, in limited, static sets. The classic ones didn't have the flash and sweep of a movie epic. So what did their boy do when admonished to view the classics of his own culture? He fast-forwarded to the blood and thunder scenes, and disrespectfully skipped through the intellectual and sensitive parts, ignoring all the things that should have begun to mean something to his developing brain.

This fast-forwarding button had begun to make his elders just a little uneasy. He was bright. He was extremely bright. They were not sure about his other attributes, or how this fascination with blood and battle played in his developing brain.

Horses, pirates, and especially dinosaurs are his current passion, he wrote to Toby. *Did I mention he's keenly disappointed to be told we don't really have horses or di-*

nosaurs on Mospheira? He was all ready to take a row-boat over there and see them, and we had to tell him they were long ago and far away, and that dinosaurs were not alive when humans appeared on old Earth.

Cajeiri had put in his request for *Captain Blood* as the birthday movie, but the dowager's staff had lately made the firm decision that pirates were not appropriate fare for a young one-day ruler. Cajeiri and his young associates had recently sent each other a series of fanciful between-decks letters about overthrowing the ship-aijiin and cruising the universe as space pirates, a plan which, whatever its lack of feasibility, entirely scandalized his grandmother.

The offering the staff has settled on for the festive occasion is The Lost World, *which has wall-to-wall dinosaurs. Presumably this will please him, since we're sure this is a version he has not seen and the dinosaurs, staff informs me, are particularly well done.*

Surely in the next few years the problem would fade: his great-grandmother seemed to think so. When the boy got old enough, the machimi plays, the ancestral art of his Ragi forebears, would touch his awakening sensibilities and adult instincts in ways peculiarly and exquisitely atevi. Then human-made movies would no longer satisfy the young rascal.

Then he would stop being the appealing young rascal he was and start becoming, well, what he ought to be, ateva to the core—which would leave the paidhi a little lonely, he had to admit it. He'd never thought to bring up a son. Even a surrogate one. And he'd had the boy on his hands for over two years. Did that qualify as fatherhood, for a man who, given his only deep romantic attachment wasn't to his own species, would never father a child?

Change of topic. Some things he didn't write to his brother, or commit even to volatile memory.

Gin and her crew invited me in for the poker game yesterday night. It's only for sugar packets, but I won ten.

*It's the math, you know. Before this voyage is over I
should have a corner on. . . .*

The door to his cabin opened. "Nandi." Narani came
in, his chief of staff: atevi, a head taller than he was, skin
which should be black as ink and eyes gold as sunset,
but the absolute of both colors had faded a bit from age.
His queued and ribboned hair was peppershot with
gray, his face mapped with years. He was the gentlest of
men . . . never mind he was, like the rest of his staff, a
Guild Assassin. "Jase-aiji advises us he will call in person in a moment."

"Will he?" He didn't see near enough of Jase Graham, whose day was his night—they met, when they
met, in the morning and twilight of their respective
days, and it was evening at the moment. He folded up
his computer. Jase's announcement of his imminent
presence was usually done from the central lift system.

Narani reached and adjusted his lace cuff, which had
fallen back and snagged on his coat. In no wise would
this good gentleman permit the Lord of the Heavens to
meet the ship's second captain at any disadvantage of
dress. If there had been time, Narani would have called
the rest of the staff and gotten him into a more formal
coat.

Bren drank off the cold remainder of his cup, when he
had satisfied his staff. Then he went out into the hall, the
main corridor on this part of five-deck, the atevi section.

Jase had already passed the section doors. Jase was in
his working uniform, blue sweater and blue coat, and in
a fair hurry.

News? Bren wondered, his heart beating a little
faster. It *wasn't* an invitation to a dinner-breakfast upstairs. Jase would have simply called down for that.

"Jase," he said, as Jase reached him, all prepared to
stand aside and show him into the cabin—to offer him
a precious cup of tea, if he could, all the courtesies of
old, yes, *friends* in his otherwise atevi universe. Jase was
the closest human tie he owned, except Toby.

"We're about to drop out," Jase said. "Emergence tomorrow on my watch, 0416.14h." Jase's eyes fairly danced with what he had come to say. "We're *there*, Bren. We'll be there, tomorrow morning, right on the button. I have it from nav, and Sabin concurs."

Sabin was senior, first-shift captain, Jase being second-shift, just preparing to go on duty about now. *Drop out* meant emerge from subspace, and *there*—

There meant home. The Earth of the atevi. The place they'd come from. Mospheira. The *aishidi'tat*. Toby. Tabini. Everything he'd left in limbo on a hasty departure a little over two years ago.

"I wanted to tell you myself," Jase said, while Bren found himself still numb, perhaps less joyful than Jase expected to see. In his daze he woke a little-used half-smile, then a laugh, in this space too dull for smiles and laughter, and clapped Jase on the shoulder.

"Home, then. Home! You're sure."

"So damned well on the button we can just about wave at the station when we arrive. So the navigator tells us."

"Is that safe?"

"Figuratively speaking."

"How figurative?"

"It's home system. Our coordinates are that good . . . not *literally* wave at them, Bren, for God's sake." Jase had a laugh of his own. "But pretty damned close. Safer, nav says, to pop in there, out of the path of the junk in outer system."

"I really don't want to think about junk in the outer system." It was a dirty and dangerous system, as solar systems went. So the spacers said.

"No worry." A second laugh, at the expense of a notoriously nervous flier, in atmosphere or out. "It'll be fine, Bren. Not a shred of a worry." Jase squeezed his arm for reassurance. "Bet you. Bet you a pint of beer. Just pack up. That's your warning, personally delivered.

I've got to get back up there. And I did ask Sabin when I notified her: you're all welcome up on the bridge once we do emerge. So get some early sleep. We're figuring we drop out at 0416h, and Sabin's coming back on shift to take over at 0330h, so you don't need to worry at all who's driving."

"God, I never would."

"You should." A grin from Jase, who was, like him, one of the three paidhiin, and a bookish sort of captain, nothing of the hands-on sort Sabin was. "I'm keeping my mouth shut while the crew does what it knows how to do. But I'll be on deck when you do come up. No sleeping through this one. I had to tell you myself. So spread the news."

"Great," he said. It was. It really was great news. After a two-year voyage and hell in between, they were *home,* or would be, tomorrow morning.

God, was it over? Was it done? Home? And Jase, for whom the planet was a destination and the ship his birth-home—Jase Graham, born and bred to this mind-numbing transit through subspace, walked briskly back the way he'd come. There was lightness in his stride, while Bren found his stomach undergoing that desperate queasiness it underwent whenever they faced an imprecise, deep-space drop—the ordinary ones that punctuated their travel between points, let alone the all-important emergence at their destination. Within waving-distance.

Was he scared? Oh, nothing at all like it.

Scared as hell, with clammy hands, this time, and he didn't know why. The notion of the navigator laying bets with Sabin for how close he could shave it, maybe.

Or maybe—

Maybe it was knowing they'd coasted along comfortably on their success at Reunion for the last year in a very static situation, everybody, human crew, Reunion refugees, and atevi allies, each on their appropriate decks, everything ruled and regulated and getting along in social stasis. They'd had a year to contemplate what they'd done, a year to get comfortable in that success.

And now they had to explain to the people back home what they'd done out there and sell their decisions to a diverse and worried world, hoping there wouldn't be panic, when they mentioned that humans weren't the only aliens out there among the stars.

"Well," he said. Jase had spoken in Ragi, he realized, so he had no need to translate for Narani, or for Jeladi, who had turned up from the servants' cabin, down the way. Both stood at a respectful distance, listening with very keen atevi hearing.

Damn, he'd forgotten—he'd completely forgotten to ask Jase to provide precise numerical data on this all-important drop. Atevi always wanted the numbers. He'd have to call up for it.

"Will you inform the dowager, nandi?" Narani asked, and of course he must—never mind Ilisidi sealed her doors against intrusion and turned surly during folded-space transits. He must tell her, and he must change his coat. And he must get those numbers.

"I shall, nadiin-ji." He included them both in the courtesy, and ducked inside with both of them behind him, Narani personally going to the closet to find the appropriate shirt and coat while he used a handheld to log on the ship's net to ask the precise navigation figures.

The answer flowed back to him: nav knew by now how passionately the atevi loved such elegant numbers, and set great store by them, and he had clearance to get that information and to pass it on. He captured it onto a removable disk, a tiny thing he held between thumb and palm as Jeladi moved in to rid him of less formal coat and shirt.

Asicho turned up, the sole female among the servants, alerted by the arcane means the whole servant establishment used. She presented him a small silver message-cylinder for his use, and Narani provided the small square of paper, on which he wrote, in a clerkly, formal hand:

Aiji-ma, may one call to present a special gift, aware as one may be of the inconvenience? One risks your displeasure to bring you the joy of excellent and auspicious news.

Hell, yes, she'd want to know. Curiosity would wake her up. He gave the little slip to Asicho, who furled it into the tiny silver case and took off in haste.

Asicho would naturally spill what she knew to the dowager's staff, who would present that little cylinder in advance of his arrival and rouse Ilisidi out of the doldrums.

Into the shirt, young Jeladi assisting, and now rotund Bindanda, cook, spy, and chief contriver of whatever needed doing, provided the knee-length coat, while Bren kept his computer disk safely in his fingers. He dropped it carefully into his coat pocket while Bindanda made sure his queue and ribbons were clear of the collar. Bindanda then fastened the five fashionable fabric-covered buttons, and Bren patted the pocket flap neatly closed.

"One is grateful, nadiin-ji," he said to his staff. The whole operation, message to coat, had taken two minutes, if that, and how could a man be less than confident, with such a staff in action? He felt far steadier.

And when he walked out the door, two shadows loomed, left and right, and immediately fell in with him—Banichi and Jago, his personal bodyguard—*bodyguard* was only a fraction of what they were, but protection, surely, first and foremost. He was a decent height for a human, and his head reached Jago's shoulder: Banichi was taller. He was rarely aware of going wired, but he was, thanks to the pocket com, which was always on, and they heard everything, all day—all night, since Jago was, well, *considerably* closer to him.

"You know, nadiin-ji," he said to them.

"One heard, nandi," Banichi said as they walked past the common dining room, on their way to the aiji-dowager's domain.

"One fears for the birthday party," Jago observed.

"Oh." His reckoning hadn't gotten that far. *Oh* didn't half express his dismay.

But they had reached Ilisidi's door, and Banichi signaled their desire to enter. Depend on it, Asicho had made it inside first, using the icy service corridors behind the row of cabins—the staff would break their necks to keep propriety and pass information as servants would in an atevi household. So it was no surprise at all that Cenedi himself, Banichi's counterpart on Ilisidi's staff, opened the door for them, almost before Banichi had pushed the button.

"Cenedi-ji, will the dowager receive a visitor?"

"Beyond a doubt," Cenedi said, and showed him past the little reception desk in the cabin Ilisidi's staff had half-curtained and remodeled into a foyer. The dowager as well as her staff used the service corridors to transit between the various cabins they had turned into an atevi-style residence in this linear human ship, and Bren proceeded to the service access as naturally as to a door, following one of Ilisidi's young men.

Beyond, then, into the cold and the dim glow of motion lights in a barren, girdered corridor ordinarily reserved for maintenance. Banichi and Jago would stay to exchange information with Cenedi, if there was anything Cenedi had not already picked up in their inter-linked communications: they were as close as two households could get, and very little needed explaining, but it was still the custom, while the Lord of the Heavens froze his bones.

Bitter cold, for a thin-limbed human nipping through the passages, but thankfully brief. He had only chilled through the outer layers of his coat before Ilisidi's man showed him, not into her library, as he had expected, but into a nearer room he hadn't yet visited, which on first sight he realized must be Cajeiri's own study, with a television and lockers and Cajeiri's distinctive sketches taped to the lockers—fairly good sketches, for a boy seven-going-on-eight. Reunion Station, complete with the hole blown in it. Sketches of Prakuyo's ship, odd-shaped and strange. His sweeping glance took in the aiji-dowager seated in the main chair, and Cajeiri standing respectfully behind her. There was a scatter of books on the floor. And cushions. He might have interrupted lessons.

"Aiji-ma," Bren said with a bow, lowering his eyes, but taking in Ilisidi's informality of dress—not the usual high-collared coat, but a mere day-coat. In the muzziness of folded space, even she gave way to comfortable practicality; and the boy was in a black sweater he might have borrowed from one of the security staff, his gangling limbs having outgrown most of last year's coats and shirts, and hems and seams being let out and let out until there was no more to give. "Aiji-ma." Straightening, with the ritual second bow. "Jase-aiji reports we are on the verge of arrival—*home*, this time, aiji-ma. Right on the doorstep of the station, Jase believes, so there will be no great time at all getting to dock."

"Indeed." A spark of lively interest. "When?"

"I have not that precise a knowledge of the schedule, aiji-ma, but Jase thinks it will be extraordinarily close to our destination, and the ship crew provides the numbers, in the thought the gift may please you." He drew the disk out of his pocket and offered it.

Ilisidi took the object with apparent satisfaction. "And do we assume the same precise imprecision as before? This 'lumpy space' of yours?"

"Not mine, aiji-ma, one begs to say. The navigators do claim this time they know where we are to a nicety surpassing all others. When . . . seems more at issue."

"Precise and imprecise at once. The 'counters will be completely scandalized. Lord Grigiji, however, will be delighted." The former were the number-counters, the numerologist-mathematicians who were somewhere between fortune-tellers and social arbiters in atevi society; the latter was the Astronomer Emeritus, confined by age and frailty to the planet, even to his mountain-top observatory, and there was so very much they had saved up to tell him on their return. "And you, Lord of the Heavens? When do you think we shall arrive?"

"The paidhi, not being expert, dares rely only on Jase's estimation, and he gives a time of 0416h, ship's reckoning. He seems extraordinarily pleased with these calculations. He calls them amazingly accurate."

"Amazingly so, then." A snort. For atevi, who worked math implicit in their language—calculated with every breath—the navigators who talked about lumpy space were indeed a test of belief. "So. That answers to when we shall reach the region. When shall we reach the station?"

He was caught with his mouth open. He closed it, since while the navigators could just about swear to the time, the location was always just a little looser. "You know I can answer you no better than ever I could, aiji-ma. But we shall certainly get underway for dock the moment we do come in, so we must stow everything. And if we reach the station with some dispatch, if the ship's chronometer bears any relation to the world's time, and if the local schedule has held as it was, we may even be able to catch the shuttle in two days and be on the planet in very short order—unless, of course, we linger on the station to please Lord Geigi."

"Excellent news." Ilisidi dragged her walking cane before her and rested her hands on the head of it, entirely pleased. "Well, well, Lord of the Heavens. So we may look forward to a good dinner."

"And as much tea as we can possibly drink, aiji-ma."

Ilisidi laughed. "Indeed. Indeed. Of a sort *you* dare drink, to be sure, paidhi-ji. Not to mention fresh fruit and meat of the season, which we have all sadly missed. We look forward to this change of menu. So. We shall begin packing. Shall we be on hand to see this arrival in the morning?"

"Jase-aiji extends the aiji-dowager an invitation to the bridge, immediately as we arrive, this from both the ship-aijiin."

"We shall advise our staff," Ilisidi said, again satisfied, as if the staff were not at this moment well ahead of them on all such details, and likely already beginning the packing and the preparation of suitable attire. "Excellent. Excellent news, nand' paidhi."

It was his cue to depart. His stated mission was accomplished. He made his bow. "Tomorrow morning, aiji-ma."

"Be it auspicious, as by all the numbers it seems to be." She looked weary and worn by the condition of space that wore on them all. But she positively smiled, rare token of her favor, and added: "Well done, paidhi-ji."

"Aiji-ma." Warmed by that rare approval, he made his retreat, back to the bone-numbing cold of the passage, where her man waited to see him back.

But not alone, as he realized within that chilly dark space. Running steps overtook him in the shadows—a boy as tall as he was, a boy whose eyes, like those of his guide, reflected like gold glass in the motion-lights of the passage.

"Nandi!" Cajeiri overtook him and made a little bow, child to adult, no matter the child was a prince of the Association. "Nandi, shall I then not have my birthday?"

Oh, such an earnest, honest face, such a thoroughly disconcerted and worried young face.

"One regrets to say it may have to be delayed," he said. "My most profound and personal regret, young aiji, but in all likelihood we shall be under a yellow caution the whole day tomorrow, which may force us to postpone the festivity at least until after we dock and disembark."

"But that will be no good, nandi! The day! My day! The very *day* makes it my birthday!"

He was, after all, despite being a lord and almost on eye level with an adult human, only seven-going-on-eight. He was heart-broken.

But being born atevi and trained as a lord by a great-grandmother firmly in favor of protocols, Cajeiri also knew that he had gone as far as he could, having presented his argument to the paidhi-aiji. He could not complain to his great-grandmother, who would offer no sympathy: straighten the shoulders, she would say. Bear it with grace.

It might be the right thing to say, to this particular boy, but a human and a diplomat tried to find a stricken child some comfort. "Well, nandi, the day itself is significant, yes, and the numbers, but among my people, understand, young aiji, birthdays can be moved a little to agree with circumstances and felicity, since the idea is to congratulate the person and have pleasure in his company. And that sentiment depends on you, not on the day itself. And your guests *are* human, and will entirely understand. Their truly significant desire is to express their wishes for your health and long life, and we shall simply adjust the numbers until everything is entirely auspicious. Narani is extraordinarily adept at such things."

"But it should be the day!"

"Even your father the aiji has been known to move a ceremony for safety. And I'm sure you shall have your presents, likely much the better for being on the station where you can enjoy abundant room. And not to forget the refreshments—I'm sure Bindanda can do ever so much better where we can find the best ingredients."

"The cake."

"You will absolutely have your cake, young aiji. A real and marvelous cake. I promise it on my word."

"But the movie, too, nand' paidhi? Shall we have that?"

"Certainly. Certainly we can manage that."

"Then it will be all right," Cajeiri said glumly, rising to a dignity the dowager would more approve. And spoiled it with a glum: "One supposes."

"But this is the station, young aiji. This is our own station." Could the boy have missed that detail? "We shall have your birthday, and then catch the next shuttle down to the planet, to Shejidan, to your father and your mother. Will you not like that?"

"Maybe."

Oh, maybe? Only maybe? He was freezing, at the moment, but this was a very distressed young lad, who evinced only minimal interest in his own parents.

"What is this doubt, young aiji? You surely wish to see your father and mother."

"Yes."

"So what should make you fret, young aiji?"

"So shall I see Artur and Bjorn and Irene and Gene after I go down to Shejidan? Shall I *ever* see them again?"

He was caught with his mouth open, ready arguments all useless. He had had all the adult arguments ready, regarding a boy's childish disappointment about a birthday—but could he possibly answer that one?

No, in all due honesty—he could not say that the little band would not be broken, this time by circumstances none of the youngsters' cleverness could overcome . . . a gravity well, human protectiveness of their children, and atevi sensibilities no different.

He was, however, an optimist. He took a longer view than a boy could. "You are no ordinary boy," he said, "and you have a father who, if you ask him in the best way, may afford a shuttle ride for your young associates, supposing their parents will agree."

"And will they allow it, nandi?"

"It may take a little argument," he said. He hated the scary dive into atmosphere they themselves had to make. He was sure every time he got back down to the planet that he might not personally have the nerve to get aboard the shuttle again. "If the shuttle has proved safe," he said, "if the trip has gotten to be routine, as likely it has—" The space program itself had been new, the equipment still uncertain, even to the day they had launched. "If it has—and there is no reason to expect otherwise—much more likely they will." He was absolutely freezing by this time, past slight shivers, the deep cold having penetrated his coat, his skin, his flesh. The warmth was leaving his bones by now, but young eyes were fixed on him, shimmering gold in the motionlights. "Young aiji, I shall have frostbite if I linger here. I have to go quickly. But I promise I shall intercede with your father and your mother with every diplomatic skill I have, and we shall do everything possible to see your associates pay you visits."

"Yes!" Cajeiri said, that disconcerting atevi *yes*, absolute, expectant, and in this instance, exultant. The topic was closed, deal done. The paidhi and he had a small secret. God help him.

"Young aiji," Bren murmured by way of parting courtesy, ducked his head and escaped out the service access into the brighter light and comparative breath-strangling heat of the dowager's foyer.

There was frost on his coat sleeves. His fingers would not bend.

"Bren-ji?" Jago was there, distressed for his condition, glowering at Ilisidi's man, who quickly shut the door as the shivers seized him.

"Perfectly fine," Bren said, trying not to let the shivers reach his voice. "I had to delay to advise the heir his festivity may be deferred. There was negotiation." A gasp for warm air, which seemed heavy as syrup, difficult to get into his lungs. He had dealt with Tabini-aiji, and marveled how often Tabini had had the better of them. The skill was evidently inheritable. He succeeded in drawing a whole breath. "I shall call on Gin-aiji, too, nadiin-ji. A matter of courtesy."

"Frozen through," Banichi said, disapproving the

staff that had not found a way to get him through the space-chilled corridor. Courtesy even yet would have fortified him with hot tea, if he asked, but he waved a disorganized protest, wishing no delays in his business. He had his thoughts collected, more or less, and staff's energies were as short in supply as drinkable tea and candy, in these latter days of the voyage.

But on his way out of the dowager's domain, paying automatic courtesies to staff, he kept ticking off in his head the little list of necessary duties, the people who needed to know, in his small society aboard a ship with over five thousand humans, all of whom knew his face, but of whom he only knew a handful.

Gin Kroger—Dr. Virginia Kroger—was their robotics expert, chief of robotics engineering, essential to their success, once upon a time, and glad to be completely useless on the way home. Gin-ji, as the Ragi language had it, nowadays spent her time at her computer, designing and tinkering, as she put it, like a teenager, enjoying a year of unprecedented leisure to create and hypothesize instead of supervise and shepherd scholarly grant requests through committees.

She designed one hell of a race car, that was certain, and the design wars and the toy car races between her engineers and his atevi staff had drawn bets from ship crew as well as bets from her own staff and the two atevi households. If explosives had been part of the rules, no question Banichi and Cenedi would carry the day—but it was sheer speed and agility, involving an obstacle course through several blocked-off corridors, so it was even odds who would win this round. The trophy, an undrunk bottle of brandy adorned with ribbons, had gone back and forth numerous times.

And dared he recall that it was not alone Cajeiri's birthday that was upset by this arrival? Bets were already laid. A great deal of planning had been done. The bottle had sat in Gin's office for two weeks. There had to be vindication.

On down the hall, past the atevi-zone security doors by the lift, and through a set of doors to the right, they reached a hall quite happy in its humanly linear arrangements, a hall that lacked compensatory wall-hangings to keep the place harmonious and the ship safe, and instead had the racing odds taped up, the whole record of events.

Both the human and the atevi wings of five-deck society lived by numbers and design, each in their own way.

There was no guard, no sentry. He knocked on Gin's door. "News," he called out. "*News,* Gin."

In the splendid informality of Mospheiran ways.

The door opened.

"I heard!" Gray-haired, age-impervious pixie Gin flung her arms about him—went so far as to pat Banichi and Jago on the arm, no matter the visible twitch of hair-triggered nerves, likely in their apprehension she might hug them. "I heard!"

"They say we're dropping out extremely close to the station," he said. "I hope this is good news. Jase stopped here, too?"

"He called, at least. Come in. Everybody come in. Can I get you a sandwich?"

It wasn't that large a cabin, but Gin was already hosting Jerry and Barnhart, amid the detritus of dinner.

"We've eaten," he said.

"Well, you can certainly drink. We should crack that bottle."

"I suppose you should. You have it."

"Pour him one. Pour *them* one," Gin said, intending Banichi and Jago to join them.

"No, in all good will, nand' Gin," Banichi said. "We shall stand. You won quite fairly."

They were on duty, freely translated. And hadn't won, and wouldn't partake. But the paidhi wasn't, well, not that much on duty. It was after dinner, and he sat down long enough to pay the courtesies and share a small glass of very excellent Midlands brandy.

"We were going to call you. We'll send half to your quarters. It's only fair."

"Perhaps," he said.

"Half and half. We won't get a chance tomorrow. Have to drink it all tonight. You'd better take half. We don't want to be hung over when we make drop."

"Sounds like a good plan," he said. "And I can't stay long. I have to get back to my staff."

"To good comrades!" Jerry proposed next. It was not quite that deadly word *friend*. And then: "To success!"

"To success," he said, lifting his small glass. And, perhaps due to that one sip of brandy, it began to truly sink in that they had indeed made it, that they were on the threshold of home, that, thanks to them, angry aliens would not show up on the world's collective doorstep— well, there were a few complications, and a great difficulty yet to enable them to cast loose from the Reunioners' past mistakes, not to mention that they still had a few human troublemakers aboard. They had rescued from certain oblivion something near five thousand people—some more grateful than others. They averted an alien war certain people's stupidity had done its best to start. And they had gotten themselves back with minimal losses.

His staff did deserve half that bottle.

"Djossi flowers," Gin said, recalling a prior conversation. "But it'll be fall. We have it all figured."

"Will it?" He had figured it too, and hoped it would be, and that the shuttle would be up there waiting for them, but he'd happily take bitter winter in their hemisphere, if it set his feet on the ground again and let him look up at a tame and healthful sun on a white sand beach.

"Absolutely," Jerry said.

"We have our invitation to come up to the bridge

soon as we get there," Bren said. "That's firm, from the top."

"Wouldn't miss it for the world," Gin said. Here, it verged on humor.

"So," Bren said, "seeing they're going to put us in so close to the station, and figuring we may have a fairly short time to dock, I wanted to issue a formal invitation now, while I have you all in reach. I want you, each and all, to visit my place on the coast, on the continent, as soon as you find it convenient. No great political problems. No fuss. It's quiet. Remote from most everywhere. Boat and swim—well, it's cold on that coast, but still, you can last a little while in the water, and there's nothing predatory in the bay to worry about. All of you. Any of you. If you have trouble getting a visa over to the mainland, give me a phone call. I intend to buy myself a boat, my own boat, with all my accumulated back pay, which I think I may have earned, and have a real vacation. Maybe sail somewhere they can't find me, oh, for at least a week."

"To vacations!" Barnhart said, lifting his glass.

So it went. He hadn't intended to stay as long as he did. But half a glass later he began to ask himself why he wanted to go back to quarters, where there was absolutely nothing urgent waiting for him, where staff knew absolutely what to do and how to pack up. He stayed a little longer, thinking, like Cajeiri, that they would all go their ways and there was no real prospect they would ever share another such evening, never again as they were. They had gotten to be family, the ones of them who had come up from the planet. He would go down with the dowager and with his own staff, Gin would go her own way, back to the hallowed halls of Mospheira's largest university, and the government. Her staff would scatter.

While Jase—Jase, who was planetary by adoption, at least—

He wasn't sure he would get Jase back on the planet

again, not when Jase had worked into the captaincy they had insisted on giving him. Jase had protested it. But he saw Jase forming ties of his own among his own shipboard cousins and kin, in ways a shipborn human had to have been set up to want very badly. He'd had no particular job that anybody understood; now he had universal respect from his cousins.

And could he fault Jase, who was understudying their senior captain, Sabin, and who was winning that hardest of all prizes, Sabin's professional acceptance?

Jase didn't know what was happening to him, yet. Jase didn't acknowledge it, but he had his own idea that Jase wasn't going to resign his captain's seat any time in the near future . . . or that if he got down to the planet, he'd find his way back to space.

"I'll miss you," Bren said to Gin, and made it inclusive. "I'll miss all of you. Take me up on the invitation. I really mean it."

"Goes without saying," Gin said, "any of you or yours, in my little digs in the city. This whole scummy group will keep in touch."

Best of intentions. Best of hopes. In his experience, people didn't ever quite get around to it . . . didn't visit him, at least, maybe because he didn't find the time to visit them, either. Something always intervened. Whatever direction he planned, events shoved him some other way. Some emergency came up. Ties grew fainter and fewer, especially to humans on Mospheira. Even his own family.

He was getting maudlin. He wasn't twenty any more. He was getting farther and farther from twenty, and he still considered himself an optimist, but lately that optimism had gotten down to a more bounded, knowledgeable optimism about his own intentions, a pragmatism regarding his own failings, and a universe-view tinged with worldly realism and personal history. He didn't *believe* in the impossible as wildly, as passionately as he once had. *Knowing* had gotten in the way of that. And what he knew depended on an experience that included betrayals, and his own significant failures to pursue personal relationships across very difficult boundaries of distance and profession.

And when he got down to thoughts like that, it was a clear signal not to have any more brandy.

"Got to go," he said after a suitable time of sitting and listening in their, admittedly, technospeak society. By now Banichi and Jago had gotten involved, since Jerry had gotten the notion to reschedule the car races, this time as a station event, and Banichi, conscious of his lord's dignity in the station environment, had demurred and thought it might not be the thing to do.

It was the first crack in their society. It had already come, and on such a small issue.

There was nothing practical to do but agree with Banichi, that their schedules were unforeseeable at present, but surely they knew why Banichi had refused, and that time wasn't the only issue.

He excused himself and his staff, thanked them one and all, made protestations of lasting correspondence, collected their half of the brandy and promised to see the engineers in the morning.

"I'll miss them," he said as they walked back into the foyer between the two wings, Jago carrying the trophy bottle. "These are very good people, nadiin-ji."

"Indeed, nandi," Banichi agreed, and Jago: "Gin might truly visit the estate."

Rely on Jago to mind-read him in a situation, even cross-culture.

"I earnestly hope she does," he said. And from that perspective—it seemed more likely. Gin was like him, married to the job, to her robots and her computers. She was over sixty and gray-haired and while the two of them had nothing in common, except this voyage—they did share lifelong passions for things that transcended the need for family ties and picket fences.

Jago was right, he decided, cheering up: if there was

one person of the lot who might show up at his door some day, it was Gin. Djossi flowers. The memory of perfume on the air. Himself and Gin, maudlin together on a certain evening in the deeps of space, far, far from home. They'd kept one another sane, in the human sense.

While these two, Banichi and Jago, had kept him solidly centered in the atevi world . . . and helped him keep a grip on what was important. Helped save his neck—uncounted times. And had a way of jerking him back to sanity.

"Time we packed the duffles," he said. "Time I finished my records."

2

This is, I hope, the final entry before I transmit this letter to you. Catching the first shuttle home is at a high priority right now, maybe not an unrealistic hope, so I'll be able to phone you on a secure line shortly after you receive the file. We're informed we're going to drop into the solar system, Jase swears, extremely close to the station—it sounds reckless to me, but Jase is very sure . . . and supposedly the area is clearer of debris than farther out would be, because of the planetary system sweeping it clean, so it will actually be safer than farther out. So I understand. I can't conceive of doing much business on the station, though there may necessarily be some meetings for me to attend to, notably including a general debriefing with Captain Ogun.

Primarily, my first duty is going to bring me downworld to inform Tabini as fast as I can, and that debriefing is going to take longest. Once that's done, I'm actually free for a while, I earnestly hope, and I can get over to the Island and see you. I just promised Gin Kroger a vacation at the estate, but I want you to come across the straits first of all, brother, just as soon as I can get a few days free—I'll stretch my time off into a month, if I have to get a decree from Tabini to do it, and we'll finally take that trip down to the reef, with no duties, no starched lace, just walk barefoot on the deck . . .

Then he wiped that out, starting with *I just promised* . . . and interposed what he knew he had to write: *I*

*want to get over to the island as soon as I can to see you
and catch up on things.*

It was the most delicate way he knew to phrase what
sat at the back of his thoughts, that he didn't know
whether their mother was still alive, that he'd ducked up
to the station without a visit to the Island the last time
he'd been on the planet, and she'd fallen critically ill
while he was setting out on this mission. Guilt gnawed
at him, for that desertion. And what could he say, not
knowing? What had he ever been able to say when they
were only a narrow strait away?

*Thanks for seeing to family, brother. I had no choice.
I had to leave.*

A thousand times, he'd had to say that to Toby. And
right now, among things he didn't know, he didn't know
whether to address his brother as *you and Jill and the
kids* the way he'd used to, because the last time he'd
talked to Toby, Jill had walked out on him, Jill having finally drawn the line in the sand about Toby kiting off to
stay a week at a time at their mother's every crisis.

The problem was, the pattern of minor health emergencies that their mother had started, planned or un-
planned, as a ploy to get her sons home more often had
extended into their mother's truly serious crises. And
he'd not been able to tell the real ones from the ones in
which he'd take emergency leave, duck over to the island, and the next morning find her risen from her bed
and making pancakes for breakfast, for "her boys,"
who'd just put their work and, in his case, the affairs of
nations on hold to get to her bedside.

Truth was, their being there *had* cured what ailed her,
since what ailed her was not having her sons with her
and not being interested in a life beyond "her boys."

Barb had shown up, late in her life, Barb, the woman
he'd nearly married . . . and failing a marriage to him,
Barb had practically moved in with his mother, not that
he'd wanted that solution. Barb had put herself in the

position of his mother's caretaker and confidant, scheming what, he was never sure, but at least their mother had had Barb, for what she was worth.

She'd had Barb and she'd had Toby, who'd gone to their mother's side even when Jill laid down the law and took the kids away with her.

So what did he say to his brother? Just ... I'm coming to the Island, as soon as I can? That covered all possibilities, including the possibility the worst had happened in their mother's case and in Jill's, and that Toby had laid it all at his door.

Toby, I have so much to talk about, so much to tell you, so much to ask. I hope to God everything's gone well at home. I've tried not to dwell on it in this letter because when I do, it takes over my thinking and magnifies in the dark, and there's been a lot of dark out here.

Enough of that. If we come in as close as they're saying, this should be the very last entry before I actually hear your voice on the phone, and I'm so looking forward to that. I'll transmit this letter as soon as possible and call you from the station, as soon as I can get to a phone.

Forgive me all my failings, which I know are many. As brothers go, you're a saint. I want to pay you back everything ...

No, strike the last paragraph. He knew he never would be able to pay Toby back what he owed. He knew that Shejidan would have work for him and he'd be lucky to get over to the Island in the first two months he was back—but he was going to fight hard for that visit to be earlier.

He was deceiving himself. Three days. Honestly speaking, except in times of intense crisis, he could almost always manage three days off. That was historically how long it took his family to run out of good will and get down to issues, which was, in his experience, just about time to head for the airport. Wasn't that what he'd always done?

He'd just depressed his high spirits. Thinking about his family reliably did that.

That was why he always wrote last to Tabini, which let him report what he'd done right, and the success they'd had, which drew his mind off the Island and Toby's problems.

Aiji-ma, Jase-aiji informs us we are about to emerge into the solar system. When we do, I shall be able to transmit this letter to you, and within a day, I hope to hear your voice. Within a handful of days I look forward to being in Shejidan again, and to making a full report of all we have seen and done.

I look forward to returning to you the young lord your son, at the completion of his seventh year, as he is pleased to remind us. We are delighted by his general good grace at the collapse of plans for a proper acknowledgment of this anniversary and hope that my lord may in person and more fitly congratulate this young man, since young man he has indeed become, as tall as I am, wise beyond his years and always your son, aiji-ma, to the dowager's satisfaction and the delight of myself and my staff. I shall forever treasure my two years with him, and hope that what small guidance I may have given him has been appropriate and useful.

Long life and health, aiji-ma, from myself and all my household.

He folded up the computer and rang for staff, looking around his little cabin, his green-sheeted, growing world for the last two years.

Jeladi showed up to help him undress for a before-bed shower—staff would have been greatly distressed if he had ducked their good offices, and in truth, if Jeladi nabbed his clothes, laundry would end up done before 0416h, items would end up in the right bags, and the exactly appropriate suit would turn up clean and ready in the morning. He gave his staff as little trouble as possible, knowing that they would have minimal rest tonight. He hadn't checked the lockers in his cabin, but he would lay bets that most of them were empty by now, void of all his small personal items, and that they had kept out only those things they thought he might use before bed, for dressing in the morning, and for whatever amount of time—hours or a day or so—it might take them to get to dock and get to their own apartment.

Their own apartment. That was a thought. His own stationside bed. It seemed impossible he could be enjoying that comfort in the near future.

He had a leisurely hot shower, slid between the sheets and ordered the lights to minimum.

Jago might not show up tonight. He wished she would: her living presence kept him from preemergence nerves, just by her being there. But that was not likely. Jago and Banichi and the whole staff would be scrambling to break down the roomful of technical equipment in their monitoring station, equipment which had grown increasingly interlaced with shipsensors. That would foreseeably take a little longer to disconnect and pack than it had to haul out of its padding and set up, and getting the crates out of cargo and all the gear into those crates was going to be a scramble.

So here he was, eyes open, staring at the ceiling in the dark, and now the thoughts started—worries about things he might need once ashore.

Worries, more substantial, about the human contingent they were bringing the station and the world—bringing not alone a pack of children intent on birthday gifts—but the population, the entire surviving population of a defunct station that had once ruled the *Phoenix* and set policy for all humans in reach. The Reunioners included the old Pilots' Guild, that had ruled the station they now governed, for starters, and when they had been in power, had so alienated his own colonist ancestors that they had dived onto the atevi planet to get away from them.

Well, the tables were entirely turned now. Atevi ruled the station, and human descendants of those refugees were the shopkeepers and a good part of the technicians on it.

It wasn't the xenophobic station the Reunioners had once ruled. And the poison of the old Pilots' Guild wouldn't spread into today's station. The station occupants and the current crew of the ship wouldn't let it.

There was hope for the Reunioners' future in the likes of Bjorn and Artur, scary as the association of the terrible five might be.

There was hope in those Reunioner kids and in their forgiving parents, who were sensibly anxious, but who had not refused the youngsters' getting together with Cajeiri. That was on one side of the equation. But they also had Braddock aboard, the former Reunion stationmaster, the former head of Reunion's branch of the Pilots' Guild, and they had to do something with him. There might be, though quiet through the voyage, certain stationers in the population who might support Braddock with sabotage and sedition. And they had no way of telling when, or if.

Which was why Braddock had spent the voyage under close guard.

But when they got to dock, they then had to figure what to do with him, since he hadn't broken any station laws, or any human laws, for that matter. And they had to do it with political finesse—their own station being a democracy, and fairly low in population.

They were bringing, in their 4078 new residents, a fair-sized voting block sharing a common culture, common problems, and common experience. *And* Braddock, with whom they had to do something. Soon.

Certainly the Reunioners would have a major and different opinion within the Pilots' Guild that existed on the atevi station, and in the long haul, he could only hope for more like Artur's parents.

He knew what he'd personally like to do with Braddock: take him down to the planet and let him loose on Mospheira, where he could join the local hate-mongers and become one of a few hundred troublemakers the government already kept an eye on, rather than a point of ferment in an immigrant population that was, depend on it, going to have their troubles adjusting to a station ruled by atevi and regulated by rules they hadn't made.

He didn't know if he could possibly justify removing Braddock to the planet. He didn't know if he had the authority just to do it. But Captain Sabin might give that order, if she retained custody of Braddock under some arcane provision of ship law. He wished he'd talked to her on that delicate topic before now, before they were suddenly short of time.

And he was sure *she* was constrained by delicate politics in that regard, because Braddock had actually been head of the main body of the Pilots' Guild and she, head of the same Guild on the ship, had simply booted him out of office and taken that post herself.

So there were considerations, even for the iron-handed senior captain of the *Phoenix*. Sabin didn't give a damn about appearances, ordinarily, but she did have to give a damn about the broader electorate on the station, when the Guild such as it was did get around to its next elections, and various issues came out.

Her reelection to the governing post she'd used a captain's authority to appropriate was fairly likely—was *almost* a certainty, unless some challenge to her blew up once they got to the station and dealt with the other ship's captain, Jules Ogun. But still, there were appearances to maintain, and there were certainly issues that could blow up, not least among them what they did with Braddock, and how the Reunioners reacted when they got onto the station and met the rules that restricted atevi-human contact and placed certain decisions wholly in atevi hands. Sabin at the head of the Guild was their best insurance that the new bloc of population wouldn't be a problem, that they'd learn the situation before demagogues took to exploiting it: she knew them; Ogun didn't. They damned sure didn't want Reunioners trying to run things, not until they'd had a long, long time to learn how the human-atevi agreements worked.

Then—then there was explaining to Tabini that they hadn't gotten to Reunion before the aliens had, that the alien kyo had taken possession of Reunion as an outpost built in what they considered their territory, and that, no, the kyo hadn't gotten their hands on the human archive—they'd wiped that from the files—but the kyo did have this very inconvenient habit of considering whatever they'd met as part of them forever. They didn't disengage. Ever.

Fortunately they were able now to talk to the kyo, who seemed willing to reason, but—

In interspecies dealings, there was always a *but.*

In this case, there was a big one. The kyo, no better at interstellar diplomacy, it seemed, than the Reunion colonists, had contacted something considerable on the other side of *their* space, something they were very much afraid of. Kyo had fairly well demonstrated their ability to slag a complex human structure. And kyo, for reasons likely as convolute as the atevi sensitivity to math, didn't relinquish any contact they'd once made. More, the kyo authority seemed, at least on very superficial examination of their attitudes, to be homogenous—without dissidence. Without a concept of permissible dissidence. This was, in interspecies relations as much as in internal politics, worrisome.

Maybe they'd swallowed their internal opposition. Or destroyed it. Or just ignored it.

Sticky. Damned sticky.

Sorry, he'd have to say to Tabini. I did the best I could. We all did. But the kyo are out there. Something else is out there. We're not sure, on the example of kyo behavior with the Reunioners, if we can keep the kyo away from us.

He'd shut his eyes without knowing he'd shut them. When he realized he had, he decided to try sleeping, finding himself very tired and not quite knowing why. Maybe it was just the letdown after a long, long voyage.

He was aware of a hand on his shoulder. Someone wanting his attention. The intercom panel was flashing red, a flood of blinking light dyeing the cabin walls, all its strands and streamers of spider plants. And he had slept.

"We are about to make the drop, nandi." It was Narani looming over him, not Jago. "Be sure you are secure."

"Indeed," he murmured. It was the predawn watches. Jago hadn't come to bed. "Is everything all right, Rani-ji?"

"Proceeding very well," Narani said. "We are nearly ready. I have put out appropriate clothing, nandi, for the event. We shall be here as soon as possible after the arrival to assist you to dress."

"Your safety comes first, nadi," he said. He felt guilty, privileged to sleep while his staff had surely been up and working through the night. But that was the order of the universe. "Go, go quickly, nadi-ji."

Narani left. Left the door open, admitting a white light that ameliorated the red flash of the panel and made the spider plants look less nightmarish. And he *was* tired, caught up out of sleep. He had no idea what time it was. If he just lifted his head he might be able to see the clock, but that effort took energy.

The siren jolted him out of a drift toward sleep, and Sabin's voice echoed from on high.

"Sabin here. We're about to make drop. Three minute warning. Take hold. Take hold, take hold."

Jago was usually beside him when they went through one of these transitions. He wasn't used to fending for himself, which, when he thought about it, was ridiculous. He ordered the room lights on, gave a fast scan of the premises—but no, Narani hadn't left the clothing on the chair as he usually did. The items must be in a locker.

Nothing was going to fly loose, nothing was going to float. He was safe. He lay back again.

And depend on Sabin, no emotion, no promises, no flourishes about homecoming, and no bets laid, nothing to indicate this wasn't just one of the many ordinary transitions.

Eyes fixed on the ceiling.

Slight feeling of floating. It wasn't that they exactly stopped spin—so Jase informed him—but that the effects of the shift did that to them. Things became highly uncertain for a moment, stomach-wrenching.

Home, he told himself. Home. And tried not to think about the circumsolar rocks.

The sight of all those spider plants lifting their tendrils at once was always too strange for words.

Then the green curtain sank and hung as before.

"We're in, cousins," Sabin's voice, uncharacteristically full of feeling this time. *"We are in."*

Emotion from Sabin. God. Unprecedented.

And he needed his clothes. Needed to move. He scrambled up, went to the bath for a quick apology to hygiene, and when he came out to dress, lo and behold, Jeladi and Bindanda had made it in, had clothes ready for him to step into, lace-bearing shirt already inserted into formal coat.

On with the boots, equally quick. He dropped into a chair and ducked his head for Jeladi to loose his hair, comb it, and rebraid it with the white ribbon of the paidhi's office, which he had never abandoned.

Ready, in record time—not a sort of thing atevi applauded, haste in preparation, but there were moments aboard the ship when haste served very well.

"Nadiin-ji," he acknowledged their effort. "Have your breakfast, cautiously. I shall make do with whatever the dowager brings along."

"By no means, nandi," Bindanda said, and took a packet from the desk-top. "One may find breakfast for the two captains, as well."

"Danda-ji, you are a treasure." He took said packet and gave a little bow to his staff, tucking it away out of sight in his lefthand coat pocket, Bindanda's little high-energy fruit and nut sticks, if he could judge by the size of it . . . and he lost no time betting Banichi and Jago were similarly provided, not to mention the dowager and her party, and Gin and Jerry. A snack in reserve was a very good idea, they had learned, in a long bridge-side vigil. Bridge crew might change shifts, but galley didn't function until the ship had gotten the all-clear. And not that he thought Sabin or, by her example, Jase, would partake, but there, they would have made the gesture.

He headed into the hall, got as far as the security station before Banichi and Jago met him, outside a room now broken down to crates, and by now the dowager and her party were out their door, joining them in the corridor, the dowager and Cenedi and Cajeiri, all of them proceeding with some dispatch down to the end of the corridor, and out.

Gin and Jerry met them at the lifts.

"May one wish the young aiji," Gin said in fairly complex Ragi, "the felicitation of completing a seventh year?"

"Nandi," Cajeiri said with a bow, with outstanding good grace for a lad deprived of his birthday party.

"Indeed," Bren said. Gin's Ragi had gotten good, but he bet she had practiced that one. "A seventh year of extraordinary nature."

"One is extremely gratified, nandi," the boy muttered, eyes downcast, in the ragged remnant of his good grace. The glum tone flirted with the dowager's displeasure. The fearsome cane tapped the floor just once, a reminder.

In that moment the lift arrived, saving the boy further compliments. Banichi and Cenedi secured the doors while they got in, the dowager first, with Cajeiri, and then Bren, and Gin and Jerry, while security folded in after and the doors shut, one of those rhythms of life,

protocol, and precedence that had operated like clock-
work in their two-year voyage, for, oh, so many trips up
and down this lift system.

"We should—" Gin began to say as the car started to
move.

Siren. *Emergency stop.* Cenedi moved to brace the
dowager and Cajeiri, Banichi moved to brace Bren, and
Jago grabbed Gin and Jerry with one arm, and flew up.
She made a terrible crash, and thumped back down
onto her feet, Gin and Jerry with her.

"Jago," Bren exclaimed, afraid she had hit the overhead.

"Of no consequence, nandi," Jago said, pressing both
Gin and Jerry against one of the recessed safety grips.
She *was* hurt, the only one of them who was hurt, to all
appearances. Bren frowned in concern.

"We have arrived," the intercom said from the ceiling
of the car, which Bren realized queasily had *not* in fact
stopped: it was the ship that had moved. *"We are at
home port. Report any injuries. The maneuver was automatic due to system traffic. We remain in a takehold condition."*

System traffic, Bren said to himself, still shaken. System traffic, for God's sake!

So much for missing space junk. Somebody had put a
damned spacecraft in their way. And where had traffic
congestion come from, in a station that derived most of
its support from the planet it orbited?

He kept his eye on Jago, who flexed her left shoulder
and looked otherwise undamaged.

The car arrived at its destination, meanwhile, as if
nothing had happened. The door opened onto the
bridge, and Jase's man Kaplan, in fatigues, reached the
door and held it open for them. "You're clear to the
shelter, ma'am, sir," Kaplan said with an awkward little
bow. "Go, go! We're still in takehold."

When ship's crew said move, moving fast was a good
idea. A padded recess existed between the lift and the

bridge, two narrow walls, just to the side of their usual observation post, for just such a purpose. "The shelter," Bren informed Banichi, in case he hadn't followed all of it, and Jago took Gin and Jerry along, Cenedi walking with the dowager and Cajeiri in the lead, all with utmost dispatch. They entered the padded area and their security took strong hold of the available handgrips, to protect their more fragile lords.

They stayed there, ready for imminent, joint-breaking movement for what might be five minutes. But the ship stayed steady. "What injury, nadi?" Bren asked Jago, who, directly asked, gave a shrug.

"Bruises, nadi." Never saying that the two humans she was trying to protect had gotten between her and the one handgrip that might have prevented her hitting the overhead.

"What just happened, nandiin?" Cajeiri asked his elders.

"One surmises," Bren said, in the absence of other answers, "that the ship dodged some sort of spacecraft. It seems we braked." He was trying to calculate the vector of their violent movement relative to the ship's axis of motion. He thought the motion might have been braking, not acceleration, but his rattled brain refused to figure the angles. Refused to function clearly. What in *hell* spacecraft was there for them to run into? Had they nearly hit the second starship, in the shipyard, the one Ogun was building?

The navigators had been so cocksure they knew their approach. And that presumably included knowing the location of the shipyard and the construction.

Kaplan showed up again, at the end of the shelter, and immediately seized a handgrip. "Is everybody all right in here? We can get a medic now. We're in a condition yellow."

Yellow wasn't quite emergency. But it was close to it.

"He asks do we need medical attention."

"We do not," Ilisidi said.

"No, nandi," Jago said, "truly, only a bruise."

A gentle move, as ships went. A small diminution of their speed. But not a move they'd planned.

"We don't," Bren translated. "We're all right."

"None of us expected that hiccup, sir," Kaplan said. "Cap'ns say they're very sorry. We're about to stand down to blue, so you can move around when it goes."

"The ship apologizes, nand' dowager," Bren translated, letting go a deep, unconsciously-held breath. "And Kaplan-nadi informs us we should be given an all-clear soon, at least a condition of moderate caution."

"And what has caused this event?" Ilisidi asked.

"The dowager asks what caused the action," Bren translated the question.

"There's *mining* craft out, sir," Kaplan said. "Best I hear, latest, there's *mining* craft, six, seven of 'em we've picked up, as is, all of 'em bots."

Bots. Bren cast a look at Gin, who looked as surprised as he was. Her robots, those would be, the craft of her design, carrying on operations full bore—certainly more of them than they'd left operational.

"That's good," Gin said. Except for their near-collision, it seemed to be good. Early on in the history of humans in this solar system, human beings had used to pilot ships in that dangerous duty, because the old Pilots' Guild hadn't been remotely interested in devoting resources to building robots to do the job, not because they couldn't, but because they wouldn't, a decision upheld for political reasons, notably keeping their volatile and angry colonial population in line. It hadn't been possible at the earlier star they'd reached, the White Star, for very real reasons, the same reasons that had killed the miners. But at the atevi world there was no such excuse: they were only interested in keeping the colonists so busy with their dangerous work that they had no time to foment revolution: it had been that bad, in the old days, and there was no Mospheiran to this day but regarded the Guild with extreme suspicion and misgivings.

Now it sounded as if the station, recently recovered, after centuries in mothballs, had gone back into full-scale mining operations, by robot, the way they should have done. The station must be needing the grosser supplies in their ship-building now—a project which would need far more supplies than they could lift from the planet's surface. Electronics, rarer metals, some ceramics: those would still come up the long, expensive climb out of atmosphere, but apparently they'd reached the stage where they needed to haul in iron and nickel from the floating junk that was so abundant up here. That meant they'd gotten the refining process out of mothballs and gotten it working.

Well. Good. Counting a kyo visitation was not beyond probability, that progress toward a second starship was very good, and they'd happily contribute the mining bots they had stowed in *Phoenix's* forward hold. It was a good thing to look as powerful and prosperous as they could. Ogun had put them ahead of schedule.

"Clear under caution," the announcement went out, generally, and Kaplan listened to the unit in his ear for a second. "You're clear to move now, sir, but get to seats fast and don't get up."

"We may sit," Bren translated that, "and should move quickly to reach our seats and belt in." The dowager and Cajeiri were nearest the seats in question, those along a section of freestanding wall—actually an acceleration buffer—at the rear of the bridge. The dowager moved with fair dispatch, taking Cajeiri with her, Cenedi and his man in close company with them and seeing them settled. "Go," Bren said to Gin, after the dowager was in, and Gin and Jerry moved out.

He came last with Banichi and Jago, and slipped quickly into a seat. In front of them, row on row of consoles and operators tracked surrounding space, the condition of the ship, the location of various items like the stray mining bots—and, one presumed, established communication with the station.

Above it all, a wide screen showed a disk-shaped light, which was—God, was it really home? Was that beautiful star in center screen their own planet shining in the sun?

There, it must be. That dimmer light was the moon. And a bright oblong light that might not be a star. It *might* be the station itself. He wondered how great a magnification that was.

Bren found himself shivering. He suddenly wanted to be there faster, faster, as fast as at all possible, to see and do all he'd been waiting so long for. And to find out that things were all right, and that all the people he wanted to find were waiting for him.

Jase and Sabin, at the far side of the bridge, were close to another bulkhead and another shelter like the one they had left, but once they began moving about in some confidence, Bren stood up judiciously, hand on a recessed takehold on the curtain wall, and caught Jase's eye.

Jase worked his way down the aisle in their direction.

"Sorry about that little surprise," Jase said. "Is everyone all right?"

"We seem to be," Bren said, finding himself a little shaky in this resumption of normalcy. "Was that just one of those things that sometimes happens?"

"I have no idea," Jase said. "We've never been where traffic was an issue, not since this ship left old Earth, far as I know. Sabin doesn't say a thing, but we've counted quite an amazing lot of these little craft. Sabin's called the station, and if the chronometer's right, it's Ogun's offshift. They're going to have to get him out of bed."

"I don't think he'll mind," Bren said.

"Not likely he will." Deep sigh. "Time lag is a pain."

"Can you make out the shipyard? Have you been able to find it?"

"That's the worrisome thing. There's no activity out there. No lights, nothing. Black as deep space."

A foreboding little chill crept down Bren's back. A

lot of robot miners. And no activity in the region that should be the focus of the effort. "That's odd." He saw a reply counter running on that image at the front of the bridge, down in the corner of the screen, now that he looked for it. It was -00:04:22 going on 23.

Four minutes without an answer. That gave a little clue about distance and magnification.

Then:

"Put it on general intercom, all crew areas, C1." That was Sabin.

". . . .just got here," came over the general address. Ogun's voice. Thank God.

"Can you respond?"

"Earth had one moon." That wasn't conversational on Sabin's part.

"Mars had two," from Ogun. Clearly an exchange of codewords. *"You're a welcome sight. How did it go?"*

"Rescue was entirely successful. We have 4078 passengers."

A little silence, a slight lagtime for the signal, but nothing significant. *"What is your situation with the atevi on board?"*

"Excellent," Sabin said. "And they're hearing you, at the moment."

"Is the dowager in good health? Is the aiji's heir safe?"

Right from human and ordinary, *hello, good to see you,* to *how is the dowager?* Odd swerve in topics. Bren's pulse picked up, and he tried not to lose a word or nuance of what he might have to translate for the dowager.

"Both are here on the bridge, safe and sound. Why, Jules?"

Why in hell, Bren wondered simultaneously, *are atevi the first issue?*

"And Mr. Cameron? Is he with you?"

"Here and able to respond if you have a question for him. Is there a problem, Jules?"

"Just checking."

"Checking, hell! What's going on over there, Jules? Is there a problem on your side?

"Did you find anything out there?"

Bren found his palms sweating. Sabin shifted her stance, leaned close to the communications console, both hands on the counter. And became uncharacteristically patient.

"Peaceful contact with a species called the kyo, a complex situation. They've been willing to talk, thanks to the atevi's good offices. Colonists are safe and rescued. We've got a lot to report. But I want answers. What is your situation, Jules? What's this set of questions? Where's a simple *glad to see you*?"

"We are immensely glad to see you. The tanks aren't finished. The ship isn't finished. Food is not in great supply here."

Worse and worse.

"Jules, why not?"

"We have an ongoing problem. Shuttles aren't flying. Haven't, for eight months. We're cut off from supply, trying to finish and fill the food production tanks on a priority basis."

Banichi had gotten to his feet. So had Jago, Cenedi, the dowager, and, necessarily, Cajeiri, followed by Gin and Jerry.

Bren gave them a sign, wait, wait.

"Why not?" Sabin asked. "Come out with it, Jules. What's happened there?"

"The government's collapsed on the mainland. The aiji is no longer communicating with us or anybody. The dish at Mogari-nai is not transmitting. Shuttles are no longer launching from the spaceports. As best the Island can figure, the aishidi'tat *is in complete turmoil and only regional governments are functioning with any efficiency at all."*

God.

"What is this?" Ilisidi demanded outright, and Bren turned quietly to translate.

"With great regret, one apprehends there has been upheaval in the *aishidi'tat* as of eight months ago, aiji-ma. Your grandson is not answering queries, Mogari-nai has shut down, and shuttles are not reaching the station with supplies, aiji-ma. The station is very short of food and rushing desperately to build independent food production facilities. Ogun-aiji is extremely glad to know you and the heir are safe."

A moment of silence. Then, *bang!* went the cane on the deck.

"Where is Lord Geigi?"

Geigi, in charge of the atevi contingent on the station. There was a question. "I shall attempt to establish contact with him," Bren said, and with a little bow went straight to Sabin, into, at the moment, dangerous territory.

"The dowager, Captain, wishes to speak to Lord Geigi as quickly as possible."

"Jules. Is Lord Geigi available? The dowager wants to talk to him."

A little delay.

"We can get him," Ogun said.

"C2," Sabin said sharply. That was the second communications post, as she was using C1's offices. "Get linked up to the station atevi and get the dowager a handheld. Get her through to whoever she wants."

Finding the handheld was a reach under the counter, for C2. Finding Lord Geigi in the middle of his night was likely to take a moment, and Bren took the handheld back to Cenedi, who would manage the technicalities of the connection for Ilisidi.

"They are trying," he informed the dowager, and met a worried, eye-level stare from Cajeiri, who asked no questions of his elders, but who clearly understood far too much.

"I'll see what I can learn from my office," Gin said, and crossed the deck to occupy another of the several communications stations, and to borrow another handheld. She would be looking for contact with the station's

Island-originated technical staff, in the Mospheiran sections of the station.

For a moment the paidhi stood in the vacuum-eye of a hurricane, in a low availability of information surrounded by total upheaval, and didn't know what direction to turn first. But Jase was his information source and Jase had moved up next to Sabin, who was still asking Ogun questions. The two voices, considerably lagged, echoed over the crew-area address.

"Is the station peaceful?"

"Yes," Ogun was able to say. *"We're holding our own up here. Everyone aboard is cooperating, in full knowledge of the seriousness of the crisis. We are in contact with the government on Mospheira, and they're arguing about whether to pull out all stops building a shuttle or maybe supply rockets, but right now the question is stalled in their legislature, and no few are arguing for an anti-missile program . . ."*

Good, loving God. The world had lost its collective mind. *Missile defense? Missiles,* coming from the mainland against Mospheira?

When he'd taken office, they'd been quarreling about routes for roads and rail transport for a continent mostly rural. Television had been a newborn scandal, an attraction threatening the popularity of the traditional machimi. There had just been airplanes.

And suddenly there were *missiles,* as a direct, profane result of the space program he'd worked for a decade to institute? Damn it all!

Cenedi was talking to Lord Geigi's head of security, meanwhile, and he picked up one side of that conversation, which Banichi and Jago could follow on their own equipment. He recalled belatedly that he carried his own small piece of ship's equipment in his pocket, that he'd picked it up when he left the apartment this morning. He pulled it out, used a fingernail to dial the setting to 2, the channel they were using to get to Geigi, and shoved it hard into his ear.

Geigi was being given a phone. He imagined a very disturbed Geigi, a plump man caught abed by the ship's return, but Geigi was never the sort to sit idly by while a situation was developing. Geigi would be at least partway dressed by now, his staff scrambling on all levels, knowing their lord would be wanting information on every front.

"To whom am I speaking?" Geigi's deep voice, unheard for two years, was unmistakable and oh, so welcome.

"I am turning the phone over to the aiji-dowager, nandi, immediately."

Cenedi did so, while, in Bren's other ear, Sabin continued in hot and heavy converse with Ogun. He hoped Gin was following the exposition, too—a chronicle of disaster and shortage on the station, with remarkably good behavior from the inhabitants, who had pitched in to conserve and work overtime. Ogun had concentrated all their in-orbit ship-building resources into miningbots, attempting to secure metals and ice, most of all to build those tanks for food production—a steep, steep production demand, with a very little seed of algaes and yeasts. The ship could have helped—if she weren't carrying four thousand more mouths to feed.

"Geigi. Geigi-ji," Ilisidi said. She never liked telephones, or fancy pocketcoms, and she tended to raise her voice when she absolutely had to use one. "One hears entirely unacceptable news."

"Aiji-ma," Geigi said. *"One is extremely glad of your safe return, particularly in present circumstances. The* aishidi'tat, *one regrets to say, has fractured."*

The Western Association. Civil war.

"And my grandson?"

"Missing, vanished. One hesitates to say—but the rumor holds he was assassinated in a conspiracy of the Kadigidi—"

"The Kadigidi!" Outrage fired Ilisidi's voice.

"And the Marid Tasigin. The assassination is uncon-

firmed, aiji-ma, and many believe the aiji is in hiding and forming plans to return. But your safe return and the heir's is exceedingly welcome to all of us on the station. Man'chi is unbroken here, on my life, aiji-ma."

Man'chi. That inexplicable emotional surety of connection and loyalty. The instinct that drove atevi society to associate together. Man'chi between Geigi and the dowager was holding fast. That down on the planet was not faring as well—if one could ever expect loyalty of the Marid Tasigin, which had always been a trouble spot in the association. The Kadigidi lord, on the other hand—if it was Murini—had been an ally.

"We are confident in your estimation," Ilisidi said. Aijiin had died, accepting such assurances from persons who then turned out to be on the other side, but Bren agreed with her assessment. The Kadigidi and the Marid Tasigin might rebel, but never the Edi, under Lord Geigi, and up here. The western peninsula, Lord Geigi's region, would hold for Tabini, even if they could not find him—a situation which, Bren insisted to himself, did not at all mean that Tabini was dead. Tabini was not an easy man to catch.

"Our situation on the station," Geigi said further, *"is at present precarious, aiji-ma, in scarcity of food, in the disheartenment which necessarily attends such a blow to the Association. We have waited for you. We have waited for you, expecting your return, while attempting to strengthen our situation, and we have broadcast messages of encouragement to supporters of the* aishidi'tat, *through the dish on Mospheira. We have asked the* presidenta *of Mospheira to recognize the* aishidi'tat *as continuing in authority aboard this station, which he has done by vote of his legislature."*

Good for Shawn Tyers. Good for him. The President was an old friend of his. The Mospheiran legislature took dynamite to move it, but move it must have, to take a firm and even risky decision.

"When did this attack happen, nandi?" Ilisidi asked.

"Eight months ago, aiji-ma." Shortly after they had set out from Reunion homeward. *"Eight months ago assassins struck in Shejidan, taking the Bujavid while the aiji was on holiday at Taiben. The Kadigidi and the Taisigini declared themselves in control, and attempted to claim that they had assassinated the aiji, but Tabini-aiji broadcast a message that he was alive and by no means recognized their occupation of the capital. The Kadigidi attempted to engage the Assassins' Guild on their side, but the Guild refused their petition and continued to regard the matter as unsettled. The aiji meanwhile went on to the coast, to Mogari-nai."*

That was the site of the big dish, the site of atevi communications with the station.

". . . but the Kadigidi struck there, as well. For several months thereafter we have heard rumors of the aiji's movements, and we do not despair of hearing from him soon, aiji-ma. He may well send word once he hears you are back."

"Or he may not," Ilisidi said, "if he is not yet prepared. He may let opposition concentrate on us."

"True," Geigi said. *"But we have not heard news lately. The Kadigidi have never since dared claim he is dead. But they may advance such a claim in desperation, Sidi-ji, now that you have arrived."*

"Well," Ilisidi said, as taken aback as Bren had ever seen her. She stood there staring at nothing in particular, and Cajeiri stood by, looking to her for answers. As they all did. "Well," she said again.

Jase, meanwhile, had been carrying on a running translation for Sabin, who stood, likewise looking at Ilisidi.

"Where," Ilisidi asked Geigi sharply, "where is Tatiseigi?"

Cajeiri's great-uncle, lord of the Atageini, sharing a boundary with the Kadigidi.

"At his estate, aiji-ma. Apparently safe. The Lady Damiri is not there."

Cajeiri's mother, who owed direct allegiance to the Atageini lord, Tatiseigi. Damiri was, very possibly, traveling with Tabini, if he was alive. She could have sheltered with her uncle, but apparently she was missing right along with Tabini, still loyal, and a constraint on her great-uncle.

"How many provinces are now joining in this rebellion?"

"Four provinces in the south, two in the east, under Lord Darudi."

"There is a head destined to fall," Ilisidi said placidly. "And Tatiseigi? His man'chi?"

"His neighbors the Kadigidi are surely watching him very closely, as if he might harbor the aiji or the consort, but he will not commit to this side or the other and they dare not touch him because of the Northern Association."

"The Northern Association holds?"

"It holds, aiji-ma."

It was worth a deep, long sigh of relief. Atevi didn't have borders. They had overlapping spheres of influence and allegiance. Within the *aishidi'tat* there were hundreds of associations of all sizes, from two or three provinces, likewise hazy in border, give or take, commonly, the loyalty of two or three families within the overlap. And if the Northern Association had held firm, rallying around Tatiseigi of the Atageini, the Midlands Association, to which the neighboring Kadigidi belonged, would be rash to make a move against Cajeiri's mother's relatives.

And *Cajeiri* arriving back in the picture gave Uncle Tatiseigi a powerful claimant to power from *his* household, which would bring all sorts of pressure within Tatiseigi's association . . . God, it had been so long since he had traced the mazes of atevi clans and allegiances, or had to wonder where the Assassins' Guild was going to come down on an issue.

Tabini missing. Assassinations. Havoc in the *aishidi'tat*.

One thing occurred to him, one primary question.

"Where are the shuttles, aiji-ma? Have they survived this disorder?"

"Excellent question," Ilisidi said, and relayed it to Geigi. "Where are the shuttles?"

"We have one shuttle docked at the station," was Geigi's very welcome answer. *"But we have no safe port to land it. The rebels hold the seacoast. We fear it may suffer attack, even if we attempt a landing on Mospheira."*

God. But they still had one functional shuttle.

One.

"Aiji-ma," Geigi said, *"I have maps. I have maps, and letters, which I can send to you for more detailed information, if the station and the ship will permit."*

Jase had translated that. They suddenly had Sabin's full attention. "Jules," Sabin said to her conversant, "Lord Geigi wants to transmit documents."

"He should send them," Bren said, "aiji-ma."

"I shall get them together," Lord Geigi said, when she ordered the transmission. *"And I shall be there to meet you when you dock, aiji-ma."*

"A cold trek and pointless," was Ilisidi's response. "Order my staff and the paidhi's to prepare our rooms and never mind coming to that abysmally uncomfortable dock. We shall meet you in decent comfort, Geigi-ji, as soon as possible. If you think of other matters, include them with your documents. I am handing this phone back now."

"Yes," Geigi said, accepting orders, and the contact went dead.

Bren stood still, numb, and glanced at Jase.

"I translated," Jase said, with a shift of the eyes toward Sabin.

"We have a problem, it seems," Sabin said. "We have a shuttle, a ship full of more mouths to feed—we do have our own ship's tanks, which should suffice to feed us all and the station, not well, but adequately, so at least we won't overburden their systems. And we have our additional miner-bots, slow as that process may be."

"We have our own manufacturing module," Gin said. "And we have some supplies. We can start assembly and programming on extant stock as soon as we dock. We can get them to work in fairly short order, and see if we can pick up the pace of their operation."

"Good," Sabin said shortly.

In one word, from high hopes and the expectation of luxury back to a situation of shortage and the necessity of mining in orbit, the condition of life of their ancestors. The condition of the great-grandfathers of the Reunioners, too, who had had to build their distant station in desolation and hazard, by their own bootstraps.

They had to break that news to four thousand-odd colonists, and still keep the lid on their patience. Four thousand desperate people who'd been promised the sun and the moon and fruit drops forever once they got to the home station—and they were back to a hardscrabble existence, with a revolution in progress down in the gravity well.

The gravity well. That long, long drop. Bren felt a sensation he hadn't felt in two years, the sensation of standing at the top of a dizzying deep pit, at the bottom of which lay business he couldn't let go its own course.

Tabini. Atevi civilization. Toby and his own family, such as he had.

"Mani-ma." Cajeiri, ever so quietly, addressing his great-grandmother. "Do you think my father and mother are still alive?"

Ilisidi gave a snort. "The Kadigidi would wish it known if not. Evidently they dare not claim it, even if they hope it to be the case, and one doubts they have so much as a good hope of being right. Likely your father and mother are alive and waiting for us to descend with force from the heavens."

"Shall we, mani-ma?"

"As soon as possible," Ilisidi said, and looked at Bren. "Shall we not?"

"How long until dock?" Bren asked the captains.

A flat stare from Sabin. "A fairly fast passage. When we get there, we're going to be letting these passengers off in small packets. Very small packets. Their quarters have to be warmed and provisioned."

They could warm a section at a time, and would, he was very sure; but they could also do it at their own speed, which was likely to be very slow. Sabin meant she was not going to have a general debarcation, no celebration, no letting their dangerous cargo loose wholesale.

And Gin Kroger had to get at her packaged robots and get the manufactury unpacked.

"I very well understand," he said with a bow of his head that was automatic by now, to atevi and to humans. "I think it wise, for what it's worth."

"Our passengers are stationers," Sabin said. "Spacers. They understand fragile systems. They won't outright riot. But small conspiracies are dangerous—with people that understand fragile systems. I'm going to request Ogun to invoke martial law on the station until we completely settle these people in—simplifying our problems of control. I trust you can make this understood among atevi. I trust there's not going to be some coup on that side of the station."

There was very little human behavior that could not be passed off among atevi with a shrug. But emotions would be running high there, too, considering the dowager's return.

"We don't likely have any Kadigidi sympathizers on station," Bren said quietly. "No. But there may be high feelings, all the same, with the return of the aiji's son, and the only general translation of martial law doesn't mean no celebration. *No one* can lay a hand on him or the dowager, no matter whose rules they violate."

"Understood," Sabin said. "That will be made very

clear to our personnel. I trust the dowager to manage hers." She drew a deep breath, set hands on hips and looked across the bridge. "We're inertial for the station. Before we make connection with the core, we've got to decide whether to run the dowager aboard at high speed, or be prepared to sit it out and establish our set of rules first. I'm inclined to get your party aboard first, if you can guarantee quiet once you're there."

"Yes," Bren said. Absolutes made him nervous as hell, but he had laid his life on Geigi's integrity often enough before this. "We'll take the fast route in, straight into the atevi section. Humans may be excited to know she's here. That's my chief worry. They'll want to see her."

"No question they'll be excited," Jase said.

Ilisidi was popular on the station, even among humans. Ilisidi always had been. And right now people were desperate for authority.

"I'd suggest we not discuss our boarding," Bren said. "If we get Geigi's men positioned near the lift, we can get into our own section fast and just not answer the outside. Stationers know better than to rush atevi security."

"You go on station with them," Sabin said to Jase. "I want you in direct liaison with Ogun."

"We can trickle the Reunioners on, three to five at a time," Jase said quietly, "Drag out the formalities, mandatory orientations—rules and records-keeping they understand. The technical problems of warming a section for occupation, they well understand."

"Register them to sponsors," Gin put in, "to *our* people, who know atevi."

It wasn't the first time Gin had put forward that idea, and they'd shot it down, not wanting to create a class difference between Mospheirans and Reunioners. But right now it made thorough sense to do it . . . a sense that might reverberate through human culture for centuries if they weren't careful.

"All that's Graham's problem," Sabin said shortly, meaning Jase had to make that decision among a thousand others, and she knew what he'd choose. "My whole concern is the security of this ship, its crew, and its supply. So are your atevi going to time out on us for an internal war, Mr. Cameron? Or can you explain to them we *might* see strangers popping into the system for a visit at any time from now on? I'd really rather have our affairs in better order when that happens."

"I intend to make that point," Bren said.

"Make it, hard. We need those shuttles. That would solve an entire array of problems. In the meantime, Ms. Kroger, I need your professional services, and will need them, urgently and constantly for the foreseeable future. Captain Ogun's got his mining operation going all-out here, but if Cameron can't get atevi resources up to us off the planet, or can't get them tomorrow, we've got the immediate problem of feeding this lot—and I'm not ready to rip the shipyard apart worse than it already is to get supply. I want Captain Ogun's tanks, Ms. Kroger. Shielded tanks and water sufficient to handle the station population indefinitely."

"Understood," Gin said.

"Then everybody get moving," Sabin said.

Bren translated for the dowager. "The ship-aijiin recommend we go below and make final preparations to leave the ship, which will be a hurried transit, aiji-ma, into a disturbed population."

"We are prepared," Ilisidi said with a wave of her hand. The dowager had acquired a certain respect for Sabin-aiji, after a difficult start—a respect particularly active whenever Sabin's opinion coincided with hers. "We are always prepared. Tell her see to her own people."

"The dowager states she is prepared for any eventuality." There were times he didn't translate all of what one side said; and there were times he did. "The aiji-dowager expects you to control the human side of this.

She is prepared to make inroads into the atevi situation."

"Go below and observe takehold," Sabin said. "The lot of you. We're not wasting any time getting in there, no time for more ferment on their side or ours, thank you."

"Aiji-ma," Bren translated that. "The ship is about to move with greater than ordinary dispatch and Sabin-aiji politely urges us all to take appropriate shelter belowdecks for a violent transit. This will speed us in before there can be further disturbance on the station or among our human passengers."

"Good," Ilisidi said sharply and headed for the lift, marking her path with energetic taps of the cane. Her great-grandson and the rest of her company could only make haste behind her to reach the doors, while the ship sounded the imminent-motion warning.

It was certainly not the homecoming they'd planned. Damn, Bren thought bleakly, taking his place inside the lift car. They'd ridden from nervous anticipation to the depths of anxiety all in an hour; and amid everything else—

Amid everything else, he thought, looking across the car at Cajeiri, there'd been no special word for a boy who'd just heard bad news about his mother and father, and who remained appallingly quiet.

What *did* he say to an atevi child? Or what should his great-grandmother have said, or what dared he say now?

The lift moved. Meanwhile the intercom gave the order: *"Maneuvers imminent. Takehold and brace for very strong movement."*

Four thousand colonists were getting that news, people unacculturated to the delicate and dangerous situation they were going to land in on the station, people whose holier-than-common-colonists attitudes were even more objectionable to the Mospheirans who were half the workforce on that station, and whose ancestors had suffered under Guild management . . . and who were going to have to sponsor the Reunioners if, as seemed likely now, Gin's plan prevailed.

Four thousand people who'd been promised paradise ended up on tighter rations than they'd had where they'd come from. And the Mospheirans, who were going to have to live with them and who'd already endured hardship since the shuttles had stopped flying, weren't going to be anywhere near as patient with their daily complaints as the ship had been.

Jerry and Gin were holding quiet, rapid-fire consultations next to him, Jerry agreeing to stay aboard the ship while Gin went to her on-station offices to take control. Banichi was holding quick converse with Cenedi.

The lift hit five-deck level and opened for them. Gin and Jerry went one way, they went another, past sentries, into the atevi section.

"Aiji-ma," Bren said, prepared to take his leave and deal with his own staff. "Nandi." For the youngster, who gravely bowed. He remained distressed for the boy, the heir, who might in some atevi minds on that station now *be* the new aiji of Shejidan; but none of them had time to discuss their situation or accommodate an eight-year-old boy's natural distress—not in a ship about to undertake maneuvers. Beyond that, he reminded himself, Cajeiri's whole being responded to man'chi, a set of emotions a human being was only minimally wired to understand. For all he knew, the boy was approaching the explosion point. Every association of the boy's life was under assault, while atevi under him and around him in the hierarchy would rally round and carry on with all the resources the battered association could rake together. God *knew* what the boy was feeling, or whether he was just numb at the moment, or how he would react when the whole expectations of the station atevi centered on him.

"Go," Ilisidi said sharply, curt dismissal, and he

strode down the corridor at all speed, Banichi and Jago in close company, down to the safety of his own quarters. Takehold racketed through the corridors. Narani waited by his cabin door, but Bren ordered him to safety.

Inside, a shocking transformation. The walls were stripped of plants now, shockingly barren. Everything was barren, even the mattress, the bed he had shared with Jago for two years, lacking sheets and blankets.

He lay down nonetheless, and Jago lay down beside him, pulled the safety netting across, preparing for what could be a scary, hard pull.

"Final warning," sounded over the general com. *"Takehold where you are."*

Engines kicked in. The force dragged at them.

"How is Cajeiri taking the news, Jago-ji?" he asked Jago, staring at the ceiling. "Can one tell?"

A slight move beside him, a shrug, it might be. "Likely still thinking on it, Bren-ji," she said.

"Can we help him?" As if the boy was a ticking bomb. "Dare we?" Then: "Should we?"

"The aiji-dowager is his only present anchor," Jago said, "and if his father should be dead, who knows? Who can know? What he feels, what he may feel, no one can predict."

Emotions, again. Emotions that connected atevi in associations, that dictated who ruled, who followed. Impassivity and formality were so much the rule of polite society; but there were currents under the still surface that he could only imagine—in the boy, and in Ilisidi herself, whose grandson was Tabini-aiji, whose allies had turned against the state she had helped build.

Engines kept up the push. For every force they put on the ship, they'd have to take it off again before they docked. It was going to be a long, rough ride, but he completely agreed with Sabin: if they got there an hour faster, the rumor mill on the station would have an hour less run-time to create problems for them.

And if they could only scare the Reunioners in their belly badly enough, without making them mad, they might have an edge in maintaining control of them. The former inhabitants of Reunion Station weren't acclimated to rough maneuvers. They had to realize now this wasn't a routine approach.

News would be spreading through the station, just one communications tech or janitor telling a cousin what was going on, and that cousin calling someone else.

Time, time, and time. It wasn't on their side.

3

A rush to dock, and intense security in their getting aboard—a quick, bone-chilling transit through the deep cold and null *g* of the mast, and on into the lift—Bren let go a desperate, shuddering breath that he realized he'd held overlong and gulped another, air burning cold and so dry it seared his lungs and set off a fit of coughing.

Himself, the dowager, Cajeiri, her security, with Banichi and Jago: they were the advance party. The rest of his own staff was still on the ship, struggling to pack up, and Jase was coming in the next batch, with Pressman, Kaplan, and a security detail, with more security due to escort them to Ogun's offices. Atevi station security was to pick *them* up at the lift exit—Geigi's men—never mind the usual hassle with customs, Sabin assured them. Just go, get the dowager and the heir safely into the atevi section, and those doors shut, with their security up and functioning. Gin Kroger was going to come in through the cargo lock, with her equipment, with another contingent of Ogun's men to see things were in order.

Then they'd worry about telling the station at large—and the Reunioners on the ship—what was going on.

The car started moving, that motion rearranging their sense of up and down—they held to the handgrips for a few breathless moments with their luggage bashing up against the ceiling until they'd exited the core. Then the feeling of gravity crept over them, settled them gradually back to a sense of where the deck was despite the movement of the car. Their baggage observed the same slow settling, floating down past them and landing with a muffled, not quite authoritative thump. Ordinarily Cajeiri would be excited and bouncing about to test the new sensations—he so enjoyed instability. But his young face was as sober and his bearing as grimly serious as his great-grandmother's while the car braked to a stop: Bren noted it with a sideward shift of his eyes, not even a glance to disturb the delicate equilibrium.

The mast-to-station lift let them out necessarily in a region not quite secure—a region completely deserted except for Geigi's own bodyguard, with sealed section doors keeping the curious away—unprecedented security, as they transited the little distance to the regular lift system and got aboard for their winding passage to the atevi section.

Cenedi input their destination, their own restricted corridor. The car moved. No one said a word. The slight warmth of the air in this car finally began to creep into cloth, to penetrate finally to flesh and bone and Bren regulated his breathing, heart racing from emotional as well as physiological demands of the bone-cold passage.

What could he say to the dowager or his staff, knowing none of the answers?

What could he possibly say that could set anything to rights, if the aiji he had served and looked to serve for the rest of his life had met overthrow and disaster?

He didn't give up on Tabini-aiji, that was one thing. He didn't admit disaster until he had no other answer left. Tabini would have gone to ground if he was outnumbered. He'd be gathering forces for some attempt to retake his post, and knowing that *Phoenix* should be back in a handful of months, he might well have waited, hoping for reports, psychological advantage, vindication.

The ship was fairly well on time, as much as a ship on a two-year voyage could be. Things hadn't been optimal at the other end, quite—but they'd been fast. So Tabini would only have waited as long as he expected to wait. And he hoped against all reason that they might get a message from Tabini once the news of their return hit the atevi countryside.

The lift stopped. The doors opened on warm air and the atevi restricted residency corridor, atevi staff lining their path on either side. There was Lord Geigi himself, with his staff, and there were the few staffers the dowager had left behind; and, most wonderful to his eyes, there were his own people, Tano and Algini foremost, joy breaking through the ordinary atevi reserve.

Tears stung his own eyes—he was that glad and that relieved to see them safe, and to be home, and he returned small bows and nods of his head, glad, so glad to be on a deck that orbited his own world, so comforted to hear the voices he'd missed for two years, so relieved to bring back his whole party safe and sound. He had gotten them this far.

"Nandi," Tano said, his voice fairly quivering with relief. "Welcome. Welcome, nandi."

"Indeed," he said. "So good to see us united, nadiinji, whatever distressing news we hear from the planet—at least we can say we have good news. We have done all we went out to do. All of us are safe and well. And you have kept the household here safe."

"It is safe, nandi," Tano said, and Algini inclined his head in simultaneous agreement. "Safe and firm in man'chi."

"Well done, very well done, nadiin." A lord did not hug his servants, though he wanted to, each and every one, wanted, humanly speaking, to hug them and go home and wrap himself in the comfort of things that were safe and just as he had left them.

Other things, unfortunately, were far from safe. And time was ticking fast.

"Lord Geigi." A deep bow to the portly lord of the Edi atevi, who met him and the dowager at once. "A welcome sight, an extraordinarily welcome sight, nandi."

"None so welcome as the sight of Sidi-ji safe and all of you with her," Lord Geigi said. "Come, come inside, as soon as you will."

"Only a moment," he said. His staff surely had a welcome prepared, longed to have him inside and safe, to tell him everything and to ask every question they could think of, but he could no more than go to his own door, could only take a moment in the longed-for surroundings to shed the essential baggage, to exchange chilled heavy coats for warm, soft lighter ones—tea in his own sitting-room was what he wanted. Hours to talk to his staff was what he wanted. A phone, to contact the planet. To phone Toby. To know what had happened down there, to people he loved.

He . . . was not the dominant issue in this transaction.

"My gratitude to all of you," he said to Tano and Algini and the assembled staff, in his own foyer. "My utmost gratitude, nadiin-ji. What can one say, to equal all the hours and devotion you have given." They were a small staff, soon to be reinforced by Narani and Bindanda, Jeladi and Asicho, with a vast amount of baggage, two years' worth, from the ship—soon to be inundated with things to stow and launder and press, with stories to hear and stories to tell, but none so critical as what had happened out in far space and no present threat as great as what had happened on the planet under their feet, to Tabini and to the space program. "One can most gladly report success. We did far more than we went out there to do. And no matter that one hears dire things—dire news that Lord Geigi has to report to us. We will take action. So will the ship-aijiin and the station-aiji."

"We understand, nandi," Tano said—security staff, Tano and Algini, not domestic, but head of domestic staff was the post Tano and Algini had devotedly held down for two years, and would hold until Narani came to take those duties. "Your staff in Shejidan, the last we knew, had held your household safe, and your office staff withdrew to the west, to Lord Geigi's province, where they have most of the critical records. No one had troubled them there, as best we know, nandi, though we have heard nothing for considerable time."

A vast relief, to hope for the safety of people whose lives might have been at risk in Shejidan . . . damn the records, though he would have been sorry to lose the work. "One is grateful. One is exceedingly grateful, nadiin-ji. Are their households safe? And are yours?"

"Again, nandi," Algini said, "the last we heard indicated no reprisals. One hopes they have called their nearest kin to join them among the Edi."

Hundreds who depended on him were all put at risk because he himself was a logical target in the coup, along with all his holdings and offices; and their families were potentially at risk. The majority of them, at least, had not realigned in the crisis—rather choosing to relocate, with all the hardship that meant, to safe territory. What did one say for such people, beyond extreme gratitude?

"Well, nadiin-ji, we must take account of our resources," he said, and saw the intensity of every face, every hushed, expectant face, hoping for a plan.

"There is a shuttle," Algini said.

"So I have heard," he said. He counted it as their most important resource, the ability to get down to the planet. There was nothing to protect them on the way—and all of them knew it. "And I have no doubt I must go down there. Do you, nadiin-ji, believe the station? Is the aiji alive?"

"One has that earnest hope, nandi," Tano said, "but we have seen no evidence and had no report beyond the initial days. Mogari-nai is down. Nothing gets up from the planet."

"We shall see what we can do about that," he said. He shrugged on the coat Algini handed him, let Tano adjust the collar and straighten his queue.

"Banichi," he said. "Jago."

No question they would attend him to the meeting, little question they would gather as much from Lord Geigi's security as he did from Lord Geigi, things of a more specific, technical nature, with times and dates, things he would wager Tano and Algini and the rest of the staff, for that matter, already knew . . . but it saved briefing-time. He had the uncomfortable notion his time here was going to be very short.

A young woman—Adaro was her name: he had by no means forgotten—opened the door for him and bowed as he left. Banichi and Jago stayed in close attendance, down what was not an ordinary station corridor, but a section that might have been, give or take paneling instead of stone, the foyer of some great house on the mainland. In this corridor, various staffs shared duty, and kept order, and maintained—his heart was glad to note it—flowers of suitable number and color, so soothing to atevi senses, soothing to his own, after so many years of living in his green retreat. Safety, those flowers said, and Peace, and Refuge, speaking as clearly as the carpets on the floor and the hangings and the tables—three in number—fortunate three—which stood each beside a door of the trinity of established great households: his, the dowager's, and lord Geigi's.

Home, it said to him in every detail. Troubled it might be, by war and upheaval: it was not the black deep, it was not the cold nowhere. It had a geography, it had a map, and he knew them as he instinctively knew the basic geometry of every atevi dwelling, and as he intimately knew the people he dealt with across the station.

He had every confidence, for instance, that Sabin would be getting details out of Captain Ogun, who'd presided over the beleaguered station and kept it fed and on an even political keel through this catastrophe.

He knew that Jase would be analyzing everything he got from Sabin and Ogun, with the ear of a man who'd spent years among atevi, and who understood significances that might float right past Sabin and Ogun themselves.

He was sure beyond any need to inquire that Gin Kroger was going to be calling down to the planet, to find out what she could from Tom Lund, down on Mospheira, to get the Mospheiran viewpoint in the crisis.

His mind swam in a sea of separate realities as he walked to Lord Geigi's door, as Banichi signalled their presence. Lord Geigi's major domo showed them in . . . he coasted, a little numb still, through the formalities. The majordomo ushered him to the drawing room, presented him to Lord Geigi in his own environment, and his mind was still half with Jase, and what Jase would likely ask Ogun, first off.

"Tea?" Geigi offered.

"It would be very welcome." Atevi custom absolutely avoided rushing into bad news. The human wanted to blurt out a dozen questions, gain a rapid-fire briefing, race over the facts to get to the worst, but no, the atevi mind said settle, sit, have a cup of tea and get oneself prepared for the details laid out in meticulous order. Tabini might be deposed, possibly dead: bad as it could be, there was still hope for resurrecting the *aishidi'tat*, and that hope lay primarily in the persons in this small drawing room.

He took the offered teacup from Geigi's servant, sipped the warm, sweet tea gratefully, reminded that even here, tea had surely become a luxury, and a generous offering. He sighed and settled back in the carved, tapestry-upholstered chair, cup in hands. Banichi and Jago had quietly gone aside, an expected absence. And the dowager must be arriving—he heard a faint stir in the rooms behind the shut door. His host, too, left him, personally to see Ilisidi in, he was sure.

Ilisidi did arrive, together with Cajeiri—a presence which might not have happened among humans, but it by no means surprised him that the heir was here. Cajeiri had his own reasons for being here, getting news firsthand—had his right, that was the point.

"Aijiin-ma," he said, the plural, and rose and bowed to both arrivals in this formal setting, receiving a courtesy in return as Ilisidi settled in a fragile chair. A swing of her cane indicated a chair beside her for her great-grandson. The several of them made a triangle of chairs with Lord Geigi's, as that stout lord took a more substantial seat.

Tea was the order, then, all around, solemnly served, solemnly accepted, a few sips drunk. Ilisidi's countenance was unreadable; Cajeiri's was solemn, quiet—if there had been words of comfort, they had been said in private. If there was lingering disturbance, it was evident only in the absence of light in the boy's eyes. The young chin was set. Hard.

A full cup down. A second served.

"We shall hear it," Ilisidi said then, and Lord Geigi lowered his cup, cradling it in his hands, and said, solemnly,

"The rebels said no word, offered no argument in advance of their move, and there was no provocation ever stated. Lady Cosadi of Talidi province had turned up in residence in the Bujavid—" That was the center of government, the residence of every lord at court. "Accepting guests into the Tasigi residence."

It was her right to bring in guests. It was always the most difficult challenge to Bujavid security. The Talidi side relations were lucky to have survived the last dust-up in the aishidi'tat. They had lived and taken their place under Tabini's tolerance.

"Cosadi," Ilisidi said. "Is that the beginning of this tale?"

"Yes," Geigi said shortly. "Cosadi."

Daughter of the late Sarini of the Marid Tasigin, of Talidi province: bad blood from the beginning—involved in one conspiracy already. And Tabini had been an enlightened ruler, and had not cut their throats.

"Mercy has its reward," Ilisidi said darkly. "Guests, is it? *Who* was scrutinizing these people?"

"That we by no means know," Geigi said. "Nor have I heard any particular blame laid on house security in the matter, nor would expect to, given who is now in charge. But it was reputedly through Cosadi that Talidi of various ill dispositions gained access to the residencies. Certainly she now stands close to the lord of the Kadigidi, who has proclaimed himself aiji in your grandson's place."

"Murini?" Quietly asked, and a thunderstroke when Geigi said:

"The very one."

"Go on," Ilisidi said, and calmly had a sip of tea.

Murini, son of the former traitor, Direiso, who had conspired with Cosadi's father to break the south and midlands out of the *aishidi'tat*. Murini, who had taken refuge with Cajeiri's great-great-uncle in the last troubles, and under that roof had proclaimed himself unswervingly loyal to Tabini. Murini had risen, after Direiso's death, and with Tabini's blessing, to be head of the Kadigidi clan.

Now Murini thought he would turn coat and rule the Association, with Cosadi's help.

There was a scoundrel from way back, Bren thought, one that had masqueraded as a victim of Direiso's plots, and an ally of the ruling house.

But, more troubling still, was the fact that Murini had sheltered with the Atageini during Direiso's uprising, and might maintain ties there. Cajeiri, having Atageini blood in his veins, now posed a serious problem to any claim Murini might make on Atageini loyalty. So great-great-uncle Tatiseigi, if his loyalty to Tabini had wavered toward that wretch Murini, now would find his own ambitions drawing him back to Tabini's side . . . if only in Murini's perceptions.

Tatiseigi's life was therefore in danger. And so was Murini's, from Tatiseigi, a canny and long-surviving man with resources of his own.

So had Murini that firmly decided the ship would never return, and that Tabini's grandmother and Tabini's son and heir would never survive the trip?

Certain significant people seemed to have relied heavily on that belief.

Or perhaps they had hoped to have everything so firmly in their hands before the ship got back that Ilisidi would necessarily arrive in a nest of enemies.

The rebels had not been able to get into orbit and take the station from Geigi, at least, and it might be because they thought they would not succeed—likely not, in unfamiliar territory, under unanticipated conditions, and involving the Mospheirans *and* the ship's crew that had stayed with Ogun. But it might also be that Tabini hadn't been taken utterly by surprise—because he refused to believe the alternative, that the rebels would have been at all content to have Geigi stay alive and powerful on the station . . .

God. His mind raced. He sipped his tea and tried to listen to the meticulous details.

"This is how it happened," Geigi said. "There had been disturbance in the provinces, certain assassinations attempted but thwarted, nothing at all unprecedented, much of it allegedly personal feuds breaking out in related sequence. Your grandson seemed to have weathered that storm, though there was active debate in the legislature and numerous petitions in court and before the Assassins' Guild, for the redress of perceived wrongs in the south—down where Direiso's failed rising had of course robbed the district of resources and projects they could have had. The recent turn of weather harmed the fishing industry. Your grandson the aiji had of course sent relief and organized construction work in that area, and this quieted the unrest, but agitators carried out sabotage and other acts, including murders and arson, to disrupt the construction and keep the population in unrest. Your grandson accordingly filed with the Assassins' Guild to take extreme action against certain of the perpetrators, and this was an ongoing debate in the Guild, where members from Talidi province employed various parliamentry tricks, ploys to stall the issue. This was the background of the night of the attack. Your grandson and his consort were safe in Taiben, but Talidi assassins passed the doors of the aiji's apartments in Shejidan, with loss of life among them, to be sure, but certain of the aiji's bodyguard and his majordomo were killed in the act."

Edo. Bren's heart sank, mourning that genteel, gentle man.

"The whole Bujavid was thrown into confusion, doors sealing, various security staffs taking measures to protect their own households, and two, the Corisi and the Canti, who were currently feuding, each going after the other in the assumption it was an attack from the other side. Your grandson and his consort were nowhere to be found, and the rumors they were dead were an early encouragement to the Kadigidi, but the aiji reappeared to the west, three days later, organizing various actions aimed at the south and attempting to rally support to Taiben. Unfortunately, the conspirators were well-organized in neighboring Kadigidi province, and crossed Atageini territory, whether with or without their consent, but certainly without resistence, to strike directly at Taiben. Your grandson and the lady consort were obliged to retreat—Taiben being by no means fortified—and they used the maze of hunting trails to escape and to drop out of sight again. I ordered my own province to take every action to reach them with aid, but they were unable to find them. Meanwhile Murini of the Kadigidi mounted a major expedition to the middle regions, and there was close to a pitched battle—impossible to advance. In default of an answer from the north or from the Atageini, my own agents moved instead to open a route for the aiji to reach the coast, and to establish a second center of government at Mogari-nai."

Site of the big dish, the communications with the station.

"But there was nothing the station could do to support us," Geigi said, "with the spaceports uncertain and the landing path of any shuttle open to attack. The Kadigidi seized the two shuttles on the ground. The personnel fled to the west and north, where, to my knowledge, they remain. The one shuttle in orbit we have kept here, for your return. Tabini-aiji and his consort reached Mogari-nai, but the dish was shortly afterward seized by the Kadigidi, who claimed to have assassinated the aiji and his household. This was never substantiated, and is, in my opinion, not at all credible."

This, in the hearing of their young son, whose face throughout remained impassive as his elders.

Bren was, himself, numb, finding difficulty connecting reason and logic to Geigi's cold, point by point account.

Why would the general populace tolerate this action against Tabini? What could the less-than-popular dissidents have done to paralyze the other districts, beyond the fact they had moved very quickly? Why had the Atageini not moved to join Lord Geigi's forces?

And had Tabini been in Taiben on a hunting trip, a holiday, his usual reason for going there—or had he been all forewarned?

"Since then," Geigi was saying, "there is no word. Since then, Murini has attempted to convene the legislature, but cannot get a quorum, various members having scattered to their estates and tightened their personal security, ignoring all messages and threats."

"Ha!" Ilisidi said in pleasure.

"The Assassins' Guild remains likewise deadlocked, with several key fatalities including, three months ago, the Guildmaster."

Stalemate. Bren read that situation well enough. The conspirators were trying to take over that Guild, that was what. Atevi were not Mospheirans, and there was more than one way to fight a war.

"Mani-ma," Cajeiri said quietly, "Geigi-nandi? Why has this person attacked us?"

Trust the child to ask the essential, simple question.

"Economics, young sir," Geigi said. "The shifts of regional economy necessary in the last decades, to build the shuttles and the ports, the shifts of regional importance due to siting of ports and new factories, the shifts of supply and purchase necessary to supply these factories—and the fact that the south had been busy fighting the aiji instead of building factories. All this change frightened people. There was great public doubt, once the ship had departed the port, that it would ever return, or that there would be any positive outcome. These things were all in the wind before the ship left. Once it did leave, and as time passed, the public found it difficult to sustain their enthusiasm for the construction projects which had created such upheaval in our lives. It became rumored that the second starship would belong to humans, not to atevi, as promised. Rumor said the aiji your father had trusted human promises which might not be kept, since the paidhi had left and all these promises now relied on the Mospheiran legislature, with its politics and interest groups. Rumor said that the *aishidi'tat* was committing far too much resource even in providing materials and food for the station, and fuel for the shuttles, while the island of Mospheira again failed delivery of the promised financial support for their side. That was the crisis. The Mospheiran *presidenta* resubmitted the budget for another vote, and it finally passed, reduced by a third. But by then very serious damage was done to good faith and reliance on Mospheiran promises. The *aishidi'tat* met and declared they would reduce their space-related budget by a greater amount—as some saw it, simple retaliation for the Mospheiran legislature's reduction of funding, a warning. But as others intended it, it was to reduce funding going specifically to certain provinces, mine, among them—my people had realized great advantage in the space program. In that poisonous atmosphere, Murini clearly found his supporters."

"Do you comprehend what Lord Geigi is saying, great-grandson?" Ilisidi asked sharply.

"The people were afraid we would never come home and that humans would take the second ship for their own. And humans didn't pay their fair share, so we would not."

"Was that wise?"

"No, mani-ma. They were squabbling like children."

Ilisidi arched an eyebrow and looked at Geigi, who drew a deep breath.

"One would concur," Geigi said. "We attempted to mediate, to give contracts to Talidi, to help them with their construction, but that was not to Cosadi's liking. She raised the issue of regional funding to gain political advantage for her point of view. *No* budget reduction would satisfy them. Nor would any word granting us sole possession of an unfinished ship, since that would not get us supply of certain necessary components from Mospheira, which had just reduced their budget. Your father was at a difficult pass, young aiji, and was attempting to negotiate across the delicate division of interests. Clearly there was no good intent among the Talidi or the Kadigidi."

"And the Atageini?" asked Ilisidi.

"One has no idea, from this remove, what Lord Tatiseigi is doing. We have no word out of the mainland, only what we gather from their broadcasts. Most of it is diatribe against Tabini-aiji and praise of Murini's governance."

"Disgusting," Ilisidi said.

Cajeiri turned a burning look on his great-grandmother, close to emotional upset.

"What shall we do, mani-ma?" Cajeiri asked.

"What shall we do?" Ilisidi echoed his question. "What have we done, first? What resources have we, Lord Geigi?"

"At first," Geigi said, "we concentrated on making our half-built starship mobile, as it is now, though extremely limited in flight. It is armed. If you should have failed to return, if enemies arrived, Ogun-aiji argued, we needed the ship for our defense. But with supply cut off, we had no choice but to turn all our efforts to food. We rationed and stockpiled at first, and now have produced yeasts, in the tanks we do have, while building others. With the ship's tanks to increase that capacity, we shall not starve. But other tanks and other robots are still under construction, and things proceed slowly. The island, after the budget crisis, is now attempting to build its own shuttle and lengthen the runway at Jackson, which can be done. But done very expensively, and certain parties had rather give that up in favor of a missile defense system against the mainland."

Distressing in the extreme. "Is Shawn Tyers still *presidenta*, Lord Geigi?"

"He is. And your return will strengthen his office immensely, nand' paidhi."

"Not enough and not soon enough, I fear, to move the legislature to act."

"We have promised the *presidenta* if Mospheira puts the shuttle as priority, we shall assure their safety from attack, but there is still great fear. The dissident factions on Mospheira have, I hear, taken to the airwaves with vehement arguments, attacking the authority of the *presidenta* Tyers, and have gained some following, perhaps much as they had five years ago, so we understand."

The Human Heritage Party. The snake they'd not quite beheaded.

"And Mercheson?" Yolanda Mercheson, the translator who had taken his place as go-between for Tabini and the station, Yolanda, whose part in these events he very much wanted to hear. "Will she be available to us? Did she even survive?"

"She was caught on the planet, on the mainland,

which has been in some measure fortunate. She traveled as far as Mogari-nai and went from there by boat to the island. She has no knowledge, as far as Ogun-aiji has been able to ascertain, regarding the outcome of affairs at Mogari-nai. She was in transit when the Kadigidi forces reached it, and has never reestablished contact with the aiji or his party. She does contact certain resistence forces in the field, but these, regrettably, have diminished or gone into hiding in recent days."

Not utterly a point of despair, that last. If Tabini had relied on the conviction the ship would return two years from its launch date, and had gone to ground to await that return, his forces would very logically have melted into the earth, to rise again only when he recalled them.

But the opposition would be hunting them in the meanwhile, and hunting them harder than ever now that any telescope on earth could testify that the ship was back.

"Doubtless," Bren said, "the whole world knows we have returned, nandiin."

"One has no doubt," Ilisidi said, and set down her teacup. "Well. And this one shuttle we do have? Is it ready?"

"It is in excellent condition. But there is no landing site safe on the mainland, aiji-ma."

"The island, then."

"It may have its own hazards," Geigi said. "There are large, armed boats out."

"But we at least approach the island over the western sea, not over the mainland," Bren said.

"This fuel." Ilisidi waggled her fingers, as over one of those inconsiderable inconveniences her subordinates might solve.

"There is fuel," Geigi said. "The shuttle is ready. The crews here have stayed in training, particularly as your return date arrived."

"Then we shall lose no time," Ilisidi said.

Were any of them surprised, either at Geigi's efficiency, the pilots' dedication, or Ilisidi's decision? No. Not in the least.

"We shall take the shuttle down," Ilisidi said, "nand' paidhi. Immediately. See to it."

"Jase," Bren said, on the line to station central via pocket com, while he walked, "the dowager wants to go down on the shuttle. Immediately, she says."

"Not surprised," Jase said. "Ogun wants *you* in his office, meanwhile, politely speaking. Senior captain's coming aboard for the conference."

He wasn't surprised by that, either.

"One hour," he said. "Can we do that?"

"Ten minutes," Jase said.

"Faster we move, the better. All right."

He hadn't even gotten to his own apartment door yet. Banichi and Jago, beside him, had heard it. They all changed course, went over to the lift and punched in new directions. His staff welcome would have to wait. If it ever happened.

Events seemed to blur past, accelerating. He was by no means sure they were doing the right things.

"It would be well," Banichi said, pushing the lift call button, "if we did hasten this, Bren-ji. Events will surely turn on our arrival, and the conspirators will know by now that the ship is here."

"One has that idea," he said. "But, nadiin-ji, we will need to clear our landing with the authorities on Mospheira, we shall need to keep it as quiet as possible, and we have lost Mogari-nai."

"They are communicating," Jago said, "by a new installation at Jackson, nandi. So we are told."

The lift arrived. They stepped in. Pieces had shifted. He could not rely on things being exactly as he had left them, not in any small particular, not after two years, not after general upheaval.

"Can Tano establish contact with Shawn Tyers?" he asked. "I need to talk to him."

"One will attempt it," Jago said, and did exactly that, on her pocket com, while the lift set into motion, taking them toward a meeting in the operational center of the station. She spoke with Tano, and waited, and by the time the lift had reached its destination:

"The *Presidenta* of Mospheira, nandi," Jago said, and handed him her pocket com, with not even the need to push a button.

"Shawn?"

"Bren?" It was surreal to hear Shawn's voice, after such incredible distances and events. *"Did you do it?"*

"We did it, no question." His own voice wanted to shake, from sheer pent-up tension. He wouldn't let it. "A lot more to discuss when we have a moment, but right now I'm asking if you can get me urgent landing clearance if we can get down there?"

"No question we can, and I advise it be soon and fast," Shawn said. *"The mainland won't be an option for your landing, not while this regime is in power. There's a sort of a navy now. And the more advance warning, the worse and the riskier."*

"Understood." Two deep breaths as he walked the corridor toward Admin, between Banichi and Jago. "We've only just docked. Listen, we're in good shape, mostly. There *is* something to worry about out there in space, way deep and far, but I'll let you work that out with the captains. I'm about to debrief with Ogun . . . I trust you're talking to Ogun, no problems."

"No problems at all in that regard," Shawn said.

"I've got to sign off. I'll be there in short order, if we're lucky."

"Got it," Shawn said. Former boss in the State Department. Ally, in what had become the only team left standing. *"I'll clear your way in all senses. You'll have clear air space and a place for you and your party, all honors. Count on it."*

"Thanks," he said. And to Banichi and Jago, handing back the phone—as if they couldn't follow most that he said in Mosphei'. "He advises we move quickly, and promises us clearance to land and a place to stay. He gave no hint of trouble on the island, but seems anxious for us to hasten our moves. He says the opposition has ships."

"Which may attempt to interfere in the landing, nandi," Banichi said. "We agree."

They reached the guarded door, and the guards on duty—one of them Jase's man, Kaplan—wasted no time letting all of them in.

Jase was inside, standing with Jules Ogun, of *Phoenix,* who'd stayed in command of the station and maintained liaison with Shawn *and* Tabini while they were off in deep space.

"Good to see you," Ogun said, leaning across the table corner with a solid handshake—certainly more warmth than when they'd parted. "Damned good to see you in one piece, sir."

"I understand we have a problem downstairs," Bren said directly, "and I hear we have a shuttle in reasonable readiness, and I have the dowager's request to launch and Tyers' clearance to land at Jackson, if we can get it fueled."

"It *is* fueled, or will be within the next two hours. We started that process when you turned up in system. Crew's kept up their sims throughout. We're not altogether cut off from the planet, but this shuttle is our one chance, Mr. Cameron. Damned hard to replace. But no other use for it now but to get you down there."

"The dowager and the heir are our best chance to stabilize the government. They're absolutely irreplaceable. And I'm going with them." He saw the frowns. "I have to be there. They'll need me."

"Dangerous," Jase said. "Damned dangerous, Bren, your going down there. You're the outsider. You're in particular danger."

"I wish we had another choice," he said. He'd come in prepared to argue up one side and down the other for his position, but no one argued, beyond Ogun's remark, such ready agreement he wished someone *would* argue, interpose objections that might make him think of critical omissions in his ideas.

But, point of fact, they had two choices—launch an information war from orbit, with the broadcast and cable in the hands of the new regime, and a lot of bloodshed likely—or get themselves down there as their supporters would expect, had almost certainly expected for months. People would commit their lives to the latter expectation, might already have swung into operations that would fail without them. In the atevi way of thinking, leaders had to show up, in person, take the risks, lay down the law, make the moves so there was no doubt of their commitment.

And the longer they waited, even by hours, the more time the opposition had to arrange something in response.

"A seat, Mr. Cameron." Ogun sat down, and Jase did, and as they settled, the door opened and Sabin came in, her coat steaming with cold and frost, straight from the core and the airlock.

Ogun rose, extended a hand to her, gave her the vacant seat next to him—senior, these two, captains under senior captain Stani Ramirez so long as Ramirez lived, and privy to far and away more than they'd ever admitted to the crew at large or to anyone else until the proof came running up on them at Reunion. Now they all knew—or hoped they knew—what Ramirez had done to the human species, poking about in alien territory, keeping a potentially hostile alien contact secret even from his own crew . . . until it swept down and half destroyed Reunion Station. Candor had not been an attribute of the Pilots' Guild, not even the benevolent part of it that managed *Phoenix* and sat guard over the station here. Not, possibly, to this hour.

"Brilliant job," Ogun said to them.

"Adequate," Sabin said. "We're alive. We've got the

ringleaders of our problems in close lockup aboard ship and plan to keep them that way indefinitely, under the circumstances. We're going to be dribbling population aboard the station, asking resident crew to sponsor the Reunioners and keep close tabs on them, no demands at all from our Mospheiran cousins onstation. They have no reason to love these people."

"Anything that slows a headlong rush to realize how short supply is, here."

"How short is it?"

"We've had serious tank problems and cycling hasn't quite kept up with the nutrient balance. We could use resupply. We could use it very urgently, or we absolutely go back on basics and short rations at that. We haven't *got* some of the critical supplies when we do get the new tanks in operation, and we're even, just among the few of us, worried about the long-range stability of the station air systems. But your people are telling me there's a big cash-in of biomass as the ship is in for overhaul."

The spider plants. The myriad spider plants, Bren thought. Bales of them. Not to mention the recycling of ship's waste for all those people. Could they possibly have that much bound up in them, that they could make a dent in station requirements?

But the ship had been nutrient rich for a long time. They'd carried an abundant supply, and they hadn't offloaded any of it. They'd taken on a good extra load from Reunion Station itself on the return flight, emergency supplies to expand their capacity to serve thousands of passengers. Was that enough?

"Meanwhile," Ogun was saying, "Mr. Cameron's got a landing lined up with Mospheira. I take it, Mr. Cameron, you have a plan."

No, he wanted to say, in all honesty. But it wasn't that black and white. "We need more information than we have, sir, more than we likely can get from here. Lord Geigi knows what happened on the mainland, but he's not in possession of enough details to give us a sure list of who to trust. So we have to go down, and go fast, before loyalties shift."

"What did happen down there, Mr. Cameron?" Sabin asked.

"In fact it looks like a long-range double cross, in the case of the scoundrel who's launched this attack on Tabini-aiji: he played the ally, he played the innocent relative caught in the last uprising, sided with Tabini, and with us, and all the while he was holding out to let Tabini beat his relatives. Then he got power over his own house, which set him up to make a try at overthrowing Tabini-aiji in the next round. Classic politics. But he'll rest uneasily now that we're back. And he'll be desperate for information, which he can't get too easily since he himself closed us off from the uplink station. That's *why* we want to move fast and continually change the data. They surely know you have one remaining shuttle that's still capable of getting us down there. They have to have formed some plan to go into action the moment *Phoenix* comes back, as we have, and in case that shuttle tries to land. That plan has to include neutralizing the dowager *and* the heir, it could mean getting boats in position to try to bring the shuttle down, which I hope is technically unlikely, and slow-moving. And our plan, quite plainly has to center on establishing a countermovement, finding out where they are, and killing them."

"So should you risk the dowager?" Ogun asked.

"If there's to be any hope of dealing with this, she has to be there. The heir has to be there. Her loyalists—and they're more than I can trace at the moment—won't understand her sitting safe on the ship or keeping the boy safe and asking them to go die for her cause while she protects herself with human allies. It's not the atevi way. They'll show up when she shows up in their circumstances, at equal risk. And they'd never respect the heir if he were held up here in safety."

"You're that sure they'll rally."

"If they don't, for that, they never would. And I believe they will, so long as they're alive and have resources. They'll be there."

"It's the best chance for our situation," Sabin said. "If you can reestablish relations with the atevi government—stabilize their situation—maybe get a new government installed, one that's pro-space—get supply moving up here. *Do* you have a plan?"

Back to that nasty question. "As you say, captain. We stabilize the situation for starters. Vindicate Tabini-aiji. *Vindicate* him, even if he's dead. It'll make a difference in the shade and shape of any government that follows him. Beyond that—I can't guarantee the outcome."

"The boy?" Sabin asked. "The heir? Or the dowager?"

"Cajeiri might succeed. He's Ragi, like his father. With the dowager as regent. Although the tashrid, their house of lords, has refused her claim before—frankly they were afraid of her in those days, because she was too closely tied to the eastern provinces. That perception of her had somewhat changed in recent years . . . but I don't know where her province has taken its stand in this current situation. So I don't know which the tashrid would choose—a regency, with Ilisidi behind the scenes, or a strong government, with Ilisidi in power, with Cajeiri still as heir-apparent."

"Still, all our eggs in one basket, taking them down there. I know, I know, everything's what *she* decides. But if he were up here, with Lord Geigi . . ."

"Geigi's Maschi, ruling an Edi population." And at Sabin's unenlightened stare: "He's not Ragi. We absolutely can't afford the perception of the boy under any influence but his own family's. We can't have him viewed as a puppet for Lord Geigi, or, God forbid, for human rule."

"God," Sabin muttered. "All right. All right. We go with it."

"Best we can do is work fast," he said. "If we get down in one piece, we'll still have to reconstitute the maintenance facilities for the shuttles and locate all the personnel, who may be in hiding—or worse. At very worst, we'll have the pilots and the shuttle we bring down. We'll have one good window to get down, and—forgive me for expressing opinions in operational matters—we should use an approach over the sea to the west, where I trust there's not going to be atevi presence armed with missiles."

"Agreed," Ogun said. "And that is what we planned. The course is laid in. You say we're assured of the runway at Jackson."

Sabin tapped a stylus on the table and frowned. "As it happens," Sabin said, "your Lord Geigi's called up the shuttle crew all on his own, and the dowager's already shifting baggage and personnel aboard, while we sit here. We know you've contacted Mospheira. We assume you have landing clearance."

Could he claim he was surprised, either at the blinding rapidity of events or by the fact humans knew everything Geigi did? "Then I'm asking your support," he said. "The station's technical support for the operation. And for whatever follows. We may need to call on you, maybe even for a limited strike from orbit. It's nothing I want to think of, but it could become necessary."

"You'll have it," Sabin said. Ogun, for his part, nodded. Of Jase, there was no doubt at all.

"Well, then I'd better go catch my shuttle," he said, with this time a glance at Jase, who'd not said a word—who gave him a direct and worried look now as he stood up to leave, as the senior captains rose. To them all, Bren gave a little bow, the atevi courtesy. But he paused for a second look at Jase, who edged around the table to intercept him—didn't say a thing, just looked at him, and he looked at Jase, the one of the captains who'd go down to the planet with him in a heartbeat.

But Jase couldn't do that. He'd gone back to space, accepted duty aboard *Phoenix,* and severed himself from Tabini's court. Jase couldn't be half the help to him on the planet that he could be up here serving as bridge and go-between.

"You know the things they need to know," Bren said. "Translate for me. Make them understand."

"I can do that."

"If anything should happen—"

"I'll work closely with Lord Geigi, in that event," Jase said, with no silly demur that nothing would possibly happen. "And with Yolanda."

Discounting all the history in *that* relationship.

He embraced Jase, patted him on the shoulder. They'd been through everything together. It was harder to part now than ever before.

"You're not even going to get a night in your own bed," Jase said.

"Luxuries go by the board, I'm afraid. I'll send up tea and fruit candy and canisters of all sorts of things, first I get the shuttles flying."

"Waiting with bated breath," Jase said. "Good luck. Good luck, Bren."

Neither language seemed apt to what he wanted to say at the moment. And there was nothing either of them could do but part company and go out their separate doors.

He left with Banichi and Jago, Jago going first outside the door, Banichi behind him, the old, carefully measured steps that were by now completely automatic. The human guards outside, knowing them, were unruffled by their ways.

"So we are boarding?" he asked them as they walked on.

"Imminently," Banichi said.

"Your staff is prepared," Jago said, "and Tano and Algini request to come down with us. So do Bindanda and Narani."

He thought about it a pace or two along the hallway. About Tano and Algini he had no question: those two were, like Banichi, like Jago, like Cenedi and Ilisidi's other bodyguards, members of the Assassins' Guild, partners, in sets, like most others.

But Narani and Bindanda, though members of that Guild, too, were no longer young. They were well suited to the warfare of the court, but not to running hard.

"What would you advise, nadiin-ji?"

"Tano and Algini would be helpful to us," Banichi said. "Narani and Bindanda would be extremely valuable to Jase-aiji."

"And they will not thank us for saying so," said Jago, "but our venture onto the continent will be no holiday in the country, Bren-ji. If we could leave *you* on the Island, and plead a Filing on Murini and his supporters without you, we would."

The legalities of the situation came home to him. One did not simply decide to attack an atevi of any high rank. "We *should* File Intent on him, shouldn't we?"

"If one can manage to get a signed letter to the mainland," Banichi said dryly. "We shall certainly attend the matter, Bren-ji. You only need fix your signature and seal to the document."

"My seal." It was on his finger. He hadn't used it in two years, except to sign notes back and forth with the dowager. Dinner invitations. Now it could request a man's life.

"One believes the dowager and Cenedi will be well before us in any Filing, nonetheless."

"We do need to send a letter." The ordinary details of atevi life flooded back into memory, the rules, the procedures. "But if we're asking a hearing, do we not automatically have protection in reaching the Guild?" If one Filed Intent, meaning an official filing of intent to assassinate, for personal or public reasons, another individual, the paper must go before the Assassins' Guild to be debated—a proceeding much like a court of law, with arguments pro and con largely coming from other members of that Guild, members in service to various houses, as well as those at large. Not infrequently it entailed an appearance before the Guild Assembly, separately, by the principals in the dispute. He recalled a provision for protection for persons summoned, or for persons attempting to File, that they could not be struck down on Guild grounds.

But that prohibition certainly left a lot of the continent under no such protection.

"Certain people may not observe the niceties, Bren-ji," Jago said. "The Guild president is dead, so Lord Geigi's people say. One doubts that assassination was easily accomplished, or without repercussions."

"Which points up," Banichi said, "that when rival ai-jiin are attempting to influence the Guild, nothing is reliable."

Appalling. The Guild, the one impartial power, in disarray.

"But Guild membership cannot be happy with the assassination."

"They will not be, Bren-ji," Jago said, "but there we are: there is no authority. The Guild is taking a position of neutrality in the dispute."

If the Assassins' Guild, offended and notoriously independent-minded, would possibly accept an Intent to remove Murini from life as well as office, it would be an incalculable advantage to the aiji-dowager in her claim on the leadership. Certain Guild members would still defend Murini, in such a case, of course—but only those in his personal man'chi, or such as might be morally persuaded to do so. Murini's personal record of double-crosses would not inspire altruists to back him. But the dowager's eastern origins would mean the same debate as had turned the tashrid against her, in the last debate of the succession, and the heir, though Ragi, was a child. The Guild was leaderless, the *aishidi'tat* was broken, and if it could not reassemble itself and make a reasonable appeal to the Guild, the Guild was not going to lash about in pointless violence that would set no legitimate leader in power—such as they had, with Murini, they had, until something strong enough to challenge Murini rose up. It was why atevi wars had become, historically, very few, once there was a unified Assassins' Guild.

"The dowager's return in itself will prompt debate in Guild Council," Banichi said, "and we shall certainly catch their notice, once we can reach the mainland. We shall get a Filing to the Guild. But bear in mind that Murini—I do *not* call him Murini-aiji—will certainly File against *you*, in particular, since it is hardly *kabiu* to file on a child."

Sobering, but not surprising, and not the first time he'd been Filed on. One never liked to contemplate the resources a wealthy lord could bring to bear . . . money which could hire certain individuals of that Guild, if they were willing to be hired. An aiji had the whole state treasury, if he could justify the budget to the tashrid, and who knew how many pro-Tabini legislators were going to dare show up to resist Murini's demands for funds?

The Guild as a whole might not budge and might be leaderless, but individuals might incline to back Murini.

"Well, we shall do the best we can," Bren said.

"Shall we advise Tano and Algini then to join us?"

"Absolutely. Tell them pack and board. I must go home first, however. I should do Narani and Bindanda at least the courtesy of a personal refusal of their offer."

"There might be time for tea," Banichi said. "It would surely please them."

They reached the section his apartment shared with Lord Geigi and the aiji-dowager—he walked up to his own door, and met Narani behind it, and formal welcome in his own foyer, with simple fresh flowers—that atevi amenity aboard station had not yet gone to recycling, and such a move would have been strongly resisted—in a heart-pleasingly suitable arrangement on the little table. He saw all the small touches of Narani's excellent taste and sensitivity to nuance, and found the whole staff had lined up as best they could manage in the little space they had.

He thanked each and every one of his people, headed by Narani, those who had voyaged with him: Bindanda, Jeladi, and Asicho; and those who had not, who had kept station here—notably Tano and Algini, whose appearance was brief, that pair doubtless already having gotten the word from Banichi or Jago that they were going with him.

"I hope I have time to sit in such splendid comfort for a moment," he said, "Rani-ji. And, Rani-ji, I must speak with you and with Bindanda, and explain myself. Will you take tea with me?"

They knew, only by that, that he was not going to agree to their going, and he detected sorrow on those two faces, the only blight on the moment.

But Narani glossed over his pain with an offer of a more comfortable coat for the voyage. He shed the coat he was wearing in favor of that one, then established himself in his favorite room, the library, where more flowers met him, if only three precious blooms.

There he waited.

Narani and Bindanda arrived with the tea service, and solemnly poured a cup for him, then for themselves. He said, "Sit with me, if you will, nadiin-ji."

They were uncomfortable as his guests, these two, who had been house staff all their careers, and who were exceedingly proud of it. But they had voyaged with him, and they had grown far less formal on the voyage. They settled deeply into the chairs, waiting to be told officially that, no, they were not going.

"I honor you extremely," he said. "And you know that I must refuse an offer which touches my deepest sentiments. I value your expertise and your wisdom, and in all honesty, nadiin-ji, I rely very much on you here, to advise Jase-aiji, to assist Lord Geigi if anything should at all happen to us in our attempt—"

"Never say so, nandi!" Narani said.

"As I shall not allow to happen, of course. But I shall need persons of level good sense to serve in this household and mediate between persons of high rank and foreign behavior, perhaps under trying conditions in situations needing decisive and wise action. That much I must have. I entrust my good name and the proper working of this house to you and to Bindanda, with the utmost confidence both will be as safe as it ever would be if I were here, and that you will never hesitate to speak for me to Lord Geigi and to Jase-aiji."

Both heads bowed, in the sober earnestness of his charge to them.

So they drank tea, and savored this taste of home, knowing that he was going to board the shuttle, and that he hoped to see them again.

Knowing the risks in the landing still set a cold lump of fear in his stomach, which even the tea and the companionship did not quite disperse.

But they finished, not too hastily, and made their courtesies, his staff far more aware of the exigencies of the schedule than he was. He had put on his comfortable coat for the descent and they added a warm if graceless outer coat for the transit to the shuttle—a transit that had never quite approached routine.

They also gave Tano and Algini two considerable packets, their initial meals aboard, since the shuttle crew was usually too busy to attend the passengers until they were considerably out along their course. Other baggage, their clothes and gear for after landing, was already en route to the shuttle.

With that, in what seemed, by atevi standards, blinding haste, they were out the door, as well organized as staff could manage for them—himself and Banichi and Jago, with Tano and Algini, now, the missing members of his bodyguard—Tano as cheerful as if they were headed for holiday, which was Tano's way, and Algini his sober, mostly silent self.

The timing of their exit was no accident, nor in any way left to chance, in the curious backstairs communication among the houses here resident. The dowager's staff turned out just behind them, so they realized when they were most of the way through the lift routings. Banichi advised him, and, bag and baggage, they waited until Ilisidi, with Cajeiri, and attended by Cenedi and his men, had arrived at the core lift, Geigi's staff attending with still more baggage, providing assistance, not that Geigi himself was going.

From that point on they made one party as they traveled upward to the core, a lift-passage in which gravity increasingly left them and the air grew increasingly burning-cold and dry. Their hand-baggage would come adrift if nudged—but no one nudged it. Eight-year-old Cajeiri stayed as grimly fixed to the handhold as he had been on the way down into the station, staring into space, occasionally casting glances at his elders, or darting a suspicious look at some particularly loud clang or thump. He took his cues from his great-grandmother, however, and refused to flinch.

It was a wretched birthday, and Bren earnestly wished there was some cheer to offer a boy who had been, in one day, advised his parents' survival was in doubt and that he must leave his agemates and companions, perhaps forever, embarking on a voyage that scared the hell out of sensible, experienced crew.

Being a boy of eight years, however, Cajeiri seemed to have run entirely out of questions and objections. At such an age, thwarted and upset at every turn, he clung grimly to the safety bar, sunk in his own thoughts, without breadth enough to his horizons to give him an adult-sized hope or fear to work on. Adults had done this, he might be thinking. Adults would fix it. Adults had better fix it, if they knew what was good for them.

This adult just hoped the shuttle got down onto the planet in one piece, for starters.

"We have our course laid," Ilisidi said, breath frosting

in the bitter cold of the car, "and we trust the *Presidenta* will attend the other details in our rapid departure, nandi."

"Supportive, aiji-ma," Bren said. "Entirely supportive, I have no doubt of that. We will doubtless have lodging as long as we wish near the landing strip. I have left the transportation arrangements for crossing the straits until after we are down—for security in communications, aiji-ma."

"Likely wise," Ilisidi said, and about then the lift stopped, requiring all aboard to resist inertia. The door gasped open, making a puff of ice crystals in floodlit dark. The burning dry cold of the dark core itself hit the lungs like a knife, making conversation, even coherent movement of muscles, a difficult, conscious effort.

No one was disposed to linger in the least. They made as rapid a transit as possible, along hand-lines rigged to take them to the appropriate entry port, through the weightless dark. Breath froze, making smaller clouds in the spotlights. Parka-clad atevi shuttle crew, spotlighted in a flood, emerged at the other end of that line to assure their safety, to take their small items of hand baggage from cold-stiffened hands, and to see them into the shuttle airlock, which itself showed as a patch of white and brilliant inner light in an otherwise enveloping dark.

"Other baggage is coming, nadiin," Tano informed the crew, "in the next lift, with Lord Geigi's staff."

As the bright light inside challenged their eyes and warm, ordinarily humid air met the lungs, it made both seeing and steady breathing difficult for a moment. The station shuttle dock had had numerous improvements on the drawing board, a pressurized tube planned, first of all, to make the transit to shuttles easier and safer, but clearly none of those things had happened, as so much had not happened in the last two years.

But in the faces of the shuttle crew, the only functional atevi shuttle crew, was an absolute commitment, a joy, even, in seeing them—a fervent hope of their situation set to rights, an absolute confidence that they were carrying the necessary answer back to a waiting world.

Bren wasn't personally that confident.

Not this time.

4

"Welcome home, nandiin," the atevi crew bade them over the intercom, just before their launch away from the station—an auspicious launch, Bren hoped, all considering. The baji-naji emblem, that portrayal of the motive principles of the universe, chance and fortune, still decorated the bulkhead of the shuttle, still reminded them the universe, always in delicate balance, had its odd moments and was subject to forces no one could restrain—that the most secure situation and the most impossible alike could fall suddenly into chaos . . . but must exit that chaos into order, the eternal swing between the two states.

Some optimist among the crew or the techs had arranged flowers in a well-secured vase on a well-secured shelf below that emblem—*life and welcome,* that arrangement meant; but one blossom came askew during undock, leaving good fortune momentarily adrift.

And in that extremity, young Cajeiri undertook a zero-g mission, on permission from his great-grandmother to chase it and restore it to its proper and fortunate place in the arrangement. It gave a too-well-behaved young lad at the bitter end of his patience a chance to be up and moving, now that the shuttle was out and away. He succeeded quickly, a triumph, then took his time returning to relative safety in the seats, to everyone's relief. Cajeiri's spirits had risen, at least enough for him to become a modest worry to his elders.

The steward then began to serve tea, a fussy, acrobatic operation, unusually early service insofar as anything in the shuttle passenger program had had time to become usual. And once they had had their tea, up front in the cockpit, the pilots greatly yearned, one was coyly informed by said steward, to hear any information they were willing to give them about their voyage to the stars.

"There were foreigners!" Cajeiri exclaimed immediately, brightening, by no means a report designed to settle the crew's curiosity, and breaching security at a stroke. Baji-naji, from order to potential chaos, in the person of a young boy. "They were nearly as tall as we are! And *huge* around!"

The steward was, of course, entranced, and at once had a thousand questions more—information for the pilots, of course.

So Ilisidi's second-senior bodyguard went forward to the shuttle cockpit to regale the whole crew with the details, by the dowager's personal dispensation, all with, of course, personal cautions against spreading the gossip. In this elite and security-conscious crew it was even foreseeable that the information would stay contained—and Ilisidi's young man remained up there for some time, doubtless questioned and requestioned until he was hoarse, and very likely enjoying his hero's status, the shuttle crew with their yearning for information on their voyage and everything that was out there, and the young Assassin just as anxious to understand the shuttle's workings and to find out in some detail how the space program had survived the troubles on the planet . . .

And whether they had allies still in any position of authority—such, at least, were the questions Bren himself was sure he would ask, and might yet ask, if the young man didn't come back with the answers. Certainly information flowed both ways up there, and meanwhile Banichi and Jago, with their own electronics, became very quiet, staring straight ahead of them, of course following all of it from their seats, and absorbing everything.

The details of the shuttle's operation, however, were not among the things Bren needed to ask anyone. Having translated the shuttle plans and most of the flight operations manual, with the assistance of his staff, and having trained the translators who had mediated the finer details of the actual operations, he knew the facts down to the length of the Jackson runway; he knew that it was 20 feet shorter than the original plan, he knew the names of the grafting bastards responsible, and he really had not rather think about that old issue right now.

He decided to divert himself with his computer, with, eventually, a nap, at least as well as a sane man could sleep on a vessel hurtling deeper and deeper into the gravitational grip of a very unforgiving planet toward a runway that wasn't quite what they'd designed.

A shuttle with all its fail-safes was still better than parachutes, he reminded himself. He had, at least, never landed the way Jase had, and the way his ancestors had landed on Mospheira in the first place—by parachute, in a little tin-can capsule. For their ancestors it had been a one-way trip, when they'd rebelled against the iron rule of the old Pilots' Guild and decided to commit themselves to an inhabited planet, since by then it had been well-established the ship was not going to find its way back home at all. *Phoenix,* the same ship on which they had just voyaged, had dropped into some anomaly of space-time, or suffered some never-revealed malfunction, and popped a station-building expedition out first of all at a deadly white star. They'd gotten away from that by the skin of their teeth, only to be told, by the ship's masters, that they had to refuel and commit to more voyages, after which, they began to comprehend, their use was to refuel the ship again and again—living a graceless, gray existence under the rule of a band of men who'd, yes, somehow survived the previous disasters, men who'd somehow not volunteered to sacrifice a thing when the better elements of the crew had given their very lives to get them free and out to this lovely green world and safer sun.

The colonists, finding there was an alternative where they'd arrived, had desperately flung themselves onto an innocent planet whose steam-age civilization naively assumed they'd arrived from their moon . . . had assumed, assumed, assumed, until they went to war with each other and every human still alive ended up in an isolated enclave on the island of Mospheira.

Hence his job, when he wasn't being Lord of the Heavens. Hence the paidhiin came into being, the translators appointed to interpret not only words, but psychology—to prevent two species who'd originally thought it was easy to understand one another from pouring their technology and their concepts into each other's heads until the system fractured.

One of a long line of paidhiin who'd served the system, trickling humanity's advanced technology into atevi hands at a sane pace, trying to make humans live lightly on the planet and not offend atevi beliefs and traditions—he'd tried, at least, to keep the faith.

But had he?

Therein lay the guilt . . . guilt that in recent hours burrowed itself a wider and wider residency under his heart, laying its foundations the moment he'd heard Tabini had gone down, and growing to a whole suite of rooms when he'd heard Geigi lay out the reasons for Tabini's downfall. Too much tech and too much change too fast had brought—not war with humans, this time—but an internal calamity to atevi, the fall of the aiji who'd pushed, lifelong, for more tech, more tech, more tech . . . and made too-quick changes in the atevi way of life to take advantage of it. At some point the paidhi was supposed to have said no, and not to have been so accommodating. That had been his *job,* for God's sake. It was why all prior paidhiin had not been so snuggly-close with the atevi leadership. Tabini had had the notion of making his people the technological equals of humans in their island enclave—a technological equality they'd all conceptualized as a good rail system, air traffic crossing the continent, maybe even a computer revolution, in his lifetime.

But then long-lost *Phoenix* had shown up from deep space, and ownership of the abandoned space station had become an issue. Tabini had been determined to secure it for his own people, entirely understandable, and he had been convinced that if humans got it up and running first they'd never relinquish it to atevi, no matter the justice of their claims. He'd had to move fast to take over leadership not only of the space station . . . but of the crisis humans confessed they'd precipitated out in deep space.

Step by step, Tabini had waded into hotter and hotter water, all for the sake of protecting his people from the changes humans brought, and the paidhi, who should have said no, wait—stop—

To this hour the paidhi just couldn't figure what else he could have done.

Average atevi, who, like Banichi, had only just figured out the earth went around the sun, or why they should care, had suddenly become critical to the planetary effort to get back into space. The mainland had the mineral resources and the manufacturing resources to do what the ship could not: supply raw materials and workers to get the space station operating again . . . and, most critically, the planet had the pilots to *fly* in atmosphere, an art the spacefarers had flatly forgotten and had no time to relearn.

Atevi had been able to get *their* manufacturing geared up to handle the crisis. The island enclave of Mospheira had still been debating the matter when the atevi's first spacecraft lifted off the runway and blasted roof tiles off the eaves of Shejidan.

Change, change, and not just change—change proceeding at breakneck speed through every aspect of atevi life. Mines and factories were opened, sudden wealth created for some districts, with shortages of critical materials and extravagant plenty of new luxuries: Mospheiran society, wrangling over regional advantage and company prerogatives, hadn't been able to do it, even with the technological advantage. Atevi society, where a strong leader could dictate where new plants were to be built, could balance the economy of regions against regions, equalize the supply and demand—and in so doing, created new values, new economy, new emphasis on manufacturing instead of handcrafting of objects valued for centuries, not even to mention such radical notions as preserved food, instead of food auspiciously and respectfully offered in season, with awareness of one's debt to the natural world . . .

Cultural change, religious change, upheaval in the relative importance of provinces and districts, not according to history but according to the mineral wealth and the siting of some new critical facility, partly by the aiji's grace, partly by the questions of where nature had put the resources. It had all worked. It had been a toboggan ride to a brave new tomorrow, and Tabini's brilliance had kept everyone prosperous, kept himself in charge, abandoned not a shred of his power and put down every attempt to unseat him . . .

And had the paidhi objected? He'd superintended Tabini's rush to modernize, confident Tabini's management of the economy was going to preserve the traditions as well as create new professions, new Guilds. He'd known he was riding the avalanche, and he'd thought he'd steered Tabini to safety. When the crisis came that called them out to Reunion, he'd left Tabini never more powerful, the Association never more prosperous, the atevi economically and politically equal to humans in every regard, even in relation to the ship-humans on the station. He'd left a people possessed of shuttlecraft and every functioning facility to land and service spacecraft, even building a starship of their own, while Mospheiran humans, across the straits from the mainland, dithered and debated and never had accomplished more than those modifications to the airport at Jackson that would serve as a reserve landing site in emergency . . . give or take the twenty feet of runway that couldn't get past certain special interests and the Jackson Municipal Golf Course.

Humans on Mospheira had continued to have mixed feelings about the space station, that was the problem underlying Mospheiran politics. Some were extremely enthusiastic about going back to space, but more were suspicious and resentful of their cousins on the ship. And like the atevi, Mospheirans had mixed feelings, too, about the changes, the haste to turn the entire economy into a space-based push for technological equality with the ship-folk, the trampling of, well, fairly old, if not ancient traditions of Mospheiran life.

He'd foreseen all the objections. He'd hoped both Shawn Tyers, the President of Mospheira, and Tabini-aiji, head of the *aishidi'tat,* the atevi government, would weather all the storms of discontent at least until they'd been able to get back from their mission to Reunion and report that all this sacrifice and striving had produced a result worth having.

He seemed to have won the bet in the case of his old friend Shawn Tyers, though Shawn's political survival when he had left had seemed more precarious. Shawn was still in office, despite the volatile politics of the island and all the pressures bearing on him.

He had been disastrously wrong, however, about the atevi side of the equation. Tabini had seemed unassailable, delicately and deftly manuvering around difficulties, as he always had, having secured the help of such unlikely individuals as his own grandmother, the aiji-dowager, a unifying power of the far east, who might have threatened his reign. He'd begotten an heir, Cajeiri, with an Atageini woman, the Atageini, historically speaking, posing one of the greatest threats to the stability of the *aishidi'tat*. He'd gotten the crochety, traditionalist head of the Atageini clan on his side. He'd put down one bad bit of trouble arising in the seafaring south and west, and engaged the gadget-loving western Lord Geigi firmly on his side, in the process, Geigi's influence being a firm bulwark against trouble in all that curve of western coast. What more could he need than those several allies? Nothing had looked remotely likely to shake Tabini from power.

But Geigi had gone up to orbit, managing the atevi side of the station, while the son of a conspirator, allowed to prosper—Tabini, lately influenced by strong Mospheiran hints that it wasn't proper or *civilized* to assassinate the relatives of people who'd tried to kill him—repaid Tabini with treachery.

Spare Murini, he'd asked Tabini. Take the chance. He'd been sensitive to the international, interspecies situation—been sensitive to any perception on the part of Mospheiran or spacefaring humans that atevi were less civilized or in any way threatening to humans. Attached to the atevi court, he'd begun to take such accusations of atevi barbarism personally; he'd begun, hadn't he, to want *his atevi* to have the respect of his species?

There had been a danger point, if he'd only seen it. But he hadn't read the winds. He had committed the oldest mistake of joint civilization on the planet—getting distracted by one issue, modernizing too fast, worst of all ignoring atevi hardwiring and ignoring the point that what humans might call barbarism was part and parcel of atevi problem-solving.

What had he tried to promote among atevi? Tolerance of out-clan powers. Therefore tolerance of foreigners. How could an enlightened ruler kill the son of a traitor, simply because of his relatives?

And now that unenlightened son of a rebel, driven, perhaps, by that emotion of man'chi which humans weren't wired to understand on a gut level, had quite naturally, from an atevi view, turned on the aiji who had spared him.

How much of the *aishidi'tat* had fractured when that happened? How much pent-up tension in the power structure had just snapped? Classic, absolutely classic atevi behavior.

And what could a human do to mend the damage, when the human in question had made the critical mistakes in the first place, and given his atevi superiors bad advice?

Ilisidi might, with some justification, ask for transport for herself and Tabini's heir back to her homeland, bidding the paidhi to stay the hell on the island. She might justly tell the paidhi to give her no more advice, certainly not of the quality he'd given Tabini. She hadn't yet mentioned the word blame, but he was sure she knew a certain amount of this situation was indeed his fault.

And there were no few atevi on the mainland who'd like to explain to him all the mistakes he'd made, he was quite sure of it. By now many of his loyal staff, maybe even Banichi and Jago themselves, were quietly questioning moves he'd made, things they'd accepted.

Now that he had an enforced time to sit and think, not even tea sat easily on his stomach, and sleep, as tired as he was, did not come, no matter how he tried, so the hours stretched on and on, in blacker and blacker thoughts. He ate a bite or two of his supper and found no desire for the rest. He drifted, belted to his seat, in a cabin never quiet—the shuttle had too many fans and pings and beeps for that—but that held a kind of a white, shapeless sound, and permitted far too much calculation.

"Bren-ji, you have not eaten," Jago observed, loose from her seat for the moment, drifting close to him.

"Later, Jago-ji," he said. "I shall have it later."

At the moment he wasn't sure he could keep another bite down.

But self-blame was a state of indulgence he could not afford. Until Ilisidi did, for well-thought reasons, tell him go to hell, he had to get his wits working and do something constructive, if he could only figure what that was.

So he decided he had best shake the vapors, satisfy Jago, and eat the damned sandwich, bite by bite. Deal with the situation at hand, avoid paralyzing doubt, and try to think of first things first. Try to learn from the mistakes. That was the truly unique view he could bring to the situation. At least he'd had experience in mistakes. He had a very good view, from the bottom of this mental pit, of what they had been, and what not to do twice.

Dry bite of tasteless sandwich. One after the other.

If atevi affairs were to get fixed, the fix had to start from the top of the hierarchy. That was the very point of man'chi. He had to find out what had happened to Tabini, the foremost atevi who'd trusted him, and set things right in that regard, if he had to shoot Murini with his own hand.

There was an ambition worth having. Too late to utterly undo the damage, but at least, if he took Murini out of the picture, as should have been done in the first place, he could free the people of a leader completely undeserving of man'chi, of anyone's man'chi—in his own admittedly human estimation.

He hadn't asked himself, in those fast-moving days when the space program had been his only focus, *why* humans felt guilty if they didn't spare their enemies, but, more importantly, he hadn't asked himself why atevi had generally felt extremely guilty if they did. He'd been feeling all warm and smug in his accomplishments in those days, too warm and smug and convinced of his own righteousness ever to ask himself that question . . . like . . . do atevi have an expectation of certain behavior on all sides, that might be worth considering?

The human word gratitude had always translated into Ragi, the dictionary blithely said so, as *kurdi, root from kur, debt.* But what did it mean, derived from the word debt? A feeling of debt for an undue kindness? Good debt or bad debt?

And how was *that* to translate into atevi actions not within, but *across* the barriers of man'chi? There was the problem.

And translators previous to him had never questioned whether application of gratitude across man'chi lines was possible—had never taken any within-and-outside-man'chi applications into account because translators before him had never been in a position to see atevi cross those boundaries. Translators before him had never dealt with an aiji as extraordinary as Tabini, whose *ambitions* had crossed those boundaries and placed him into situations where inside and outside man'chi critically mattered. He hadn't seen it. Bang! Right in the face, and he hadn't seen it. None of his predecessors had suggested there might be a problem with the word, that concept, that assumption.

Welcome home, Bren Cameron. Welcome home, on the day all the mistakes suddenly made a difference. Bring the computer up, open the dictionary paidhiin had spent centuries building, and put a significant question mark not only beside that word *kurdi,* but add a note that every emotional and relational word in the dictionary deserved a number one and a number two entry, an inside meaning and an outside meaning.

He'd let his dictionary-making duties slip, thinking they didn't matter so much as his flashier, newer ones. Lord of the Heavens, he'd become. But where was the clue to his problems? Lurking, as always, in the dictionary, right where he'd begun.

The shuttle made its insertion into atmosphere on a route they'd never used before, so everything was tense. The station confirmed they had clearance from their landing site at Jackson, and from Mospheiran air traffic control in general—it was another worry, that some lunatic Mospheiran with an airplane might take exception to their landing or just, in great admiration, take the unprecedented chance to see a shuttle landing. Both sides of the strait had their patented craziness, and a man who wanted to think about such things could fret himself into deeper and deeper indigestion.

Jago noticed it, and inquired again: "Are you ill, Bren-ji?"

She had put away a fair amount of the offered prelanding snack, and for answer, he simply gave her his dessert, a prettily wrapped bit of cake. "Would you, Jago-ji? I fear I may weigh my stomach down."

She knew him. She knew he was worrying. She likely knew he was scared spitless. She floated across the aisle and back a row and shared her acquired pastry with Banichi. Then the two of them gave him analytical looks, and put their heads together and conferred.

The conference drifted up the aisle—literally, as Banichi and Jago floated forward—to Cenedi. Dared one wonder—or worry—that his anxiety might then drift over to the dowager, and reach the eight-year-old heir?

Bren felt his ears grow hot, a flush of thoroughly human embarrassment, and he shot Banichi and Jago a fretful look, trying to get them to desist from advising Cenedi. He signaled Jago, who pretended not to see. Now *they* were worried because he was worried, and because he had not informed them why.

His bodyguard was a delicately balanced, edged weapon. It was outright wrong to handle such an instrument with anything but precision and caution, and he had leaked human emotion into their situation. He had upset their calculations of the risks, not told them the nature of his worries, possibly tipped them toward distrust of the Mospheirans they might have to deal with.

Well, he could at least patch that problem. He insisted, caught Jago's eye, and when she had drifted back to him:

"Have no concern for my surly disposition or my appetite, nadi-ji. Flying always upsets me. I particularly dislike it when there may be missiles aimed at us. Imagination quite thoroughly upsets my stomach. But I have confidence in our landing and great confidence in Mospheirans on the ground."

"Do we rely securely upon the *Presidenta*?"

She was still ready, ready as Tabini had been, along with all their security, to take his word as truth, when his judgement was necessarily at issue in this whole business, whether he was at all reliable in his estimates of his own people, when he'd been so badly mistaken in reactions on the mainland. But there was no room for second thoughts. Gravity had them. They were headed irrevocably for Jackson, with no other landing site in the whole world available, carrying the most precious cargo atevi had, in the dowager and the (at present) bored, over-sugared, and over-stressed heir of the *aishidi'tat*.

The paidhi needed to get solid control of his own nerves, that was what. He could only think so many moves ahead, or go crazy trying to calculate the variables to a nicety. There *was* no calculation possible at present, except that they had to get down and get transportation to a place where they could gather more information.

"We may rely on Shawn," he said. "The *Presidenta* remains a strong associate, reliable and, as far as I know, firmly seated in his power. I wish I might tell you the next steps we shall take, but I have been reluctant to discuss any specifics with him, for fear of interception by some less well-disposed party. We shall land, I suppose we shall spend the night near the landing field to consider our options and gather information, and by some means, in the morning, I expect, we shall cross to the continent as rapidly as we can. I trust the *Presidenta* will arrange a boat—that would be my preference."

"Safer," Jago agreed. "Slower transit, but one believes all of us agree. There will be surveillance, but surely more boats than planes go about the strait, particularly under these circumstances. I shall present it to the others."

"Do so, Jago-ji," he said, and she sailed forward, pulled herself down to a secure place in the seats forward and spoke gravely to Banichi and Cenedi, who had continued their conference, and doubtless were committing certain key things to memory. It seemed likely a plan was in formation up there—even, likely, a plan as to what they should do if all the paidhi's assurances fell apart entirely and they were met with gunfire or treachery at highest levels.

The paidhi was out of his element in martial affairs. What his bodyguard was doing up there was certainly more constructive than what he was doing, sitting back, fretting, and nursing his indigestion. High time he opened his computer and set about his own reasonable preparation, raking up details of officials on Mospheira, recalling those in various offices, down to their contact numbers and home addresses. He did that, reminded himself of accesses to certain lords on the mainland, then unbelted and drifted up near the dowager. Floating there, tucking down somewhat into a vacant seat, he asked her in detail about various lords on the mainland, with her estimation of their web of man'chi, and that of their households, to whom they paid allegiance, and of what history, with what marriages and inheritances, reestablishing his command of that mathematics of trust and old grievances.

Certainly young Cajeiri listened with more personal interest than a human child might have mustered, absorbing a set of old, old feuds and seemingly pointless begats, marriages, and business dealings of people he'd never met, most of them now dead. His young lips clamped tight on questions he by now knew not to ask, wisely declining to interrupt the conference of his elders, eyes sparking at this and that name he might remotely know, or a light of understanding dawning at a particular reason this clan avoided that one.

When Ilisidi began enumerating the members of the Atageini household, and included two sisters of Cajeiri's mother, and an illicit affair and illegitimate child in the extreme youth of Damiri's youngest sister, Lady Meisi, his young eyes grew as round as moons.

"Who, mani-ma?"

"Deiaja."

"She is my cousin, mani-ma?" Cajeiri exclaimed—Cajeiri having resided under great-great-uncle Tatiseigi's roof, not so long before their mission launched.

"And being half Kadigidi, and ill-advised, she is a scoundrel of a youngster," Ilisidi said darkly, "and a thoroughly bad influence, I have no doubt."

"She brought me cakes," Cajeiri said, "when greatuncle said I had to stay in my room. I never heard she was my close cousin."

Ilisidi had lifted a brow at the business of the cakes, and actually seemed to muse on that small point for an instant before she frowned darkly. "One may read the winds of decades in a tree. Young, it bends to every fickle breeze. Old—it leans increasingly to the persistent summer winds of its growing seasons. Have you never marked this tendency in trees, young aiji?"

"I never have, mani-ma."

"Do so in future," Ilisidi said sharply. "Consider the winds that continually blow in the Atageini household, from what direction, and how strong. Grow wise."

"I should rather have had Artur and Gene come down with me! I might rely on them more than the Atageini, at any time!"

Oh, damn, Bren thought, inwardly bracing himself for a very wintry wind, indeed. *That* small rebellion was certainly not well considered, coming amid Ilisidi's remarks about childhood and growing.

"And so you do not trust Deiaja as much these days as once you did."

"You say we should not rely on her. But the Atageini . . ."

"The Atageini remain questionable."

"Not my mother, mani-ma!"

"Children arrive into such difficult situations. Being born to patch a rift, one necessarily spends years at the bottom of it, looking up and seeing far less of the landscape than one might otherwise see. A wise child will take the word of those with a wider view."

A young jaw clenched. "Can I not trust my mother, mani-ma?"

"Do you trust me, young sir?"

"You are the aiji-dowager. I suppose you are still the aiji-dowager, mani-ma, even if my father is—my father is—"

"I remain the aiji-dowager and shall remain, so long as I draw breath, young sir. As you will be the sole occupant of that untidy rift so long as you live: *plan* on it, and get as many reports from those who saw it form. As you grow taller, you will see more of the landscape. Do you understand me? Need I make it plainer, and leave less to your imagination?"

"No, mani-ma, one need not." A duck of the imperial head, a momentary downward glance. And up again, with a thrust of the bottom lip. "But I could absolutely rely on Artur and Gene, mani-ma. They are very clever."

"They are humans, boy."

"You rely on the paidhi-aiji, mani-ma, so I could rely on them!"

Time for the paidhi-aiji, a bystander, to duck his head, cling to his seat, and above all not to think unhappy thoughts about what grief the dowager's reliance on him had brought to the world.

"Impertinent youth, to dare compare two untried boys with the paidhi-aiji."

"They may be reliable, mani-ma, when they grow up," Cajeiri protested.

"When they have grown up," Ilisidi said, "and when you have acquired an adult mind, great-grandson—then give us your mature opinion. Until then, profoundly apologize to the paidhi-aiji."

Bren looked off toward the staff consultations, quite sure he would surprise an unseemly sulk if he glanced toward Cajeiri. He waited for the dutiful, soulless, "One apologizes, nandi."

And didn't hear it.

"*Bren-nandi* was eight, once, and he grew to a more fortunate year, mani-ma. So even did my great-grandmother."

"Impertinent boy!"

"But it is true you were eight once, and you grew up wise and clever. So they might, and I might."

"Too impertinent by far," Ilisidi said. "Wait until we stand again on solid ground, young gentleman. Then we will see if substance accompanies that sauce."

"Yes, mani-ma," Cajeiri said, and added, under his breath and with a forward glance: "One does respect the paidhi-aiji at all times."

"One is grateful, nandi," Bren ventured to murmur, as Ilisidi waved the imitation of a blow toward Cajeiri's ear.

"Intolerable," Ilisidi said. "And growing more impertinent by the day. We shall be glad to deliver him to his father."

Fortunately phrased, auspicious wish. He personally took heart from the notion that the dowager, knowing her own people, and with her own ambition, had not given up on finding Tabini alive.

Nor, apparently, had she given up supporting him.

But he had gathered all he was going to for the moment. The mood was broken.

And somewhere in the exchange of names, the gathering of reference points and names he had not thought

of in years, he found himself sunk back into those referents as he went back to his seat. The dowager's analogy
of standing in a rift was apt. He had been brought in to
bridge a rift of his own—and was it entirely his fault if
even Tabini, who had a thoroughly atevi set of instincts,
had misjudged a situation in relying on him so much?
They'd known what they were doing was dangerous,
hastening the trickle of technology into a spring flood in
response to trouble on the island, incursions onto the
mainland, and—and the arrival of the ship from its
centuries-long absence. In the press of events, a good
number of atevi had come to agree with their actions.
Even the dowager, prominent among the environmen-
talist and traditionalist element, still approved what
they had done, to the extent of going into space herself
and attempting to assert atevi authority over their own
world and its surrounding space.

He found himself traveling down old, old mental
channels instead of meeting blank walls. This lord and
that lord might be relied upon to thus and such a degree, as in past crises, and if that lord stayed loyal to the
Ragi atevi, so would this other lord, very likely, give or
take a cousin married across a certain dubious clan
boundary—

It all grew familiar to him again, like putting on an
old, comfortable coat. They weren't advancing into unreadable chaos. They were coming home—*home,* whatever its current condition, and there were resources he
would be so busy laying his hands on, he wouldn't have
time to panic. They *had* resources with them, for that
matter, and if saving the mainland government meant
setting Ilisidi at the head of the *aishidi'tat* until they
could find Tabini, there were northern and central and
eastern lords that would approve that stopgap measure
in a heartbeat. There were lords he was sure that would
approve any aiji at all who wasn't a usurping duplicitous
Kadigidi backed by detested southerners. There was a
solid center to the *aishidi'tat* that would accept compro-

mises of every sort to gain the reestablishment of a solid, known power in place of Murini, who had no majority, only a coalition of powers that sooner or later would cut his throat and fight for power of their own, taking everything down to chaos with him.

Oh, yes, count on it: each and every one of the lords of the west would have a grand plan how to avoid chaos in the south. Each and every plan would favor their own interests—altruism did not run strong outside man'chi—but atevi also had their ways of coming to a workable arrangement, pragmatic in the extreme, and faster-moving than the Mospheiran legislature on its best behavior.

The lords already knew what had to be done to establish a lasting order: put power back in the hands of a non-regional authority, a clan with no particular regional axe to grind, which was exactly the position the Ragi atevi had satisifed, in the person of Tabini-aiji, wherever he was—or in the person of his heir or a regent for that heir. It was Tabini's line that had been able to build the *aishidi'tat*. It was only Tabini's line that could hold its neutrality in regional disputes—or at least, convince the participants of that neutrality.

He felt better, thinking of that. Tabini, for one thing, would not have had every hand against him, only a critical few. He would have had support. He likely still had.

He called Banichi and Jago, with Tano and Algini, into proximity, to trade what they had gotten from Cenedi for what he had gotten from the dowager, and thereby to point up certain lords as likely and certain others as dubious in their usefulness.

"Most of all," he said, "and key to the situation in the central provinces, we need to ascertain what position the Atageini have taken."

"Not forgetting we must also arrange something to protect Atageini interests, and Lord Geigi's province in the west, nandi," Banichi said. "They will have been under attack already."

"And to ascertain the position of the aiji-dowager's neighbors to the east," Jago added.

Ilisidi's neighbors, to the far east, were a band of hidebound conservatives who had been dubious enough they had any reasonable place in the *aishidi'tat* in the first place, and who had acquiesced to it because Ilisidi had dragged them into it and linked their interests to her influence in the government.

"They may have grown doubtful and restive in her absence, nadiin-ji," he said. "But she is back, now. They may need to be informed of that fact. Perhaps convinced of it."

"One thinks," Tano began to say. But the steward had just appeared from the cockpit.

"Nandiin," that person said, "we are entering the rough part of our trip. Kindly secure all items and take safety measures."

Belt in, that meant, and get the computer safely into the under-seat locker. They were going in.

Their conference broke up. Jago came to sit by him, a comfort in a landing process he truly, truly dreaded.

And one he only wished had become routine.

They were about to come in over the western sea, which meant driving through the coastal weather systems, over a very worrisome central mountain range, itself a breeder of weather, to a landing at a short municipal airport on the opposite coast of Mospheira, an airport the crew had never seen before except in maps. Which was twenty feet shorter than it was supposed to be.

"Jago-ji, a message for the pilots. Remind them courteously that the runway is shorter than at Shejidan." He gave her the precise measurement in atevi reckoning, and watched as she sailed forward and delivered the warning.

"They have the chart, Bren-ji," Jago said, settling back in beside him. "The numbers agree."

"Very good, very good, nadi-ji." He briefly touched

her hand, swore he was not going to grip it, white-knuckling the whole way down. He was going to relax.

Engines kicked.

God, God, God, he hated descent.

5

Tires squealed. Bren thought about that unapproved twenty feet of runway and clung, white-knuckled, to the armrest, Jago beside him. He did not grip her arm. He refused to. They'd made it over the mountains. They couldn't crack up now.

Big reverse thrust. Was that planned? Bren held his breath. Even Jago had put a hand to the seat in front of her, and imposed an arm between his face and the next row.

"The short runway," he breathed, feeling their speed considerably slowed, seeing, on the monitor above the baji-naji emblem, that unlikeliest of sights, the skyline of Jackson beyond the end of the runway.

That skyline. His family. Obligations unsatisfied. Old enemies. The Heritage Party. Gaylord Hanks. Deana.

His mother. His brother, Toby. He hadn't transmitted the letters. He had them both on his computer.

They reached a stop, still on the runway, but he couldn't see pavement. He dared draw a whole breath.

"We have arrived," the pilot said from the cockpit. "Nand' paidhi, we have need of translation."

They needed him. Someone needed him. The pilots spoke Mosphei' enough for routine problems, and had gotten down by means of computers talking to computers, but he immediately had a critical job to do, and he ought to be in the cockpit, if he could get his shaking knees to bear his weight. It felt as if he'd eaten a very heavy meal, or suddenly gained twenty pounds—he probably *had* gained twenty pounds, being back on Earth. He saw that flat horizon on the screen, and it looked strange to him, after two years. Every horizon was going to go the other way to his eye, possibly disturbing his balance. *That,* he suddenly realized, was what had felt so strange about the Jackson skyline. It wasn't a picture on his computer screen. It was real. His body knew it was.

He levered himself out of the seat, walked—walked down the aisle toward the baji-naji emblem, past his fellow passengers gathering their personal items, passed through the cockpit door.

Lofty windshields showed the whole flat earth in front of the shuttle's nose. He shied from the sight, took an offered com plug from the copilot, stuck it in his ear—it both received, off the bones of his skull, and transmitted, and he heard the accents of his own homeland talking to them, advising them of routine details, the approach of a tow truck, the query whether they'd need any special assistance. They would have to sit still in a period of routine cool-down. Hazmat personnel would approach, going over them with instruments. Mospheira wished them a welcome in, the first shuttle landing in history.

He relayed. He answered. The shivers attacked him and slowly dissipated in the scurry of various agencies assisting and trying to get the Jackson main runway clear of their presence, because while they sat cooling down, planes were in a holding pattern over Bretano and Sutherland, maybe not even knowing the reason they'd been held up.

He settled down to wait with the crew, translated arrangements for the tow, and balanced on an armrest as the tow moved them off the runway onto a taxiway. Then there were arrangements for the ladder to move in, and advisement a bus would pick them up.

But Mospheiran military security cut in with their

own arrangements, and an advisement that the President was waiting for them.

Shawn? Bren found his heart beating harder—anticipation, now, anticipation of a meeting he hadn't had in years with a man he'd used to deal with, oh, three and four times a day when they'd both been in the State Department.

"I do understand," he said to them. "Please understand I have the aiji-dowager with me, with her own security, and her grandchild of eight years, never mind he's as tall as I am, who's very tired and very stressed and should be given allowances. I'll inform them as I'm informing you, weapons will be in evidence on both sides, but peaceful intent is understood and expected, in all good will. Please don't anyone encroach on the dowager's space, and particularly understand you are dealing with a young boy, no matter how tall he is, and with very protective security. Our security likewise will maintain watch over our baggage. Expect this."

A hesitation. A slight hesitation.

A new voice. *"This is Colonel Brown. We understand your situation. We're instructed to accommodate atevi customs in all particulars. Come on out as soon as ground ops gives you clearance."*

"Thank you, sir."

The shuttle ticked and popped and boomed, cooling down. Beside him, the crew were busy checking readouts, making changes on the touch-screens and with the switches, setting everything, presumably, for the shuttle to be shut down and held. It would have to sit, under guard, and it had to remain accessible by the crew, a point he raised with Mospheiran security. It was their only way back to space until they could ascertain what might have happened to the other shuttles grounded on the mainland, with the very survival of equipment, maintenance staff and crew far from certain.

"No problem, sir," the answer came back. *"That's understood."*

No problem, no problem, no problem. Shawn had given orders and obstacles fell down as soon as they came up. He felt he could draw a breath.

And pay courtesy where it was due.

"Excellent job, nadiin," he said to the crew. "Thank you. One requests you will come with us wherever they assign us, share quarters with us, and maintain yourselves ready to return to space, as soon as we can clear up the difficulties. The *Presidenta's* own men will put a constant watch on the shuttle. You need not worry. I say so in utmost confidence."

There were respectful nods, quiet acceptance. "One request, nand' paidhi," the pilot said, "if it were possible to send regards to our households on the mainland when you cross over."

"One would be extremely pleased to convey such sentiments," Bren said fervently. These several young men had been stuck in orbit, away from their own parents, wives, associations, since the trouble had stranded them, while the *aishidi'tat* underwent a violent upheaval, and, as the only shuttle crew likely current in operations, they would be handed the first mission back to the station once conditions permitted it, a shuttle prepped, what was just as scary, by inexperienced Mospheiran ground crews, unless they were fortunate enough to smuggle atevi maintenance over here. "With my personal regards and I am very sure, with the aiji's, we will look to your households. One absolutely understands your situation, and I convey the extreme respects of all of us. We will by no means forget you."

"Nandi." There were bows, expressions of gratitude, that *kurdi* word, all around, and he left the cockpit with the sure determination to do something for these men—work some miracle to reward their devotion, their professionalism, their man'chi to the program.

"The *Presidenta* himself has come to meet us," Bren

reported to the dowager, who, amid the debarcation preparations of her staff, pursed her lips and looked satisfied as well as—dared one surmise what she would never admit—absolutely exhausted?

"Excellent," she declared. Cajeiri, standing at his seat beside her, looked to be both frayed at the edges and brimming with questions, all of which were desperate, but he asked not a one of them, except, "Shall we go out soon, nand' Bren?"

"As soon as the hull cools, young sir. We have two constraints: the need to be across the straits quickly, so that our enemies have little time to organize a reception, and the need to gather as much information as possible from sources on Mospheira, who have come here to meet us." Not only Cajeiri, but the dowager was listening. Ilisidi was patient only because it was *her* question as much as Cajeiri's. "One hopes the *Presidenta* will provide informational files we can take with us. But we must accept the *Presidenta*'s kind hospitality for the night, to recover our equilibrium on the earth. Walking is not as easy to deal with, as long as we have been in space."

"An extreme inconvenience," Ilisidi muttered, frustrated and doubtless feeling the change of gravity in all her arthritic joints, not to mention added labor for her heart. "Sit down to wait, great-grandson. Cease fidgeting."

"Mani-ma." Cajeiri sat.

Bren found his way aft, where staffs were in last-moment conference, where he could pass on his own immediate information to Jago, who turned up to gather it.

"The dowager is not in favor of long delay," he said quietly, speaking frankly. "Nor am I. But we must acclimate to the world, if only for a few hours, and get some sleep, and I hope for a great deal of organized information that may be useful to us, from the local government. The *Presidenta*, Shawn Tyers, is meeting us. One would not be surprised to have Yolanda Mercheson pay us a visit, she being on this side of the strait, and likely very interested in a return flight." He glanced anxiously toward Cenedi, who represented the dowager's interests and rarely disputed her opinions or her wishes. "I very much fear for the dowager's well-being if we attempt to ignore our physical limits and press ahead too fast. I know we risk losing the advantage of surprise, but if we risk her health—we risk everything."

Jago nodded, leaning on the seat, eye to eye with him. "This is in his mind, too, Bren-ji, be assured. That, and we all entertain the hope you mention, of resources here."

"We shall sleep in a secure place, I have no doubt of the *Presidenta*'s hospitality. They have had enough domestic stress that they are no strangers to security requirements."

"I shall inform the others," she said.

So that was handled. Bren went back up the aisle to gather up his small amount of luggage, his computer, his duffle with changes of clothes and other items Narani had packed for him. The rest of their luggage was back in the cargo compartment, and there was a fair amount of it, their staffs' gear, not to mention the clothes and items the dowager had brought.

"Nandiin," the pilot said, appearing in the doorway, "they are moving a scissor-lift to the hatch. One believes they intend us to debark."

The language barrier persisted. But they were cooled down sufficiently, it seemed, and checked for hazardous leaks. He gathered up the baggage he would handle and piled it in his seat, then went forward to attend Ilisidi and allow her the proper precedence down the aisle to the hatch.

"About time," she said. Cenedi had also gone forward, and attended her, offering his arm, but the notion that the dowager was about to meet human notions of hospitality . . . that was daunting. He was in charge of that, he feared. Every courtesy would necessarily come through translation.

The steward moved aft to open the outer hatch. Banichi and four of Ilisidi's young men had stayed back there, two of the latter to see to the baggage, the rest to attend the door when it opened, Bren was sure.

Ilisidi walked down the aisle, with Cenedi, lips tight, and young Cajeiri came close behind, with two others of her bodyguard carrying her personal baggage.

So Bren fell in, carrying his own bags. Tano snatched them as he passed, and fell in behind him, with Jago and Algini.

The hatch opened. Air wafted in. The dowager and her party exited onto the quaking lift platform, and he followed, flinching at the flat world. A wave of malodorous heat from the shuttle walls warred with cool and fresh wind off the sea, air as moist as the shuttle's atmosphere was dry and cold. The side nearest the shuttle felt like the breath of an oven, baking their backs.

And the blue and gray horizons dizzily went on forever, with Mt. Adam Thomas drifting like a vision above a haze in the distance, real, and solid, in flat perspective that warred with recent reality and yet quickly seemed right to memory, if not the inner ear. He stood near the dowager, as their security piled their baggage onto the lift. He gave one hand to the rail and offered one to her vicinity, if not touching her, just as the lift started into motion.

She stood fast, jaw set, stubbornly refusing assistance, even from Cenedi. Cajeiri caught her arm, clever lad. The platform shuddered and descended.

Vehicles came into their view, airport emergency vehicles, and with them was a gray limousine with the presidential seal, along with its own entourage of black security cars. Emergency crews waited near their vehicles, and a cluster of suits and uniforms stood to the fore. Bren spied Shawn's familiar face, saw with a little shock that he'd gone gray, in so short a time in the presidency.

The lift bumped to the ground. Cenedi put himself at Ilisidi's side as they walked off the edge, Ilisidi using the cane carefully but decisively, Cajeiri on her left, as they reached the tarmac. Bren followed, set himself decorously to the side, bowed.

"Aiji-ma, allow me to present Shawn Tyers, *Presidenta* of Mospheira." Change of languages. "Mr. President, the aiji-dowager and her great-grandson Cajeiri, son of Tabini-aiji."

Shawn gave a measured little nod of his head, a meeting of equals—Shawn had spent his days in the State Department and no one could have a firmer grasp of the protocols, the little dance of who was introduced to whom first and to what degree heads nodded or eyes lowered. Host nation for the island enclave, atevi took slight precedence in any encounter—few encounters as there had ever been on this soil, since the War of the Landing.

"Welcome, nandiin," Shawn said, in Ragi—carefully, and fortunate in number. He *had* run State, and the paidhi's office. Then in Mosphei': "Tell the dowager that that's the safe limit of my command of the language, but the delegation is most cordially welcome for as long as they choose to stay. We have safe and appropriate quarters at the airport hotel, should she wish, and cars to take them there."

He rendered that: "The *Presidenta* most happily welcomes you and offers transport. Will the dowager, he asks, be pleased to accept his hospitality and refreshment in appropriately arranged quarters nearby, for however long his guests may please to advantage themselves of his hospitality?"

Ilisidi considered the offering—Ilisidi, whose aged bones were doubtless aching with earthly gravity. "Tell him this is our shuttle. Let him by no means mistake that fact."

He bowed. And rendered it: "The dowager accepts with utmost gratitude, and requests Mospheira set a round-the-clock guard over the shuttle, which she regards as a vital atevi asset. Only crew should have access, at their pleasure, also round-the-clock. Crew will attend us to the hotel, along with our security. They will lodge there and come and go as they please, escorted by your security as far as the shuttle perimeter."

Shawn understood exactly what the dowager meant. He smiled, graciously enough, and gave a slight nod. "Understood." He swept a gesture at his own bodyguard, toward the waiting cars. "Everybody."

Everybody was not so easily rendered, when it came to fitting tall atevi into human-sized conveyances, along with their carefully-watched baggage and equipment. There was the bus for the airport crew, and that also went into service for baggage and shuttle crew transport, accompanied by two of Ilisidi's young men.

The rest of them eased into Shawn's limosine—no great problem for himself and Ilisidi and Cajeiri, near human sized, but only Cenedi could get in besides, in the facing seats. He settled beside Shawn himself, leaving his aide to ride beside the driver. Banichi and Jago, Tano and Algini, together with the rest of Cenedi's men, all parceled themselves out into other cars, having to duck their heads uncomfortably, and the vehicles whipped off at considerable speed down the frontage of airport buildings and onto a road leading outward.

"Most happy to have you safe," Shawn ventured, filling an awkward silence in the crowded vehicle.

Bren translated, improving it to: "He expresses all possible felicitations on the dowager's safe return."

Ilisidi frowned and muttered, "Has he any useful news?"

"She asks news," he rendered that surly utterance. "I fear she won't consent to stay here more than the night. She wants transport to the mainland, and information that can set her on the other shore as well-prepared as possible. I have to concur. Our enemies won't waste time setting up opposition to a landing."

Shawn absorbed that. More than the gray hair—he'd added a few lines in his face in the last two years.

"Does she intend to confront Murini-aiji militarily?"

"Not aiji," Ilisidi said sharply.

Shawn quickly inclined his head, a slight apology. "Pardon."

"She doesn't acknowledge Murini's claim," Bren said quietly. "No offense on either side. The dowager will do what makes sense in atevi terms. I doubt she knows yet exactly what, though contacting allies figures somewhere in the plan. Crossing, preferably by boat. Quietly. Inserting our group onto the mainland. Quietly. Then all hell may break loose as we secure a foothold, or we may proceed more quietly. We don't know. That's where information would come in very handy. Have you possibly heard from Tabini-aiji?"

"No. Unhappily, no. Ms. Mercheson made it here. I'm sure she'll want to report, but I don't think she knows any more than I do."

"What of the central provinces, the Atageini?"

"We don't know the details of who's allied to whom," Shawn said. "We only know who's come out in public as supporting Murini—mostly southerners, and the Kadigidi in the central association. For the rest, we don't know who's fence-sitting and who's biding their time."

"We have Lord Geigi's information, which we'll share with you, but it's not current."

"I have a file for you," Shawn said. "And our current codes." Shawn hadn't entrusted this item to an aide. He reached into his own inner coat pocket and handed him a small data reader. "I don't trust your old accesses. Don't use them. This is up to date. Accesses that can get that computer of yours into whatever it needs. Guard it with your life."

"Runs by itself?"

"D-socket. If it can get a phone connection, it can get to Red Level. Your new codes are activated as of this hour. I trust you haven't let the old ones loose in any unreliable places."

"No. I haven't." It was far better than he'd hoped for. A profound trust, when he'd technically stopped working for Shawn years ago. "And won't. The file is in it?"

"Yes. The information we have is thin, from a couple of north shore sources. For God's sake, protect it. The recessed point on the back—that's the security wipe. Punch that and everything's gone."

"Just thank God it's got one." He put the small black unit into his pocket. Miniaturized to a marvel. "The *Presidenta* has given us a great courtesy, extreme access and all his best information, nand' dowager, contained in this small item which will connect us to him through my computer."

That drew a deep inclination, a regal bow of the head. "Say to him that we shall remember this great courtesy, nand' paidhi."

"She is—'" He began to say *grateful,* and, with a little coldness at heart, hesitated on that word. "Very favorably impressed."

The car braked outside the service entry to the airport hotel—the utilitarian service entry, pavement spotted with grease and a couple of trash bins brimming over, was *not* where he would have presented the aiji-dowager and the heir, but there they were, the human notion of security, and not that far off atevi requirements. He hastened to get out, wanting everyone under cover as quickly as possible.

"This is the appointed stop," he called out, as Banichi and Jago exited the car behind, with the other vehicles pulling up close. "We shall take a lift inside, among common folk of no likely ill intent. Above all, no deadly force, nadiin-ji."

Atevi security and ordinary airport hotel guests, many of whom might have had their flights cancelled by the unannounced shuttle landing. And security wasn't his only worry. He turned his attention to the aiji-dowager getting out. She waved off his assistance, used her cane, anticipating Shawn's exit from the other door, and by now his security, her security and Shawn's security were all over the entry, taking possession of cars, service entry, and, just inside, the hotel kitchen, with startled staff. Shawn's security held the door for them as atevi security entered. Somewhere a pan dropped, a horrid racket, and the perpetrator lived.

"Service lift, sir," one of Shawn's people said, and they reached it, dispersing security, human and atevi, along their route, and then folding it in behind them, with the exhausted shuttle crew bringing up the rear with all the baggage.

"That will all come with us," Bren said sharply, when Shawn's people tried to hold it at the lift in favor of people first. "Shawn." Forgetting himself. "Mr. President, we need those bags with us at all times."

"Absolutely," Shawn said, waving off his own men's efforts. "Rely on them, Jim. They'll manage." Shawn's men were doing a splendid job so far, not coming between Ilisidi's security and Ilisidi, and managing to hold the door of the lift for them, so that even the dowager found no reason to scowl.

Inside, with the dowager, Cajeiri, her security, Banichi and Jago, with baggage, plus Shawn and his aide and two of his men, the first load as the lift ascended, under key . . . up and up, to a destination which proved to be, indeed, the penthouses, not altogether unexplored territory to his eye. He'd been here for official meetings and the like, had stayed in more than one of the several suites, each with a formal room between. Comfortable rooms, large beds and a grand view, even by the dowager's exacting standards. He'd had a relieved sense of where they were likely going when Shawn had said hotel, and the place had been, as Shawn had assured him, suitably arranged. There were flowers by the lift, flowers in the formal room, harmonious, even *kabiu*: *suitable* for high-ranking guests. Remarkable. University and the current paidhiin-designates had probably swung into action. And very, very welcome. The dowager drew an easier breath. Everyone did.

"The southern suite, nandi," Bren said, motioning to the right—he was able to recommend it, having lodged there before, himself—"has an extraordinary and pleasant view."

Ilisidi walked forward slowly, absorbing the environs, Cajeiri close beside her, Cenedi and Banichi to the fore. Bren opened the door of the suite.

"Perfectly adequate," Ilisidi said, on a mere glance inside. A note of exhaustion had thinned her voice. Cajeiri's arm had became a constant support under her hand, like the cane on the other side, and one might suspect a haystack in a barn might have sufficed at the moment. The view was wasted. "We shall sit, nand' paidhi. We wish to sit down."

"She is extremely tired," Bren said.

"Not surprisingly so," Shawn said, and motioned toward the sitting room that ended the corridor in a half-circle of broad windows, blazing daylight. "The hotel has laid a buffet, tea, fruit, and sandwiches, if it can pass her security. Mine has watched it, start to finish. If it doesn't suit, she can order any service she may wish."

"Nand' dowager," he said, extending an arm in that direction, "chairs, tea, fruit and sandwiches in the sitting room, provided as a courtesy by this establishment. The *Presidenta*'s security has passed it and swears to its safety."

"Excellent," she said, and forged grimly ahead, her cane in one hand, Cajeiri's arm under the other, Cenedi in close attendance, as they walked into that sunlit room. The window held a broad view of the mountains, snowy Mt. Adam Thomas framed in the lesser peaks, its flanks shaded with a skirt of cloud in an otherwise blue sky.

Home, that mountain said to him, as nothing else on Mospheira. The buffet spread below, table upon table of elegantly offered food, tastes they had not enjoyed in a very long time. And even with hot tea and the longed-for chair at hand, Ilisidi lingered standing, gazing at that view ... Ilisidi, who loved the world and its natural state.

And whose species had owned this island once, before humans came.

She settled slowly, painfully, into a chair which faced that view. She gazed on it, while her staff moved to bring her tea and offerings from the buffet.

Shawn gave a little bow and settled in a chair and Bren sat, staff doing the serving—staff and Cajeiri, who sampled an item or two then contentedly served himself a heaping plateful of little sandwiches and sweets.

Shawn cannily said not a word of business, nor did he. No one, in fact, spoke, or disturbed the dowager's contemplation of that view for some minutes after tea and refreshments were served. The air they breathed here was unprocessed air, rich with moisture, with smells that had nothing of the machine about them. The food offering they had was simple, the world's exquisite flavors, and Bren luxuriated in the tastes of smoked fish and cheese and fresh fruit, wonderful things, with hot tea. He found his hands shaking with fatigue, and he both wanted every detail of what Shawn had to say, and dreaded hearing it, most of all having to cope with it and make decisions. He already had a wealth of things packed into the back of his mind, an overstuffed baggage of personal and national emergencies and anxieties, things he hoped, in part, Shawn's files covered without overmuch coming at him in conversation.

The dowager finished. Definitively set down her teacup. "Thank the *Presidenta*," she said, "nand' paidhi, and ask how fast he can get us to the mainland."

"Nandi. Mr. President, the aiji-dowager very much appreciates the hospitality and asks for your assistance in reaching the mainland safely and as soon as possible."

"Tell her we're honored by her sentiment, and we could try by air, but there are air and sea patrols out from time to time. There is no safe landing site for a plane except perhaps up in the north, or out on the southern peninsula, Lord Geigi's territory."

He translated that.

"A boat," Ilisidi said, "and the central coast, south of Mogari-nai."

He translated. And added: "You could shadow us by sea."

"We could," Shawn said, "and it has advantages. Murini's people don't have a firm grip on the coast and might have trouble positioning agents."

"He offers all assistance, aiji-ma, and offers the protection of patrol boats, with, no doubt, air, if we need it."

A wave of an aged hand. "More tea," she said. "The details are for Cenedi to determine."

"She takes it under advisement," Bren said. "She does favor the idea. Our security staff will consider our options."

"Then I won't linger long," Shawn said. "I can't manage any lengthy visit without extensive noise, unfortunately, and I've got a press conference to manage. You have your contact numbers. Your access is active. Your phone installation on this floor is State Department, secure. If I stay much longer, the news is going to speculate outrageously, as if it hasn't already."

"Hardly possible to stop air traffic at Jackson and stay unobtrusive, I know." Unbridled news access was one great drawback of their landing site. But the drawbacks on the mainland were far worse. "The shuttle crew will continue to come and go to the spacecraft. They'll need extremely good and determined security for it, or we'll have the curious out there taking souvenirs."

Shawn's mouth twitched. "Absolutely." He rose, a slight breach of etiquette, but one Ilisidi passed with a nod. "My respects, nandi. Bren, I'll be out of here before we have news cameras in the lobby; I'll go do a media show over by the shuttle, answer questions—distract the mob and promise them more at my office. The story I'm giving out is that you're all here in refuge, you plan to enter into extensive consultations and gather essential items before returning to the station—the shuttle will have a showy pre-launch checkover, under close security. That'll keep them busy."

He could imagine the controversy in the legislature, motions proposed, resolutions offered, all the usual fears of atevi taking over the island they'd used to own, radical notions of appropriating the shuttle as human-owned, if they could. Most of all, Mospheirans feared getting dragged into an atevi conflict, with dark memories of the only war they'd ever fought.

"You're going to have your hands full," he said to Shawn.

"That's what I do for a living," Shawn said wryly, and offered a hand to him, a warm, old-times handclasp, before a parting bow to the dowager and the heir. "Good luck to you, nand' dowager."

"Baji-naji," Bren rendered it: the flex in the universe. Things possible. Things falling by chance and fortune. Without chaos and upheaval, the universe stagnated.

"Baji-naji," she repeated, the only answer, and nodded graciously, even going so far as to rise, painful as it was, and with Cajeiri's help, to respect the withdrawal of their host.

"Ma'am." Shawn was truly touched. He bowed very deeply, and took his security with him, except a pair of marines that stood by the lift.

"We take the *Presidenta* for an ally," Ilisidi murmured, "despite the opinion of certain in the legislature."

"He is that, nandi. As good a one as we could possibly ask. He has among other things established a cover for us, as if we were conferring here, and as if we plan to return to the station."

"Clever gentleman." Ilisidi nodded approval, leaning on her stick. "Well, well, but we shall want quiet passage across the straits."

"As soon as we can arrange it, nand' 'Sidi," Cenedi said.

"Do so." She gazed past them, as she stood, looking toward the windows, toward the view of whitecapped mountains. "Tell me, nand' paidhi."

"Aiji-ma?"

"What mountain is that?"

"Mount Adam Thomas, aiji-ma."

She stood staring outward a long, long moment at the mountain that he'd regarded as his, his, from his first childhood view of it.

"A grand view," she said. "A very grand view."

Curiously, Bren thought, he had never heard any ateva literature mention the loss of the island and its special places, places important to them. But atevi were not given to mourning the impossible and the unattainable.

"Noburanjiru," Ilisidi said. "Noburanjiru is its name."

Grandmother of Snows. Center of an entire atevi culture, now displaced to the mainland, lodging generally on the north coast, where they were fishermen. It was the mountain where he'd learned to ski, where he'd spent as much of his off-time as he could—and couldn't, these days. Hadn't been up there for years. He had a vision of his own, white, unbroken crust, above the snowline, a view that went on for miles.

"Well, well," she said, "I have seen it. I shall rest. Perhaps I shall have a nap."

"Assuredly," Cenedi said to her, in the surrounding hush, and offered his arm. "Assuredly, nandi."

Her chosen rooms would have that view, too. Bren was glad of that—glad, in a regretful sort of way—because atevi, lifetimes ago, had ceded something precious and sacred, to stop the War that was killing both nations.

Humans built lodges up there. Built restaurants and ski lifts that he increasingly suspected didn't belong up there, when atevi of Ilisidi's persuasion would have made pilgrimages.

He was home, after a fashion—*he* was home, and had not, in the haste and the normalcy of these people around him, even thought of the view outward, Jackson, and what it held . . . the buildings, the traffic, as normal to him as breathing, and as alien as the face of the moon these days. Ilisidi would never see that side of human Mospheira. He remained a little stunned, thinking of that fact, her reality, and his: he felt dazed, as much of the voyage down had involved a strange mix of feelings, fear of falling and mortal longing for the earth; knowledge of the textures, the details of the place he'd lived, and seeing them—a sense of remote strangeness. He was home and he wasn't. He wasn't the same. He never could be. That mountain up there—he saw it through atevi eyes, and the memory of the ski resorts lodged in his heart with a certain guilt.

Ilisidi left the sitting area, then. Everyone stood quietly as Ilisidi walked, leaning on her cane, and her great-grandson's arm about her, toward her suite. Two of her young men went after her, to see to her needs. She looked at the end of her strength. It was the first time ever he'd seen her falter. And it scared him.

Scared them all, he thought.

He let go a slow breath, cast a glance at his own staff, asking himself whether tomorrow would be far too soon to move, and wondering how much strain the return to terrestrial gravity might have put on Ilisidi's frame and on her heart. And every day they delayed—the danger of interception grew worse.

Of all hazards he had taken into account—Ilisidi failing them was one he hadn't reckoned on.

But the aiji-dowager was also the one of them able to

wave a hand, say, See to it, and repair to her bed to cope
with the change in gravity. The paidhi and her staff had
to plan the details, where to land, what to do next.

He felt drained.

He went and got a fruit juice, and indicated to staff
that they should make free of the table.

Staff closed in, and for a few moments food was piled
onto plates and those platefuls demolished. They were
all bone-tired, all famished, sleeping only by quick
snatches ever since the ship had arrived. They'd suffered
the hours of docking, hauling luggage, attending meetings, and catching the shuttle, and the way down had
been one long planning session, reviewing maps, reading reports. Now they were down, they were alive, they
had a few hours to catch their collective breaths, and all
of a sudden even atevi shoulders sagged, and conversation died in favor of refueling, massively.

Bren found his own moment of quiet, in sheer exhaustion, and decided he might pick a suite for himself—the one next to Ilisidi's, he thought, still in his
chair. He desperately wanted to go make a personal
phone call. State-secured line, Shawn had said. He could
take five minutes, five minutes to call, to find out—

But in the moment he got to his feet to go do that,
Banichi got up, set down his plate and went back down
the hall in that very purposeful way that said something
disturbing was going on in the hall. Jago and Cenedi and
then others set their meals aside. A stir near the lifts,
Bren observed, rising. A young woman in sweater and
trousers had come up on the lift. An amber-haired
young woman he'd, yes, very much expected to see before too much time had passed.

Yolanda Mercheson. Jase's former partner. The
woman who'd taken over his job as paidhi-aiji, advisor
and translator to Tabini-aiji for the duration of his mission in space. Staff knew her very well, and made no
move to stop her as she arrived, giving a little nod to
Banichi and Jago, who were old, old acquaintances.

"Bren," she said. She didn't offer a hand. It might be protocol, since he was in atevi dress; or it might just be Yolanda, who was not the warmest soul in creation. She didn't bow, either.

"Yolanda." He did offer his hand, and received a decently solid handshake. "Glad you made it out."

"Did all I could," she said in shipspeak, her native accent, near to Mosphei', but not the same. "Situation blew up." Defensively, brusquely, as if she'd very much dreaded this meeting with him. He felt obliged to say the civil thing, that it wasn't her fault.

He felt obliged, and became aware that he entertained a deeply-buried anger at Yolanda. She was competent. But she hated the planet. Hated Mospheira. Hated the atevi. Hated everything that had dragged her into the job, and away from the shipboard life that Jase, equally unwilling, had been drafted into. "Doubt I could have done better," he told her, obliged to courtesy, and tried not to blame her for what he subconsciously laid at her doorstep. There was no question that fault in this disaster must be widely distributed, that he had set up the situation she inherited. He'd left her in charge, having no one else to rely on, and he couldn't blame Yolanda if his ticking bomb blew on her watch. He might have stopped it; perhaps arrogantly, he clung to the belief he could have done something better. But she couldn't. And hadn't.

On her side, Yolanda probably equally resented the fact he'd set her up in an untenable situation, knew she'd not been able to keep the forces in balance, and blamed him.

So he shook her hand gravely and offered her tea, which she refused—atevi would never refuse such a peace offering, but she wasn't atevi and aggressively didn't observe the forms, not with him.

Angry. Oh, yes. No question she was. Angry and defensive, in a room full of atevi all of whom paid her the courtesy of a bow, whose government she'd failed, utterly, within months of taking up the paidhi-aiji's duty.

"I had a briefing this morning from Captain Ogun," she said to him. "Seems the Reunion business is settled, to your credit. Congratulations."

"Fairly settled," he said. It wasn't settled, not by half, and he didn't miss the bitterness in that *congratulations.* "We're not alone in space."

"Is what isn't settled out there coming here?"

"It may well," he said, meaning aliens of unpredictable disposition. "But we're talking to them. We've gotten them to talk."

She drew a breath and let it go. "*You're* talking to them."

"We have the very beginnings of a civilized exchange," he said. "We have every hope it's going to work out." Looking at her, he saw the unhappiness in her expression, the intensity of feeling she awarded to nothing but news of her ship. "With luck, we'll solve this one, and get you home."

Bullseye. Politeness on either hand flew like cannonshot, right to the most sensitive spots.

"Did the best I could, Bren."

What could he say? I know you did? That was, in itself, a damning remark. He settled on, "It was a hellish situation. One I'd pushed to the limit. Beyond the limit, apparently. You don't have to say it."

"Tabini didn't indicate to me there was any trouble. But he wanted me to go to Mogari-nai."

"*Did* he? Just before this blew up?"

"The night before. I didn't get time to go. Well, I did, actually. I was supposed to leave at dawn, from the lodge in Taiben. That's what didn't happen on schedule."

"So he was warned."

"Maybe. But it was short warning. The Taiben trip was in a hurry from the beginning, no apparent planning, just pack and go. And for some reason, after we got there, *I* was supposed to get to Mogari-nai, and he didn't explain."

"Have a cup of tea, have a sandwich and come back and sit down. We need to talk."

She looked somewhat relieved at the reception, and did pour herself a cup of tea, then came back and sat down in a chair next to his, a little table between them, staff continuing their depredations on the buffet on the other side of the room.

"I brought you a report," she said. "Everything I have. Everything I could think of." She pulled a disk from her belt-pocket and laid it on the table. He reached, took it, and pocketed it himself.

"I'm going to have a lot of reading."

"I know the President was just here. I'm supposing he's told you everything he knows, which is mostly what I told him. And what we still get from fishermen on the north shore."

"How much of our business is hitting the news?"

"Plenty. The shuttle landing. The news has been following the crisis on the mainland, with all sorts of speculation. There's a lot of nervousness. There's talk of war."

"Damn." He wanted to change to Ragi, so that what she said would be available to the rest present, who hovered around the windows, blotting out the mountain view and the daylight, keen atevi ears doubtless hoping for information. But if she was more comfortable in shipspeak, so be it. It was more important that she spend her mental energy entirely on recollection, and that her vocabulary be completely accurate.

"The President asked me to come here. So did Captain Ogun."

"You've been in routine communication with the station."

"Frequent communication. I'm spending my time mediating with President Tyers, these days. Trying to do something about the earth to orbit situation. Trying to persuade your people to spend their money on shuttle facilities, not missiles. With only partial success."

Not wholly surprising. She hadn't told him anything he didn't already know. He hadn't intended to do interviews, most of all wasn't in a mood to coddle Yolanda's upset mood. He wanted to lie flat on his bed for an hour. Wanted to make a phone call. Wanted to think about their immediate situation. But he was obliged to salve ruffled feelings, assure Yolanda he was on her side, offer appropriate sympathies, because the woman wasn't happy and never had been, not by his experience.

"I regret to say," he said quietly, "the shuttle is grounded. We have to get the mainland not to shoot at it. We have to get it prepped, and crew alone can't do it. We consider ourselves lucky to have gotten down in one piece."

A little compression of her lower lip. A crease between the eyebrows. "I understand that." When it was the dearest wish she had, to be on that shuttle homebound as fast as they could possibly turn it around. *I'm not a fool,* that tone said. "But by your leave—and the President's, and Captain Ogun's—I'd like to take up residency on this floor, next to the shuttle crew. To translate for them. To be here, with a military guard, to make sure the shuttle stays safe. I have my luggage." *To be on that shuttle when first it lifts,* he read her intention. He didn't disagree with that. And it was fait accompli. She nodded back to the lift, where, indeed, a single bag stood.

Living on a world for two years, and that was the sum of what she'd accumulated. The sum of what she valued on the planet, he surmised uncharitably.

He'd brought down an entire entourage, with enough baggage for a small war; but then, Yolanda had always been a solitary sort. She had formed a liaison with Jase and broken it off, bitterly, when Jase got an appointment she wanted. And that was it, socially, for Yolanda. Pity the atevi shuttle crew.

"We won't be here," he said. "But if you could get a communications system set up in this place, something between us and Ogun, if you talk to the crew and make sure the local authorities keep the shuttle under guard, that would be extraordinarily helpful."

"No problem. I'm gathering the President gave orders. I can be eyes-on for the immediate area."

Good, he said to himself. Yolanda cooperative could be useful. He dared the harder question. "What happened, with Tabini? What do you think triggered it?"

Her lips went to a thin line. "There was no one trigger, that I was able to figure. No reason, but Murini's ambition, and a public brouhaha over funding and districts. I think it was a long-running plot. It organized, got people into position over a period of months . . . maybe starting with your leaving, when they could talk a bit more freely about human influence. When the blowup came, like I said, we were already in the country. I was all packed to get to Mogari-nai. I was to leave in the morning, just to go out there, as if somehow I was supposed to get some special message from Ogun, or be in position to pass him something. But I woke up in the middle of the night with shooting going on in the hallways. The staff—your staff—threw me into atevi-style clothes, got me into a stairwell, and got me out into the garden, then to another stairs, and down to the outside. After that it was a lot of dodging and clambering around in the woods. The two men I was with got me as far as the garage, passed me to a woman who drove me off through the woods—I wasn't trusting her much, but she got me to a farm, and a service truck, which drove all night into the country. And after that, after that, it was just a succession of farm trucks and small waystops." A deep breath. Roads were far from extensive in the open country. There would have been detours, roundabout approaches. "At a certain point," she said, "at a certain point the driver left the truck and didn't show up for hours, and I just pulled my hood up and walked down the road. I walked three more days before I got to the coast, mostly walking at night. Trying to be mistaken for a kid, if anyone spotted me. Finally I stole a truck that was unattended at a rail depot. Learned to drive the thing in a few klicks. I got to Mogari-nai, and they told me Tabini and Damiri had disappeared, that Murini was claiming they were dead, and he was setting up as aiji in Shejidan."

Yolanda hadn't had an easy time of it. No question. He couldn't blame her in the least.

"Any evidence what did happen?"

Shake of the head. "The contact got me down to the harbor, and put me in a boat with a woman to run it, and that was all. Later I gathered from independent radio and shortwave, that Ragi atevi were in confusion, certain lords assassinated, or claimed to be assassinated . . ."

"Who's gone?"

"Parigi. Celaso."

Two stalwarts of Tabini's court.

"Others had scattered from Shejidan to their estates," Yolanda said, "which was probably how I got away—that they were tracking everybody at once, and I wasn't the most dangerous to them. Instead of following me, they were probably chasing Tabini, and he was probably leading them in circles in the woods. Me, I just opted for Mospheira and made it. Once we lost sight of land I was seasick."

He made a dutifully sympathetic face.

"But just after I got aboard—the boat had a radio, and we got radio messages that went out of there to Geigi's people and up north, and back to Shejidan, trying to rally help for Tabini. I wanted the boat to turn around. But the woman running it pretended she didn't understand me—she spoke some kind of dialect I had trouble with—and we didn't communicate, and I didn't think I could take over the boat in the middle of all that water. I just had myself, and my com unit, but I couldn't reach the ship, because Mogari-nai just shut down, and all I was getting was Jackson and Bretano."

"They'd have been onto his heels fast, if he did appear at Mogari-nai. He wouldn't have lingered there, only long enough to send out advisements to Ogun and Geigi and to his own supporters on the ground."

"That's what I told myself. That's the reason I didn't make a try to take over the boat. But there's been nothing else like that since. And they're claiming it wasn't the aiji talking from Mogari-nai, that it was one of his staff, and they're claiming the station has launched capsules down by parachute, to infiltrate the countryside, would you believe? That's a complete lie. But they've hyped that to the skies and put a bounty on supposed foreigners. Which I think is their way of covering their people searching every barn and warehouse and arresting the individuals they're looking for, all Tabini's supporters. It's not going to make it easy if you're going over there."

"Lovely," he said. The countryside overrun with searchers after every vestige of Tabini's administration, all transport become suspect, Assassins of the Kadigidi man'chi out on the hunt in the central regions and those of the Marid Tasigin in the south. He looked unintendedly at Banichi, and particularly at Jago, who understood far more of shipspeak and Mosphei' than she commonly let on. She might have followed the gist of it much more closely than Banichi, and neither of them looked happy with what they heard.

"I wrote all the detail I know in that file," Yolanda said. "I've had my evenings to sit and rehearse the whole mess, for months now. I think it's complete. I was waiting for you. I've been waiting."

He never could warm to Yolanda. He came as close as he had ever come, counting what she *had* done. That bit about turning the boat around to go back to the mainland he wasn't sure he wholly believed, but then again, Yolanda was tough at unexpected moments, tough as nails, if she wanted something; and she might have gone back to rescue Tabini and Damiri—if her linguistic skills had been up to it. But with some of the north coast dialects, and maybe with the boat's owner being deliberately obtuse, she had ample excuse for failing. Seasickness. Vertigo. Terror. Jase had gone green when he'd realized what a distance of water was under their feet, aboard a small boat.

"You're of course welcome to stay here," he said. "They're clearly feeding us well. And you're behind double security. You can relax."

"First time, frankly, that I'll sleep the night through."

"Trouble here in Jackson?" He would be surprised. There were rabble-rousers, and Yolanda, solo, didn't know to what extent she was protected.

A little diffidence. "The Heritage Party has surfaced again, causing all sorts of hell. Both our names have been tossed about, with no good intent."

"I'm not surprised."

"They're demanding Mospheira's officials up in orbit take over the station, which of course the captains aren't going to have happen; and Lord Geigi isn't going to have happen, and I doubt those people up there would even contemplate doing. But down here, you and I are representatives of the agencies the Heritagers think deprived them of their rights, that caused all this on the mainland. We're the devils. They're the light. Send ten cred to their fund to keep their message on the air and write your representative so the President, who's in league with the enemy, doesn't call up the home guard to shut down the program and arrest Gaylord Hanks."

"God." Gaylord Hanks, whose daughter Deana had gotten herself an appointment to the paidhi's office and proceeded to create a small war on the mainland. She'd died in the effort to create absolute mayhem, one of the things which had surely contributed to the current situation—and Gaylord Hanks undoubtedly carried a personal grudge for his daughter's fate.

"So I don't open my mail," Yolanda said with a deep, shaky sigh, "or maintain any office where I can be reached. I don't feel safe in Jackson or Bretano. There's no private apartment I can get where I feel safe, if you want the truth. And if you wouldn't let me stay here, I'd get a room downstairs."

It didn't make him feel easier for his own family, or for his being in the news again.

"Well," he said, "the fix for it all is on the mainland. Where I've got to go."

"Anything I can do," she said, not meeting his eyes.

"Take care of the shuttle. And count on the shuttle crew to support you."

"I heard the dowager was with you. And Tabini's son, too?"

"Both, yes. The dowager's resting. Cajeiri's gone to lie down, perforce. Exhausted, though he won't admit it."

"You look more than a little frayed around the edges yourself."

"I'm fine." That was a lie, too. But he didn't at all do the physical work the crew and the staff had done, not to mention Ilisidi, or a boy whose high energy came in frenetic spurts. "I'll brief the staff on what you've told me, particularly as soon as I have a chance to sit down and go through the notes. Is there anything but that bag you'd like to send after?"

"That's all. I'll take lunch, gladly enough. I've got my computer, I've got my com unit. I'll trust if the crew's here, they have some kind of a link up to the station, too."

"They do. No problem with that." He suddenly found himself flagging, done, physically exhausted at the thought of having to go over all the details again with Banichi and Jago. Which he probably should do, nonetheless. Events might come rushing down on them, leaving no leisure for explanations. He might forget things. But he wasn't sure, now that he thought of it, that he had the energy to last another hour, or that he could make sense in either language. The dowager had had the right idea, heading for bed while there was a chance, and before the news spread.

He put a hand on the chair arm, pushing himself to his feet. Yolanda rose. "I'll see to the things I can," she said. "Don't worry about what's happening here."

"My staff . . . they're done in, themselves. Good thing we didn't plunge off for a crossing forthwith . . . Nadiin-ji, have you followed any of what we said? Mercheson-paidhi felt more at ease in her native language, for precision of expression, and says she believes Tabini-aiji was warned only by a few hours, not knowing the threat was so close. She was supposed to precede him to Mogari-nai, was hastened out during a violent attack, sent on to Mogari-nai, and with no further explanation, she was hastened onto a boat. She heard then that Tabini-aiji had also arrived at Mogari-nai—but his few radio transmissions ceased from that source within a few hours and now she has no notion what may have happened there."

"One did follow a certain few details, nandiin," Jago admitted. "And if Mercheson-paidhi will repeat her information for us in Ragi, we shall take notes."

"One will gladly do so," Yolanda murmured, with commendable courtesies, "with apologies, Jago-ji."

Maybe he looked as ready to fall on his face as he felt. He hated to leave his weary staff to endure one more briefing, but murmured a courtesy of his own and let Jago take Yolanda back down the hall, presumably to retrieve the duffle she had abandoned to the military guard near the lift.

"One might sleep," Banichi said, touching his arm. "One observes you have not slept much on the flight, Bren-ji."

"I never sleep on airplanes," Bren muttered. Which was not quite true. But it wasn't restful sleep. Banichi could sleep under the most amazing circumstances, and doubtless had, at least for an intermittent hour or so. So, likely, had the rest of them. And it was true they looked fresher than he felt. "An hour or so," he conceded. "I take it as good sense."

"Undoubtedly good sense, nandi," Banichi said, as alert and bright as he was not.

But it was not bed he had first on his mind. He picked the other suite that had a view of the mountains and betook himself to that, immediately to the phone.

He knew his mother's number. He both longed to call it and dreaded the call, not knowing what might have been the outcome of her last trip to hospital, two years past, not knowing if she had lived through that crisis. He had a choice of her number, or his brother Toby's, up the coast, on the North Shore.

He decided on fortitude, and called his mother's number, not even trying to think what he would say to her after his desertion, beyond hello, I'm back.

But the number, the lifelong number, was no longer working.

He clicked the button down, severing the connection, desolate. Even if she'd gone to some care facility, she'd have retained that lifelong number. And now it was just silence on the other end. And he knew he'd failed her. She was gone. Just gone. And he wouldn't blame Toby for not speaking to him.

There was a lump in his throat. But he didn't take for granted, ever again, that there would be time, that there would be a second chance. He rang Toby's number. And it at least rang. And rang. And rang.

And clicked. *"Toby Cameron here."*

"Toby, thank God."

"Bren?"

"I'm on the planet."

"I know you are, you silly duck. I'm downstairs."

"What?"

"Downstairs in the hotel, in the lobby. The guards won't let me upstairs."

"My God." He slammed the phone down and exited the room so fast his bodyguard and Ilisidi's jumped to alert; and so did the marine guards down the way. He stopped half a beat.

"My brother," he said to Banichi, and was off down the hall to the military guard. "My brother's coming up. Toby Cameron. Tell the people down there to let him into the lift."

The guards looked dubious, but one of them called down on his personal unit. "John? Have you got a Mr. Cameron down there?"

He didn't hear clearly what the other side said, but the guard said, "Send him up," and Bren folded his arms into a clench to keep the shivers at bay, not wanting to pace while the lift came up, but not knowing anything else to do with himself. His own bodyguard attended him, close at hand—they might be why the guards had folded. He thought so. He hadn't been coherent.

The lift ascended. Stopped. The door opened. Toby was there, Toby, in a casual jacket, sun-browned, scrubbed and shaved and anxious to see him. He flung his arms around his brother, Toby gave him a bone-cracking hug, and they just stood occupying the lift doorway for a moment, until it beeped a protest and they broke it up and moved into the hall.

"So good to see you," Toby said, holding him by the arms.

"How did you know?"

"Oh, it's been all over the news. Amateur astronomers saw the ship had come back. Then the morning news said the shuttle was coming down. That you were on it. Indefinite whether you were coming down at Bretano or Jackson—I reserved a ticket to Bretano from here in case, but I bet on Jackson, and I brought the boat over. I saw you come in as I was coming into the harbor."

"I can't believe it. Damn, it's good to see you." His bodyguard knew Toby. Knew him well. Word was spreading to the few staff that didn't know him, he was quite sure. "Come on. Come sit down."

"The President was here, I gather."

"Met us when we landed." He had Toby by the arm, unwilling to let him go, and walked him down the hall toward his chosen rooms. "A quick move, up there. We weren't sure we wouldn't be shot at coming down, if we didn't. At least that's how we understand things stand."

"It's been dicey. Things have gone completely to hell on the mainland, by all reports."

"I'm getting that impression." He showed Toby into his suite, offered a chair. "Tea?"

"I'm fine," Toby said. "No fuss." A small silence. "Bren, we lost mum."

He dropped into the other chair. "I'd tried to call her. Before I called you. But the number'd gone invalid. I thought that might have been the case."

"Not long after you left," Toby said. "About a week."

He didn't think the news would hit him that hard. He'd expected it. He'd known it had probably happened, two years ago. But he still felt sick at his stomach, guilty for the last visit not made, a skipped phone call, on a day when he'd had the chance and ducked out to get back into orbit. There'd been so many emergencies. There'd been so many false alarms. He'd put so much off onto Toby. Handle it, brother. Brother, I need you. Brother, I can't get there. Can you possibly?

"She asked about you," Toby said quietly. "I said you'd called."

"That was a lie."

"It was what she needed to hear. And I knew you would have called, if you could. I just glossed that bit."

"You glossed everything, the last number of years.

You glossed the whole last ten years. I don't know what I'd have done without you. I didn't know whether you'd be speaking to me when I got back."

Toby shook his head. "You should never, ever have thought that."

There was another small silence. Breathing wasn't easy.

"So did you do it?" Toby asked. "Did you get the big problem solved out there?"

"We got the problem to talk to us," he said, got a breath and chased the topics he lived with. "And this isn't for public knowledge, Toby. I think it's going to get into the news soon, but I don't want it to spill yet. We established relations with a species called the kyo. They weren't at all happy about the ship poking about in their business—they blew a bloody great hole in Reunion Station and they were all set to finish the job, except we talked them into just taking possession of it and letting us get the population off. They're technologically ahead of us in some ways, they're dangerous, and we got the station population safely out of their territory, humanity pretty well disengaged from them, the local Archive destroyed, which was another part of our job, but they did get the station itself, they got every other record aboard, and they're watching us, even though they're negotiating and probably studying us. They could show up here. I don't know when." He didn't say what else the kyo had told them: that there was something more worrisome still on the other kyo border. That information was deeply classified information, and he wasn't sure when or if he was going to let that detail hit the evening news.

And God help him, even while he was trying to figure how to explain things to Toby, his hindbrain was working on a plot to use that restricted information to scare hell out of certain factions on the island and among the atevi on the mainland. There was no decency at all in the automatic functions of his hindbrain. He just went on calculating and finagling, while trying to tell his brother as much truth as he thought he could, about something that had already cost their family dearly.

"Sounds like you've been busy the last two years," Toby said, understatement.

"Busy. Busy with a ship full of refugees who *still* don't know how serious their situation was." That led into the kind of trouble said refugees might pose the current local station population, and that was a topic he didn't want to get into. "How are *you?*" he asked, the thing he truly wanted to know. And the next painful question: "Did you get back with Jill?"

"No," Toby said. Just, no, when there were two kids involved, and Toby's whole life. "I gave her the house, the kids, I kept the boat . . ."

"I'm glad you kept the boat."

"She sold the house. Couldn't stand to live in North Shore any longer."

Bitterness in that. Jill had been the one who wanted to live on North Shore, far from their mother, which had led to their mother's deep unhappiness and isolation, and a lot else that had gone wrong, with him living on the mainland. But apparently that effort, like everything else, hadn't worked out for Jill.

"Are you happy?" Bren ventured to ask.

"Actually—yes. I am happy," Toby said. "What about you?"

He didn't live the kind of life where he expected to find that question coming back at him, as if he could sum everything up in the fact he owned a boat, or a house with a white picket fence. Or a wife. Or kids. He'd just never gone that direction—had skittered all over the map with his life, from obscure, ignored atevi court official to Lord of the Heavens, and was lovers with Jago, for what physical needs he had. No children there. Nor ever going to be.

He supposed he was happy. He was alive. Banichi and Jago were. Toby was. He'd be happier at the moment if he thought Tabini was, which he wasn't at all sure about. He'd be happier if he didn't have the business on the mainland looming ahead of him, and the prospect of everything their return might bring down on a peaceful countryside. But—

"Happy," he said. "I think I'm happy. Happy being back. Happy seeing you again. Happy to have all my people safe. Except the mainland's in a mess. And there are people I care about over there who have their neck in a noose—increasingly so, as the news of our landing spreads."

"I take it you're going across."

"Fast as I can." He couldn't even apologize for the desertion. "I have to."

"I brought the boat."

He blinked. Twice. "No. I couldn't possibly—"

"She's small, she's quiet, she has full instruments, and I know the atevi coast."

"Damn, Toby."

"Look, it's a family outing. I've been waiting for this fishing trip for two years."

Toby's humor broke out unexpectedly, and it got right through his guard. He missed a beat in their argument, and Toby said, with a slap on his shoulder,

"Deal, then."

"For God's sake, no, it's not. We're arranging for the military to run us over there. People with guns and engines to stand off an atevi patrol boat. Or an air attack."

"Noisy. Let the navy just keep a radar watch and be noisy somewhere between them and us. We'll make it in when no one's looking. I'm even provisioned, if you don't mind hot dogs and chili. I can set you ashore with food in hand. I've got a whole box of survival rations. Where precisely do you want to go?"

He had no intention of listening to Toby. But he envisioned Toby's fishing boat, the sort that was ordinary traffic on the waters of the strait, then envisioned, as Toby said, a noisy military move.

And, unhappily, he knew which he'd rather be on, given the certainty their enemies would have intercepted the news broadcasts which had detailed their landing. There was more than enough time for Murini's crew to position Assassins on the coast, people who moved quietly and secretly, more than enough time for the Kadigidi to toughen the surveillance around Lord Geigi's estate. That around his own, he was sure was constant and thorough. A military escort bringing them in on a fair landing on the coast could do nothing to protect them. Only secrecy and surprise could do that.

"You're wavering," Toby said, reading his face. "You're wavering, brother. I have you."

"Damn it, lend me the boat!"

"Lend you my boat, so you can run her in and abandon her on the mainland?"

"And leave *you* safe on shore this side of the strait."

"While you wreck my boat? No, thank you, brother! I'll get you there. I'll get you there and get out again with my boat, with room to spare. I've made a fine study of the tides and the shallows over the last dozen years, with that nice set of charts I picked up over at your place. I know what I'm doing. I've got charts our military doesn't have."

He gazed at Toby, at a face he'd so longed to see. "No."

"I know the risk," Toby said. "You've done what you want with your life. You've made the grand gestures. For God's sake, give me the chance for mine."

Got him dead on. He sat there a moment not saying anything.

"So," Toby said. "We're going."

"Toby. If anything should happen to you—"

"Sure, sure, mutual. When do you want to leave?"

He made his career persuading the powers of earth and heavens. And his own brother nailed him.

"It's not a done deal. I have to talk to Banichi."

Meaning Banichi, Jago, and the whole atevi contingent. "Not to mention the dowager."

"You think she'll want to come ashore on a Mospheiran navy ship? How would that look?"

Got him again. He heaved a slow sigh. "I'll see if Shawn will give me a few boats for a screen and a diversion."

"I've no doubt he will. But it's not our problem. We can leave after dark, just get everybody into a couple of vans and pull up at the dock. My crew had her at the fueling dock when I left. We're at dock C, number 2, easy to pull up and get right aboard."

"Your crew. Who else have you snagged into this crazy venture? Not one of the kids, for God's sake."

"Barb."

His heart thumped. "God."

"You aren't involved with her any longer."

"No," he managed to say. "No." Barb, who'd been his lover for years, who'd broken with him, married and divorced Paul Saarinson, taken care of his mum with a daughter's devotion, and pursued him with a forlorn hope of renewing their relationship, right up until he left the planet . . . and now she'd gotten her hooks into Toby? He started to say: *It's certainly over on* my *side* . . . and then had sinking second thoughts, that it wasn't a very good thing to say to a brother who might, God help them, have gotten himself emotionally involved with Barb.

Toby was entitled, wasn't he? Toby knew very well what the relationship between him and Barb had been, and wasn't, and then Jill had left him, and he could picture it: Toby and Barb both had been taking care of mum when he'd left, two desperately unhappy people in an unhappy situation—

"You're not upset," Toby said.

"I haven't got a right in the world to be upset."

"You're damned right you don't," Toby said, with the

slightest amount of territoriality, serious warning, one of the few Toby had ever laid down with him.

"I'll wish you both the happiest and the best," he said, "fervently." And he thought to himself that if Barb made a play for him on that boat and hurt Toby, he'd kill her. "I'll behave. Absolutely. Nothing but good thoughts."

"Good," Toby said, and took his promise at that, and the deal was done.

It was a quick council following, Toby describing the yacht's speed under power and under wind, for their staff's benefit, and Tano suggesting precisely, if they were going in by boat, where they might hope to put in unseen—the northern coast, a region which, though not Ragi, would hold no sympathy for the south, and Tano had connections there. It was a region of independent fishermen, practicing *kabiu*—seasonally appropriate— catch, people whose small boats supplied the tables of the wealthy and philosophically conservative houses, and who were not greatly interfered with, in consequence, in any political upheaval.

"We shall be one boat among many," was Tano's summation of the matter.

One boat among many. They would be relatively unarmed, vulnerable to spies and ambush both on the approach and after they landed, but that would be their situation wherever they went on the mainland.

The particular beach, Naigi, was the recessed shore of a region where Toby had fished before, a stretch of small islands and stony reefs. Tano had been there. There was a consultation of maps, a discussion of neighboring villages.

It was not a place inviting to boats of deep draft, another good point.

Yolanda arrived in the conference. "I've provided a short list of names in that area," she said. "I have no way of knowing whether they're still reliable."

"The worst thing," Banichi said, "will be to make a

move and hesitate. It would lose lives of those who may attempt to support us. We are here. We have transport, nandi. We should go."

There was a simple way of looking at it: if anyone did attempt to organize anything on the mainland in their support, they could not leave them exposed and unsupported, and they dared not go asking for support in every possible place, for fear of Kadigidi assassins moving in on the situation.

"We should move as soon as possible," Banichi said, "and get as far from our landing as possible. If the dowager agrees."

Cenedi agreed, and went and waked the dowager, who, Cenedi quickly reported, ordered them to gather only their necessary baggage, and by all means, depart as soon as the night was dark enough.

Plenty of time, then, to reach Shawn, not by phone, but by the services of one of their marine guards, who simply went downstairs with a sealed note, got into a car and took the twenty-minute drive to the Presidential residence.

Shawn interrupted his supper with his wife to send a message back by the same courier: *The escort will act with all prudence and cooperation. The shuttle is under marine guard and will remain so around the clock, come what may. Give whatever orders you need regarding supplies and support. This man has his instructions, and the authority to do what you need. Good luck, Bren, to you and all those with you.*

Meanwhile they had done their re-packing, unnecessary personal items stowed in Yolanda's care, the shuttle crew briefed—and privately informed of Yolanda's limits of authority.

The only remaining difficulty was getting over to the marina, and for that the marines were ready: four large vans and an escort turned up at the hotel service entrance, out between the trash bins. Marine guards stood by to assure their safety from the curious in the hotel—

no few curtains parted on floors above, letting out seams of light, but they proceeded in the dark, except the lights of the vans, and they packed in as quickly as possible, Toby accompanying them and all their baggage piled aboard, for the brief transit from the hotel to the waterfront.

Masts stood like a winter forest beyond the dark glass as they turned in at the marina gate, the dockside floodlit, boats standing white on an invisible black surface, as if they floated in space. The vans ripped along past the ghostly shapes of yachts some of which Bren knew—the extravagant *Idler* was one, and the broad-beamed and somewhat elderly *Somerset*—the *Somerset* had used to take school children out on harbor tours, happy remembrance, incongruous on this nighttime and furtive mission.

The vans braked softly and smoothly, at the edge of a small floating dock.

Toby led the way out of the van, led the way down the heaving boards toward a smallish, smartly-kept vessel among the rich and extravagant, a boat rigged for blue water fishing, not cocktail gatherings. It was not the boat Toby had once had, Bren saw, but a new one. The *Brighter Days,* was the name on her stern. A ship's boat rode behind her, at separate tie.

The dowager walked down the boards with Cajeiri and Cenedi, using her cane, but briskly, with a fierce and renewed energy—a curious sight for her, surely, to find such a large gathering of lordly boats: one or two was more the rule on the atevi coast, yachts tending to tie up at widely scattered estates. But for all that, it might have been one of the larger towns on the other side, with a working boat, a fisherman, bound out under lights, a freighter offloading on the shabbier side of the harbor, in the distance.

And the city lights, the high rises—nothing at all like that on the mainland, where tiled roofs gathered, all dull red, showing very little light at night except the corner lanterns on streets as winding and idiosyncratic as they had been for a thousand years.

Towers, glittering with lights. Streets laid out on a grid, relentless, as strange to atevi eyes as the architecture of a kyo ship.

A long journey, there and here. And another, in the dead of night.

Toby reached the boat first, ran aboard and ran out a little gangway, with a safety rope, no less—on the old boat it had been a thick, springy plank. Bren moved up close behind, not sure whether he would dare lay a hand on the aiji-dowager if she should falter, but ready to help if she did.

No need to worry. The dowager waved all of them off and crossed onto the deck quite handily. It was Cajeiri that had to make a grab for the rope, and Cenedi grabbed him instantly and pulled him aboard.

"New boat," Bren said to Toby in going aboard.

"My great indulgence," Toby said. "The marriage was going. We split the investments."

"Very nice." The whole of Toby's finance. Everything was in this boat. And Toby lent it to a hazardous effort that could get it shot up, could take him and all of them to the bottom. He walked the afterdeck, looking apprehensively around him—and, next to the boom, had a sudden thought of Cajeiri and that lethal item. "Young sir." He snagged the heir unceremoniously—the boy seemed a little dazed. "This large horizontal timber is the boom. When the ship maneuvers, this may sweep across the deck very fast without warning. You may not hear it. It might sweep an unwary person right overboard or do him mortal injury. Kindly keep an eye to it at all times and stay out of its path."

"Shall we spread the sails now, nandi?" Cajeiri asked, bright-eyed in the dark, with a whole boatload of unfamiliarity about him—but he had seen all those movies. "Do we have cannon?"

"We have no cannon. We have our bodyguards' pis-

tols. And whether we spread the sails—there are two—
that depends on the winds, young sir. We have an engine
as well." Then he lost his train of thought completely,
seeing Barb come up the dark companionway onto the
dimly lit deck, a trim and casual Barb, with her formerly
shoulder-length hair in bouncy short curls. She wore
cut-off denims and a striped sweater—every inch the
Saturday boater.

She saw him. And stopped cold.

"Good to see you," he said as they confronted each
other, a lie, but he was trying to be civil. "Toby told me
you were here."

"Bren." As if she didn't know what to say beyond
that. Meanwhile Toby was trying to communicate in
sign language and mangled Ragi where things had to be
stowed, and Bren gratefully realized he had a job to do,
directing duffles into bins and nooks, explaining where
life-preservers were located, where the emergency supplies were, all the regulation things—and indicating to
Ilisidi the stairs down to a comfortable bunk, a cabin of
her own.

"A seat," Ilisidi said, contrarily, "on the deck, nand'
paidhi. We enjoy the sea air."

And the foreign goings-on, he thought. Those sharp
eyes missed nothing, not even in the dark, where, one
had to recall, atevi eyes were very able. They shimmered
gold in the indirect light of the deck lantern, like the
eyes of a mask, and the fire died and resumed again as
she swung a glance to her great-grandson. "Boy! Stay
away from the rail. Find a place and sit down!"

A sheltered bench beside the companionway, against
the wall, a blanket for a wrap against the wind that
would be fierce and cold once they started moving, although, Bren recalled, the dowager favored breakfasts
on the balcony in Malguri's ice-cold winds. She inhaled
deeply as he settled her into that seat, her cane nestled
between her knees, pleased, he thought, pleased and

somber in the occasion. He had no wish to intrude into those thoughts, and went to help Toby.

No chance. Toby bounded ashore to unmoor them, tossed in the buffers as Barb started up the engine, a deep thunder and a rush of water. Toby hopped aboard, hauled in the gangway with an economy of motion and took the wheel as the boat began to drift away from the dock, bringing them away with a smooth, easy authority.

A team. Clearly. Bren stood against the rail, watched the water in front of them, the white curl of a little bow-wave, the space between the moored yachts reflecting a slight sheen of the few marina lights as they moved down the clear center of the aisle. Masts shifted past them, lines against the light.

Their own running lights flicked on. The bow light. There were rules, and they didn't make themselves conspicuous by the breach of them, though their own lights blinded them and it would have been easier to steer by starlight. Barb had moved forward, past the deckhouse, to take up watch in the bows, and stayed there until they nosed into the open waterway.

Now Toby throttled up, and they ran the outward channel, just a fishing boat getting an early start, to any casually inquisitive eye.

They passed the breakwater, a tumbled mass of broken city pavings, and now Toby kicked the speed up full, getting them well away from the marina, well out into the dark. Wind swept over the deck, cold as winter ice.

Banichi and Jago had found a place to sit, on the life-jacket locker. Tano and Algini had gone forward, likewise some of Ilisidi's men, and Cajeiri, leaving the bench seat near the companionway, immediately worked his way forward, too, into the teeth of the wind and the chill, staggering a little, this child who had grown accustomed to dice games in free fall and tumbling about like a *wi'itikin* in flight—he had yet to find his land legs again, let alone take his first boat trip and find sea legs, and Ilisidi's bodyguard was watching him closely everywhere he went. Cenedi got to his feet and quietly signaled one of his men to stay close to him.

Then Toby shut the engine down, walked over and began to hoist the sail. Bren twitched, almost moved to help his brother, old, old teamwork, that—he had taken a step in that direction, full of enthusiasm. But Barb turned up out of the dark, got in before him, working with Toby, all their moves coordinated—laughter passing between them, laughter which belonged to them, together.

A lot had happened. A great lot had happened, while he'd been gone.

The sail snapped taut—Cajeiri had run back to marvel at it, staggering hazardously against the rail in the process. The boat leaned, steadied to a different motion. The wind began to sing to them.

No right, he said to himself, no right to say a thing, or to insinuate himself into that partnership of Toby's and Barb's, not so early in his return, not while things were still fragile and both Toby and Barb were still defensive. He knew Barb, knew there was a streak of jealousy, sensed she'd moved particularly fast to get back and lend Toby a hand, nothing chance or unthought about it. He only sat and watched, letting Barb have her way, wishing his brother had twigged to that move, a little glad, on the other hand, if he hadn't. He didn't want to foul them up, didn't want Barb's worse qualities to get to the fore, things Toby might never yet have seen. Might never see. At the breakup, when it came, they'd both brought their worst attributes to the fray, he and Barb both. They'd seen behaviors in each other he hoped the world would never see again.

A feeling meanwhile crept up from the deck, that familiar thrumming sound of the wind in the rigging. The vibration carried into the bones, the gut, bringing him memories of past trips, past expeditions, fishing on the coast, a wealth of smells and sounds and sensations—it might have been a decade ago. The whole world might have been different, pristine, less complicated.

The wind moved, and the sea moved, and they moved over it, reestablishing a connection to the planet itself. Home, he told himself. Everything could be solved, in a breath of that cold air.

Had there been a voyage? Was there a space station and a ship swinging overhead? Was the whole world changed? He was back. He had never left. Nothing had changed.

Except him. Except what he knew, and what he had on his shoulders to do.

He drew a deep breath and hung isolated, between worlds, waiting for the sunrise to come over a planetary rim. Then his eyes shut, once, twice. He wrapped his arms about himself and slept his way to dawn.

6

Sunrise still held a favorable breeze—indicative of weather moving toward the continent, in this season, and the *Brighter Days* ran before the wind with a continual hum of rigging and hull. It was a glorious motion, an enveloping rush of water.

And it was impossible to keep Cajeiri out of the works: Algini, taking his turn at Cajeiri-watch, took the young rascal in charge before breakfast, assuring he stayed aboard and uninjured, explaining the tackle and the working of the sail, explaining—Algini having once lived near the sea—how a wind not exactly aft drove the boat forward, and the mathematics of it all. Cajeiri sopped it up like a sponge—his other guards had not been so knowledgeable—and dogged Algini's steps like a worshipful shadow.

Breakfast—chili hot from the galley—met universal approval, even from the dowager, who thought this strange spicy offering might go well on eggs, if they had had any.

Afterward Algini put out a line, baited it, set Cajeiri in charge of it, and the boy promised fish for lunch.

It was tight quarters, over all: everyone wanted to be on deck at all times, and atevi even trying to watch their elbows took up more room than the ten humans who might have been quite comfortable on the boat. Bren was constantly cold—Jago and Banichi found occasion to stand close to him, warming him and blocking the wind.

But the dowager, who had sailed often enough in her youth in Malguri, left her bench, and rose and walked about the tilting deck, to everyone's acute concern, no one but Cenedi daring to keep close to her.

Within the hour, Cajeiri actually hooked a fair-sized fish, and all but fell in from excitement. It took Algini and one of Cenedi's men to get it unhooked, not without getting a hand finned, but Cajeiri was triumphant, and admired his pretty fish, until it escaped across the deck to considerable excitement. Algini picked it up, and Cajeiri proclaimed it was a brave fish and ought to go free. So back to the sea it went, to universal relief. And the line went back in the water.

So they sat or stood and absorbed the sunlight, in a sea devoid of other ships, from horizon to hazy blue horizon. "Bren-ji," Jago ventured, when Banichi had gone aft to talk with Tano, "this woman Barb. Is this a common name?"

The question. The very pointed question. Jago had once upon a time urged him to File Intent against Barb, back when Barb had been a trouble to his life. Jago had offered to take out Barb herself, except he had, in a little alarm, realized Jago was perfectly serious and told her that this was not the human custom.

Now he found no cover at all.

"It is a common name, Jago-ji, but this is indeed Barb."

"And she has made a liaison with your brother?" Very little floored Jago, but this seemed to reach some limit of good taste . . . he parsed it in atevi terms, and it came out worse than with humans—man'chi might be involved. A family breach among atevi was beyond serious.

"It seems so," he said, and on a quick breath, Jago giving a very dark look toward Barb, he touched Jago lightly on the arm and drew her over to the forward rail, in a small space of privacy. "I know this will be confusing, Jago-ji. You know that my mother has died."

"One had feared so, Bren-ji. One offers whatever words are appropriate, with deep concern for your well-being." But it did not relate to Barb: the silent objection was there, simmering under her patience.

"Thank you. Thank you, Jago-ji." Touching her hand. "One appreciates the sentiment. It was no great shock, but a profound loss, all the same. And this is what I have to explain. It does connect. Barb, in her own way, Barb had become a close associate of my mother during her illness, since I was absent. And that was a good thing. Toby, meanwhile, Toby had attempted to assist our mother, and was absent from his household. His wife took offense and left him, taking the children with her."

"They were hers?" Under atevi law, children were arranged for, and contracted for, and went with the contracting parent under the marriage agreement. Nor was marriage always permanent. Nor was there love, that troublesome human word. There was that other thing, man'chi, which followed kinship lines more than it followed sexual attraction and finance.

He let go a deep, despairing sigh. "Humans make no such contracts. They assume husband and wife share man'chi. And no, she had no particular right to take the children, but their man'chi seemed to be to their mother, so they went, and left Toby at a time of crisis."

"One recalls the facts of the case." Jago had been privy to the details of a great deal of it, once upon a time, and seen him frown and worry over it, though, he recalled, he had not troubled her with overmuch explanation. The only thing she had known for certain, he put it together, was that Barb, a problem to him, had been taking care of his mother for reasons unfathomable to the atevi mind.

"Toby's wife, Jago-ji, did not sympathize with our mother in her wish to have her household about her. She insisted Toby move to the north coast. This was about the time I took up the paidhi's office, which upset my mother greatly. Toby had moved away. I moved away. She had no servants, nor anyone close to her. She wanted us back. I could by no means cross the strait at will; for Toby, it was a shorter flight. And our mother found a way to have emergencies. This became a serious matter between Toby and his wife. Our mother abused Toby's devotion, I cannot pretend otherwise; and when she became old and sick, Toby's wife was not willing to view the situation as anything but the old quarrel. Her man'chi to Toby fractured. In such cases, one splits the property—and the children. Toby gave the wife the house, which she sold, and kept the boat into which he put all his fortune. And I suppose—I suppose when our mother died, Barb had no man'chi but to him, and he had no one but her."

"This is difficult, Bren-ji," Jago said, whether that she meant it was a difficult situation, or difficult for her to comprehend.

"I have a deep man'chi to my brother. He risks his boat, and his life, in offering to assist us. And Barb—Barb has come with him to work the boat as she has evidently been doing—it is, apparently, their household, and it may be—it may be that she wishes to be sure the man'chi between Toby and me does not supercede that between her and Toby. So she came. So she wishes to maintain her influence. I trust this is her motive. She will not let me touch the boat."

That apparently made sense. But it brought a frown.

"If she brings him happiness, Jago-ji, and settles herself with him longterm—" Talking it out, having to translate it into terms Jago could comprehend, somehow took the sting out of his heart. "If she treats him well, Jago-ji, I shall never remember any quarrel with her. I would honor her as my brother's wife, and be respectful of her and him."

"Then you believe, nandi, that she has come on this voyage to support him as well as to maintain her hold."

"She would. She has courage, Jago-ji. She always had.

She wanted the glamorous life, when I was coming and going often from the mainland, with a great deal of my resources to spend. Then when I grew more involved with the aiji's affairs and my coming and going grew more irregular, and sometimes fraught with public controversy, even assassination attempts—she wanted quiet and safety. You know she married once, a man who could provide that comfort. That contract was brief. Now, it seems she has chosen Toby, and the boat. I think it the best choice she ever made. Toby is an excellent man."

"We all think extremely well of nand' Toby," she said, undoubtedly speaking for the staff, and added with a slight lift of the brow: "I shall accept her presence if she behaves well."

"Do," he said, laying his hand on hers, and then, thinking that, above all else, Jago had some reason to wonder what she would never ask: "But, Jago-ji, my regard is entirely for you. You need never wonder. You have no equal, in that regard."

She cleared her throat quietly, both hands on the rail. Dared one believe she had wondered where Barb stood with him? Dared one think, dared one believe—possibly—Jago might be just a little jealous?

"Shall I protect this person?" Jago asked, out of her generous heart.

"As you would Toby, Jago-ji. But only as you would Toby."

"Yes," she said, that absolute agreement, and seemed peculiarly satisfied with that equation he established, Barb with Toby, a set, an established set she could indeed figure. He looked at her—the wind fluttering the ends of her braid, her dark face now completely calm and satisfied as she gazed out at the onrushing sea, and his heart warmed. Jago could by no means imagine what he felt; no more than he could quite grasp what she felt, that attachment that settled her whole universe into order around him and her duty more surely than love had a right to order his. He wished he could feel what she felt, for just ten minutes. His universe was so often chaotic, his certainties far fewer, his loyalties pulled in so many conflicting directions, always had been, until he felt habitually stretched to the breaking point.

But he'd known, when he became—romantically, on his side, at least—involved with Jago, whose sole statement, relayed through Banichi, was that she was attracted to his hair—he'd known that he'd gotten into territory with her he never would entirely understand. It involved a constant element of experimentation on her side, along with a kind of commitment fiercer and more lasting, he suspected, than a human could find outside parental love . . . sex having apparently nothing to do with it. He brought his badly-battered sense of human romantic involvement; she brought her own healthy and solid atevi attachment to her appointed leader; and they patched together an arrangement that he at least hoped satisfied both of them in all the healthy ways. He had never wanted to hold her to him if their arrangement ever became a burden to her, emotionally or otherwise . . . including if she wanted children, an impossibility between them—though one supposed two years with Cajeiri might have altered that, if the notion had ever taken root. He never wanted to hold her longer than entertained them both, but he knew, looking at her now, that she'd made herself ever so comfortable a spot in his heart—a comfort he never wanted to give up, not for any human connection that might explode into his chemical awareness.

He thought her notion toward him might be the same, that atevi fondness for well-worn places, comfortable associations, ancestral items, everything forever in place, *hers*, with every sense of permanency.

So now she had met her rival, and had heard the hierarchy of man'chi laid out in his own words.

So in her atevi universe, maybe—maybe it had reassured her and made her content. She looked to be. But what could he know? He was the translator, but certain things forever baffled him.

They talked about inconsequential things as the water rushed past the bow. They constantly meant something else. He wanted her, now that they had talked about their relationship—it had put him in mind of certain things and there was absolutely no place of privacy to be had, unless one counted the cabins below, which were exceedingly small for an ateva's comfort, and *everybody* would know why they went below. He didn't want to see his brother's amused look. Or the dowager's.

Or worst of all, Barb's. And that realization almost made him inclined to do it anyway, but he would not embarrass Jago, not run the risk, however remote.

He contented himself with being next to her, with feeling her warmth in the chill wind.

In that state of affairs, Toby came up to them.

"I figure to put us into Naigi Shoals," Toby said, "if that suits. The wind will hold fair long enough. It's likely to come up a real blow by tomorrow, and I'd rather be away from the shore. That area is pretty deserted, except for fishermen. And I'd rather run by sail, conserving fuel."

"He proposes a landing in the Naigi shallows," Bren translated. "Near Cobo. And says the wind alone will carry us there."

"One will propose it to the others," Jago said.

"She says they'll discuss it," Bren said, and was not surprised when Jago left to do just that, Banichi and Cenedi alike being very familiar with all that coast, and Tano even more so.

"Damn, it's good to see your face," Toby said, for no reason, except they'd had only yesterday evening to talk, and so much to say, and no time, and topics—

God, so many topics they'd skirted round, that had to be said sometime.

"Good to see yours—I wrote you a letter. It's—it's way too long to print out, unless you just happen to have a couple of reams of paper aboard. I'm not kidding. It's about a thousand pages. But I have the file. I wrote you every day I was gone. You and Tabini, each a letter, just my thoughts, day to day, what I was doing, where I was, as much as I knew at the time . . ."

"I'd like to have it."

"I'll give it to you before I leave. I imagine parts of it might better be classified. And I'll leave it to you whether you want to take on that burden. If you want me to edit it and give it to you later, I will. But I'd like you to have the whole copy. So you understand."

"I'd like the whole copy, too," Toby said. "If there's stuff to know—I want to know, if you can trust me with it. I'd rather know, and then maybe I can be some help."

"I trust you. I just know what it can mean to your life to carry that kind of information. It could mean watching over your shoulder until everything in that letter ceases to be secret, and maybe after that, if you've gotten involved in my business. I'm not sure it's worth it. I'm not sure it's worth it for Barb, and don't just drop it on her. She knows how to keep a secret." The sinking thought came to him that he might, in giving Toby that letter, be driving an unintended wedge between them. "Use your own discretion, but if you tell her it exists, she'll want to see it."

"Do I want her to see it?"

"There's nothing in there about her, nothing bad, nothing good, either. It's about us. Where we were. And that's plenty dangerous. When I wrote it, I didn't know what they'd classify and what not, and now that this has blown up on the mainland—I don't know. I think I'm going to blow it wide and see where the pieces fall. But I have to think about that. And if you don't want it, if you don't want the whole question, in consideration of Barb—I'll understand. I should have given a copy to

Shawn, for the information in it. I'd intended to clean the private stuff out and do that, and now there's not going to be time."

"I know what to edit."

"And that means getting into it. And getting Barb into it. The more I think about it—hell, Toby, I'm risking your boat, I'm risking your neck and hers—I never meant to risk your peace of mind and your private life."

Toby's hand landed on his shoulder, squeezed hard. "You worry too much."

"I worry for a living. I have to think of these things. And they're real considerations."

"I know they are. So what's the classified part?"

"Aliens."

"That they're a threat?"

"The ones we met, nothing imminent. Not to be trifled with, but probably manageable. But there's more than the kyo out there. A much wider universe than we ever imagined existed. A new referent. A new way of thinking. Hazards we may already be involved in."

"So what's a letter between brothers more or less? Is the news out there that bad?"

"It may be good, or bad, or the usual scary mix of things. It'll still touch off the crazies."

"Oh, God, everything touches off the crazies. That's why they're crazy. Give me your letter, silly brother. I don't have that much paper, but I've got a computer aboard, for my charts."

He opened his coat and took out a disc from an inner pocket of his coat, where he carried that, and Tabini's letter. He gave the right one to Toby. He was extremely careful about that transaction.

"This little thing," Toby said. "Doesn't look dangerous to me."

"Don't let anybody see it until you've read it end to end. That's all I ask. You've had a rough enough time being related to me, brother. I really, really don't want to make it worse."

Toby pocketed the disk and patted the pocket. "I secretly enjoy it."

"God, I don't know how you could."

"Oh, look at us, now. Good excuse for a fishing trip, good view of a forbidden coast, breaking the law with a naval escort off beyond that horizon . . . and knowing there's something useful I can do about the current messed-up state of the world. What more could I ask?"

"A brother who shows up when it's really important."

Toby grabbed his arm, hauled him around, never mind the boatful of atevi that went from relaxed to high alert. "Don't you ever say that, Bren."

"A discussion of brothers, nadiin-ji," Bren said over the rush of the water, and more quietly, to Toby, who had let him go. "I won't say it, but I still think it. Don't meddle with my load of guilt, Toby. It looks like hell, but I've got it pretty well balanced by now."

"Don't joke."

"I'm not joking."

"The hell. What happened with mum was what had to happen, sooner or later, the course of nature, happens to us all, and no, as happened, you couldn't possibly have been there, or you couldn't have gone and done whatever you've done out there. What happened between me and Jill was my doing, my business, our business—Jill undertook a warfare the same as mum, to have me disavow everybody but her own circle. I must have picked her out of my subconscious, a familiar style of dealing with people, something I understood by upbringing. God only knows. But she and mum were a real bad match."

"I won't argue with you."

"And Barb's not like that. She's not Jill."

Oh, God, he most of all didn't want to tread that territory. He didn't want to claim to know her the way he did. But he did know her. "The reason we didn't get along was the job, brother, just the job."

"She's not possessive."

Not possessive yet, he thought, Toby was wrong about that: Barb was exactly like Jill, exactly like their mother. At least—he said to himself—she had been of that stamp. She'd gotten along perfectly with their mother, understood exactly what grief their mother had, at war with Jill.

But he carefully, determinedly, gave Barb credit for improvement over the years, most of it a matter of growing up, dealing with the consequences of her choices, after he'd gotten as far from Barb as he could get. She was entirely agreeable, if she was getting what she wanted, exactly like their mother. She was adept at making the environment constantly tense if she wasn't getting what she wanted, exactly like Jill, and on one level his conscience told him he was a coward not to say exactly that to Toby, right now, while he had the chance and before Toby got himself into another bad relationship. But half of all that had been wrong in his relationship with Barb . . . was him, and his being constantly on the mainland; and constantly resenting the demands their mother put on him, and recognizing that game all too well—he knew that, too. If Toby and Barb shared a boat and were never apart—they might be happy. They could be happy. Could he help, by breaking that up with what he thought he knew?

"Is there a problem?" Toby asked, going defensive, and worried.

"She's Barb, that's all you can say. The fire's completely cold between us, not even an ember left alight. That's no problem of that sort; but we never got a chance to make a decent friendship after we broke up. I'll do my level best to do that now. For your sake. You can tell her that, if you like."

Toby let go a breath, so wonderfully open, so transparent and honest, all the way to the depths, his brother, two things which he wasn't, and couldn't be for two minutes running.

"I'll do better than my level best," he said. "We'll work it out. Don't worry about it."

But *he* worried about it. There was one more thing Barb liked, different than their mother, and Jill. She liked the spice of drama in her life. She couldn't pass up the opportunity for a little excitement. And if Barb pulled one of her shifts of attraction from Toby to him, just to see the sparks fly, he didn't know what he'd do. The stability Barb demanded in her partners had never had to apply to Barb.

A thought which he shut down, except the determination to have a talk with Barb and lay down the rules of engagement—or non-engagement, as the case might be.

"Tell you what," he said to Toby, "if you have any lingering doubt, believe this: Jago will keep us honest. I *have* an attachment. You know that." Half humorously: "And believe me, Jago's not to cross."

Toby shifted a glance aft. Jago was not in view. But his shoulders relaxed as he leaned against the rail. "I hope you're happy, Bren. And I'm not criticizing. Jago is special. She's very special. And I really hope you're happy. Contented, in the human sense."

"Mutual," he said, glad to escape the topic, and leaned there beside his brother, while Barb steered the boat and Jago—did whatever Jago did. Rested, perhaps. Perhaps just watched Barb like a predator watching prey. One never forgot, either, that Jago's hearing was far more acute than humans were used to reckoning, and she understood Mosphei' much better than humans were used to being understood.

Had she overheard? The rush of the water was very loud. Probably she hadn't. He let it go. There was honesty between him and Jago, such that he could outright ask her, and they could discuss what Toby had said—remarkable, wonderful in relationships he'd had. He let go the tension.

Peace, for about half a minute.

A commotion, Cajeiri's exclamation, and a sharp word from Ilisidi, involving venom, and cutting a line.

"Stingfish," Bren cried, without even seeing the situation, and shoved away from the rail to get back past the deck house, which blocked their view. Toby was right behind him.

Cenedi had snagged the fishing line, it seemed, and with a flash of a knife sent Cajeiri's orange-spotted, finny prize back into the sea, hook and all, to the relief of all aboard.

"But I had no chance to see it!" Cajeiri protested.

"Fortunate," Ilisidi said dryly, from her seat against the cabin wall. "Foolish boy."

"But, mani-ma, Cenedi cut my line!"

"Nand' Toby can show you how to rig another hook to the line, young sir," Bren said, "a valuable skill for a fisherman." Water was scattered over the white deck, right across Ilisidi's sitting-area, from what must have been a considerable inboard swing of the snaky animal in question, with lethal side spines and an equally lethal bite of needlelike teeth, had the boy attempted to disengage the hook. "And when we have an opportunity, I shall show you a detailed picture of the creature—which, if it had bitten your great-grandmother, would have grieved us all."

A stamp of the formidable cane on the deck. "*We* would not be so foolish as to be bitten. One does not say the same for a willful boy."

"Mani-ma." A bow. A very measured bow. Oh, we are not behaving well today, Bren thought. The boy was as tired as the rest of them, and desperately trying, after the frantic habit of youth, to be entertained, but patience and good humor was in very short supply.

Ilisidi had noticed this sluggishness of respect, too, and arched a brow, and stared at the young rebel, her lips a thin line.

"Where are you, boy?"

The jutting lip faltered. Tucked in.

"Answer."

"On a boat, mani-ma."

"As if to say, a *ship*. And *that* is the ship-aiji, more, the *owner* of this boat, which we are not. We are guests of a person placing himself at great risk in transporting us. Does this fact suggest anything?"

A moment of silence, in which Cajeiri shrank half a handspan and drew a deep breath.

"Need we suggest it?" Ilisidi said sharply.

"One apologizes, nandiin." Delivered very quietly, with a bow of the head, from a boy who looked, now the energy had gone out of him, frayed, running on nervous energy, and, yes, terribly scared, when the whole ship had reacted to a creature he had flailing on the end of a line he had had no particular skill to manage. "I did not intend disrespect."

"Bow," Bren said, nudging Toby, who managed it, and Cajeiri bowed to Toby, and the dowager nodded, and matters were patched.

"This boy is tired," Ilisidi said. "Nawari-ji. See him to a bed and tuck him in."

Indignation. "I do not need to be tucked in, mani-ma!"

"He does not need to be tucked in," Ilisidi said serenely, "but will benefit from a little rest."

"Nandiin." With a bow and a great deal of dignity the young rebel laid aside his pole and departed to the companionway, one of Ilisidi's young men at his heels.

The deck was silent meanwhile. Barb, at the wheel, kept clear of the business, watching with apprehension, decidedly.

And then things went back to ordinary, the staff relaxing, Ilisidi enjoying the sunlight, hands on her cane, eyes shut.

Toby cast Bren a worried look.

"There are rules," Bren said carefully, since Ilisidi herself understood more Mosphei' than was at the present comfortable. "He's doing very well. But he's only eight."

Toby gave a deep breath, on edge, clearly, and perhaps recalling his time about the mainland shore, where people had been on holiday and relaxed, as relaxed as atevi staff could be. The whole picture of atevi manners had never been available to him, and was not, now. It might not seem Ilisidi had been understanding, even kindly, in her handling of a boy whose temper and self-command had just snapped, and snapped because he was a child who'd been snatched from a world of routine and order into a world that had grown very remote from him. But Ilisidi was not cruel. Two years ago, at six, Cajeiri had had no independence. Now he had begun to run certain things—being tall as a human adult and strong and dexterous enough to do things for himself. But on the earth—and under present circumstances—he was obliged to take fast, concentrated advice from his great-grandmother, and become very much more adult, for his own safety's sake, overnight . . . not mentioning the fact his physical strength was enough to do serious damage.

"This boy," Bren said in a low voice, as they turned and leaned on the rail, "may be aiji within the week. He will have life and death in his hands. Indulgence is nowhere on his horizon."

"You think Tabini is really gone?"

"I don't know," Bren said. "No one knows." He moved the conversation back to the side of the boat and forward, under the white noise of the water, recalling atevi hearing. "She learned a great deal of our language on the voyage."

Understanding dawned. Toby nodded, gave him a look, then leaned beside him on the bow rail, the white froth rushing along below them.

Long silence, then. Conversation on old memories, winter on the mountain, school days. Their mother's cooking. The whereabouts of their father, who never ventured back into their lives, not even lately. That was a lost cause. They both knew that.

The wind shifted, and Toby looked up at the sail, and quickly left to see to the trim. Bren thought of going with him, handling the boat just for a moment, but, again, Barb was back there, and they'd clearly worked out that smooth teamwork, Barb and Toby had. He chose not to interpose his own skills.

A full day of such running, and half the night, and they'd work into the shoreline isles under cover of darkness. He might, extraneous thought, get off the boat without dealing with Barb, postponing all such dealings until he got back from the mainland—granting he would ever get back. He could duck below for an hour, get some sleep, and let his staff relax, more to the point, which they would not be able to do with emotional tension on the deck: they weren't wired to ignore a situation that their nervous systems told them was unresolved between him and Barb. God knew there would be no violence, but their nerves, already taut, would resonate to every twitch and gesture and look, especially since he was sure by now Banichi also knew that was *the* Barb.

And the last thing he wanted between him and Toby at this imminent parting was Barb. He didn't want to go below, into the close dark. He thought he just ought to bed down as Ilisidi had done, on deck, wrap up in a blanket somewhere where no one would step on him. He could lie near the bow, and just listen to the water. That would be good. There was a decided nip in the air. But only enough to remind him the planet wasn't temperature-regulated, not on a local scale.

"Bren."

Barb. Barb had slipped up on him, masked by the rush of water, the very person he hadn't wanted to deal with. He stared at her, frozen for the instant, caught between a desire not to deal with her civilly and the fact that he'd promised Toby peace.

"Barb?"

"I'm sorry about your mother. It was two years ago

for me. I know it was only yesterday you heard. So I'm sorry."

"Accepted."

"You're upset that you weren't there. She accepted that."

"The hell she did. She never forgave me. She blamed me to her last breath because I wasn't there. Let's have the truth."

"She did that," Barb conceded. "But it doesn't mean she didn't love you."

That hit to the quick, that *love* word, that sentiment humans needed, and atevi didn't understand. He felt an angry sting in his eyes and turned his face to the wind, his eyes to the horizon, unwilling to have Barb come at him on that topic.

"You know there were things she wanted in her life," Barb said, unstoppable, "and that didn't happen, and she'd have been disloyal to her hopes to ever give in. One of them was your father. She never would deal with him again. But she never stopped loving him."

"Not that I ever heard." And didn't want to hear. Barb had no business in their family business. But she'd been there, at a time when their mother might have confided things. He hadn't.

"She was stubborn," Barb said, "just like you. She held on to her hopes and wouldn't admit any other situation. Like you. Yes, of course she wanted you there. If she hadn't, if she'd ever let you go, she'd have been letting you go in the emotional sense, and she wouldn't ever do that. It was her kind of loyalty. Is that what you want to hear from me?"

"It's no good to tell *you* that I did what I could. You know me. I'm very limited in that regard."

"I accept it," she said. "I've learned to accept it."

"Doesn't matter." He didn't like the direction this was going, and wasn't going to talk about love and devotion with Barb.

"Maybe it doesn't, to you," she said. "But I think it does."

"Doesn't, Barb. Leave it. Leave it alone."

"I couldn't be her. I couldn't live with you. That's the truth."

That was the truth he wanted. He looked at her this time. The years and the sun had put little fine lines beside her eyes. She wasn't a vapor-brained kid any more. "You learned the hard way."

"Did that."

"So let's all try to get it right this time," he said, while the wind blew at both of them, whipping hair and clothing. "For Toby's sake. You and I used to be friends. It was better while we were friends, before we began talking about love and the future and the rest of it. Before we ever slept together, we had fun. We liked life. Anything in the middle is a long voyage ago for me. Let's have it that way again. Can we do that? Because I'm telling you, I can't accept anything else."

"Because you're her son, and you don't accept anything but what you choose to accept. I know that."

That was a hit below the belt.

"I'm grateful you were there to help her. If you want thanks for that—thank you."

"It wasn't hard."

"I've never understood why you did it. You had nothing in common that I could figure."

"She needed someone. So did I. She helped me see things. She helped me understand you."

That was worth a laugh. "She didn't understand me. She never figured me out."

"She understood you much better than you think."

"Well, good. I'm glad. But take your sights off me, Barb. I swear to you, if you ever hurt Toby, I'll be your enemy."

"I know that, too."

"Do you, now?" He discovered he didn't trust her,

hadn't trusted her all these years, and might have been right after all. "Don't mistake me, Barb. Don't play games with this situation. You like stirring the pot, right. That's fine. Don't stir this one."

"I'll tell you something. What I was looking for in you—I've found, in him."

Maybe she meant that to sting. Maybe he was supposed to be jealous of Toby. It badly missed its target, if that was the case. He was only disgusted with her.

"No games, Barb."

"None of yours, either, Bren. No more promises to me *or him* for what you can't do."

"That—that, I've gotten wiser about." She'd set him suddenly on the wrong foot, taken away the impetus.

"I love him, Bren."

"You'd better."

"It's not the glitter and champagne it was with you, showing up now and again for a fantasy night at a hotel. Toby's a mug of hot tea in a cold morning, that's what I think of when I think of him. He's a week on the water, fishing. Just us. He's happy. So am I."

Curious, that what she saw of Toby was the life he wanted at his own core, or thought he did, and the life he had, by scattered days that he treasured through the days of office and court. What she said she loved about Toby was his own daydream reality.

But what she'd gotten from one Bren Cameron had been the hard security, the rush from this meeting to that, the contests of power, the secrecy, then a few stolen moments of the sequin-spangled glamor he'd thought she thrived on.

And here she was, older, wearing denims, with her hair in windblown curls, her immaculate complexion getting little frown-lines from the sun.

A mug of tea and a boat, was it? That was Toby, for sure. Ambitions had certainly changed.

But so had his.

"I wish you both three thousand years." It was what atevi said. "I hope it's all smooth sailing."

"Oh, not smooth sailing." For a second he saw Barb laugh, honestly laugh, and those sun-lines were in evidence at the edges of her eyes. "We have our storms. But we sail through them. Always. We *like* the lightning."

"Then you take care of him," he said, disarmed. "Enjoy things with him. Laugh like that."

"You mean that?"

"Damned right I mean it."

She stood on her toes, suddenly kissed him on the cheek. He didn't flinch, but he wondered whether Toby was, in fact, out of viewing perspective, back at the wheel. He didn't kiss her back, just patted her arm.

It was a decent test. Attraction toward Barb wasn't anywhere in his reaction. Just worry for Toby.

Jago had seen it, however, Jago not letting him out of her sight for a moment. Barb passed by her on her way aft, but Jago looked straight at him the while, then walked up and leaned on the rail beside him.

"She was confirming a truce," he said.

"Indeed," Jago said blandly.

Damn Barb, he thought.

"This is the channel," Toby said, drawing a black line along a treacherous series of shoals. It was Naigi district. "Get in, get out. You can reach Cobo village from this beach, which is mostly sea-grass. The little bay is particularly nice for redfish."

Bren translated. Except about the redfish. They all—all but Cajeiri, who was fast asleep—huddled on deck in the dark, the chart secured behind a plastic cover with a faint glow underneath, and marked over with erasable pen.

That Toby owned such a precise chart, lettered over in Mosphei', had passed without comment from Ilisidi, but being related to the possessor of said contraband,

Bren suffered a twinge of minor guilt under Ilisidi's sideward glance.

"My brother has fished illicitly, aiji-ma," he admitted, while security looked over the situation and discussed the area.

"He has not," Ilisidi said with a wave of her hand. "He has our permission."

"One is grateful," he said, bowing his head, and by then security had reached a favorable conclusion.

"We can manage, nandiin," Cenedi said. "We have a name, one Lord Geigi personally recommends."

"Then let us do it," Ilisidi said sharply, slightly under-lit by the table as she leaned close for a look. "Toby-nandi handles this boat very well. We have every confidence. Douse this light."

It went out.

"They agree," Bren said to Toby. "And you have the grant of a fishing license, and the right to this chart."

Toby cast him a second, questioning look, with a little quirk of impish humor. Toby knew . . . damn him, he'd known what he was challenging, bringing that chart out into plain view, and had known, too, that he'd get away with it.

"Light off the starboard quarter," Tano said.

Bren looked. He couldn't see it. Out in the open sea, there was every chance that light was some fishing boat, like themselves, only more honest. Or their naval escort, which had never come into view. But they could afford no chances.

"If they're atevi, they may well have seen us," he said. "Toby, Barb, Tano's seen a light out there, starboard quarter."

"Wind's fair," Toby said, and fair it was, bearing on the *Brighter Days'* best sailing point. They could go in, or shy off.

Shying off would only make it likelier they'd be spotted.

"I still don't see it," Barb said, looking out into the dark.

"Trust Tano's eyes," Bren said. "We have this chance to get ashore. Any dithering around about it only gives the opposition time and warning. We'd better use it. But, God, Toby, be careful getting out."

"I'm the model of caution," Toby said. Damn him, he was enjoying this. It was like their days on the mountain. Beat you to the bottom, brother. Downhill on skis.

No Jill, now. With the boat's wheel in his hands and the west wind blowing, Toby was free, these days, freer than in years. And it showed. It youthened him by the hour.

"Scoundrel," Bren said under his breath, sure that Toby heard him, since Toby gave him a grin.

He found a grin of his own in reply, thinking, damn, if we die, we die moving, don't we, not sitting still and letting our lives fade out?

Deep breath, as Toby steered them for the unseen coast, and the wind sang in the rigging.

That boat out there, if it had seen them, might be radioing someone in a better position to cut them off. They could only hope it was one of Shawn's, though Shawn's people were supposed to be doing something slightly noisy to the south, running a navy vessel into forbidden waters near Geigi's estate, and running out again as if they'd dropped someone off.

It wasn't a very sophisticated ruse, that feint by sea. But the other side would have to spend energy reacting to it. The opposition had to expect something, with the starship in dock and the shuttle down. He only hoped nobody got killed making it look real.

The coast was a dim line on the horizon by sundown, a sunset that reflected off a layer of cloud at their backs. That cloud went iron gray as the sun slipped away, and left them running an iron-gray sea on sail alone, that rocky coast bisected by their bow.

"Piece of cake," Toby called it. Bren eyed the rollers that came in there and broke on rocks and wished they could have done this by daylight.

They had their runabout, a light shell of a thing with, Toby swore, enough motor to handle the surf inbound, if not out. But a buoyancy rating for humans was not the same as a rating for that number of atevi. The boat could handle at most three of them at a time, and that meant getting a number of them ashore first, with weapons, to be sure they could land the rest, and one person continually fighting that surf back and forth with the boat.

"I can get it in and out," Barb said, "and I'm light."

It was the best, the logical choice, granted she could handle the boat, and Toby didn't object. Bren just bit his lip and waited, watching, as the rocks and the surf became quite distinct in what was now a panoramic view of the coast.

There were no lights ashore. They showed none. They brought the sails down, fired up the engine, brought the boat up close to the stern ladder, and Barb went down to take the tiller, taking a heavy extra fuel can Toby let down to her.

Banichi and Jago opted to be first in, first to take up position on that shore, to guard the rest of them coming in. And they had life-jackets that they'd have to hold to: they were far too small for atevi. "Take care," Bren wished them, "take great care, nadiin-ji."

Baggage and armament filled up whatever room they had left. The little boat motor purred quietly into action and Bren went to the side rail and watched, lip caught in his teeth the entire time the little boat washed in with the surf and let out two people he desperately cared about.

Toby worked the engine to keep them in position—they didn't drop anchor, just kept a visual fix.

The little boat came back through the surf, rode through light as a shell, with fair expertise. Bren heaved a sigh of relief. Cenedi committed his two juniormost, Toby had another tank filled, traded the empty, and off they went, another lengthy passage. A light crossed the sky, in the distance, a plane, but far from them.

Barb came back, and another exchange of fuel tanks. Then Tano and Algini went with her.

Bren gripped the rail and watched until they were safely ashore, paced, and realized he was pacing. The next load was more supply.

Bren went to stand by Toby. Just to stand there for a while. "Goes without saying," he said. "But shouldn't go unsaid, how much I owe you."

"Wouldn't have missed this for the world," Toby said, and they stood there a while more, spending the agonizing wait content in each other's company, in idiot remarks about the weather.

"Where are you going next?" Toby asked him.

"Don't know," he said. "Depends on what we find. We have names, people we may be able to rely on."

"You be damned careful about it," Toby said.

"Oh, yes," he said, and heaved a pent breath.

Two more of Cenedi's men went the long, slow trip.

"Wish I could go in with you," Toby said out of a long silence.

"I'm glad you're going back," he said, "and, brother?"

"Yes?"

"*Go* home. I'll phone when I can. Don't hang around this coast to watch. When they know where we got in, they'll be over this place like gnats on jam."

"And where I am, they'll think that's where you got in."

"Don't even say it, don't think about running a diversion, Toby. Leave that to the military. Don't give me one more thing to worry about. Promise me."

"I promise," Toby said, but Toby would lie, in extremity. So would he. It was, he thought, a damned nasty habit in their family.

"Wouldn't help us anyway," he said to Toby. "We'll be away from this coast fast as we can find transport, that's the one thing I can say."

"Just don't take chances, Bren."

"Mutual."

This trip it was Cenedi and the dowager. "You will go with Lord Bren," Ilisidi said to Cajeiri, buckling on a life preserver. "And you will do exactly what he says."

"Yes, mani-ma," Cajeiri said.

After the dowager left there was no restraining the boy. It was a thousand questions, most of them, in some form, Where are we, and Where are we going, nandi? It seemed forever while the boat clawed its way back through the surf. Forever, and far too short a time to talk to Toby, once Cajeiri was in his care. He had things he wanted to say, none of them quite finding words, none of them that he managed to say, except, when Barb came back and took on her last spare fuel can, "I want to see you on the holidays."

"Think you can settle things by then?"

"I've got, what, four months? Sure. Time enough." It was a jibe in the face of fate. He resisted superstition. "Just when you get out of here, *go*."

"I'm going to marry her, Bren."

He swallowed every objection. Every thought of objection. "Good," he said. "Good. If you're happy—that's what I care about. Go home and do that."

The little boat bumped the hull. He had to take Cajeiri down the ladder. He stopped to hug his brother long and hard, and to try to fill up all the missed chances in one long breath. "Luck," Toby said.

Then it was down the ladder, Cajeiri last, and unsteady when he hit the cockleshell of a boat, rocking as it was in the chop. Bren yanked Cajeiri down onto a seat and sat down, himself.

"Can you swim, young sir?" Bren asked him, checking the fastening of the life preserver, that at least fit Cajeiri's young body.

"A little," Cajeiri said.

Which meant not at all in this rough sea. "Then stay still in center of the boat. Precisely in the center. Neither of us wants to fall in."

"We're off," Barb said cheerfully. "They're kind of

disappearing into the rocks, out there, but they're waiting for you."

"Good," he said. He didn't know how to make conversation with Barb, let alone now, when everything in the world was riding on their getting inshore and Toby getting out again. He did as he'd told Cajeiri to do, centered himself in the boat and held on for the ride. Barb had her hands full, and the bow smacked down with fierce jolts as they went, white water boiling past the sides. Spray drenched them.

"May one turn around?" Cajeiri asked, wanting a better view.

"Keep your weight centered, young gentleman, and you may turn."

Cajeiri did, quickly, as they rode the waves in, with ominous dark rocks on one hand and the other.

The engine throttled back, then Barb shoved the throttle hard, and they knifed through the boiling white.

A single dark figure waited for them as their keel hissed up onto the shingle—Cenedi, by the silver in his hair. Cenedi gave his hand to Cajeiri and pulled him out. Tossed the life preserver back aboard.

"Bren?" Barb said. "Be careful."

He shed his own life preserver, Toby's gear. "Make him happy," he said to her while she was switching fuel tanks, last thing before he cleared the boat and ran up the shingle to the rocks.

He didn't look back until he was in shadow, with Cenedi and Cajeiri and the rest of them, with all their gear. Then he looked over the top of a rounded boulder and saw the runabout fighting the surf. He watched, wet and freezing in the wind, until he saw the boat meet up with the *Brighter Days*—he couldn't see Barb get out or Toby help her, but that was what he figured was happening.

He watched, chilled through, aware Jago had thrown a thermal sheet around him, watched as they began to move. Watched as she turned for the open sea.

"Good luck," he mouthed, and, feeling a hand on his shoulder and a presence behind him, looked back at Banichi, who was urging him to get up and move.

He did that—looked back again, but now the boat was only a wedge of white behind the surf, headed home.

7

They gathered in a small rocky slot well up on the headland, the dowager struggling considerably at the last of the climb up a rugged slope. She sat down on a rock under the overhang of a branch, and leaned both hands against her cane. One was not supposed to notice this fact, but Cenedi quietly proffered a small cup of water from his flask, and she took it gladly enough.

It was the darkest part of the night. The cloud that had filmed the west at sunset swept on across the sky and blotted out the stars above them. That made it more difficult to see, but it also made it harder for them to be seen, and that gave them a little time to catch their breath and to reconnoiter.

"We must get transport to come to us," Cenedi said to them. "We are moving too slowly. If we can find a place for a few of us to wait—" Cenedi would never say that the dowager and the boy and likely the paidhi-aiji were the *few of us* in question, but Bren had no difficulty understanding there might be theft, mayhem, even casualties in the process of acquiring that transport, actions in which the few might be an inconvenience. They were at a crossroads of their plans, either to find a secure place where they might leave their weaker members in fortified safety, with allies, while the rest of them attempted to raise support—or go all together. Bren was not unhappy when Banichi supported the principle of stealth and rapid movement, which was their Guild's general preference, and all of them going together into the interior.

"We have several names," Cenedi said, "for this area. Dur remains one possibility, nadiin, but our adversaries will watch that."

There were staunch allies in that particular district, for certain, somewhat to the north of them, and they might have gone there if they had run into opposition. Dur was an isolated place, the sort of place in which one could hide, but from which they could not maneuver with any aggressive rapidity at all—not unless they wanted to try an escape by air, in a small plane, and Bren sincerely hoped not to have to do that.

"Desari is our choice, then," Banichi said, and others seemed to agree this name represented a good idea. "Two of us will go. We should." That was in the dual, as Banichi put it, meaning himself and Jago.

Bren was less happy with that, but to this council— all of them were out of the Assassins' Guild—he was necessarily a spectator, not a useful contributor of suggestions. They had spent their voyage down memorizing and arguing resources, and likewise used their voyage across the straits, laying these plans. When Toby had suggested this coast, and Cobo village, they had immediately known where he was proposing to land them and what resources they might have here, before they had approved the idea.

Now they were the ones with the information and the plan, which turned out not to be Cobo, evidently, but another village in the area and the paidhi could only wait, wait sometimes sitting on an uncompromising and chilly rock, sometimes sitting against it, resolved not to move about or stand up, for fear of attracting attention. Silence was all he could contribute to the situation. Ilisidi had lain down to nap on the lumpy, but less chill, bulk of their personal baggage. Cajeiri had completely flagged and gone to sleep on the icy damp ground, buffered by baggage. Cenedi and his men rested, catnapping by turns, cleaning weapons, speaking only in necessity.

But, damn it, he never could nap under such situations, even if he knew it was the sane thing to do. He sat there in one position or the other and fretted, and had a candy bar he'd stowed in his pocket, and listened to the sea, that vast, powerful sound that in principle seemed so quiet, and wasn't. It could mask their small sounds. It could mask ambush. He felt deaf.

Tano and Algini came and sat by him, his protection, still. They went to sleep for maybe half an hour, taking turns with Cenedi's men.

Bren just stared at the horizon, as a faint, faint glow began in the east, and grew, and grew, casting the lumpy horizon into relief, and slowly bringing reality to the landscape around them, rounded rocks and clumps of sea grass, small shrubs and a fairly precipitate slope behind their little camp.

Daylight. And the mainland. It seemed surreal.

Light grew. And with it, all at once, every ateva but Ilisidi and the boy suddenly stirred, opened eyes, looked in the same direction, an eerie simultaneity, a warning. They sat up, reached for weapons. Bren reconsidered his position, whether he had enough cover. He didn't ask what was happening, or what their senses had perceived. He didn't make a sound. Didn't twitch a muscle, not risking even a scuff of dead grass.

Came a distant thrum, then a motor, some sort of vehicle, something of size, by the pitch of it. And he stayed quite, quite still, knowing that whatever he heard, the atevi around him heard more than he did. It could be a chance traveler. It could be trouble.

Cajeiri sat up suddenly, blinking and confused. Cenedi immediately signaled silence. Weapons were in evidence all around, and Cajeiri quietly touched his great-grandmother's foot.

She woke, and Cenedi assisted her to sit up, as he moved Ilisidi and Cajeiri ever so quietly to a sheltered place behind the rocks. The paidhi was supposed to see to his own welfare, and the paidhi had no idea except to keep low and not move.

The noise kept on, a low gear, straining, and it was coming toward them.

Are we that close to a road? Bren wondered, as the racket grew and grew. Is it coming overland? He dared not put his head up to see what was going on, but Algini edged up among the rocks and got a look.

And stood up, as the racket and clatter crescendoed to a ridiculous level.

If Algini stood up, everybody could have a look. It was a battered old market truck, and Banichi was driving, Jago occupying the other seat. The side of the truck said, in weathered blue and red paint, *Desigien Association,* and it had made a fairly long, laborious track across the grassy headland, leaving tracks in the grass.

It came to a stop, and Banichi set the brake, and the two of them got out, beckoning them to come, hurry it up. Banichi and Jago were not in uniform—were in bulky country jackets and loose trousers, even their pigtails tied up with leather cord.

Bren gathered up his computer, his personal baggage, and Tano and Algini gathered up their own gear and Banichi's and Jago's, while Cajeiri and Cenedi assisted the dowager to rise and negotiate the rocky path toward the truck.

Baggage went unceremoniously into the truck bed ahead of them, except the computer, which Bren kept close, except the guns and ammunition, which various other people kept close. And the truck was atevi-scale. Cenedi got up onto the bed and bent over to assist the dowager up, and Nawari made a step of his joined hands, so that she could manage it, Cajeiri hovering behind, in case he needed to administer an indelicate push.

There was no need. The dowager, once aboard, went to the heap of baggage near the cab and sat down quite nicely. Cajeiri got up and wandered noisily around the truck bed, looking for a permissable spot, and Ilisidi beckoned sharply for him to join her sitting on the baggage.

Bren hitched his computer higher onto his shoulder and tried to climb up the metal rungs. Algini extended a hand from above and Jago, appearing below him, shoved from behind.

He turned and looked down over the tail of the bed. "Did we steal it?" he asked Jago.

"Borrowed, nandi," she said. "We shall leave it at the railhead for its owners." She clambered up. "There is a tarp, nadiin-ji. Regretfully, we must use it. Heads down."

She hauled the oily, dirty thing from its position bunched against the rear of the cab, and and began spreading it out of its stiff folds, back along the slatted side-rails. Tano, from the other side, moved to help, and it spread like a tent over them. Bren sat down, as they all must, below the level of the side panels, their daylight cut out again in favor of oil-smelling dark and the vibration of the still-running truck engine.

"Are you well, nandi?" Cenedi asked Ilisidi, off toward the cab end, and Ilisidi answered, practically: "It will be warmer under the tarp, at least, Nedi-ji."

There was some to-do, Cenedi and others evidently rearranging baggage to make Ilisidi a more comfortable place—she was not so tall that she had to bend her head, at least—and meanwhile the tarp was being tied down from above, lashed across with ropes, made into a snug container.

The truck smelled unpleasantly like fish.

Springs gave. Doors banged, forward. A moment later the truck lurched into gear and growled and lumbered into a turn.

They were leaving tracks that would persist in the tall grass, evident from the air. But trucks such as this one came and went without benefit of roads all the time in the country, heavy-tired, following tracks to fishing traps and boats. They had no choice but some such transport, given that the dowager was not up to the kind of brisk hike Banichi and Jago had taken last night, at what toll on unaccustomed muscles Bren could only imagine, and at what risk to the village in question, which one assumed had lent the truck knowingly to help them.

One assumed so, at least.

They jounced and bounced downhill for a long, winding trek, before they came to more level ground, and gravel under the tires. Likely they had come down to a common market route. The mainland had far fewer roads than Mospheira. By the name on the door, this one truck likely belonged to the whole village of Desigien, which meant any one in the village might use it to haul net, wood, supplies, or, daily, fish, or ice—Bren dimly recalled that an ice plant existed, central between Desigien and several other coastal villages, an essential item for fishermen who hoped to get their catch to market. They would truck it daily to the railhead at—where was it?

Adaran, Adaran was the name, whence it went to larger markets, even to Shejidan itself. If people in the district went visiting, they would walk generally, or take the local bus, which provided social connection for the little association, and that bus might run only twice a day, life proceeding at a slower pace out in the villages. And outside of such buses and one or two trucks such as this one for the whole village, that was the whole need for roads. Such interdistrict roads as existed would parallel the railroad right-of-way, village-to-market roads that were, generally, informally maintained, and persisting so far along the rail as frequent need kept wearing down the weeds.

He knew. He'd once had the job of surveying the rail systems, advising the aiji where expansion would or would not better serve the area ... in those ages-ago and innocent days, so it seemed, when rail and a nascent air service was the whole story of atevi and Mospheiran transport. The office of the paidhi had read the histories of waste and pollution, and wanted to avoid the excesses of old Earth, wisely so, considering how passion-

ately atevi felt about spoiling the landscape. The paidhiin of a prior day had advised the aijiin in Shejidan to
go on as they had been going before the Landing, to link
their provinces by rail, not road, to make orderly, minimal corridors for village-to-town transport that very little disturbed the environment, that kept the little
associations as inward-focused as they had begun,
above all not sprawling along transportation lines in
ways that would absolutely destroy the atevi pattern of
life, and with it, atevi social structure. Wise, wise decisions that gave them this little truck, this little-used
road.

Circles. Interlocking circles. And no one went far by
truck or bus. If they took their little truck out of district,
it would look increasingly out of place, the farther it
went from its origin. It could by no means serve them all
the way to Shejidan. The train was where they were
going. And how they were going to get aboard that
without a fuss ...

"Will we ride the train?" Cajeiri asked, as they
bounced painfully about in potholes and what might be
ruts, or simply an abundance of rocks amid the gravel.
"Are we going to drive all the way to Shejidan?"

"We will take the train, young sir," Cenedi's voice
said in the darkness. And because there was an obvious
next question, for which Cajeiri could be heard drawing
breath: "As far as Taiben."

Taiben, it was. The aiji's estate. If there was one place
they might find trouble, nearly as efficiently as at Shejidan, Taiben was a likely place.

But it was a sprawling estate, almost a province unto
itself, a maze of hunting paths and woods in which they
might even lose this truck—if they could get fuel
enough to get them there. He wished they could do
without the train.

"Listen to me," Ilisidi said, sternly, "listen, great-
grandson, and remember a name. Desari. Remember
this name, and be in debt to this village. Lord Geigi once

rescued this man Desari and his daughter at sea when their boat engine failed, and when they had drifted for days, likely to die. Geigi recommended Desari of Desigien as a name to rely on, since every year that he could, on the anniversary of the rescue, this Desari has sent Lord Geigi a gift, so I have it from Geigi. So the debt remains, until Geigi might call on him. This will discharge the debt to Geigi, and place it on us in his place."

"On the Ragi."

"On all the Ragi," Ilisidi said. "And you must remember it, boy, for another generation, a debt to him, and his whole association. The risk we have asked of them is considerable."

"Our enemies could see the name on the truck."

"Exactly so, if we make a mistake, and they will be in grave danger. What is the name, boy?"

"Desari," Cajeiri said. "Desari. From this coast. From Desigien. But, mani-ma, will this Desari come with us on the train?"

"No," Cenedi said. "He would be little help."

"But," said Cajeiri.

"Give us rest, great-grandson. An honest truck does not jabber as it proceeds along the road. We should be an ordinary truck, full of fish. Who knows who might hear, along the road?"

"Who would be listening, mani-ma?"

"*Hush*, I say!"

There was silence, then, none of them brooking the dowager's exhausted annoyance for a very long, bumpy ride. Bren felt himself bruised, his own baggage having gone to cushion Ilisidi, and protected his computer in his arms, which somewhat kept him stable.

There was a whole world of things which, he thought suddenly, no, the boy didn't automatically know, simply by being born atevi. He'd been very young when he'd been shunted off to Taiben, and then again sent off to his great-great-uncle Tatiseigi's estate at age five, scarcely informed about the world at large, scarcely philosophical when, scarcely six, he'd gotten a little freedom of the grounds and learned to ride.

That had been a disaster, involving wet concrete and a very large patio, and uncle Tatiseigi's great indignation.

Then the lad had been whisked off to space to get an education. To get an education, his father had said.

In what? Hacking the ship's computer? Talking to hostile foreigners? Cajeiri was quite precocious in those regards . . . but what had they taught him? A fondness for dinosaurs?

They might, if they had been wiser, spent a little more time on the ordinary arts of going unseen, on natural history and most of all on atevi classics, which might have taught him that badgering his great-grandmother was not productive of harmony.

Not to mention the boy's lack of knowledge about the world itself. How could he know how this truck fit into a village on the coast? How could he know how the roads lay, or how they all went to rail lines?

The boy had, literally, dropped in out of space onto his own planet, naïve regarding the weather, regarding the geography, naïve in many ways regarding Ragi rural society, and, the paidhi supposed, ignorant of the fabric of traditional atevi life which ought to trigger appropriate atevi twitches in young atevi nerves—if those nerves hadn't been jangled by too much sugar and too many humans and no contact at all with the planet. He'd done his most critical growing in a linear human corridor only partially jury-rigged into a dwelling of atevi pattern. He'd entertained himself with movies and cultivated human children. The atevi world—it had its rhythms, its seasonally proper foods, its rules of etiquette and ethics, all the social graces that appeased volatile tempers and stiff regional pride. The boy had had the dowager to hammer the traditional courtesies and social conventions into his head, but had the nerves ever gotten triggered in the right ways, at the right times, in the very basic sense?

One could have a very deep unease, given what Cajeiri didn't know, what they'd robbed him of, in taking him to space. The boy had no ingrained concept of how profound the bond had been between Geigi and that fisherman, the situation that allowed this debt to be passed up the lines of man'chi, from Lord Geigi to Geigi's lords. Up, in the direction of wealth and ability—but never down, onto the shoulders of a poor man, who could discharge his debt by convincing his village to lend a truck.

But obligating the lord forever. And thence never to be discharged. That had been what Ilisidi had been trying to be sure of—that the young lord would know that name, remember the debt in his own generation, if hers failed that man. That was what the paidhi dimly grasped.

But had the boy? Cajeiri had sunk into quiet, and probably, in such silent times—Bren feared—was remembering the ship, not his uncle Tatiseigi's estate, not the Bujavid, or Taiben. He was, one very much suspected, thinking about the human company he'd left behind, since he had few enough memories of any other associations.

Can Gene and Artur go with me? Not just a boyish question. Desperation. Attachment, in a bond even the human paidhi had to think was unhealthy. The right social nerves just hadn't gotten the right trigger at the right times, and the boy was more than a little lost, getting instruction, but missing any emotional connection. He knew all the right social moves the way he memorized the provincial capitals and their lords, but not why those moves had to be made.

Dared one think . . . a sociopath, if one let one's thoughts wander far, far down an unpleasant track?

Impossible. A good and willing kid. Angry. Hurt. Exhausted. The dowager shoved lectures at him, and he argued, he defended his ground, he increasingly annoyed his grandmother, who probably had a better sense of what was going on with the child than he possibly could. His own advice certainly couldn't help the boy.

The fish—God, the fish had been a moment. He afforded himself a wan laugh, in silence. But having to fish, having to have an activity, that was the frenetic energy the boy had, that explored things and then sent him dashing back to great-grandmama when the world threatened him . . .

That flocking instinct? Man'chi in its early expression? Maybe dashing back to adults was the normal part and the brash, aggressive exploration was what he'd picked up from his human associates.

Maybe a human just didn't know how to judge the boy, and ought not to say a thing.

While Jago, who knew less about children than she knew about field-stripping her guns, had expressed concern during their voyage, but seemed to indicate there was not much to do about Cajeiri's isolation, except to keep him happy and to discourage him from the human Archive. Banichi had said, what was it? That the boy was going to have to stand still long enough to be aiji in Shejidan, and that was by no means a given.

The brakes began a prolonged squeal.

"Keep utterly still," he heard Cenedi say, doubtless aiming that at the boy, and the truck bumped and heaved to a stop.

Conversation reached them from outside the tarp, questions about their use of the truck, from someone who definitely didn't recognize their right to have it, or to be here. Bren held his breath, held utterly still.

"Picking up driftwood, nadi," he heard Jago said, in a country accent he'd never heard her use, "to make lamps."

"Lamps, is it?" he heard from that strange voice.

"Driftwood lamps, nadi," she said, "which sell quite well in Shejidan."

"Who authorized you to have this truck?"

The wrong answer could damn the man and the whole village who'd helped them. Could cost lives.

"The council, nadi," Jago said, "for a consideration. A fee for the wood and for the hire of the truck."

"Papers," the man said.

"Here," Banichi said, and got out, a creaking of springs and the opening of the door.

Thump. *That* was the truck door on Jago's side, and a second thump, as something hit the ground.

"Good move," Banichi said, and one formed a picture of that truck door opening and bashing right into a man, perhaps a local security patrol, who'd gotten too inquisitive.

There was some to-do outside, a series of small movements.

"Best take him along," Banichi said. "He may be local."

The logic in that was clear, that they wanted no blood on their ally's hands, and the man who'd come afoul of two Assassins was still, courteously enough, alive.

Banichi came around to lower the tailgate, letting in daylight and a welcome waft of cool air.

"One regrets to report an inquisitive nuisance," Banichi said, "and a problem. We propose, nand' dowager, to put the local constable aboard, and leave him where we leave the truck, for our ally's sake, for peace in the district. We believe he is not Desigien village, but perhaps a neighbor from Cobo."

"Do so," Ilisidi said. "How far are we from the rail?"

"Not far, nand' dowager. The train comes into the station just after dark, and will pick up the local railcar, which is our best hope. We are to leave the truck in its ordinary spot, which is by the depot north wall, where we can move safely after dark. After that the ride may be much cooler, nandiin, one regrets to say."

One formed a picture. The local car would carry fish. And ice.

Their unwanted passenger came to in the dark, blind-folded and gagged, and thumped around, kicking and protesting, until Cenedi's men got hold of him.

"You will live, nadi," Nawari's voice said pleasantly in the dark. "Be patient. We mean no particular harm to you and we shall return the truck, the use of which we took."

A deal of muffled outcry, then. And a quick subsidence after.

Everyone had to be quiet. Cenedi had said that while their passenger was still unconscious. Particularly the dowager, the heir, and the stray human had to keep quiet, their voices being far too remarkable.

"The drug has taken effect," Nawari said, "but we should not rely on it. It has its hazard, nandiin-ji."

There was silence. So on they rolled, with one bound, gagged constable heavily sedated, from that store of small nastinesses the Assassins' Guild sometimes used. Finesse, Banichi called it.

They maintained particular silence, as the truck rolled slowly over smooth, and therefore well-maintained, road, which indicated a populated, frequently-traveled region. It was probably a picturesque village they had come to. They were probably not in Desigien, but at Adaran, at the railhead, and the Desigien truck sitting still and waiting for the train was probably not that unlikely an evening event.

Banichi got out of the truck, and asked, near the side: "How are things?"

"Our guest is sedated," Cenedi said. "We shall renew the dose every half hour. We are monitoring him carefully."

"We are at the station, parked at the appropriate place. There is no shade, one regrets to say. How is the dowager?"

"Hot and cross, nadi," Ilisidi snapped. "But it seems we all are hot and cross, and will freeze tonight. Cease talking. Take no chances."

"Yes," Banichi said simply, and got back into the truck cab, for a long, long wait.

It was a very long, uncomfortable silence, in the stifling, oil-smelling heat of the sun on the canvas above their heads. Once and twice again someone administered another dose of sedative, and reported they still had a steady pulse.

Someone approached the truck, a slow scuff of gravel. That someone, a female person, went as far as the door of the truck and spoke quietly and respectfully to Banichi and Jago. She said something about having walked here, and being the driver, and taking the truck back.

"When the train leaves," Banichi answered that person. "Come back then. Do not associate yourself with us, for your own safety."

"What of the fish?" Jago asked.

"We have everything on yesterday's ice, nadi," the female person said. "Some days the truck breaks down. We will bring the catch in tomorrow night. We shall make up for it. Thank you for asking."

"We have an unexpected problem," Banichi said. "The constable met us on the road and questioned us. He is sedated. Back there. Would you know who would properly be on the road above Cobo village, asking us questions?"

"I by no means know, nadi," was the answer. "But the Cobo constable would not be wandering around up on the ridge."

Banichi said, "Come have a look at him."

The truck rocked. Steps moved around to the tailgate, and Banichi lifted the tarp. Sunlight came in, and a young girl stood with Banichi and Jago, a pretty young girl with astonished eyes.

"Aiji-ma?" she said reverently.

"Nandiin," Banichi said, "this is Ruso, our associate's daughter. And the driver. We would not let her drive it here."

"We are grateful," Ilisidi said, from the deep recesses, where the angled light glimmered off atevi eyes. "We regret the inconvenience. Show her this man."

Nawari, a shadow against the light, turned their unconscious prisoner's face.

"Dataini," was the immediate, frightened-sounding answer. "Dataini. His wife is Tasigin. He is the new constable."

"The new constable?" Banichi asked.

"Here in Adaran. Since—" Ruso's eyes moved uneasily toward the dowager and back. "Since the new authority, in Shejidan."

"And where is the old Adaran constable, Rusonadi?" Ilisidi asked.

"Gone back to fishing, aiji-ma, since they took his authority away."

"We give it back. Do you suppose, if you found him this evening, he might deal with this man?"

Ruso's eyes were very large. "I think he would run that risk, if it was your order, aiji-ma. But the wife has relatives."

"See to it," Ilisidi said with a wave of her hand, and Banichi lowered the tarp, taking the light away. A low-pitched discussion followed, outside, how they would leave this Dataini in the truck, well-secured, and how Ruso must go to the former constable in this town, and take measures to take Dataini's wife into custody too, before she could realize her husband was missing and make a phone call to whatever regional authority was overseeing this remote fishing district.

The counterrevolution had started. And the young driver, Ruso, had volunteered in harm's way, with time and force of the essence. It was not the move Banichi would have advocated if they were going to take months dealing with this.

God, Bren thought, we may have to deal with Kadigidi appointees in districts where we're going, not to mention the cities. It was an unfortunate possibility that these new authorities were still compiling their own list of everyone within the man'chi of Tabini's household and Geigi's, Geigi being aiji up on the station, and in an otherwise unassailable position ... threaten those under his protection, since they could not reach Geigi.

This could be a problem, Bren said to himself. This could be a real problem.

"Is there water, mani-ma?" Cajeiri asked. "Might we just leave the corner of the tarp up a little?"

"Hush," Ilisidi said sharply, and there was renewed quiet, in which they could still hear the discussion with Ruso, a discussion in which it seemed there was some sort of written instruction, some commitment to paper that they had found in the dash panel of the truck, and a pricked finger—blood could work, where wax was lacking, however imperfectly, impressing a mark from Banichi's Guild ring. It was an Assassin's signature they were producing for the girl, a request with legal force, when Banichi was acting in his protective capacity. His own authority at least matched any village constable's.

"There," he heard Banichi say. "Let the Adaran constable carry that for a warrant, and gather deputies, as many as he can."

They moved away, then, and by the give of springs, sat on the front bumper, Banichi, Jago, and the girl from Desigien together, as it seemed, looking, as they would, like country folk holding a bored conversation. Things grew quiet for while.

"There was almost certainly a phone call that put that man out on the road," Cenedi said. "Someone, at sea or on land, saw nand' Toby's boat. When the constable does not phone back with a report, there may be an inquiry sent on more than a local level."

"Good we are not staying the night," Ilisidi said.

Other footsteps approached the truck. Whoever was sitting on the bumper did not get up, but Ruso, clever girl, told whoever had come up that these were her cousins from down the coast, that they had sailed up to beg the loan of a net, their own village having suffered extremely in a recent storm. Converse went on and on, mostly Ruso speaking in that local lilt, and the conversation up there settled to the usual grumbling about the weather, the fish, daringly, to the market since the trouble. Others gathered, and for a time the truck rocked to bodies leaning against it, all complaining bitterly about market prices and the attitude of the owners of the ice plant, who thought their profits should stay the same, no matter what the depressed market did to the villages.

The talk dwindled, then, some conversants going off to a local watering hole, inviting Ruso and her supposed cousins to join them, but Ruso said she would stay with the truck.

"Now who would steal it, nadi," one laughed, "or filch one of your fish?"

"The new constable, for all I know," she said, a bit of boldness that made Bren's heart skip a beat.

"You have a point, Ruso-ji," the speaker said, and voices and presence retreated.

There was a collective sigh of relief, audible in the dark. Their prisoner stirred, and went out again, to everyone's relief.

Bren pillowed his head on his arms and tried to catch a nap beside Tano and Algini. He shut his eyes, tried to ignore the heat, hoped that Toby had gotten well away from the coast by now.

Hoped that the constable's wife expected him to be out at all hours.

He did sleep a little. He came to in utter dark and much cooler air, no light even from the edges of the tarp, with the noise of a train in the distance. Everybody was stirring about, and he sat up, sore in every joint from resting on bare boards—he could only imagine how Ilisidi fared.

"We are ready, nandi," Tano said, close beside him.

The train chugged to a stop, passed them, so that they must be alongside the cars. There was a good deal of hallooing and fuss up and down, and Ruso—Bren had gotten to recognize her voice—talked to someone, some talk of ice, a bill, and papers, and then she came back again, saying her cousins would help her load, there was no need of any other. There was a great deal of rattling about, rolling of large doors, cursing and thumps, as something loaded on noisily in their vicinity. It sounded like steel drums.

This diminished, finally, and whoever it was trundled off with the rattle of an empty pull-truck. There followed a period of silence, in which the unconscious constable stirred, and went out yet again, this time gagged and tied to an upright of the truck slats.

"When?" Cajeiri whispered miserably, teeth chattering. "When shall we move, mani-ma? What if we miss the train?"

"Hush," Ilisidi hissed.

Abruptly someone pulled loose the ropes and freed the back of the tarp. Jago was there, in the dark, outlined in the light of a lantern somewhere distant, to the side.

"Quickly, aiji-ma." Jago held up the edge of the tarp as two of Cenedi's men rolled out to assist the dowager. Bren snagged his computer and Tano and Algini worked past him to get at the baggage. Cenedi and Nawari and Cajeiri himself helped Ilisidi to the end of the truck bed, simply sliding her inventively if unceremoniously toward the rear on a piece of baggage. Cenedi then jumped out and lifted her down in his arms, ever so carefully, himself no youngster, but he accepted no help doing it.

"I do not believe I shall walk," Ilisidi said.

"This way," Banichi said, and marked a destination with his flashlight, shining the beam along the waiting row of cars, onto the one fairly near their truck, with its door open.

Nawari clambered into the dark boxcar and knelt on the edge. Cenedi handed Ilisidi up to him, and Tano flung baggage in and jumped aboard to the side, pulling Cajeiri up after him. Bren slid off the end of the truck and tried to help Algini with the baggage, but Jago took over that job. "Get aboard, Bren-ji, quickly."

He was the most conspicuous item in their company. He'd just spent two years where he was ordinary, and he found his protective instincts were dulled, rusted, right along with his wits. He moved quickly, made a try at getting up onto the waist-high deck of the car, computer and all. He couldn't make it, and tried again. Tano hauled him aboard by the back of his coat.

Scrambling out of the way on the wooden deck, leaning his back against the boxcar's wall, he checked his pocket. He had not lost his gun. His eyes, accustomed to the dark, made out the surrounds, the source of a pervading chill. It was what they had expected, a wooden refrigerator car, stacked high with dim blocks of ice, with crates of, yes, another village's fish, already loaded, on their way to morning market somewhere along the rail line.

Banichi was last in, and slid the door to after him. Ruso helped shove it, brave girl.

"Good luck, aijiin-ma," she said fervently, and the door shut with a thump.

Dark came with it, and persisted, until Cenedi produced a penlight and helped arrange seating for the dowager against the wall, on a pile of baggage.

"It smells like fish in here," Cajeiri complained.

"They *are* fish," Ilisidi said. "Hush."

"Mani-ma." A pained whisper, next, which no one could fail to hear. "I have need of the convenience."

"That can be attended, young sir," Cenedi said, and took the young lad toward a dark, opposite corner of the car, which, fortunately, had plenty of gaps between the boards.

There was mortified silence after Cajeiri returned, silence except for a trembling sigh, as the youngster collapsed onto the wet and mildly fishy floor to sit against the wall, elbows on knees, hands wrapped about his head, a thoroughly miserable picture.

Bren paid his own visit to that small corner. So did others. Life seemed a great deal more bearable, afterward.

The train fired up and slowly, slowly, without the blast of a whistle to disturb the village in the dead of night, got itself into motion, gathering speed with a regular thump of wheels along the rails.

"Ruso says the train will stop briefly for mail at Sidonin," Banichi said, settling down with a sigh, "which should be just before dawn."

Sidonin. Next to the Ragi estate of Taiben. It wouldn't have been a preferred strategy, in Bren's reckoning of things, to go straight to the heart of the trouble.

But staying aboard into full daylight, when the train reached some town market center, didn't seem a good idea.

There was a sort of breakfast by flashlight, if one counted Toby's food bars, slightly crushed by sitting on them—they were glad to have them, even so, and washed them down with melted mouthfuls of fishy ice, to conserve the little left in their water-flasks. The train sounded like one of the old-fashioned sort, a steam-powered relic, which rocked along at a fairly sedate clip, whistling eerily at lonely points of hazard.

The chill of the ice had come welcome after the truckbed, at first, but Bren found the chill seeping into his bones after an hour. He sat in near complete dark, now that necessary moving about was done. His hands and feet and backside grew increasingly numb, the faint taste of fish persisted in his mouth, and he was increasingly convinced those cereal bars would remind him of that fishy taste as long as he lived.

Distaste wouldn't survive the next pangs of hunger, he said to himself. An upset stomach was the least of his worries. A meal at all was better than none. And he had actually gotten a little sleep in the truck, and caught a little more, in the surreal spaces between blasts of the whistle. He found a way to pillow his head on his computer case, and hoped the fishy smell would not embed itself in his clothes.

Eventually, at one waking, there seemed a ghostly gray light coming in the seam of the door, and they were still thumping along. Banichi and Jago had gotten back into uniform. Ilisidi had bestirred herself, and gotten up onto her feet in the brisk cold. She walked about, relying on her stick for balance, waving off Cajeiri's well-meaning assistance and Cenedi's offered arm. Cenedi had arranged a sort of a chair for her, consisting of their waterproof luggage atop blocks of ice of suitable height, and she had rested in the best arrangement of all of them. He was heartened to see her up and moving steadily, if slowly. What it cost the dowager in pain he had no idea, but she was on her feet, and refusing to give up. And if she could, no one else could complain. He began to rub life back into knees and ribs and elbows, and thought about hot tea, which was as remote as the space station.

Squeal of iron wheels. The train began to slow gradually, braking, with attendant squeak and thump and rattle. Cenedi leapt up immediately to steady the dowager, who allowed him to see her to her seat.

"Are we supposed to stop, nadiin?" Cajeiri asked worriedly.

"Likely," Nawari said, extremely curt, and shushed the question.

The dowager had settled and perched braced with her cane as the train slowed to a stop.

Sidonin, one hoped, the mail stop, edge of the Central Association.

In Sidonin, there was more than a chance of a hostile constable. In the territory of the Central Association, an hour or so by rail from Kadigidi territory, their opposition would have set up shop in far more elaborate fashion than in Adaran, on the coast. Not only a constable, but likely the town authorities as well.

Banichi and Tano heaved the door back while the train was still slowing to a stop. It was the faintest of dawn light, and a lantern showed, when Bren took a quick look outside.

No chance that they could jump out before the train reached the station and avoid the possibility of being spotted. It was a long way down, next to the hazard of the track. Ilisidi couldn't do it. Cajeiri couldn't. He didn't know if he could. For the dowager's sake—at least for hers, they had to wait for a full stop and get down in better order.

Guns were a real likelihood, in that case. Bren patted his pocket and drew a deep breath. Slower. Slower. Slower. Thump-thump-thump.

Wheeze and stop. Banichi and Jago jumped down onto the graveled slant. Nawari and his mate followed.

And any employees of the rail line who saw Assassins' Guild black suddenly in evidence beside their train at this hour of the morning were likely to be looking for cover, fast. Bystanders were safe during a Guild operation—if they ducked fast and avoided involvement. Things had to be finessed, Banichi's favorite word, and that meant delicacy, and avoiding the simply feckless and unfortunate.

Two more of Ilisidi's men heaved baggage down. Bren passed his computer down to Jago, who shouldered it and held up her arms to steady him as he jumped.

He landed hard. Needles lanced pain through every bone in his cold feet, and he collided with her. He bit his lip, apologized, trying not to fold in pain, and to walk on the edges of his feet, simultaneously looking around and orienting himself on the railroad siding, a steep, gravelly bank, a cluster of small buildings with a faint electric light on the porch. People moved in that light, people they didn't want to notice them.

They lifted the dowager down gently, silently. Cajeiri simply scrambled over the threshold of the doorway and lit on the gravel on young, strong feet.

The people down there didn't look to have seen them. Better still, off to the rear of that building there was a small bus parked, one of the sort that served train passengers, to reach town center and other means of transport.

Tano signed in that direction, and Banichi waved them on. Tano and Algini sprinted silently across that dirt yard, and had the door of the bus open in a few seconds, whether or not it had been locked. Before the rest of them could cross the intervening distance, Nawari carrying the dowager at a near run, Algini had gotten under the hood and had the bus started, a startlingly loud noise.

Cenedi helped them get Ilisidi aboard, shoved Cajeiri after, and then shoved Bren up the steps, following after. Nawari heaved baggage into the back door. Two of Cenedi's men got up onto the roof rack, a great deal of bumping and thumping—carrying rifles, Bren suspected, settling into a bench seat, watching for his own team to come aboard before someone down at the station came to investigate. Or opened fire.

Jago got in. Banichi followed, Tano and Algini followed, Tano closed the door and Algini slid behind the wheel. Jago remained standing, hanging with her elbow about the protective rail next to Algini, who floored it and turned the wheel vigorously. Banichi braced himself with a wide stance in mid-aisle, watching the rear view.

Bren, clinging to the seat in front of him, behind Cajeiri and the dowager, looked back and saw lights bouncing in the rear window, people running, shadows in the night. Red and blue lights flashed, emergency vehicles.

Algini swerved onto a gravel road that paralleled the tracks, throwing Bren hard against the window-side. Swerved again, up and over the rails behind the rear of the train, then dived down the other side of the tracks, skidded onto a service road in a spatter of gravel— whatever track they followed would follow the railroad, no likelier than roads along the coast to persist for very far, but it got them out of there, and kept them going, and a second look back showed dark behind them, no sign of red lights, just a light at the rear of the train.

The bus ran flat out on the rutted road, bouncing over potholes and sending gravel flying where it took a turn—the men up on the roof must be clinging for their lives.

Somebody back there at the station had to have made a phone call to higher authority, getting instructions, calling for reinforcements, maybe light aircraft.

Jago had a map. That was the paper. She held on with an elbow, tilted the paper to the dim light from the instrument panel, gave instructions, and Algini took a turn to the right, onto a track rougher than the last.

Right. Where did a right turn lead them? He'd remembered where Sidonin was, near the edge of its association, and the rail here served several provinces, skimming along the hazy join that was the atevi concept of a border. They were maybe within forty k of that area of hazy authority, within fifty or sixty, possibly, of Taiben district, which ought to offer safety, maybe a hope of finding Tabini—or run them right into an occupying presence, Taiben being the heart of Ragi territory, and the Ragi Association being the very center of Tabini's power . . .

Logically the Kadigidi might have posted observers and controls and guards along this very road, which began to have all the look of a farm-to-market route, maybe one that got Taiben goods to Sidonin's rail station, and vice versa—he didn't know. When they'd come to the lodge, they'd come in from the south and east, never the west.

Daylight had begun to fill in some details in the landscape. He saw tall grass, scrub, occasional deciduous growth. Taiben was forest intermittent with sweeping grassland. Hunting territory, with the aiji's own hunting lodge deep in its territory, a rustic former hall sometimes converted for tourists and ordinary hunters, what time the aiji was not in residence. The place was a warren of hunting trails, abundant in game, with rugged hills, areas where no one lived, rugged terrain and rolling meadow where no one was allowed to hunt or to enter at all, no one but Taiben rangers, overseeing the heart and core of the district, or Tabini-aiji himself, who never fired a gun there.

Good memories, good memories thrown into jeopardy on this rough and half-lit road. A fool had to know where they'd gone. And the Kadigidi had to have watchers out . . . whether or not they'd be strong enough to interfere with a Taiben move or one from the railway at Sidonin, they'd know, they'd be set up with guns . . .

As long as no one got aircraft up looking for them . . . as long as nobody started dropping grenades. They made a very conspicuous target; and if there was an ounce of speed to be gotten out of the bus, Algini was looking for it.

He clung to the seat as they swerved, saw Cajeiri actually trying to sleep in the seat ahead, head against the window, and bouncing from time to time as they hit a particularly deep pothole, but wedging in the tighter the harder the bumps. The dowager, beside him, had Banichi in the aisle, quietly bracing her in the worst stretches But the boy beside her fell asleep, mouth open—Cajeiri was that tired, and the motion of the bus finally did it, maybe the illusion of having gotten away, when nothing else had lulled him.

Bren gazed at him, the momentary focus of very worried thoughts. Felt sorry for him.

Hell of a birthday, kid. Hell of a few days.

And what the boy didn't know about their present situation had the paidhi's stomach in an upheaval. Speed over stealth. Speed, over the chance of bogging down in a sniper war while their opposition called for air support, and them with the dowager, afoot in rough terrain . . . he had enough of an idea of the reasoning in their security's choices to keep his stomach in a knot, and his eyes sweeping what he could see of the road past Banichi, dreading the sight of a roadblock, the moment at which their two on the roof might open fire.

Fifty k to a dubious safety in which they couldn't even guarantee the heart of Taiben was still in allied hands. This whole desperate venture could come to grief in the next five minutes.

The road passed trees, passed trees on either hand, and by now the dawn showed more than one tree or two deep, a thicket, a forest. Their road bounced, rolled, pitched, and swerved left and right. Branches raked the overhead, hazarding their pair on the roof.

And with a soft gasp of brakes, Algini slowed the bus, and stopped.

The men on the roof got down. Tano opened the door, Banichi got off the bus and did not get back aboard, conferring out in the dim dawn with the two from the roof.

Then those two boarded and Banichi did not. Banichi wasn't there. Bren looked left and right out the windows.

Where has he gone? Bren wondered. But maybe it was as simple as a call of nature.

In front of him, Cajeiri moaned and turned sideways in the seat, seeking more room for his limbs. The dowager sat still, waiting.

Then the bus started to move again, and Banichi was not aboard. Nawari had gotten up and moved into position to brace the dowager.

It was too much. Bren stood up, using the seat safety grips as he edged past Nawari to one he could ask, to Jago, who was still hanging with her map, at Algini's side.

"Are we onto Taiben's lands, Jago-ji?" he asked.

"Well onto them," Jago said. "Unfortunately . . . the tank is nearing bottom. It was only half full when we left."

"At least they're not on top of us," he said, just glad to be alive and in something like daylight. "Where did Banichi go?"

Jago stooped and gave a look out the windshield. "A

short hike, to a message drop. We shall pick him up when the trail winds back across the hill."

"A message drop?" How in reason had they arranged that? And with whom?

"We have no great reason to hope it is active, nandi," Jago said, "but if anyone has escaped into the woods, there are such places. There always have been. We were in the aiji's service, before we came to yours."

In Tabini's personal service, and likely in and out of Taiben and perhaps privy to its defensive secrets . . . neither of them had ever alluded to that knowledge, not even in crisis.

Which meant Banichi took the lead here. Cenedi was, like Ilisidi, from the east, from across the continental divide . . . and might know many things . . . but maybe not Taiben.

"You are not supposed to know where these places are, Bren-ji. Not even all the Taiben folk do, but the lodge director, his assistant, the aiji's personal guard. As we were, previously, of course, in that number. If the lodge staff has escaped, and gotten to the drops, they will leave word, and break into cells, and use the drops to communicate between cells, avoiding any transmissions that might be traced. We shall see if the system is active."

The road turned, the bus exiting the woods and running along the grassy side of the hill. Forest fire had denuded the farther slopes. But that was old damage. Young trees were coming back, a thick bluegreen growth half a man's height.

Brush scraped the fenders, and grass brushed the undercarriage. Their road might lead to one of the villages, but it had not been much used this season.

A figure popped out of the brush at the next turn, and Bren's heart thumped. But it was Banichi, waiting for them, and the bus slowed.

Banichi waved at them, signed for them to turn, and there was no place to turn, but in among the trees, deep into brush.

Algini did it, and Bren steadied himself by a grip on Jago's rail. Brush scraped the windows. Algini drove it in solidly, plowing down undergrowth, breaking his way through until the bus was enmeshed in brush. Algini reached and opened the door, which Banichi had to pry open, breaking a branch.

Another man appeared in the woods, at Banichi's back. "Look out!" Bren called out, heart in his mouth, and then felt foolish, because there were two more, and then a fourth, and Banichi seemed quite easy in their presence.

"Allies, Bren-ji," Jago said, patting his arm, folded her map in a few practiced moves, and climbed down. Cenedi was ready to follow.

Bren negotiated the steps after Cenedi, having to cling to the rail, on tall, tall steps, to be sure his weary legs stayed under him. The ground seemed to be pitching and rolling, and he was hungry, and dizzy, thirsty, and absolutely exhausted from sheer worry.

"Keimi-nadi," Banichi said, "I present Cenedi, chief of security to the aiji-dowager."

"Nadi." Keimi was an older man, in country clothes, with scratches on his face and graying hair straying from its queue. But there was no country accent. "Welcome. Welcome to the aiji-dowager, and to the paidhi."

"Nadi." Bren gave a nod of his head. More watchers had appeared, women and men, even a couple of children. The woods was populated.

"Along with ourselves," Cenedi said, "we have brought trouble. This bus, for which our opposition will be searching by every possible means."

"We should get away from this area," Keimi said. "And will. Is the dowager able to ride?"

"Able to ride?" That small stir in the aisle of the bus at their backs was not another of their security, it was Ilisidi herself who forged her way to the door, above the steps, with every intent of descending. "Able to ride?"

Ilisidi said indignantly. "Bury me, the day I am unable to ride. Have you mecheiti?"

"We have sixteen, aiji-ma, scattered about for safety. Sixteen, and their gear, and can get others."

"Excellent." Ilisidi wanted to descend, and lowered her cane to the steps. Cenedi reached to assist her, and when he had her in reach, lifted her by the waist and set her on the ground, where she planted her cane and, leaning on it, surveyed the gathering that had materialized out of the dawn woods.

"Nadiin-ji, where is my grandson?"

People looked at one another in dismay, and Keimi bit his lip.

"Say it," Ilisidi snapped with a thump of that cane. "Is he dead, or is he alive?"

"We by no means know, nand' dowager. The aiji was here when the trouble began at Shejidan, and there was some talk of going back to the capital, but he sent the paidhi—Mercheson-paidhi—to Mogari-nai, and then followed, and came back. But he left."

"He came back from Mogari-nai," Ilisidi said. Bren's heart lifted. *There* was news. "And where did he go?"

"He refused to say, nand' dowager. His guard said it was for safety."

"He had his guard with him."

"He had Deisi and Majidi, nand' dowager. He did not have the other two. One fears—"

"And my mother?" Cajeiri asked, pressing forward. "Was my mother with him?"

"Cajeiri-nandi?" Keimi asked. The boy had been four when Taiben last saw him. "Nandi, Damiri-daja was with the aiji, in good health. And we do know they left eastward, with Deisi and Majidi."

"Alone?" the dowager interrupted sharply.

"We wished to send a larger guard, aiji-ma. We all would have gone. We could not persuade the aiji your grandson. He said he would move more quietly."

"Toward the east," Ilisidi mused, and Bren drew a deep breath, thinking: either into Damiri's home territory, Atageini land, relying her great-uncle Tatiseigi's having stayed on Tabini's side in this mess—or past the Atageini and past Kadigidi territory, into deeper wilderness.

Or straight at Kadigidi borders, to strike at the heart of the enemy, Bren thought with a chill. On one level it would be like Tabini, not to depart without retaliation—but, God, against tremendous odds, and refusing Taiben's offer, and with Damiri.

Instinct said no, that wasn't what he had done, not with Damiri on his hands, not with the ship due to show up with answers, with the dowager, with his heir. He'd want to minimize damage, want to keep his losses low, his strength intact, and organize.

"Then we shall assume he is waiting for us," Ilisidi said, echoing his own estimation. "We have committed the coastal association at Desigien. Now we have contacted you. Attack will surely follow in both instances, if the scoundrels setting up in Shejidan have begun to track us. We were approached by one of their people in Desigien territory, and we assume there are others of his ilk in other villages. We have brought you this ungainly bus, laying tracks all the way, which we had rather not have done, but we had little choice—we have come in from the rail station, with an unfortunate lot of racket, and we fear they will follow."

"It will not find us, dowager-ji. We are never where it comes. And those they send here do not come back."

Historic guerilla war, the way atevi had fought from the dawn of time, before the Assassins' Guild had risen up to make it a conflict of professionals. These were not of that guild. They were foresters. They were there, they were not, they scattered and they reconverged on a timetable that had nothing to do with clocks. Bren had no idea what their capabilities were, and he would put his money on the Assassins, in a contest, but tracking them—the edge was with the Taiben folk.

"Come, nandiin," Keimi said, and moved a branch aside. Others held the brush back, making a hazy path through the thicket, one that the dowager followed, with Cenedi, with Cajeiri, and all of them followed, baggage hauled out of the bus, ported along. Bren carried his computer, and Jago carried her duffle and his just behind him, the men taking two bags apiece, their bulk a hard load in the thicket, and the rangers helped, holding branches aside, making a corridor for them, leading them by ways that became, imperceptibly, a trail, broad, free of branches.

Brush ahead of them cracked, however, with a noise that left no doubt of a presence in the woods, and at a distance, a mecheita made that soft, disgusted sound that, once heard, one never forgot.

Mecheiti. Four-footed transport that left far less trace in Taiben's wide lands than a stolen bus. In a moment more, around a bend of the trail, a rider sat waiting with a number of saddled mecheiti, tall, rough-looking beasts, golden brown to sable, and possessed of two hand-span long tusks that ordinarily were capped, in domestic mecheiti, for safety of bystanders.

These were not. The tusks were bare, and dangerous, and all the herd went under saddle, reins simply lapped about saddle rings, but they were not led—and would not stray off, not even if shots were flying. It was all follow-the-leader in a crisis, the impulse that made a charge of these beasts so formidable.

The sole rider slid down off that leader, a scarred, ear-bitten creature, and, maintaining a careful hold on the halter, he bowed to Ilisidi and offered her the rein.

She can't, Bren thought in dread. She hasn't the strength, and, dammit, she won't admit it.

"Sidi-ji," Cenedi said, offering his hand.

Ilisidi ignored him, took the rein and the quirt, administered a whack to the impervious red-brown shoulder, a second whack, and a tug at the rein. The mecheita swung its tusked head around, snorted, stopped short by the handler while it inhaled the scent of someone strange, a diminutive someone who tapped its foreleg, now that she had its attention, tapped it hard behind, and took no nonsense.

Second snort. It had the scent, it had the signal, and that foreleg obediently shot out, the shoulder dipped, and, with Cenedi's slight boost, Ilisidi grasped the saddle ring with the quirt-hand, got her foot squarely in the mounting-stirrup, and used the momentum of the mecheita's sudden rise to land astride, not to pitch over the other shoulder—thank God, not to pitch off, as the paidhi had so notoriously done on one occasion. Ilisidi was up, she had the rein in one hand, the quirt in the other, and she was secure. More, she no longer struggled to walk: she had four fast legs under her. The mecheita in question gave an explosive sigh, acknowledging an expert hand in charge, no showy moves, just little taps of the quirt at the right time and an unfamiliar mecheita circled out of the way under complete control.

It was a knack the paidhi oh, so wished he had—because the next matter at hand was for him to get up on one of these beasts, and not to be ripped up by those tusks or pitched onto his head.

"Nand' paidhi?" Keimi had loosed the rein on a smallish mecheita, pulled the requisite quirt from its secure place, and offered him transport.

He took the offered rein and the quirt in hand, and had no shame at all in using Banichi's help to get up, no need for the beast to make violent moves or even to kneel: Banichi threw him upward, he landed astride, did not pitch over the other way, and settled. He had the rein, and the creature turned its head on its snaky neck, one limpid, treacherous eye measuring its likely chances of unseating him. The ivory tusks gleamed in the forest shadow.

Timidity with these beasts was lethal. He resolutely tapped its shoulder, took his chance and tapped the hindquarters, to make it swing back out of the way. It answered his signal, wonderful beast, and even stood still while Jago passed his computer up to him.

That was as far as he had to manage. The beast need not move until the leader moved, would not stray, and he settled the strap over his head, as secure as he could be. His personal duffle he saw loaded onto another mecheita, baggage lashed to the saddles of three additional mecheiti, before all was done. When their company was all settled aboard, there were still left five mecheiti for the oldest and the youngest of Keimi's party—and those five mounts turned out to accommodate seven, since children doubled up. Adults clearly meant to walk—wherever they were going.

Keimi led off at a brisk walk on the broad trail, branched off to the right when there was a choice and kept them moving, downhill and up again.

No one said, even yet, where they were going, and it was too difficult to ask, strung out as they were, the mecheiti assuming their habitual order in the herd. They were heading to another of the drop points, Bren was fairly sure. On his legs' account he hoped for a short ride: none of them had ridden in years, and even Cajeiri's young body was going to feel it in an hour, let alone the dowager's and Cenedi's. But for their safety's sake, he hoped it was a long way from the bus, which sat like a signpost in the brush. Getting the dowager clear away from it was a priority that needed no questions.

The Taiben rangers were no fools, and as they moved out, one could suspect other, well-armed parties might well move in to watch that bus and wait for someone from the opposition to come investigating . . . and if the Sidonin authorities were no fools, they might hesitate to take the chance themselves. If the Kadigidi tried it, they could be sure their quarry was not likely to be sitting there waiting to be caught. In the upshot of the whole affair, very likely local authorities in Sidonin would, after a little show of anger for Murini-aiji's consumption, send someone to the Taibeni under truce and negotiate to get their bus back, oh, in a few days, when the dust had settled.

By then—by then, their party might be a long way gone from the area. Maybe by then they would have gained news of Tabini. Maybe they would be rallying supporters for a return to power and the chain of dominoes they had started in Adaran might fall here, too.

That thought lent a giddy feeling of freedom, with the willing strength of the animal under him, with the rhythm of movement and the creak of leather, the home sun's light sifting through bluegreen leaves above and about them.

This was Taiben. This was where he and Tabini had started all those years ago, a simple hunting trip, the gift of a forbidden firearm. Thoughts started picking up details, old memories, people, places, connections remade. Resources. Possibilities.

8

Whistles began to sound through the woods, faintly carrying beyond hills and thickets—the source might have been at the next turn of the trail, or far, far off. Cajeiri looked over his shoulder, startled, when first they heard them, and then as Keimi answered with a similar whistle, Cajeiri settled in again, perhaps some deep memory of having heard those whistles before, in the earliest years of his young life.

They were watched, but the watchers were their own, protective. Keimi's easy attitude said he believed they were safe, and Banichi's said he believed Keimi, so Bren felt reassured enough.

The mecheiti hit their best traveling stride on trails well-used and clear of overhead entanglement—not forest creatures, but perfectly capable in that environment. Their party took only small breaks for rest, and at last let the mecheiti water at a small forest stream, where they themselves drank as much as they wanted, water that tasted not of immaculate filters, but of the woods where it flowed. Clear and cold, it held the slight mineral tang of stone and the slight flavor of good clean moss. Bren washed his face with it, taking in the chill and the smell of the deep springs that fed it—shivered, happy in the sensations.

Cajeiri spat out his first mouthful in sheer surprise, but he looked around him, saw everyone else drinking, and then drank without complaint, wise lad. He, too, washed, and wiped his hair back—a long strand had escaped its queue, and, dampened, made a trailing streamer beside his face. He stuck it behind his ear and hugged his arms about him, sitting like a lump on the mossy bank, a very weary boy, not so full of questions now, not in the last two hours.

But two teenaged Taibeni drank near him, turning shy looks in his direction, and then offered him a bit to eat, one of those little nut and fruit bars Bren would have been glad to have, remembering his own time in Taiben. Cajeiri clearly had his doubts of the irregular, much-handled roll, and Bren watched, wondering if he should say something, as, indeed, their difficult Cajeiri, whose delicate palate had balked at unprocessed water, hesitated between courtesy and suspicion. The boy of the pair held it out nonetheless, insisting with a motion of his hand and an earnest look. Cajeiri hesitantly took it, took a bite, and a bigger bite, then ate the whole sweet, and washed it down with a double handful of the despised spring water.

"Thank you, nadiin," Cajeiri said, and two heads bobbed in respect, the three of them crouching there, three youngsters on the mossy edge. Good, Bren thought, seeing Cajeiri relax and trust those who ought to be trusted.

And when they were underway again, the two Taibeni, who had been walking to the rear of their column, now walked alongside Cajeiri's mecheita, keeping the pace with strong, determined strides, looking up with just now and again a little youthful chatter, a protective attitude—they were older—and occasionally the necessity to dodge a stray sapling. Cajeiri began to ask questions: where do you live, how long have you been here, how did you find us? In Cajeiri, this flow of questions was a heartening sign.

Considering how the saddle hurt now, it was remarkably good spirits. Bren bore his own discomfort, looking at the dowager, wondered how she was bearing up, and whether she was going to manage another long stretch of this traveling.

He was very much wondering that, several hours on, in late afternoon, when another few whistles came from somewhere ahead. Keimi answered that whistle, and before long, in a little cleft in the wooded hill, they met other rangers camped. There was a herd of mecheiti, all under saddle, a greater number than the five rangers who waited there . . . for them, it seemed.

Now they had mecheiti enough for all of them to ride.

"How did they know to meet us?" Cajeiri asked his young guides, and there were answers, a conversation that strayed into the trail system—interesting to know, but by now Bren was thinking obsessively only of his backside, and wondering if it was going to be less painful just to keep going at greater speed, wherever they were going, all of them on mecheiti, or whether they might, please God, stop now, spend the night, and stop moving, never mind the hour of mortal pain when they got into the saddle tomorrow morning. He had reached the limit, legs two years unaccustomed even to long walks, let alone this abuse, and the conference of rangers afoot and mounted passed in a haze of absolute misery.

No one had yet uttered a word about their destination, which might be here, or days off, but likely all this hurry was to meant put distance between them and the bus, and any likelihood of the opposition tracking Ilisidi and the boy. They might have been riding in circles for all appearances—at least it had been uphill and downhill and around bends and through low spots, getting only to more forest, which, in Taiben, covered half the province.

Cajeiri, however, asked, "Are we staying, nadiin? Are we getting down now?"

Try, "Where are we? What are we doing here?" Bren

thought, but he wanted detail that wouldn't bear shouting up and down a moving column. He thought his staff might have an idea. He hoped they did. It was beyond the paidhi's need to know.

They stayed stopped for a long conversation, out of earshot. Then Cenedi got off, and began to help the dowager to dismount.

So they were getting down, for a while, at least. With a profound sigh and a hope of at least an hour to sit on unmoving ground, Bren expertly secured the rein, slipped his quirt into its loop, slipped his leg over and slid down the mecheita's side.

Mistake. Bad mistake. His legs buckled, his ankle gave on soft ground, and for a precarious moment he was in that worst of positions with mecheiti, flat on his back on the ground, dazedly looking up at his mecheita's underside. Banichi and Jago appeared out of nowhere, Banichi to seize the mecheita's halter, Jago to haul him to his feet and brush off his clothes.

"The paidhi is exhausted," Ilisidi said from a distance, having witnessed his tumble, and perhaps finding in his mishap her own excuse. "We shall rest here."

Their guides tried to suggest Ilisidi sit and rest, but Ilisidi had her cane in hand and walked—walked in wide, aimless patterns, as far as the clear space allowed.

Not unwise, Bren thought. He walked a bit himself, trying to keep his legs under him, trying to get circulation back to his nether regions, and not to let the ankle give. Careless of dignity at this point, he swung his arms and bent and stretched, feeling the pain already, and knowing it would be worse before it was better. He owned, he very much recalled, a saddle more to his proportions. Unfortunately that saddle was, like the mecheita he owned, off in Malguri, at the other end of the continent, and for now, and in public, the only cure he could apply was three tablets of mild painkiller, which he carried in his baggage.

He swallowed the dose, washed it down with spring

water, then sank down gingerly on a decaying log near the baggage, in the general area where the rest of them were gathering, to wait for it to take effect. The rangers had set up a small stove, and were heating water, for tea, one ever so earnestly hoped. He watched as other utensils appeared from various baggage. Food appeared.

His appetite began to override the pain. Food, hot food, and not concentrate bars. The fire seemed reckless, if they were being followed. The smell of smoke carried. But a hot meal was oh, so welcome. He resisted second-guessing the rangers' judgement.

There were other whistles in the woods, some near, some far. Their guides fell utterly silent and listened for a bit.

"There has been no investigation of the bus, nandiin," Keimi said, standing by the edge of the clearing. "The Sidonin authority evidently is not particularly zealous. We shall likely receive a message by hand, from another direction. We shall let them retrieve the bus, eventually."

A whistle sounded startlingly close to them. One of Keimi's people answered it, and meanwhile business around the stove went on as if nothing alarming had happened. Tea was served, soup was on to boil, water supplied from the spring, in a pot that otherwise served as a packing container. And someone out in the woods was watching, guarding them.

"Mind, we have a human guest," Ilisidi had said, when they were putting together the meal, and she had her staff watch, personally, every item and spice that went into the stew, for which Bren was entirely grateful. It smelled better and better. Anything would have appealed to him, laden with alkaloids or not, and he would, he thought, have died mostly happy if he could only get a bowlful of what was preparing.

Some little noise attracted their own bodyguards' attention. "We have others arriving, nandiin," Keimi said, and Assassins relaxed. Hands left weapons.

In a while more, indeed, while they were ladling out the contents of the pot, which turned out to be a thick stew presented as a sauce on hardtack, other riders turned up, three of them, a woman, two men, these all in mottled dark green not unlike the leaves, on dark, well-kept mecheiti.

There were introductions, and the dowager stayed seated, but she inclined her head courteously to each—whose names, it turned out, she already knew.

"Nand' dowager," they addressed Ilisidi, with great respect. It appeared, by what conversation flowed, and by the exchange of bows with the two youngsters that had settled by Cajeiri, that these were the parents of the two teenagers, and now they were on much more formal behavior. The elders recalled that they had known Cajeiri as a babe in arms, not the sort of thing a young lad of any species liked to hear recalled in front of his new friends.

But there they were, in the heart of Taiben, where Cajeiri had spent much of his babyhood. And the two teenagers recalled they had met Cajeiri then, if one could meet a toddler in any social sense.

So it was old acquaintance. The chatter went on, in a tumble of particulars for a second or two, entirely displacing adult business, until Ilisidi meaningfully cleared her throat. "There is a better sitting place over near the spring, great-grandson."

"Mani-ma." Cajeiri gratefully took the hint and took his two teenaged conversants with him, out of the stream of adult conversation.

"His father's son," the older man of the arriving party said. His name was Jeiniri—Bren had noted it; and the woman was his partner in service, Deiso. Those two were the parents. The other man, Cori, was Deiso's brother.

"In very many ways," Ilisidi said, "he is his father's son." Some quiet current ran in that exchange that Bren could not quite gather, but there was a little tension in the air, and eyes were quickly downcast.

Is there some problem in this meeting? he asked himself, and cast a worried glance at his own staff, who were busy with their supper. Is there some news passed, some particular difficulty, that brought this pair in?

Or have they come in to retrieve their teenaged youngsters from our vicinity? It was a dangerous vicinity, he had no question of that, and it made sense they would feel some awkwardness in saying so. The aiji-dowager and her great-grandson being the gravitational center of that danger, sensible parents would want those two and all the rest of the young children and elderly away from them. It would be a relief, to have the vulnerable part of their band withdraw to safety.

So here went another set of youngsters out of Cajeiri's reach, he thought, if they did that, and he was sorry, immensely sorry they could not send Cajeiri to safety too.

They finished eating. They took tea, a solemn, quiet time.

Community was established. Food and tea had gone the rounds. Then it was permissible to get down to barefaced questions.

"How many of the staff survive, nadiin?" Cenedi asked their hosts directly. "One apprehends they are fairly well scattered."

"The lodge is mostly intact, nadi," Keimi said. "And the Kadigidi have attempted to base there, but to no good, not for them."

That covered bloody actions, Bren thought.

And still that strange reserve.

"You wonder, do you not," Ilisidi said sharply, "who claims the succession." Her mouth made a hard line, and she leaned on her cane, which rested at a steep angle before her. All around the fire, eyes fixed mostly on the ground. And the cane lifted, pointing. *"There* is the succession, nadiin, should it come to that." The cane angled toward the spring, and Cajeiri.

A scarcely perceptible tension breathed out of the

newcomers as they followed that indication. *Not* an eastern claimant, then, but an heir of the central provinces, a Ragi like themselves; and no proclamation in the solemn halls of government provoked more tension or more relief than this. Bren himself found his breath stopped, and when they looked back to Ilisidi, Taibeni heads bowed in deep, deep respect.

"Nand' dowager," Keimi said solemnly.

That old, old divide between east and west, that had once, in the previous aiji's death, voted Tabini into office, passing over Ilisidi: too eastern, too much a foreigner to manage the Western Association. It had been a bitter dose.

And Ilisidi knew these people, knew where their man'chi lay, and gained everything in one stroke. The whole atmosphere had changed.

"So what happened here, nadiin?" Ilisidi asked, leaning on that cane again. "And where is he?"

A small silence.

"The aiji," Keimi said, "had come to the lodge for safety. He had intended to send Mercheson-paidhi to Mogari-nai, and he intended to follow, when news came that Murini of the Kadigidi had conducted assassinations in the legislature itself, and lords had scattered for immediate safety. Sabotage was aimed at the shuttles, and Tabini-aiji dispatched staff immediately to prevent that. He intended, himself, to go to Mogari-nai and communicate directly with Ogun-aiji up on the station. The shuttles could not launch: they were in preparation, as best we understand, but we have never heard that they launched."

Bad news. Terrible news.

And Tabini had made a critical choice, to neglect all other matters and protect the shuttle fleet, as an irreplaceable connection to the space station, to his mission, to the ship and its business. Some atevi might not understand that, might not forgive it, in an aiji who had already committed so ruinously much effort into the space program, to join with humans.

"It was suggested by the staff," Deiso said further, "that he be on one shuttle, and that some of us would go with him. He refused, nand' dowager, and said it was impossible, anyway. He said that he belonged to the earth, and that he would never expect us to die for him while he sat safe in the heavens. By all we know, the spaceport is still in provincial hands, the shuttle grounded, but intact, and the crews in hiding. The Kadigidi have taken the shuttle facility at Shejidan, however, and maintain a guard there."

A profound relief. The investment, the unique materials, the irreplaceable staff . . . protected, thus far. But now that the ship was back at the station, the Kadigidi and their supporters would know that the shuttle there and the one on Mospheira represented a dire threat to them. Destroying it, or taking control of it, would become a priority.

"And where is my grandson?" Ilisidi asked.

"No one knows, aiji-ma, but he left eastward—whether skirting through Atageini lands, or more directly inward, we do not know."

A border where there was only uneasy peace, an old, old feud within the Ragi Association—not often a bloody one—that had been patched within the larger Western Association, the aishidi'tat, first by pragmatic diplomacy, then by the marriage of Tabini-aiji to an Atageini consort . . . Cajeiri's mother.

And Cajeiri, with his two companions, had quietly gotten up and moved back to stand nearby, listening, lip bit between his teeth.

"The dowager proposes to go ask Lord Tatiseigi where his man'chi lies," Cenedi said, and Bren's heart did two little thuds.

But of course. Of course that question had to be posed, and posed face to face, if it was to have the best chance of a favorable response. Man'chi worked that way. Ilsidi could ask that question by phone, supposing they found a phone, and that would indeed shock her former lover to a certain degree, perhaps jolt him enough to get the truth out of him. But he might equally as well puff himself up and take personal meaning out of the fact that she had used the phone, not confronting him—and then the shock would diminish into recalcitrance at best. Nothing on earth would match the emotional impact of personal appearance, on Atageini land, and very little could match Ilsidi's force if she got inside his guard. If there was anything calculated to catch the old gentleman at a disadvantage, if there was any appearance of the old regime capable of shaking him to his emotional core—Ilsidi could.

And Ilsidi with the advantage of guardianship over Cajeiri, half Atageini, himself, and destined to rule, by what Ilsidi had just declared—canny politician that she was . . . oh, damned right she had a hand to play.

If they lived long enough. If the Atageini had stayed free of Kadigidi forces. If, if, and if.

Granted they had set something in motion back in Adaran, and stirred things up at Sidonin. They were about to do something far, far more dangerous.

He decided on another cup of tea and kept quiet. This was an atevi matter, and not one where the paidhi-aiji owned a particularly valid theory of how to proceed. *This* choice depended on emotional hard-wiring, the psychology of the business—it was ninety percent psychology, where it involved convincing people to risk their lives to support an eight-year-old successor. The same way the mecheiti stayed, unrestrained, where their leader stayed, this group just sitting round the fire was doing something, arguing things, exerting persuasions and enlisting arguments that human nerves might perceive, but couldn't quite feel.

Excitement was in the air, resolution in the direction of glances, the attitude of heads, the expression in golden eyes, shimmering the other side of the small gas flame. Dusk had settled deep as they heated more water for another, easier round of tea.

The fate of the *aishidi'tat* was potentially being decided, right here, between one great player and a handful of lesser ones. Tabini's choice under threat had been to come to them, and even absent, he had for months been a nebulous presence, whether dead or alive, sustaining them in their fight. With Ilisidi and the boy came an emotional pressure that Ilisidi, canny as she was, seized, directed, bent to her own purpose.

One saw how she had survived coups and assassinations—why she was alive and many of her enemies were dust.

"Tea?" one of Keimi's people asked, and poured for him. He sipped it, feeling, despite the painkiller, the early twinges of what was going to be a truly excruciating day in the saddle tomorrow. Cajeiri had dropped down to sit with the two teens, all of them listening, questions in abeyance, feeling—God knew what.

Sometimes the paidhi's job was best done by keeping his mouth firmly shut.

The folk of Taiben seemed at least not to forget him, in his silence. He had to refuse another serving of hardtack, but he sopped up several cups of tea before he reached capacity. And the discussion went not that much longer before Ilisidi declared she was tired and wished to sleep.

Bren was glad enough to lie down. He was unwilling for Jago to lie beside him and make their relationship that apparent to strangers—it was her dignity he was thinking of, in settling in a narrow spot, between two tree roots. But she sat with Banichi and Cenedi and the rest in a second conference with the three latest-come rangers—perhaps asking particulars of trails, quasi-boundaries, and affiliations, not to mention rumors from outside . . . all that sort of thing their Guild would be interested to know, on which they did their job.

Trust at least when his staff slept, they would sleep, under ranger guard, far more soundly than he would, with half-formed speculations and useless plans swarming through his head.

"But they will come here now, nadiin," he heard Banichi point out. "They will not ignore our landing. They must suspect our route."

Comforting, Bren thought to himself. He shifted onto his back and stared at the branches moving gently above his head, against a sky ragged with cloud. A wind was getting up, that line of cloud, perhaps, that they had seen at sea, now reaching the mainland. It might rain.

He heard the distant voices of Banichi's conference, heard small rush of water flowing, and, nearer at hand, eight-year-old Cajeiri astonishing two teenagers with the account of how he had gone aboard an alien spaceship, and how their kyo had been extremely fond of Bindanda's teacakes . . .

Far too much information to be scattering around the countryside. Information, in strictest sense, that should be classified. Information that he could use to his own advantage.

But it was late for that now. And as Cajeiri told it, the kyo, who could slag a space station with their weaponry, were in fact capable of reason. The boy had helped find that aspect of them. He was a hero in his own right, and was certainly basking in the admiration of his audience. Would he cheat the boy of that, with a request to keep it all quiet?

No, he would not.

He shut his eyes, still alive—he reminded himself— still alive after the shuttle ride, still alive after a very remarkable stretch of hours in which their only rest had been slow baking under the tarp, and slow freezing on blocks of ice, and a long ride on a very uncomfortable saddle, all in the fear of being shot or captured. The ground still felt as if it was moving under him, still with the thump and clack of the rails, or the thump and heave of the boat cutting through water, or the shuttle's tires rolling rapidly down the pavement.

Just too damned much moving in the last few days. And too little real sleep. At the very edge of oblivion he forgot where he was, except he was down, and they'd landed, and the wind was moving, and atevi voices were around him. Jago was close by. And the mecheiti were ripping the leaves off trees.

He could trust that, he decided. The solid earth was reliable. He finally let go all defenses, and did sleep, deeply.

He waked by daylight, with people moving about, with breakfast cooking, an aroma of crisping meat. As sore as he had anticipated being, he took three more pills, then set himself to rights, straightened his by now disreputable queue, shaved the old-fashioned way—no servants to comb his hair, dress him, all the quick attentions that had started most of his days in recent years. He missed Narani and Bindanda—missed their society and their quick briefing on everything in the household. But he found something morally refreshing, being sore in very inconvenient places, sitting on a rock beside a gurgling spring.

Jago brought him hot tea, his one special attention, and dropped to her haunches in front of him.

"How are you this morning, Bren-ji?"

"Very well, really. Will we ride today?"

"We must, Bren-ji," she said.

"If the dowager can do it, nadi-ji, I certainly have no cause to complain."

Jago folded her arms across her knees and leaned close. "We have a plan, Bren-ji, a dangerous plan. The dowager wishes to inquire at Tirnamardi."

Tatiseigi's country estate, about half a day's ride out of Heitisi, the cluster of medium-sized towns that was the economic center of the Atageini holdings. Dangerous didn't begin to describe it. "I heard, last night."

"There is a relatively safe approach," Jago said, "through the hunting reserve, which is contiguous with this woods, which both Taiben and the Atageini manage."

As the animals they hunted were in common, so certain territory overlapped, and game-chase became a matter of hazy rights and who protested—civilly, at least modestly civilly, recently. One hoped it persisted.

"From there," Jago said in a low voice, "we may be able to reach our Guild."

Oh, *now* it got dangerous.

"By phone?" he asked, doubting it.

"It would be far better, Bren-ji, if we were to go ourselves."

He didn't like it. She knew he didn't like it. He reserved a thought to himself: If you go, I go, and he was sure they'd try to outmaneuver him unless he strictly forbade it.

"What do you think, Jago-ji? Is venturing to Shejidan a good idea?"

Jago looked at the ground, then at him. "We consider this a risk, and we have reservations as to whether to attempt Tirnamardi, or to bypass Atageini territory and keep within Taiben. The whole question is where Lord Tatiseigi stands in the current crisis. The dowager is firm in her notion. Cenedi has doubts, too."

"Cajeiri will be at risk."

A second hesitation. "Not from Lord Tatiseigi," she said. "Nor, we think, would the dowager be. You, on the other hand, Bren-ji—"

"Have no particular favor in his sight. I know. I enjoy very little favor from the majority of the population of the mainland, at the moment, one would think."

He had never been particularly acceptable to this very conservative lord, who disliked human influence and all modern intrusions.

"There is misperception, perhaps."

Loyally put. He did not think, however, that he had yet reached the foundations of Jago's thinking.

"Do you, personally, think that Tabini-aiji is dead?" he asked.

"We have had no proof," she said, and that was a delicate, revelatory matter: they had seen no proof they accepted, and therefore had no emotional disconnection of man'chi. They were, she and Banichi, still functioning as if their highest man'chi of all was intact, and that opinion would color all others, affect all other decisions, define all other logic—whether to go to the Guild, whether to bend every effort to empower Ilisidi, whether to agree to this mission entering Tatiseigi's lands.

"If I were not with you," he said—delicate, delicate, to probe an ateva's man'chi too deeply— "would you now leave the dowager, Jago-ji?"

"Unlikely that we would," she said. "But what she is doing, Bren-ji, places the heir and all his aspirations in Lord Tatiseigi's hands. That notion has to be reckoned with. If Tabini-aiji is alive, this risk is a serious consideration, and we are not able to prevent the dowager doing it."

He hadn't quite seen through to that unhappy fact.

"Tatiseigi has," he developed her thought, "every personal interest in seeing Cajeiri sit in Shejidan."

"And that means he has proportionately less interest in seeing Tabini alive."

"God." In Mosphei'. He loosened the wilted lace at his throat. "But his interests cannot involve alienating Cajeiri by attacking his father. That move the boy would never forgive."

"That would be one constraint on him, nandi—besides the operational difficulty of such a move, the fact that the camp opposing the aiji does not place any reliance on him, and, perhaps, whatever regard he holds for Lady Damiri. There is a complex of reasons. Also, Tabini would move to get Cajeiri back, if Tatiseigi were to take him in his charge, and Tabini-aiji with his guard is no small threat. If Lord Tatiseigi made a move to lay personal claim to the heir, then everyone would take sides. Violently."

The denouement of the machimi, the moment in the play where loyalties suddenly came crystal-clear, and atevi had to act.

"Tatiseigi's ambition is abated, not dead, Bren-ji. This is our thinking. He has always aspired to rule."

"And he cannot. If the tashrid would not elect the dowager, they would never elect him."

"The tashrid may have suffered changes in membership, during the present troubles."

"That is so."

"The boy, however, with him as regent—would have far less trouble being confirmed. If his father were dead, and Damiri being Atageini—Tatiseigi would indeed rise in importance. This move of the dowager's, bringing us under his roof, is fraught with hazards."

"Do you think, Jago-ji, that the dowager herself might be in more danger than she thinks?"

"Possibly." A frown creased Jago's brow. "Possibly so, Bren-ji. Sometimes, lacking certain instincts, you do see astonishingly clearly."

"Not lacking my own species' instincts, I assure you, and this hazard is understandable. Can we not talk her out of it? Can you reason with Cenedi?"

"Cenedi has tried to persuade her: he wishes to settle her in Taiben and then venture against the Kadigidi himself. Cenedi himself knows the risk, knows your man'chi. He would not blame us for withdrawing from this venture and trying to find Tabini. Nor, I think, would the dowager herself blame us."

It was an absolute wilderness, the forest of atevi emotions, atevi decisions, atevi snap judgements, all rooted in urges humans didn't feel at that depth, at that intensity. "She is counting, is she not, Jago-ji, on the boy having a strong emotional force with his uncle?"

"Counting very heavily on her own, one believes,

nandi, considering the boy's last emotional impact on his uncle was set in a wide expanse of concrete."

He was caught off guard. Laughed, a brief sneeze of laughter, despite the grimness of the situation. Tatiseigi was a notorious curmudgeon, who had suffered considerably from public amusement at the incident in question. And one did fear Tatiseigi would not find Cajeiri that much improved, not from his conservative point of view—a sober thought which instantly killed the laughter, and did nothing to form a rational conclusion. If Jago was perplexed, caught between two loyalties, he was caught in his own. He had their welfare at heart, and the boy's. And Tabini's, granted the aiji was still alive. And he had the whole outcome to consider, and the whole human-atevi-kyo problem to weigh into the equation.

While Ilisidi, damn her, had always been an incredibly nervy, canny player in atevi politics, and he had no wish to undermine her best effort, if she could shock the fence-sitting lord into alliance. There he met his own division of common sense and emotion. She might be making a monumental mistake. Or a very smart move.

But at the bottom of the stack, on the scale at which they operated, he had no right to choose personal safety. He was a resource, a resource of information and defense for the fallen regime, one it could no more afford to lose than it could afford to lose Ilisidi or Cajeiri, if Tabini himself was alive. But in order to be useful, he had to be active and get the information public in the most credible way. He had his own reputation to restore, and if he could not defend their mission and its outcome to one fairly civilized old man under Ilisidi's influence, he stood precious little chance of persuading the rest of the continent.

"One cannot hide in the bushes," he said. "We did not come back from space to do that, Jago-ji. One has no real idea how to find Tabini. One rather thinks he may find us if we can make just a modest amount of noise and if Atageini territory is open to him. And the things that Tabini did that were right, that were essential—that succeeded—these things have to be vindicated to the public at large, do they not, Jago-ji? If I were to separate from Ilisidi, I, as much as you, need to go to Shejidan. I need to speak to your Guild, and to the legislature. I need to give people the information I have. I have to defend Tabini's decisions for everyone to hear. Words, Jago, words are my whole defense. Words stand a chance of changing minds. I have to gain what respect I can recover, starting, one supposes, with this very influential lord."

A moment of silence, then, Jago's gold gaze steady and honest. "You are not necessarily wrong, Bren-ji."

"Good."

"So," Jago said, "our way from here—"

"Lies through Atageini territory," Bren said. "So our intent may have diverged ever so slightly from the dowager's, but our path logically does not."

"One concurs, Bren-ji," Jago said. "I shall tell Banichi."

She did not go back to the conference. She went and sat apart from that gathering, on a rock, arms on her knees, waiting. In a little time Banichi came and squatted near her.

Bren continued fussing with his lace and dusting his boots. The conference at the fireside broke up, and the young people, who had been settled in their own conspiracy over near the mecheiti, began to look for saddles. Cajeiri was limping a little this morning. He didn't complain overmuch about it, doggedly maintaining his dignity, one suspected, particularly in front of the two older youngsters, who were inured to the saddle, and who had likely never in their lives felt this particular pain.

Ilisidi had to be helped up to her feet, but she walked and stood, somehow, shaking off assistance, and ordered Nawari to saddle her mecheita.

Bren figured he had best go see to his own gear. He

thought he could tell which mecheita he had ridden yesterday, and which was its tack, and no one else objected to his selection of gear. Tano and Algini left consultations and hurried to help him. He decided he was very grateful for that, having disgraced himself last evening, and having no wish to contest the creature's tusks, as sore as he already was.

Meanwhile the small side conference between Banichi and Jago had broken up fairly inconspicuously, as Banichi and Jago sought their own tack and Banichi found the means to talk to Tano and Algini.

And did the dowager take note that there had been a planning session of his own staff, or did Cenedi possibly miss it? Bren took the rein from Tano. He gritted his teeth and got into the saddle, with Algini's help.

Pain was bearable, if it was familiar pain. It would pass in an hour or so, even without the painkiller to hasten the hour. A little gentle riding would bring its own numbness.

Their direction was the same direction they had been tending yesterday. Cajeiri and Deiso's two teenagers all rode together now, the ranger youngsters riding with considerable skill, compelling their mecheiti to ignore their ordinary order, likely with their parents' beasts, and stay near Cajeiri, an argument that occasionally annoyed the rest of the column, but they had their way and stayed.

For his own part, he was very glad to be somewhat behind, and to have his mecheita bored and quiescent. He rode quietly in line, seeing Banichi and Jago conferring with Cenedi up ahead, a conversation undoubtedly being overheard by the dowager. There might be close questions, or implied close questions from Cenedi, about the private conference, and Banichi might even answer them fairly honestly, since their intentions, while somewhat separate, lay in the same direction. It was safer to have Cenedi well-acquainted with their notions and their logic.

The dowager did not comment on the matter. Bren watched, unable to hear those quiet voices above the general movement of the mecheiti. It was a peaceful ride, a quiet ride, few people speaking even to immediate companions, and it was only belatedly that he realized the oldest rider and the youngest children were no longer with them. The whistles from elsewhere in the woods continued, fewer in number, but perfectly audible.

Toward afternoon: "We are inside Atageini lands now," Jago rode back to tell him.

He had noticed an upright stone a moment ago. He had learned to pay attention to anomalies, even when he had no idea what they might be.

And he had not heard a whistle in at least an hour.

"One remarks a certain silence here," he said to her.

"The rangers will not signal near this boundary," Jago said. "Atageini hunters cross here. None recently, by the look of things."

"Does that indicate, nadi-ji, that the Atageini avoid crossing into Taiben?"

"It is worth remarking, nandi. We have no word of any hostilities, however, and none of any intrusions."

"Inform my ignorance, Jago-ji. What do you think it would it mean?"

"Possibly that Lord Tatiseigi wishes no incident with Taiben in these perilous times. Possibly he wishes none of his hunters be caught and questioned by the Taibeni, which might give away too much of his intentions and his position, even if his intention is to stay neutral. And possibly some installation hereabouts has frightened the game away and there is nothing to bring hunters here."

"Electronic surveillance?"

"We have picked up a signal."

The subtler elements of Guild technology, which he was sure some of their staff carried, and the nastier elements of Guild actions possible on the border they were crossing. Wires. Traps. Not likely to stop others of the same Guild, but enough to slow them down.

He had noted Cenedi had traded mounts with Ilisidi this morning, taking the more fractious herd-leader for himself. Banichi had also pushed his mecheita up ahead of Ilisidi's, he and Cenedi riding first and second in the column the last few minutes, a small indication of worry. Theirs were very experienced eyes, apt to spot specific things even a ranger might not, and that the mecheiti might sense, but not know the danger.

He himself knew entirely too much about such devices, and their more lethal adjuncts, which were ordinarily deployed in secure places in Shejidan. One scarcely expected them to be placed out here in the depths of the woods, where roaming animals might trip them too often, with bloody result, not to mention the provocation it posed against Taiben.

And it was not without significance, he was sure, that Jago stayed closer by him now, with Tano and Algini staying very close behind him. Ever since they had passed that stone, their progress had acquired the caution of Guild very much on the alert.

The woods thinned, and there was open land visible, beyond the screen of trees. They were still within forest, riding that ridge of low hills, Bren recalled from his railroad-building days, which was the nebulous boundary between Taiben and the Atageini.

Soon, sure enough, they exited the woods onto open meadow, and took a downward pitch, now firmly within Atageini territory and evidently free of monitoring or threat. From the broad slope of the high meadow, they could see a village, an Atageini village, far down and across extensive grassland, past winding brown hedgerows, into cultivated fields gold with ripened crops or dead brown with harvested stubble. A little haze overlay equally grassy hills beyond.

It all had a quaint look, as many small villages did, hereabouts, little places nestled in sheltered nooks, not all of them to this day using electric lights. One saw no electric lines in this province, no more than in Taiben: installations like the monitoring equipment they suspected back there had to be battery-powered. The siting of the railroad right of way had been a particularly bitter controversy here, and in Taiben, and the train when it did go through had been slowed by Atageini insistence that the tracks, where allowed, should follow old farm-to-market routes. It meant a curving, inefficient progress that prevented trains going as fast through Atageini territory as they ran elsewhere . . . and they ran not at all through Taiben, except on the very border. He knew the whole untidy history. He had had to mediate a dispute on the junction of two regional rail lines that had, finally, *finally* gotten Atageini permission to lay track to that set of villages.

No sign of the disputed rail from their vantage. Only isolated copses of woods and rolling meadow, intermittent with plowed fields, until it grew too dark even for atevi eyes to be sure there were no traps.

Then they settled down for another camp, and, daringly, a hot cup of tea, a hot bowl of soup.

And another dose of analgesic.

Beside the little stove, Keimi and his remaining people announced their intention of going back in the morning, back to Taiben land, back to organize a second meeting with Ilisidi once she left this territory and proceeded northward to gather support there, as she intended to do.

And, in the conversation that followed supper and tea, there were statements of gratitude, hopes for their success, concerns for their welfare. It was all the Taibeni could offer at this point: Taiben rangers were persona non grata where they were, already. The district had a long, long history of cross-border forays and, before the aishidi'tat, of outright warfare.

So they would be commiting themselves to Ilisidi's plan in the morning. Bren found himself a flat place where no one would tread on him and went to bed early, absolutely exhausted. Traps, wires, old feuds . . . he had reached that stage of exhaustion and compliance when even terror for his life and the world's welfare were no barrier to sleep, deep as a pit and dreamless, so far as he could remember.

He lifted his head, startled, when he heard stirring about, when daylight was at least faintly discernible to human eyes. His head objected to the sudden elevation. His eyes wanted to shut. He wanted to drop back down to the uncompromising ground and lie there another day, perhaps a week. An experimental movement of one leg convinced him that the saddle was, oh, no, not going to be comfortable today at all.

But staff had more important things on their minds this morning than playing servant to him. The Taibeni were to leave them. He levered himself up on his hands and knees, and got up, brushing off the clothes that by now were truly showing signs of wear. He had loosened his queue. He rebraided and tied it. He had neglected to take his boots off, and now he was sorry for it, but he limped about a sluggish morning routine, trying to make himself look as presentable as possible—the dignity of a lord was a protection to his staff, and he did as much as he could for himself, shaving, picking small bits of detritus off his coat, the effects of sleeping under a tree that shed.

"How are you this morning, Bren-ji?" Jago brought him a cup of tea from the Taibeni stove, abundantly steaming in the morning chill.

"Awake," he said, fumbling with the analgesic. Human-specific. He had no help for his companions. "Minimally awake, Jago-ji." She had been with him long enough to know he never, ever waked as she did, full of energy, whether or not it was daylight—he wondered where she got the moral strength, this morning. He wondered, too, that they had heated the stove, but it was bitterly chill this morning, and he supposed it would cool rapidly for packing.

Beyond anything, he was grateful for the hot tea, and washed down a nutrient bar and his pills. The knees were not quite so bad as yesterday. The seat was, if possible, worse.

He was so muzzy-headed with early waking and breakfast he failed to realize when the stove was packed up, failed to see the preparations for separate departure going on apace, but he saw Keimi and his people were saddling up, going.

So Cajeiri was losing his two companions, Deiso's youngsters. He saw looks being exchanged, saw a glum unhappiness in Cajeiri's countenance, as the boy stood with hands locked behind him, watching the separation of baggage.

The two young people kept looking back at him, too, while packing and beginning to saddle up. They spoke together. And Cajeiri never stopped gazing at them, with a dejection in his whole bearing that bespoke more than a childish disappointment.

The young woman took a hesitant step toward Cajeiri, away, then went back to her father and mother, and bent in a profound bow.

"We wish to go with the young aiji," the girl said distressedly. Not I, *we*. "We have to, father."

The father was clearly distressed. So was his partner, and the uncle. But he said something Bren could not hear, and spoke to the girl, and then went and spoke to his son. So did the others of the family.

Then the two came back to Cajeiri and bowed, choosing to go with him, evidently, with parental permission, the girl and then the boy extending their hands to his, emotions brimming over in the moment so that eavesdropping on them seemed all but indecent.

Dared one think—?

Because a curious thing was proceeding. Cajeiri gripped their hands one after the other, and bit his lip fiercely, and looked as moved as it was possible for a reserved young lad to be in public.

Man'chi. That emotion. That binding force, that sense of other-self. What had almost been broken was made whole all in an instant: it was a choice of directions and attachments, and there wasn't a damned thing a father or a mother with safety concerns or a great-grandmother with her own plans could do about it.

A little chill went over him. Do I see what I think I see? he wondered, and was too embarrassed to look toward his own staff, who themselves felt such an intimate thing for him. He'd never actually seen it work—well, there had been the time he had bolted from cover to reach Banichi and Jago under fire, an action that so scandalized their concept of proper behavior that Jago had been willing to shake his teeth out. He had been lucky enough to gain a staff he could absolutely trust, and, from his side, love, but the shift of loyalties had generally been so subtle and so internal with him and his staff, all of them sober, older creatures than teenagers, and while he never doubted deep emotion was there—and felt it—he had never seen a case of man'chi shifting, except in the machimi plays.

But the fact was—those two young people were utterly honest, and Cajeiri was, and there it all was, a life-choice. They hadn't broken bonds with their family, but they'd formed something else, something that had, in a day, taken over their lives, totally shifted their focus. They were about at that stage when humans hit first love, and had to be counseled and persuaded against tidal forces that could shipwreck their whole lives . . .

Nothing of sexual attraction, here, not in man'chi. But clearly it was a sort of chemistry, and a choice might be just as problematic—for Taibeni youngsters dragged into danger of their lives and a Ragi prince who, two years from now, might have made a more mature, political judgement.

"Young persons," Ilisidi said severely.

"Mani-ma." Cajeiri pulled his young followers over to Ilisidi, and they bowed, and he bowed, all of which she accepted with a deep frown.

"This will be dangerous, nadiin," she said to them.

"Yes, aiji-ma," the young man said.

"Names."

"Antaro, aiji-ma," the girl said; and, "Jegari, aiji-ma," the boy, both under Ilisidi's head to foot scrutiny.

"What, sixteen?"

"Fifteen, nearly sixteen, aiji-ma." The boy answered.

Twice Cajeiri's age. That made no difference in what they felt. It by no means affected rank, or precedence.

"So," Ilisidi said, and gave a nod and leaned on her cane, then looked at the parents, another exchange of bows, hers and theirs.

And Cajeiri—Cajeiri was incredibly happy, solemn, but his whole being aglow as he went off with his companions—from dejected, he hurried to deal with his own mecheita, to make himself ready, to do everything himself. They wanted to help him, but let him manage what an eight-year-old could.

Jago turned up at Bren's side, to help him saddle up. So did Tano. They looked solemn, themselves.

He looked a question at them, but they had no immediate answer. There were some things which, if he asked them a plain question, would be several days explaining, and no greater understanding at the end.

Now, God, the parents had to be upset—but they showed no inclination to go along. How could they, if the next ride took them down into Atageini territory, where their presence would not help negotiations at all?

Neither, the thought occurred to him, would this young pair.

Damn, he thought, arriving at, perhaps, the thoughts that were racing through several atevi minds, but never, of course, the young minds in question.

"Nandi." Algini had his mecheita saddled for him. He took Tano's help getting up, and hit the saddle with, oh, the expected pain. In the periphery of his vision he saw, to be sure, a leave-taking, Cajeiri with the two Taibeni youngsters, after which Keimi and the parents and everyone else rode away, back toward Taiben lands.

There was a moment of quiet. Then a burst of energy as Cajeiri went to mount up, with his associates' help, as if the whole world was made new around them. The dowager accepted Cenedi's assistance to mount, and, curiously, to Bren's eye, she had a satisfaction about her this morning that said, indeed, she was not that displeased, not nearly as much as their situation might indicate.

So there were still nuances he failed to understand.

They started off, the young people planted firmly in the center of the column, with the dowager, and with him. For a while he listened to Nawari instructing the young people, advising the new arrivals what to do and what contingencies to consider if they should come under fire.

And the dowager sternly advising Cajeiri that if he picked shelter, he should now adjust his thinking and pick shelter wide enough for three.

Hell of a thing, he said to himself. Hell of a thing for three kids to have to think of. The older generation had a few things to answer for.

But then—under different circumstances, they might not have met at all. Man'chi might have fallen out differently. Tabini and Damiri and Ilisidi herself might have carefully managed what susceptible young persons came into contact with the heir, at what times, with careful consideration as to what associations they represented and what possible alliances they brought.

What governs what attraction takes hold? he wondered, without answers. What sets off the spark, that hits one hard at eight, and the other two blithely unattached to any loyalty but their parents, evidently, until they're midteens?

They hit a long slope, bound downward, now, into the

treeless meadowlands. A herd of teigi grazed in the distance. They would not be legitimate prey for another few months, in the atevi rules of season, but the teigi had no instinctive knowledge of seasons and *kabiu*. Heads went up and the herd bounded off at the first whisper of their presence. The wind had been out of the north, across the slope, though it had been shifting, and now it came full around out of the west, at their backs, in some force. A little spatter of rain came down on them, quickly abated, but with hints of thunder behind them.

They rode down one meadow and up to the crest of a long roll of the land, where they had their first view of the eastern mountains, a blue haze in the distance, above a long slant of meadow and cultivated fields, even the brown stripe of a farm-to-market road. That would lead to some larger town.

They avoided that direction. Wind and rain-spatter at their backs, they turned northeast, toward the heart of Atageini territory, deeper and deeper.

Further and further onto the tolerance and mercy of Lord Tatiseigi, who surely knew by now that intruders had crossed his borders.

Deeper and deeper into danger, the frail dowager, an eight-year-old boy and a pair of Taibeni children—and a human, whom Lord Tatiseigi had only grudgingly tolerated in the first place. Vulnerable, he kept thinking. And vulnerability was entirely unlike Ilisidi—on whom a supplicant's role sat very, very strangely.

God, he thought. She wouldn't. Would she?

Would Ilisidi, to protect her great-grandson and secure her own bloodline in the succession, harbor any notion of abandoning Tabini as aiji and joining with Tatiseigi in a coup, a shift of man'chi as sudden, as illogical, and as catastrophic as what he had just witnessed? She had always wanted to rule.

It was a turn straight out of the machimi. Too damn

many movies. He was far out of the habit of the classic drama. His thinking had gone into human lines, which had governed politics on the ship. Down here the priorities were very, very different.

"Do I see worry on your face, paidhi-ji?"

"One relies, as ever, on your honesty, aiji-ma. Are we going to Tirnamardi to fight, to negotiate—" Never leave a logical set at ill-omened two. She knew there was a third thing coming. "Or to make new arrangements?"

An aged map of lines rearranged itself subtly, a wicked gleam in her eye. "No one else would dare ask such a question, paidhi."

"Because atevi follow, aiji-ma. Humans have to figure out the path."

"Some follow us. Some follow others."

"But the paidhi has no instinct to tell him which way the wind is blowing, aiji-ma. One assumes there is logic in what you do. May I know what it is?"

"Purity defines you, paidhi-ji. As far as you travel, it always defines you."

His face flushed slightly. He could not help it. He was indeed very naïve, in certain regards, and knew it, and Ilisidi smiled at him, a subtle smile.

"What you witnessed makes you think of such things, does it, paidhi-aiji?"

"It teaches me. It makes me question what I know."

"We value you," she said. "Our compass. Our true lodestone of virtue."

"One is glad of some usefulness, aiji-ma." He was not comforted. The old spark had entered the dowager's eye this morning, ever since that turn of events in the camp. Ilisidi in this mode was dangerous. Lethal.

And sometimes frighteningly honest. She reached out a hand and touched his arm.

"Protect the truth, paidhi-ji. Do not swerve from that. We wondered when, not if, you would come to consult us about the future."

His face still burned.

"And what future, aiji-ma? One regrets not to know, but one has no understanding at all."

"Nor will you. Nor can you. Nor can we. We will know when we see Tatiseigi."

Was it all that nebulous, that much a dice throw, that even Tatiseigi himself would not know until then? Tatiseigi would have to see her. They would have to size one another up, for resolution, strength—and plans, which might include one or the other of them making a power grab.

Or at least thinking about taking hostages.

She rode forward, leaving him, having said as much as she chose to say. He reined back a little.

"It was well done, Bren-ji," Jago said, riding next to him. "Well done, to speak to her. She had questions about what you might be thinking, which she may have satisfied."

"I had to try," he said. "But I learned absolutely nothing. Except that a great deal is still up in the air."

"Up in the air," Jago said, amused, sometimes, by his translation of Mosphei' idiom. "Baji-naji," she rendered it, the dice-fall of the universe, the give and take in the design.

The design always survived. The pieces might not.

There was quiet in the column after that. The youngsters talked in whispers even human ears could detect over the general noise of movement.

They took to the trees again, a wooded district, Cenedi still leading. When they came out again, on a ridge overlooking a broad expanse of cultivated land, and the distant cluster of small towns, visible clear to the swell of horizon that obscured the eastern mountains, the sun was behind the woods at their backs, and the light was growing dim with twilight. The cloud had begun to rumble with thunder, advising them that clearing the edge of the trees and getting to the lowlands might be a good idea.

Bren absolutely had no idea where they were now. He asked Jago, who gave him village names.

"Within an hour's ride of estate land," she said, "at the pace we set."

"That close." He was dismayed. He had rather thought they would be getting wet tonight, camping in the open. He was not that much encouraged to know they were that close.

He hoped to God they didn't run into trouble. He fished after another analgesic. He was sure everyone in the party was suffering, excepting, of course, Antaro and Jegari, who were disgustingly blithe and bright even at this late hour.

At least Cajeiri had someone specifically looking after him and answering his questions, providing him the instinctual moves his two years on the ship hadn't taught him. Besides them, Nawari was back there, bringing up the rear, protection for the youngsters.

No question that Cenedi, who had been all his career with Ilisidi, was going to stay with her, no matter what happened: he would not divert himself to care for anyone else, come hell or high water, as the saying went.

God, he hoped Tatiseigi had not turned coat.

They started downhill again, and their trail broadened toward dusk, broadened and joined a true road, even a maintained road. The air grew cooler as the sun sank, cooler to the point of chill, with a beginning drizzle, and Bren buttoned his coat.

Another space of riding, and a dark wall, a hedge, loomed across the road, in the gathering dark. He looked concentratedly at it and saw a dim barrier in their path. A gate. A metal-grilled gate.

The estate border. Beyond it—they were on Tirnamardi's grounds, however far they extended.

"Traps, Tano-ji?" he asked.

"Possibly," Tano said. Algini had ridden up to speak to Banichi some few moments ago, not unprecedented in their trip, but Algini had a particular expertise in nasty devices. Of Cenedi's men, only Nawari still hung to the rear.

And Cenedi checked their pace markedly, the closer they came to that gate. At a certain point something exploded with an electric snap, and Bren jumped, the mecheiti all jumped, and he fought to bring his beast under control.

"What happened?" The dark and the misting rain obscured the riders ahead into twilight shadows. He was afraid for Banichi and Algini, foremost; and Cenedi: there might be worse. Or they had set something off.

Jago had drawn closer to him. "A discouragement to approach, Bren-ji, not lethal. One never likes to surprise a guard—unless one intends to remove him."

"Someone is there?" In the gathering dark, in the rain, at this remote remove, he had not expected it.

"Assuredly," Jago said. "And Banichi did not care to approach unheard. That watcher will pay close attention now."

"We shall ride right up to the gate?"

"We shall ride up. He will come out."

Bren bit his lip. The watcher was coming to them, that was to say.

And of a sudden, atevi eyes being the better in the dusk: "Tell your lord he has visitors!" Cenedi shouted into the night.

"Who are you, nadi?" a distant voice asked, somewhere behind the gate, and by now the fore of their column had stopped, the rest of them drifting to a halt behind. They were all too exposed, in Bren's anxious calculation. And in a heartbeat and a glance, he was not sure where Banichi had gotten to, or Algini.

"Escort to a lady of the lord's personal acquaintance. Tell him so, nadi!"

"I shall relay that, nadi, but best if I had a name!"

A two-heartbeat pause, then, from Cenedi: "Say he will remember when lightning hit the boat."

"Lightning hit the boat." Bren could hear the disbelieving mutter from here, in the general hush. Mecheiti snorted and shifted, his own included, and he kept the rein just short of taut, tapping slightly with his quirt to restrain a sideward motion, while someone up there was making a phone call.

"Should we move off the road, Jago-ji?"

"Best stay in the saddle. Keep the quirt ready, Bren-ji. If we move, we move."

There was a small pause. The guard was undoubtedly Guild, undoubtedly had communications with a station somewhere inside the Atageini house, and was asking questions. He was likely not alone, either. It was not the atevi habit that he be out here alone, and one rather thought that in all the brush grown up against the wall, and overtopping it, there might be a gun aimed at them, as somewhere out there Banichi and Algini had moved into protective position.

"Nandi," the other side called back, this time in a tone of astonishment, "Lord Tatiseigi is bringing the car."

"No need for that," Cenedi said, "if you open the gates, nadi. We can meet him halfway."

There was another small delay. Then the gates yielded outward with a sullen creak of iron.

Bren drew a deep, deep breath. He asked, on its outflow: "Is this good, Jago-ji?"

And her amused answer: "Certainly better than the alternatives."

9

It was a well-maintained and level road, probably, Bren thought, the route by which the lord's vehicles, when used, would make the trip to the rural market or to the much-debated train station. Rain spatted down, windblown, and lightning lit the rain-pocked dirt under the mecheiti's feet.

And far in the distance two headlights gleamed, wending their way toward them.

Cajeiri and his two companions came up the column, taking advantage of the wider road, to reach the dowager.

"Is that my great-uncle, mani-ma?" Great-uncle, in the polite imprecision of ordinary usage, was easier and more intimate. He was great-uncle to Cajeiri's mother.

"It should be, indeed, young gentleman. Straighten your collar."

"Mani-ma." Cajeiri quickly adjusted the wildly-flying lace.

Bren did a little tidying of his own. And he was very conscious of the gun in his pocket. He was sure all their staff was on the alert. They had only the gatekeepers' word that the oncoming car represented a welcome at all.

And the guards had shut the gate behind them.

Further and further into the estate, as that car wended toward them, its headlights at times aimed off into shrubbery, at other times casting diffuse light down onto the road in front of them, at last close enough to spotlight the slanting rain-drops.

"Should there be any unanticipated trouble for us, great-grandson," the dowager said, speaking in the fortunate first-three-plural, "ride for the outer gate. Rely on Nawari. He will open it."

"Yes, mani-ma."

The motorcar was not the most modern and efficient, but certainly it sounded impressive. It had probably gone into service in Wilson's tenure as paidhi, and probably it had traveled less than the distance from Jackson to the north shore in all its years of operation: Bren reckoned so, knowing Tatiseigi's ways.

It blinded them with its lights as it rumbled up to them, and the mecheiti were far from happy with its racket. They milled about and the sky took that moment to add thunder to the mix.

The car braked. A door opened, and a guard bailed out and moved quickly, bringing a move of hands to weapons, but indeed, it was only to open the passenger door and to assist an elderly gentleman to exit into the rain.

Tatiseigi himself, grim old man, outlined in the headlights: he advanced a few paces, squinting and shading his eyes.

Ilisidi rode forward, keeping her mecheita under tight rein, its uncapped tusks a hazard to everyone it might encounter, no respecter of elderly lords.

" 'Sidi-ji," the old man said, frowning into the rain. "It is you."

"It certainly is," Ilisidi said sharply, "and a pretty mess the world is in, when your gates are shut and guarded by lethal devices, nandi. Is my rascal grandson here?"

"No," Tatiseigi said. "No. He has been, but he is not. But you are back from this gallivanting about the heavens. And is that half-grown boy my nephew?"

"One offers deepest respect, great-uncle." Cajeiri was doing very well controlling a restive and annoyed mecheita, which detested facing the lights and that rumbling engine. "Has there been news from my mother, great-uncle?"

Very damned precocious, for eight. But then, Cajeiri had had his great-grandmother for a tutor non-stop for two years, and lost no time seizing the moral initiative.

"No news," Tatiseigi said shortly, and somewhat rudely. One was not strictly obliged to courtesy with a forward child, and the old man was being rained upon. "Come to the hall for questions. Come to the hall. The deluge is coming. You might ride with me, 'Sidi-ji."

"Too much effort to get down and get in and get out," Ilisidi said. "These old bones prefer a short, painful ride. But a glass of brandy and supper would come very welcome when we arrive, not to mention a warm bath, Tati-ji."

"Then come ahead. Both are available. Is that the paidhi with you?"

"It is, nandi," Bren said for himself.

"Instigator of this mess," Tatiseigi muttered, like a curse, and turned away, headed for his car.

So. It was certainly clear where he stood, and abundantly clear, too, the paidhi could stand out in the oncoming rain for all Tatiseigi cared, but at least Tatiseigi did not exclude him from the invitation ... whatever his next intentions.

"He is old," Jago said, not that it moderated the old man's discourtesy. The old had license, and some used that license freely.

"He is justified," Bren said in a low voice. "He is completely justified, as far as things on the ground go, Jago-ji. One fears there is no remedy for his opinion except our setting things back in place."

Not mentioning there was no particular reluctance to commit assassination under one's own roof.

Right now they had only Taiben's advice, predicated on Taiben's devotedly favorable opinion of the fallen regime. This ... this would be the less pleasing side of the matter. Especially as regarded the paidhi-aiji and his influence.

Tatiseigi had gotten in. The car awkwardly executed a turn, mangling a shrub in the process, and lumbered off down the road.

"I wish to try to convince this gentleman, Jago-ji. I wonder if I can do it."

"Easier to move a mountain," was Jago's grim judgement. The man was notorious in the senate and elsewhere as the stiffest-necked, most hidebound lord in the west.

"We shall get the truth from this lord at least," he said. "And if it should be a hard truth, so much the better for my pursuing it here, under the dowager's auspices. I doubt he will poison me in her company."

"One believes she would take strong offense," Jago said, not at her happiest. "One hopes this is the case, Bren-ji."

"Be easy, nadi, no matter what he says to me. I shall be glad to hear anything the lord wants to say to me, no matter how insulting, no matter how wrong. How else shall I understand what people think?"

"Indeed," Jago muttered, not happy with the notion. "The same with his staff, nandi. We shall learn what we can, and politely tolerate what we would never tolerate. Shall we tell others of our Guild, if they ask, the things we have seen, the reasons for our actions?"

It was worth not a moment of consideration. "Yes," he said. It was what they had to do, ultimately, and the Guild on Tatiseigi's staff would ask those who had dealt with them. The Guild in Shejidan would need to know, above all else, and they would gather information on a situation—they would constantly gather information, and it needed to be consistent at every level.

They followed the car, no more rapidly than they had formerly ridden, and over the second hill the house itself came into view, lights gleaming through the rain.

House: fortress, rather, not quite in the sense that Malguri was a fortress, of a much older origin; but the Atageini stronghold, Tirnamardi, was a white limestone sprawl of wings and towers, some of which might have snipers at the windows, in such anxious times. The building dated from the age of gunpowder, and even had a cannon or two about the premises, which, he had heard, still fired on festive occasions, and once in the last thirty years, in a territorial dispute with Taiben, making a point, if doing harm only to a tree or two.

The old lord, disdaining modernity, had probably laid in a supply of cannonballs for the current crisis.

The place showed yellow lights from ornate windows, lights that cast rectangles on formally pruned shrubbery and, yes, a cobblestone approach, which the mecheiti intensely disliked under their pads. They protested, and Cajeiri's tended off toward the topiary hedge, intending to cross onto the clipped lawn. Jegari and Antaro rode between, and forestalled it quite deftly.

The car pulled up ahead of them. The great double doors of the house opened wide, and servants poured out onto the steps carrying electric lanterns, no floodlights installed, nothing to scar that historic facade. Gas lights had been the rule here until ten years ago, and the lord had, ever so reluctantly, modernized, only because the gas pipes had gotten too old to be safe, and electrification had been, the deciding point, cheaper to install than new gas pipes.

The lilies of the Atageini ran along the carved stone frame of the doorway atop those steps, tall, leafy stems in bas relief and graceful nodding blooms at the corners, fully defined. Lilies figured at intervals across the facade, and were—he had not noticed it—emblazoned on the black door of the car from which Tatiseigi emerged . . . parsimonious on technology, profligate with artists, so the reputation of the house was.

Damiri's ancestral home. But there was no news of

her, the old man had said. *Has been, but not.* Like a will of the wisp, Tabini's progress through the countryside.

Servants hurried to take charge of the mecheiti, who had generally formed predatory intentions against the lush, low topiary hedge. After one mistake, the servants singled out the leader as, not Ilisidi's, but Cenedi's. Once they had that increasingly cantankerous mecheita adequately under control from the ground, it was time for all the riders to secure the reins and get down.

Bren's mecheita had its own ambitions toward the nearby hedge. He whacked it hard with his quirt. His blow might have been a stray breeze, the tug at the rein a mere nuisance. Its mind was set; it was dark, it was thundering and raining, the mecheiti knew they were stopping and there should be food in the offing. And with the servants starting to lead the herd off, if he did not get down before they led the leader away, he would be swept ignominiously away, unable to get down before they stopped at the stables, which was not the entry to Lord Tatiseigi's house he wanted. He slipped his leg across the bow of the serpentine neck, grasped the saddle for safety, and slid down the towering side, holding onto the leathers as he went.

He at least kept his footing on the wet cobbles. Annoyed, his mecheita swung its head back toward him with a dangerous pass of those formidable lower-jaw tusks, then, seeing the herd moving, ignored him for a stolen mouthful of carefully-pruned hedge on the way. He defended the foliage with a whack of the quirt, risking his life and swatting it twice. It moved on.

Jago came hurrying back belatedly to rescue him from the responsibility, the house servants trying to shy other mecheiti off the hedges and only adding to the chaos. But the herd leader was clearly being quirted off into the dark, now. Bren got out of the path of two others, forced his legs to bear him, and felt Jago's hand on his arm, firm and steady.

Thunder echoed off the walls.

"Dry lodgings," Bren said breathlessly, attempting good cheer, but, God, he was done in. When he asked his limbs to walk, his knees and ankles were entirely unreliable under him. Too much sitting. Too much space travel. And earth's gravity, reminding him what he did weigh.

Ahead of them, Tatiseigi had gone up the lily-bordered steps with Ilisidi, into the warm electric lamplight inside. Staff had followed. So had Cajeiri, and his two. He climbed, Banichi and the rest of his staff ahead of him, Jago steering him, where no one would notice.

They were, thank God, shallow steps. He reached the top, followed the dowager and her bodyguard, and the three youngsters into a lighted foyer, so warm it stole his breath. The walls had a lily fresco that jogged a dazed memory hard—they were exactly, he realized, like the lilies of the Atageini in their apartment in the Bujavid. Lilies were prominent everywhere, in bronze on a cabinet, worked into the sconces, rendered in marble around the border of the floor. A visitor was to be aware at every instant under what roof he had come, and know how rich, how powerful this ancient clan was.

Inside, under the many-shadowed lights of the chandelier, there were the necessary greetings, Ilisidi to their host, the formal presentation of her great-grandson—and a scowl on Tatiseigi's face as he looked over the two young people attending the heir, young people *not,* evidently, to his taste.

"Taibeni," he said.

"In man'chi to the young lord, nandi," Ilisidi said sharply—if she and Tatiseigi had had fur, it would have bristled. "And under my protection."

"They will stay *with* the young lord," Tatiseigi said, "and only under those conditions, is it clear, nephew?"

"Yes, great-uncle."

None of them were fit for polite company, except the two Taibeni, who were at least clean. As for the rest of them, no amount of small fussing could order their clothing into anything like good grace. They, and their baggage, were dripping onto the marble. There were the traces of the dirty, oily truck, of fishy ice, of slobbering mecheiti, sweat, stove soot, forest leaves, and God knew what else, all tracked into this immaculate hall, along with mud from the rain. But Tatiseigi's mood had been, for him, warm, even cordial—until he spotted the two Taibeni. Encouraging, Bren said to himself, and noted that there was, unlike their bodyguards' martial look in this hall, no sign of weapons among the staff, some of which were uniformed Guild. House servants had arrived, too, looking at them from the inside stairs, sizing up the job in some dismay, one might imagine, though nothing showed on their faces.

"We shall accept responsibility for these young people," Ilisidi said. "But we stand in need of baths. Baths, Tati-ji. Even before brandy. Before supper. One does hope there will be supper."

"By all means." Appearing a little mollified, Tatiseigi made a movement of his hand. A servant ran up the marble stairs at high speed. There would be hot water only if the boilers were up. In places of this age, predating the human presence on the planet, boilers were the standard, and they did not operate at all hours. One would assume that if there was hot water, it would go first to the dowager.

Maids among the servants made deep bows, ready to escort the dowager and, odd woman in their party, Jago, upstairs.

"Young gentleman," Tatiseigi said to Cajeiri, "you will use my own bath." A signal honor, to a close kinsman, and with a slight disgust: "With your Taibeni. The rest of you, there is a bath backstairs."

That, in Bren's ears, certainly said where he belonged, in the mudroom, the bath the house would use coming in from the hunt. And Jago, who had matter-of-factly started to join the dowager in retreat, did not. She came back to him, and with Banichi, Tano, and Algini, formed part of a very unkempt and undigestible lump in the center of the immaculate foyer.

Tatiseigi scowled, and Bren gave a polite, measured bow—his staff knew. His staff understood it was not a case of saying the hell with it and taking the insult and the bath, which might or might not have hot water. He had to stand his ground or lose, here in the hall.

Jago, however, was not the only one of the women to stop. The dowager fixed the old reprobate with a chill glance.

"Ah," Tatiseigi said, as if he were the most forgetful old man in the world. "Yes. The paidhi."

"The Lord of the Heavens, Tati-ji, has prevented a swarm of foreigners from the far heavens descending on us in fully justified rage, a situation which we shall discuss in far greater detail over brandy. He has urgent business in the capital. But he has stopped here to pay you particular courtesy."

Lord Tatiseigi turned a glance in his direction, a very prickly sort of glance, and it was time to follow the dowager's statement in his own hall with a blithe and extremely courteous deference.

"With great appreciation, nandi," Bren said, "for the good will of your lordship, under threat from the Kadigidi, which I am certain you disdain. One is particularly sensible that certain persons would hold the paidhi's presence here as a statement of defiance, and certainly you run a risk, to open your doors to me. But I have every confidence the lord of the Atageini sets his own policy."

Tatiseigi's nostrils flared. A deep breath, a calculation in old, canny eyes. I know your infernal tricks, those eyes informed him. I know your flattery. My behavior will be my own, too.

But the respect was at least some face-saving to a lord who had, doubtless before his staff frequently, and loudly, cursed the paidhi and his human influence for years. Tatiseigi was so incredibly conservative and fa-

mously *kabiu* that the Kadigidi and the rebels in Shejidan themselves would hesitate to move against this
house, a pillar of atevi culture, a bulwark against the
very changes the rebellion publicly decried and wished
to undo.

"The paidhi," Tatiseigi said. "The white rooms, nand'
paidhi. Appropriate, one may say. There is a bath."

White being the paidhi's color. The neutral. The
houseless. The impartial interpreter and advisor.

Bren bowed, slightly more deeply than courtesy dictated. The old man's bitter insult was strangely comforting. Tatiseigi was angry with him. Tatiseigi had never
been pleased with him, not from the beginning. And he
argued, and made the dowager make a personal intervention for his welcome here ... politics, politics. And a
certain level of forthright detestation of him and the
Taibeni. Whatever the strength of that old bond between Tatiseigi and the dowager, it still held; humans
were still despised in this household, and on that frank
detestation his safety seemed more likely. Treachery did
not wear such evident resentment.

A manservant turned up to direct them up the stairs
and deal with details, and Banichi and Tano and Algini
went with him up the stairs, Jago going ahead of them to
resume company with the dowager and the maidser-
vant. Cajeiri and his young friends walked behind the
dowager, accompanied by another young man, and with
them, far in the lead, a old man who might be one of
Tatiseigi's bodyguard, but not wearing Guild leather, or
carrying evident weapons.

Not the most cordial welcome, as it had evolved, but
the room was lordly and the bath was glorious, fit for
ten atevi at once. The manservant turned certain taps
and went elsewhere to open up other lines in the antiquated system. Soon the pipe gurgled, then gave forth
an explosion of air, then an abundant flow of cold, then
warm, but never quite hot water gushing in with consid-

erable force, hot water either piped in from another boiler or stolen from the distant heating system, or put at a secondary priority to the dowager's and Cajeiri's baths, as some of these older houses could arrange. Whatever the water-source, it was warm, it was clean, there was soap, and the flow from the two gold-plated faucets was capable of filling such a huge bath in short order.

Within the time it took them to shake the worst of the dirt off onto the tiles, it had become a very deep bath, sufficient for a human to float and for the all gentlemen of his staff to get in at once, no formalities, no objections, no precedences here.

He was ineffably glad to be rid of the clothes he had worn since the hotel, garments which he surrendered to the servants with apology. Bruises showed in amazing number on his pale skin, polka dots from head to foot. It took a truly bad bruise to show on his atevi companions, but there were a few that did, not to mention small cuts and scrapes.

He scrubbed the dirt he could see, slipped off the tile seat that ran the circumference of the tub, and ducked his head completely underwater, surfaced in bliss and used the provided soap to work up a thick lather. His hair and body felt as if he had picked up passengers. If there were, he cast them adrift. A good deal of scrubbing finally got the lingering smell of fish off his hands . . . he swore he'd imagined it, since the train, but now he was absolutely convinced it was gone from him and from his companions, replaced by the strong herbal scent of old-fashioned handmade soap. He scrubbed days of dirt from under his nails, and ducked under to rinse, hair streaming about his shoulders, until lack of air made him surface.

"Good," Banichi said. "You have not drowned."

"Clean," he said with a sigh. Banichi at the moment was white-haired and spotted with lather, and bent

under the water to rinse, sending islands of froth scud-
ding on the waves Tano and Algini raised.

There was no deep conversation, none, what with the
lord's sharp-eared servants popping into and out of the
room, carrying this, bringing that, soap, towels, lotions,
every excuse and a hundred trips into the suite. But they
needed no conversation. Exhaustion ruled. His staff had
been as long out of the saddle as he had in their long
voyage, they were surely as sore as he was, and, given
their profession, they'd been at a level of tension and
alertness he could only imagine for the last number of
days. That alertness was still not quite abated, the quick
reaction, the dart of attention to a suspicious noise in
the bedroom. It was notable that, in Tatiseigi's oh, so
proper house, his staff hadn't allowed the house servants to come near their weapons or their personal baggage, which sat defiantly, not in the master bedroom, but
piled in the corner of the bath with them, in a dry spot
on the tiles, tides from the filled tub occasionally wash-
ing near it, despite repeated indignant assurances from
the staff that the baggage would be perfectly safe and
untouched in the bedroom.

Seeing where they had disposed their critical items,
Bren had put his gun there, too, with its ammunition,
with his computer, with his personal bag. So there
everything sat, sacrosanct, if in danger of water, still
muddy, but with that in their control, they knew nothing
could be added or subtracted. They felt ever so much
safer, collectively.

The laundry and cleaning staff, meanwhile, had a
major job on their hands, if they meant to restore rav-
aged clothes, scratched and rain-spattered leather, lace
that had long since lost its starch and its whiteness. He
had a change of clothes, but of coats he had only one, a
formal one, and his staff owned only the coats they
wore, which were in need of treatment they habitually
attended to themselves. God knew what he would do if

they had to ride with another load of frozen fish, or where he was going to get another pair of trousers his size—not to mention the boots, of which he had only the one pair, and those were in the hands of the servants. He had to muster something sufficiently respectable for this house, if they had to pay the courtesies and join Ilisidi downstairs, and oh, he dreaded that.

He shut his eyes. A shadow bent over him. A servant offered him a cordial glass on a tray.

He cast a brief, questioning look across the tub to Banichi, who blinked placidly, a signal Banichi judged it should be all right. He took it, then, but asked what it was. "Gija, nandi," the servant said.

Safe. No alkaloids. He nodded and sipped the fruit-tasting item, which had a considerable alcohol content.

This staff had never in their lives had to wonder whether there was an alkaloid in certain foodstuffs, since it provided only a nice tang for them. They might make such a mistake in utter innocence. It became his own concern, to eat and drink only things he could identify and keep to simple foods, if his own cook had not prepared the meal—and Bindanda was up on the station, sleeping peacefully in his own bed at this hour, one hoped.

He sipped the drink, arms on the tiled rim, and felt the slow fire spread down his throat, into his stomach, through his veins. The atevi notion of a small drink was a bit excessive for a human and he left a percentage in the glass, when he abandoned it on the edge.

God, he didn't want to move again. He didn't know how long the painkiller would hold out. He had no blisters, at least. He'd wondered, this last few hours.

"Do you intend to go down to dinner, nandi?" Banichi asked him.

"I heard no invitation," he said. And it was a question, now that he considered it, whether to let Ilisidi work her charm solo—she had it in abundance if she wished to use it—on her old flame, Tatiseigi. But food—food was one thing this house could provide them.

"One can easily plead indisposition," Banichi said. "Your staff is certainly ready to plead indisposition."

This from a man who could still lift him with one hand and fight his way out of the house unaided. But it was also the justified complaint of a staff who'd run long and hard. And a reminder that he, like the rest of them, might not be at his sharpest, going into an encounter where sharp wits would be everything.

"Nadi," he said to the seniormost servant, who had drifted into the bath to retrieve the glass, "one has the suspicion that we would intrude on the reunion of old association in the lower hall. One hesitates to place greater burdens on an already accommodating host, and we are, when all else is said, exhausted. Might we impose on the generosity of our host to request a small, private dinner here in our rooms, for me and my staff?"

"Certainly, nand' paidhi. One is warned the paidhi has special requirements."

"My staff will certainly appreciate the full range of offerings of the season," he said, "with profound thanks and compliments to the chef, for whatever courtesy he may extend to such an uninvited arrival, and one is certainly appreciative if he will consider my not inconsiderable difficulties of diet. One only asks modest accommodation, simple bread without seasonings for me, a simply grilled and salted meat of the season—such would be extraordinarily appreciated, nadi. A bottle of common brandy, nothing at all extraordinary. We shall all stand in debt of your lord. And there may be one other person sharing this meal, if she should come back."

A bow from the servant. He had kept his requests very limited, his instruction clear and easily handled, consideration for a chef already discommoded by an unexpected arrival—even Bindanda had his limits of endurance, and a lordly request from a human guest for particular favors and special cooking instructions would not meet with favor under this roof, he was quite sure.

He wished the servant staff, at least, to report the house guests as well-behaved.

There were robes provided—his reached the floor, and had to have the sleeves rolled up threefold, so that he looked like a child playing dress-up. His staff helped him with the sleeves, laughing the while, then wiped down their muddy baggage, using a pile of soft white towels, wiped down their coats, as well, and broke out the small store of leather treatment they carried in their gear, a comfortingly domestic task, the air filled with the sharp, oily smell of the bottle. Servants only gingerly offered to assist and provide cleaning cloths—the Guild rarely permitted another staff to touch their personal gear, which had an amazing array of small pockets and reinforced seams, not to mention outright weaponry and wires. Damp hair went up into queues, a stubbled human face benefitted by a shave and lotion, and over all, they presented a more civilized appearance by the time dinner arrived, borne by a procession of servants.

And the offering evidenced a chef in decent temper, or one severely instructed to maintain the dignity of the house. His requested meat of the season turned out to be a massive grilled fish, perfectly prepared, with a domed loaf of crusty hot bread, in a warm clay container to conserve the heat, with a very nice southern fruit wine in a sealed and sweating bottle. The meal for Banichi, Tano, and Algini was a savory game roast with gravy, with spiced vegetables, fresh greens of the season, and a lovely iced fruit dessert, which happily they all could share. Not to mention a very nice bottle of brandy, as if the great lord would possess anything less.

"I had thought Jago would join us by now, nadi," he said to Banichi.

"She likely will attend the dowager to dinner," Banichi said. "She will attempt to manage it, Cenedi permitting."

Jago would stand formal guard so their separate staff might have a report of the doings down there, Bren thought. A very good idea. The pocket coms were useless except as walkietalkies, in a place where there was no supporting network. They were obliged to sit ignorant, this rainy evening, of all that was happening elsewhere. The world which had been so tightly knit around them, themselves aware of every tic and twitch on any deck, around the clock, in every circumstance, was far away, floating in space and out of reach. Here, separated for an hour from Jago and the dowager, their world began to develop dark pockets of delayed or no information.

But it was also a *kabiu* house, and, on the side of Jago's continued attendance on the dowager, it was not particularly graceful for Jago to show up in their male society to sleep—he realized that the moment he thought of it. The old lord would not have male-female teams on his staff. That Jago slept with a human—the old lord would have a conniption, a whole litter of them, if what was likely common gossip in the capital turned out to be reality under his roof.

Prickly old man, devotedly maintaining a life in the previous century, a dragging anchor on change in the *aishidi'tat*—but not, evidently, following the Kadigidi, who only put on a show of old-fashioned attitudes. It was not so much that Tatiseigi had ever been deeply loyal to Tabini. It was that this old man would insist, if there was no Tabini, *he,* not his upstart neighbors the Kadigidi, had the right to govern the mainland, at least the central part of it, where people of his own opinion lived. It was centuries-old ambition, he had the picture quite clear—ancient ambition, and a grand-nephew who, in his day, might bring absolute power to the Atageini bloodline.

One could only hope Cajeiri did not regale his uncle at supper, downstairs tonight, with his opinions on humans and racing-cars.

But that was trouble Ilisidi would be there to handle—quite deftly, giving up nothing, the paidhi was sure.

And a delicate, wonderful fish, with bread dipped in salted oil, the light, iced wine, the like of which he had not tasted literally in years—all these things combined to persuade the paidhi that it was a very, very good thing he had stayed in his room. He was by no means qualified for diplomacy, tonight. If he had sat at the table downstairs he might have fallen asleep in the soup course, and a drink of wine would have completely finished him. As it was, he only tasted the wonderful dessert, and apologetically took to his bed, face down. Banichi, Tano, and Algini were, except for the dessert, of the same mind, and Tano and Algini bedded down together in the adjacent bedroom, while Banichi was about to take the guard post aside from the small foyer, where a cot could be let down.

"Share the bed," he said to Banichi. "I rattle around in it anyway, Banichi-ji." It was a very large mattress, even by atevi standards, and he probably could have fitted Tano and Algini in for good measure, if they had not already settled.

The fact was, it made him feel safe. Safe, and watched over, when the circumstances of the house were not as safe as they could wish. His head was reeling from the wine and the half glass of brandy. He wasn't up to conversation, or questions, and too stupid to judge reassurances. It was enough to know that Banichi was there, and he wished Jago were, too. Having her out of his sight and elsewhere in this place made him marginally anxious, but if trouble was to come tonight, he relied on Jago to make it heard from one end of the house to the other, and on Banichi and the rest to handle it, no matter the odds.

"I hope we have clothes tomorrow," he murmured.

The bed shook to Banichi's silent, short laugh. "One would expect they will have attended the laundry, Brenji. We have told the staff you would perhaps attend breakfast. With enough bleach, staff may even be able to restore the lace."

"Very good," he murmured. "Ever so good, Banichi-ji." And he went straight to sleep.

There were, indeed, clothes in the morning. The staff had even darned a small rip and drawn in the pulled threads where thorns and brush had snagged his coat. The shirt was bleached white, the modest lace was immaculately starched, his boots were polished, and even the white ribbon for his queue was washed and pressed despite its frays and snags, not to mention there were clean stockings and linen. Bren dressed himself as far as the shirt, but getting the hair braided properly and ribboned was a difficult operation even if he were less stiff.

"Here," Tano said. "Let me do it, nandi."

"Bren," he said decisively. "One wishes the staff would always call me more familiarly, in private, Tano-ji, if it would not distress you."

"It would by no means distress us," Tano said. And quick, deft plaiting secured the braid, with its ribbon. With a pat on his shoulder, Tano pronounced him fit for public appearance.

Staff's uniforms were fit, everything done to perfection, everyone feeling very much better, it was certain, after a night's sleep and clean clothing. Even the stiffness was somewhat abated this morning—it still warranted sitting a little gingerly, but not so much as before.

A servant appeared, with a formal message scroll, an invitation to breakfast on the terrace.

"I have no means to reply in kind," Bren answered the servant, "but advise your lord I shall be there, and I thank him for his gracious invitation."

Message cylinder. One small item he had neglected to pack. He'd left it—the mind jolted between worlds—in the bowl on the table in his quarters aboard *Phoenix*. Staff had packed it. It must be in his apartment on station. He was very loath to lose it.

And if he was taking up brain cells mourning lost personal items, he knew he was dodging thinking about what he was going to do downstairs. Nervous about the meeting? Oh, not a little. He had had no report yet from Jago. He caught himself pacing while Banichi restored a number of arcane items to his jacket's inner pockets and then to the hollow seam of his right boot.

Odd, he thought, as the small pile of strange objects diminished. As long as they'd been together, he'd never seen the whole array. It was curious, some of the pieces, though the uses for almost invisible wire were disturbing to think of.

A rap at the door. Jago's signal. Thank God. Algini let her in, and she had fared as well, clean and polished, as immaculate as she might walk the halls of the Bujavid.

"Nandi." A bow. "Nadiin."

"How did it go, Jago-ji?"

A slight glance at the ceiling, warning they might be overheard, far from surprising in a modern great house, and not, reasonably, in this one. "The conference last night was interesting," Jago said, her eyes sparkling. "Lord Tatiseigi, nadiin-ji, firmly believes the aiji is alive."

Indeed astonishing that Tatiseigi should say so, when he had everything to gain by hiding that belief—if he entertained personal ambitions of supplanting Tabini with a young and pliant Cajeiri. Maybe the old reprobate was in fact on the up and up. Maybe Ilisidi had gotten good behavior out of him.

Maybe there were motives he hadn't thought of.

Damn, it was altogether what he'd tried to avoid doing, immersing himself in possibilities before listening to what might be going on at the breakfast table.

"What did the dowager say to that supposition, Jago-ji?"

"That she would not tell Cajeiri until there is something certain."

"Cajeiri did not attend last night?"

"No. He dined in, with his staff, and Nawari."

He approved of Ilisidi's caution. Atevi or human, the

boy had feelings for his father and mother, and sending them soaring and then crashing on every tidbit of news was not good, not at all good for an adult, let alone an eight-year-old.

"Does our host say where Tabini-aiji is?" Banichi asked.

Jago put her hands in her jacket pockets, with another cautionary glance at the ceiling. "Nand' Tatiseigi maintains that the aiji sent Mercheson-paidhi ahead of him to Mogari-nai. He followed her route as far as the coast, then when it was attacked, returned to Taiben, then here."

Exactly as the Taibeni had said—except the detail about Tabini coming back to Tirnamardi.

"He and Damiri-daja stayed here three days, with certain staff, and then two staffers left, and all the rest of them left shortly after. There has been no word since. The aiji did not say where he was going, nadiin."

"One would not expect it," Banichi said. "Nor should we discuss our opinions of his whereabouts under this roof."

"Indeed," Jago said. They were speaking for eaves-droppers' consumption. Listening devices. Jago had confirmed it, and she might well be the one of the team carrying electronic means of knowing for sure. Tatiseigi favored antiquated lighting—but this said nothing about Guild members in the household, who, one reasonably presumed, would not use centuries-old equipment.

But this news—this news, if it was true and even if Tatiseigi only believed it to be true—this affected how they dealt with the old man, and the turns things might now take. He was keenly aware that he himself had become an issue, because of his advice to Tabini, and that it was likely a very hot issue under this roof. He personally had two choices, as he saw it—personally absorb the blame for everything Tabini had done, which left Tabini looking weak and reliant on bad advice—or vindicate himself, and thereby vindicate Tabini in the eyes of a lord who had voted against the space program, decried the shift in economy, hated modern technology, human culture, foreigners in general, and had taken a position in those regards, publicly and loudly, for years.

"Would it be possible," he said to his staff, putting the final touches on his lace cuffs, "rather than us trying to go personally to Shejidan, for us to urge members of nand' Tatiseigi's staff to go for us, and notify the Guild that we are intent on reaching them—even ask them to put a hold on Guild actions until we can arrive?"

It was a legal question, on one side of the coin. It was a question of lordly opinion on the other, as to whether Tatiseigi would honestly cooperate with an effort on Tabini's behalf—and, presumably, Damiri's.

"It would be technically possible," Banichi said, "legally possible. Tatiseigi certainly has standing in the question, as a relative."

"It might save lives," Tano said. "Through them, we might obtain a safe conduct for the paidhi. If he asked that, it might work."

"Saving our own lives, among others," Jago said.

"The Guild, debating its course of action," Banichi said, "is only doing so as a subterfuge. They wish not to support Murini as legitimate, not to support Tabini-aiji either, until questions are resolved. They will debate, at all hours of session, if someone has to stand and recite poetry to continue the flow of words—as I imagine they must have read several volumes in by now. All this is a way of remaining neutral, and it will be impossible for them to dissolve the session until they can vote one way or the other, if the question has been put—they will be reasonably anxious to find some resolution. The traitors have not persuaded them to end debate, and one suspects that now the Kadigidi themselves are urgently raising their offers and making promises they would not make otherwise, ceding portions of their authority to the Guild—which the Guild seems to have been wise enough to ignore. If we convince them to send for the paidhi to testify, this would represent a break of a sort ominous for the other side. They might try to do something about it, at very, very great risk of offending the Guild."

Bren asked, out of his own musings: "Might Tabini himself have asked them to stalemate, knowing he could not carry the vote until we came back?"

Banichi thought about that. So did all his staff. "It would certainly be a canny move," Banichi said. "His own staff has evidently taken a heavy strike. It would have impaired his ability to take direct action. Worse, he may have suspected treachery from the inside."

Who, possibly, would be a traitor on Tabini's staff? Bren asked himself, and dared not ask aloud, nor did Banichi's glance at the peripheries of the room encourage another question—not in the very house that was most suspect. If there had been treachery, he would lay odds it would never be one of the men who'd been with Tabini forever, not those Guild members born into his man'chi. No. It had to be someone who'd come into the household from outside. Staff acquisitions were rare.

Except—except most of Tabini's own original staff were male. A lady needed female staff; Ilisidi's preference for 'her young men' was the scandalous exception, since her husband's death, since she had achieved the status of aiji-dowager, and moved in staff from Malguri, and gave not a damn for propriety.

Damiri's staff, on the other hand, was Atageini and, proper to a lady, female. Staff from her own home, persons close to her, had come with her when she married Tabini . . . Bindanda, of his own staff, was one of the handful Tatiseigi had sent, and he knew it, and by now he was sure Bindanda knew he knew . . .

And, God, if only, he thought, if only the dish at Mogari-nai were up, and Bindanda were able to report to Tatiseigi his experiences directly—things might be much easier.

But as for spies in Tabini's house, and ways information might have flowed, and those by whom a lethal strike might have been organized—

This house, this province, had bordered the Kadigidi since medieval times. And who knew how many and how deep the cross-connections of all sorts that had grown between Atageini and Kadigidi, over centuries?

That certainly wasn't a topic he wanted to raise where they might be overheard.

It could mean Tatiseigi himself was in danger, a life the Kadigidi could take at any time, a life preserved from assassination in the specific hope he would serve as a magnet for intrigue, and maybe in the hope he might be a lure to draw Tabini in. Their coming here, their welcome, could tilt a delicate balance.

Tatseigi had not apparently suffered any Kadigidi attack here, even when Tabini had been here—if he had, it would surely have made conversation last night, in Jago's hearing. Which could also mean that the conspirators had not been able to get a spy back into this house from Shejidan in time to advise them of Tabini's presence here, before he was gone again.

Or—it could mean that the initial coup that took Tabini from power had Atageini fingerprints somewhere around the edges of it, and things were not so safe here as they seemed. He could not believe that Tatiseigi would have ceded political control to an upstart like Murini. He could not believe Lady Damiri herself would ever have betrayed Tabini—in the machimi, betrayal from a previously well-disposed spouse was absolutely classic, but she had no motive, and her man'chi to her great-uncle had always been more a case of exasperated tolerance—her parents were dead, her great-uncle was her clan head, and she had been his ward, which had put her in constant contention with the old man as she reached her majority—and her own more modern opinions.

Besides, Damiri being the mother of the heir, and

factually outstripping her uncle in power in the nation at large, she had no motive to strike at the very power she shared with Tabini ...

No motive, that was, unless she had taken violent offense at Tabini shipping their child out on a starship, to be thoroughly taught and indoctrinated by his conservative great-grandmother Ilisidi on the way.

Had Tabini even consulted her in that move? He would have believed Tabini would not act without her, on that matter, but—

Tatiseigi, on the other hand—dismissing treachery originating from Cajeiri's mother—Tatiseigi had a massive array of unsatisfied ambitions, and a family history of desire for rule. His surest path to power logically involved setting Cajeiri in power in Shejidan, and that was already the appointed succession, if Tabini only stayed in power, and it was nowhere in the picture if Murini established his own line. Tatiseigi's other concerns must involve keeping Damiri from supplanting him inside the clan—which she had never pressed to do, likely having no wish to be encumbered by clan affairs and a populace which shared its lord's attitudes toward technology.

As to whether Tabini's sending the boy off to space would have particularly alienated Tatiseigi, one had to consider that Tatiseigi had far rather see the boy under Ilisidi's conservative tutelage than in Tabini's, Tabini-aiji notoriously promoting one Bren Cameron to extravagant office, and accepting everything modern, with sudden extra-terrestrial ambitions.

But ... but ... but. Tatiseigi had hosted Tabini here since the overthrow, and hadn't killed him, or Damiri.

Which circled back to Damiri's reasons.

Atevi didn't marry for life, not often; but those two had always seemed so apt, so close and permanent a pair—and to have relinquished their son for a particularly formative couple of years ...

Never mind that the paidhi, who was now persona non grata most everywhere that had once approved him, if he read the signs, had also had a hand in the boy's teaching. Tatiseigi would have been happy enough believing Ilisidi was in charge of the boy—but not at all happy considering the boy was also under the paidhi's instruction.

Damn it. His stomach was upset. He didn't want to consider Cajeiri's mother among the suspects, but had to, for self-preservation, because it *was* absolutely classic; and considering where they lodged at the moment, he didn't want to suspect Tatiseigi of being in on it, or of lying when he said Tabini was alive.

Most likely suspect in any treason, Atageini servants: he certainly couldn't rule out one of Damiri's maids as the infiltrator, likely someone who was secretly Guild, and likely someone with some still more secret man'chi to the Kadigidi that had somehow deceived first Tatiseigi's, then Tabini's very canny staff, for years and years. That would have meant there had been a traitor on Tatiseigi's staff even before Murini, even back before the traitor Direiso's tenure over the Kadigidi . . . because assuredly nobody with a taint could get in afterward.

And if Tatiseigi had made one mistake—who knew but what the Kadigidi might have other allies under this roof at the moment? It was perfectly reasonable for the neighboring Kadigidi to try to infiltrate, and it was perfectly possible for them to have done it for centuries, all with a view to maneuvering the Atageini politically or gaining useful information at critical junctures. It went on all the time, to various degrees. It was simply the atevi way of coexisting with the neighbors and knowing what they were doing—usually not across so bitter a dividing line as Kadigidi and Atageini, but spies did get in, spies got caught, feuds sprang up and died down over time. The Atageini might be doing exactly the same thing over in Kadigidi territory. And, God, if he went on, he would be suspecting Ilisidi herself of fomenting the coup, which was utterly unlikely . . . nothing that would ever put Murini in power.

One could say the same, actually, about her ever putting Tatiseigi in power, when he thought of it that way.

And he, meanwhile, had to go to breakfast with the old scoundrel.

"We had better go," he said, taking a last look in the mirror.

"We shall watch the room, Bren-ji," Tano said.

"Should anything happen—"

Banichi cleared his throat and made several rapid handsigns. One of them, Bren knew, meant the team should go fast, probably in prearranged directions, with prearranged priorities. It was not the paidhi's business to ask.

Tatiseigi was his problem.

So down the hall they went, down the stairs, and to the lower-level balcony, where an Atageini servant directed them to a right turn, down through a dining room. The double doors at the end of the room were open, and Ilisidi and Tatiseigi were already at breakfast out there, with suitable attendance of bodyguards lined up formally along the end of the dining room . . . including, one could not but notice, young Antaro, meaning that Cajeiri was at breakfast, meaning that the younger set had, just like their elders, prudently seen to room security, one of them remaining behind to keep the premises secure . . . and meaning that uncle Tatiseigi was probably annoyed as hell.

Not fools, the two Taibeni youngsters, Bren said to himself. He approved, though he worried about youngsters who might think they could take action in crisis, and who might get themselves in the way of Guild action, trammeling up his bodyguard and Ilisidi's, who did know what they were doing.

But—in the light of his thoughts of the morning— might one think that uncle Tatiseigi had reasons to think *spies?*

He walked out the double doors, onto a terrace under morning sun, a painted railing of—what else?—

wrought-brass lilies, and a beautifully laid table, with a large bouquet of seasonal flowers, mostly mauve, with sprigs of evergreen, three in number, which said a wealth of things, if the paidhi had the skill to unravel it—he almost did, if he had had one more level of his brain to spare for wondering. Their host was there, Ilisidi, and Cajeiri, demanding instant attention.

He went to the empty chair, bowed slightly. "Apologies, nandiin, for my tardiness." Nods. He sat down. Servants moved to offer him eggs—those, he accepted, since they were in the shell, and free of sauces. Toast was perfectly fine, and oh, so good—and steaming tea, which came most welcome of all in the bracing chill.

"My compliments to the staff and the cook," he said, the proper courtesy, "who have done extravagantly hard work to make a visitor comfortable and safe."

"Indeed," Tatiseigi said. "We should hardly wish to poison a guest."

"We favor nand' Bren extremely," Cajeiri said sharply, out of turn, "and if someone poisoned him we would take it very ill."

Silent attention followed this pointed remark, not exactly what Bren would have chosen as a conversation opener.

"We thank the young gentleman," Bren said, "but we have no complaint at all. Lord Tatiseigi's hospitality is flawless."

Ilisidi snorted, but made no comment.

This was not going at all well. Bren reached for toast for his eggs, wondering what he had walked into, and dared not intervene in the tension between the dowager and her former—one thought, former—lover. If this was something like a domestic dispute in progress, a stray human was by no means welcome.

"The paidhi recognizes our delicate position," Tatiseigi said, "does he not? We have inconvenience on every border. Delicate alliances are rendered precarious by your arrival. Our very lives are at hazard, not to mention the interests of the central provinces, which we have carefully safeguarded."

"May one assume our grandson and his consort quitted this place under their host's invitation?"

"No such thing!" Tatiseigi banged down his spoon, and tea quivered in the cups. "Perverse woman!"

"One deems it an entirely fair question," Ilisidi said. She trisected a hardboiled egg with surgical precision, speared a portion and popped it into her mouth. "Under the circumstances of such extreme threat as you describe, one considers even the Atageini might tremble, with southern scoundrels in the ascendant, possessed of records and resources in the capital."

"Piffle," Tatiseigi snorted. "*You* will give them another half year of unity, 'Sidi-ji. You invigorate them by your presence. If you had frittered away any more time in the heavens they would have been at each others' throats."

"And the whole region would collapse in bloody ruin, which would by no means be to your advantage, Tati-ji."

"The Atageini need nothing from the outside. We never have!"

Another snort. "Nor does Malguri." Her own holding, which had equally primitive plumbing. "But our walls are ill-prepared for war, this century. One had rather not stand siege from airplanes."

"There would be no such siege. There would not have been, if you had stayed up in—wherever it is, up there."

"Oh, say on! Do you think the Kadigidi will go on flattering an old fool?"

"Disagreeable woman!"

"So you say throats will be cut in the capital, once the conspirators fall out. Granted, of course, granted, and they will. But whose throats, say. And where are the knives being sharpened? The southerners are the foreigners in these central regions, here at invitation. And which of the central provinces have bedded down closest with these southern fools? And who will do the throat-cutting when complacency takes hold? The Kadigidi will cry 'Foreigners on our land!' and be at them in short order. Will they not, Tati-ji? And *they* will rouse up the central provinces, and *they* will lead, taking an even firmer grip than they have now, while you have no daughter of your house married into *that* line, do you, Tati-ji?"

"Damn your nattering! This is breakfast, no time for business! You insult my table!"

"I merely point out—"

"Oh, point out and point out, do! Do you say we are fools who never saw these matters for ourselves!"

"Absolutely not. We have come under your roof, have we not? We had every confidence that the Atageini would not be swayed by Kadigidi blandishments. These are excellent preserves, Tati-ji."

Tatiseigi took a mouthful of eggs. "Empty flattery, and you mean not a word of it."

"Everyone can do with a little flattery, so long as it stays close to truth. You were always too wise for your neighbors. And remain so, we believe. Or we would not have come here first and foremost."

"Not first! You sojourned with the Taibeni!"

"Taiben lies between your land and the coast, Tati-ji, and always has. We received assistance, yes. Would you expect otherwise? But we came to you, having received a report—from the Taibeni—that you held out very bravely."

"Ha! One doubts those are the words."

"An approximation. In these times, Taiben respects you, and respects your borders. And joins you in disapprobation of your neighbors to the east."

"The Kadigidi are fools and troublemakers. And bed down with other fools. That whelp of Direiso's . . ."

"Murini."

". . . had the extreme effrontery to write a letter to this house, under his seal, attempting to enlist us."

Ilisidi pursed her lips, above the rim of her cup. "Did you pitch his man onto the step, Tati-ji?"

"I was very cordial, and temporized." Another spoonful of sauce. The paidhi ate very quietly, meanwhile, listening to all this extraordinary flow of confidences and not rattling so much as a cup. Cajeiri sat likewise quiet, those keen ears taking in everything, remarkable patience for a boy. Definitely, Bren thought, Cajeiri showed the qualities that created his father.

"So what was the gist of this impertinent letter?" Ilisidi asked.

"They wanted to use the Atageini name, can you imagine? We explained to these fools that since a daughter of this house is their quarry, we would either take command of the search and the campaign or we would tastefully abstain and make our demands clear if they should find her. For some reason they did not immediately cede the search to us, and seemed confused by our rebuke."

Ilisidi snorted, short, dark laughter. "Wicked man."

"This generation has no sense. Do you hear, great-grandnephew?"

"Sir." Cajeiri was caught with a mouthful of toast.

"Why are they fools?"

A rapid swallow. "Because the Atageini hate them, and they wrote a stupid letter, grand-uncle."

"Not the answer, boy. They are out of touch with *kabiu*. Their hearts are dead. They have lost touch with the earth, with the seasons. Like humans. They practice flower-arrangement as if that was the be-all, and conceive that I would help them."

"Nand' Bren understands *kabiu*," Cajeiri said, seizing on the casual slight, ignoring the central issue. "Much better than any Kadigidi."

"Does he?" Tatiseigi's pale gold eyes swung toward Bren, questioning, hostile, and Bren, wishing for invisibility, gave a little nod to the old lord. "Do you, paidhi?"

"Enough to know flower-arrangement is a manifestation of respect for the earth and the numbers of life, nandi, and that the mind and the heart surely improve with a deeper understanding of such issues." He had no wish at all to debate the old man, or to become the centerpiece of argument, but Cajeiri had taken him for a shield . . . hell, for a weapon. "As, for instance, your arrangement, the three sprigs, fortunate in number, honor yourself, the dowager, your young kinsman, the evergreen lasting in all seasons."

"Ha!" Tatiseigi said, caught out in his little grim humor. "He knows by rote. Like my great-grandnephew, who has doubtless read all the books. Where does one learn *kabiu* up in the ether of the heavens? Where are flowers, where are stones, where is the sun?"

"One sees the stars," Cajeiri said firmly. "Which behave together, all connected to each other and to us."

"Ha," Tatiseigi said again. A wonder if Tatiseigi knew or cared that the earth went around the sun. "Stars, indeed. Can you say your seasons, youngster? Or do you even remember them?"

"We could say the seasons when we were six!" Cajeiri said, leaning forward, and using that autocratic pronoun. "And we have also seen very many stars, nandi, and have a notebook with their numbers and their motions."

"And the numbers of the earth, young sir, and the numbers even of this room? Can you declare those?"

"The small wildflower in the arrangement, sir, is surely because of my mother, as if she were at the table, since lilies are not in season. But I see nothing here for my father. My great-grandmother, and nand' Bren, and I are at this table for him, fortunate three, and since Bren has no representation at all, perhaps the addition of a remembrance for him would have upset the favorable numbers of our breakfast—since you are at the table, and you clearly do not count yourself for my father, sir, which would make it four, without ameliora-

tion in the bouquet, which you did not add. Am I right,
mani-ma?"

The only trace of the child, that last appeal to his
great-grandmother, who arched her brows and pursed
her lips.

"Precocious boy!" Tatiseigi was annoyed, and would
not have taken such a rebuke from an adult.

"One has noted the arrangment," Ilisidi said, and no,
the paidhi could not have read that much of it, except
that lilies were out of season, and that in this *kabiu*
household nothing out of season would appear out of a
hothouse.

"Damned precocious. Is this disrespect your teaching, or the paidhi's?"

"I told you I would not neglect the graceful arts, Tati-ji."

"And courtesy? Where is respect of his elders?"

"I am very respectful, nandi," Cajeiri said. "And offer
regret for the patio."

The mecheita incident, with the wet cement.

"Precocious, I say!" It was not a compliment. Profile
stared at profile across the table, that Atageini jaw set
hard—on both sides of the equation.

"Where are my mother and my father, nandi? If you
know, we request you say."

It was the uncle who broke the stare and looked at Ilisidi, whose face was perfectly serene.

"Have we an answer to give the child, nandi?"

"No, we have not an answer. Your grandson offered
me none. Likely he failed to tell my niece, either. They
kited off into the night without warning or courtesy."

"Afoot, nandi? In a vehicle?"

"On mecheiti, as they came."

"Ha." Ilisidi nodded sagely.

Mecheiti meant an overland route, off the roads,
which made them hard to track by ordinary means.

Aircraft, on the other hand . . .

"For all I know," Tatiseigi said, "they crossed the corner of Kadigidi land and headed for the high hills."

Not impossible. But dangerous. Deadly dangerous.

"Excuse a question, nandi." Bren felt he needed to ask. "Have there been planes up?"

"Not over Atageini land, we assure you! Noisy contraptions. Not over our land."

So they could not track Tabini by that means, not close at hand, and that might have let him get into the hills—or even circle back into Taiben. He might have been there, and the people of Taiben would not have betrayed his presence, not until he had given personal consent, which their hasty passage might not have allowed.

It might be wise for Ilisidi and Cajeiri to set up here and let Tabini come to them, if he could—if they could keep the peace with Uncle Tatiseigi in the meanwhile. But there might be lives already at risk on the coast. A counter-revolution would be a delicate thing, easily crushed, unless something busied the Kadigidi very quickly, and stirred up maximum trouble.

The paidhi, in that regard, had a job to do. *He* had to overcome the Kadigidi arguments, had to prove that Tabini was not wrong to have relied on his advice. And if he could not convince this old man, who had accepted him under his roof, he had no chance at all in places where he might be less favorably regarded.

"One wishes cautiously to advance a plan of action, nandiin." Bren's throat constricted unexpectedly, and his hands sweated. "I feel I should not impose my presence here overlong. That I should go to the capital, to the Guild, to present the case for our mission, to say what we have found, to justify my advice to the aiji, which it seems I must do."

"Suicide," Ilisidi said sharply.

"*Is* there a justification for bad advice?" Tatiseigi retorted. "Is there any justification for this overthrow of *kabiu*, this intrusion of belching machines and smoke into our skies? Is there any justification for this general corruption of our traditions, setting our young people grasping after human toys, is there any justification for *television* and rushing across the country in an afternoon, scaring the game and ruining perfectly good land with racketing airports?"

There it was in a nutshell. Justifiable, considering all that atevi had already let slip, precariously close to forgetting certain imperatives. For a moment he saw no argument on his side at all. What had been done in the heavens, humans could have done.

He could have done. If he ever could have gotten into space without atevi industry behind him, and could not have had that without Tabini's strong backing, and that had been the beginning of all the changes, and the present trouble.

There was a chain of justification. Difficult as it was, the reasons were unavoidable, if egocentric—because there *was* no one but a person skilled in cross-species logic who could have seen the problem.

And it had taken a seven-year-old atevi prince to make the kyo believe their intentions.

"With the aiji-dowager's leave," he began, "I do wish to justify it, sir, and beg your indulgence to begin under this roof."

"No," Ilisidi said sharply. "You will never convince him. He is set against it. He is convinced I have lost my senses and soared off to the heavens with my great-grandson, intending to corrupt him and turn him human."

"Well?" Tatiseigi asked, with a jut of that Atageini jaw. "And you bring him back here with two ragamuffins from Taiben, no less—Taiben! No doubt they have poached in our woods, and now eye the household silver."

"I am Ragi," Cajeiri's higher voice said, "and you are my great-great-uncle, and great-grandmother is Malguri! And you should not speak badly of my father and my mother!"

There was a small, shocked silence.

"The world is changing," Ilisidi said. "Living things

do change, Tati-ji. Even the hills change. *Kabiu* itself moves slowly, but it does move, as the very earth moves. Baji-naji. There is always room to flex, or a thing *breaks,* Tati-ji."

Around the flank and uncomfortably up from behind. Tatiseigi looked disquieted, and very much out of sorts.

"Look at this boy," Ilisidi said, "half Atageini, and tell me there is no connection. He has your jaw, Tati-ji."

"Clearly!"

Ilisidi took up her napkin. "We shall discuss this without the boy."

"To be sure." Tatiseigi was still irate, but the thunder and the fury sank, a temporary lull, like a pause in a storm that had only had its initial run. "To be sure. Take the paidhi with you."

Tatiseigi laid aside his own napkin. Breakfast was over. There were courtesies, bows, as they rose. Bren had the notion he had just been in a war, and wished only to clear the area without complete disaster.

"Nand' Bren," Cajeiri said, and fixed him with an eye-level stare. That was all he said, just an acknowledgement of his presence, and the boy's disquiet, perhaps, at certain transactions.

"Nandi," he said, and let everyone including Tatiseigi precede him off the balcony, back into the hall. He was cold, chilled through. He was always cold at these open-air breakfasts. He walked out to collect his bodyguard and retraced his steps with them through the halls, with every confidence that they had heard everything that passed out there . . . staff on the next floor might have heard a good part of it.

Upstairs, then, and behind their own doors, where Tano and Algini had kept things safe and secure.

"It did not go well, nadiin-ji," he said, "but it was not disastrous. No one was assassinated."

Banichi thought it funny. He was less sure. His efforts to persuade Tatiseigi had gotten him nowhere, Ilisidi had some agenda of her own, or Tatiseigi had, and the boy, defending him, had annoyed the old man . . . all of which was predictible, now that he thought about it. He should not be glum about the situation—raw fear might be appropriate, but glumness was hardly warranted, when his companions had behaved exactly as they might be expected to behave.

Which argued, perhaps, that going into a critical debate with Cajeiri at hand was not the best choice.

Wind blew through open windows, wind stirring the gauzy inner draperies, and carrying all the scents of the earth.

He had had a night's sleep, even a decent night's sleep. But when he tried to think about what to say to Lord Tatiseigi, if he could get a quiet meeting, it completely refused to take shape in his brain, as if that was not what he ought to be thinking about, as if the whole world was pulling at his sleeve, wanting his attention, refusing to deal logically, or at least, refusing to deal in human logic. He wanted to throw himself into bed, pull the covers up around his ears and lie there getting warm and digesting a too-large breakfast—desire for the tastes had led him to overindulge, and he had eaten to appear uninvolved while the barbs flew—but the desire for sleep was not a desire for sleep. He knew himself, that the instant his head hit the pillows he would start processing the things he had heard, sifting them for every nuance, regretting things not said, and things said. It was his job to parse such things: something in what the dowager and Tatiseigi had said, or something he had picked up elsewhere this morning or last night, had begun to make a nest in his subconscious. If he went to bed, he would have to undress, to save the clothes; if he delayed to undress, he might lose the thought. And right now the safest place for him was a large, well-padded chair in the sitting area, and not letting those subconscious thoughts surface and distract him from what he, dammit, needed to think about. It could be as foreign to the problem as a remembrance of something Barb had said. He began to wonder if it was something he had eaten or drunk, the somnolence was so urgent, so absolutely pressing.

He sat, finding warmth in the well-padded chair, attempted to distract himself with a view of the land and sky outside, all veiled in blowing gauze, but he kept seeing the metal and plastics of the ship. He kept thinking of Jase, who had a food-short population on his hands, and tanks to get into operation, and who would have loved half of the breakfast he had just had. Of Barb. Of Toby, at the wheel of his boat. Crack of sails in a stiff breeze.

Shuttle runway. Wheels down.

He had done precious little good down there, except to serve as a lightning rod for Tatiseigi's irritations. Or possibly to provoke them. He had no idea whether Tatiseigi had included him in the breakfast of his own volition, or whether Ilisidi had insisted on it to annoy the old man.

Or to have a lightning-rod handy, to prevent topics being raised which *she* had no wish to discuss at the moment.

Should he send a message to the old man, request an audience independent of Ilisidi? He had not the least idea what to do now. He heard his staff talking quietly in the bedroom. He supposed that was a debrief and a strategy session. He ought to participate. He ought to have a brilliant idea what to do from here, and whether he ought to stay here, and urge the dowager to stay here, where there was at least reasonable protection— or whether he should go to Shejidan and present the untried arguments before Banichi's Guild.

He knew what he had rather *not* do—which was to go to Shejidan. But it was fear that held that opinion. Logic might dictate otherwise, if he could summon the will to think straight.

Too much breakfast, too much comfort here.

He had to talk to his staff, once they'd had a chance to talk to everyone else, once Ilisidi had a chance, canny as she was, to figure what Tatiseigi knew or didn't know. He was dimbrained because he had an adrenaline charge shoving his brain into all-out effort, he had a critical lack of information, and every instinct was telling him not to press Tatiseigi too hard, that there was a current flowing between Tatiseigi and Ilisidi that was critical, that he should not interrupt.

Waiting. Waiting was the very devil.

10

He must have dozed, sitting there in the armchair, tucked up against the slight cool breeze from the open window. He came awake with the passage of a shadow between him and the light, and saw Banichi standing between him and the windows. Jago was with him. Tano and Algini were behind them.

"Nadiin-ji?" He sorted his wits for relevant recent information and remembered breakfast, and a post-breakfast conference in progress among his staff.

"We have a plan, Bren-ji."

Wonderful. A plan. He so much wanted a plan. He had failed to come up with one, and he was sure Banichi's was going to involve his staff doing something that would risk their lives.

He mustered the wit and fortitude to say no to those gathered, earnest faces.

"Sit down, please, nadiin." He wanted a quiet conference, one in which they did not cut out his sunlight, or loom over him with superior force. "One hopes it by no means involves your going to Sheijidan without me."

Not a twitch. "No, Bren-ji." From Banichi. "It involves Lord Tatiseigi's men going there."

"One would hardly count on his assisting us."

"For the dowager's sake," Jago said. "One believes he would order it for her. Not for us, never for us, but possibly for her."

"In Shejidan," Tano said, "his messengers can enter the Guild Hall reasonably unremarked, under far less threat of hostile measures from the Kadigidi. And they can present the facts of the heir's claim."

"But to claim the succession—that would seem as if the Atageini think Tabini is dead, nadiin-ji." He was far from sure that turning their support from Tabini to Cajeiri was a good idea. "And would it not look as if we support that theory?"

"Much as if," Banichi allowed. "But if Atageini representatives can get the debate in the Guild centered on that topic, bypassing all the suspended question of their support for Tabini-aiji, and if, through that debate, we can inject evidence backing Tabini-aiji's policies, there is some hope of presenting the report. By that means, the Atageini might prepare Guild support for the aiji's position should he appear."

His mind hared off in twenty different directions at once, Tabini's safety, Tabini's reaction, even Tabini's sense of betrayal if he should appear to support Cajeiri's claim.

Most of all, the volatile controversy of his own influence in the administration . . . because his influence was going to be the sticking-point in any presentation a third party made to the Guild regarding the mission that had cost the *aishidi'tat* so much. From the atevi end of the telescope, thinking what the Atageini might say, he saw the situation much more clearly. Very honest people viewed him as a long-standing and pernicious influence on Tabini-aiji, a human, an interloper whose advice was primarily responsible for all the difficulties the *aishidi'tat* was in now. Very honest people had reasons to support some other authority, no matter how objectionable on all other grounds.

Small wonder he hadn't been able to persuade his brain to come up with the right words: *he* was the problem, and nobody he intended to speak to was going to hear him except through a filter that said all his past advice had been wrong, no matter how well-intentioned. *That* was what his better sense was trying to tell him. It was why the Guild hadn't backed Tabini against this insurgency—and why in hell would it then listen to the paidhi's arguments?

He drew a deep breath, facing these unpleasant truths. "But if all they hear, nadiin, is that I am here with the heir, what can they think? And if they cannot be made to understand that our judgement regarding the space program was correct and cannot be assured that their sacrifice was necessary—I am not sure Cajeiri will win any case with your Guild or with the legislature. If they cast Tabini aside because they detest my influence—where has *Cajeiri* been, but with me, for the last two years?"

"The paidhi has many allies," Tano said staunchly, "who hold a very different opinion of his actions. People will rise to support us, nandi. I have no doubt. They only want to choose the right moment."

Certainly he had faithful staff, in his apartment in the Bujavid—who were likely dispossessed, if not worse. He had a secretarial staff, an entire office in Shejidan, loyal, gentle people who might have lost their jobs and found it precious hard to find others—if not worse. And he could not imagine that band of dedicated individuals facing down Tasigin assassins with a stack of contradictory records and soft protestations about right and reason and cross-species logic.

"I am not so sanguine about their chances of surviving the present troubles," he said. "And if I cannot persuade Lord Tatiseigi—or even persuade him to listen to me—"

About the mission to Reunion, no chance. Not as things now stood.

But about the boy's rights, and therefore Tatiseigi's rights, and the need to advance them forcefully . . .

"He would want the boy to make that claim, would he not, nadiin-ji?"

"Exactly so," Banichi said. "Exactly so, Bren-ji."

"Endangering him."

"He is already in danger, in danger, and without Guild protection, excepting those of us under this roof."

"And what is there to support him, Banichi-ji?"

"The backing of Lord Tatiseigi, and a letter from the paidhi-aiji," Banichi said, with an uncharacteristic leap of faith. Faith placed in *him,* God help them all.

And if the plight of his long-suffering on-world staff was a burden on his heart, that earnest look from Banichi, of all people, lowered a crushing, overwhelming weight onto his shoulders.

"What could one reasonably say in a letter to convince those who have been injured by my advice, Banichi-ji? I hoped to speak to Lord Tatiseigi after breakfast. I could not even secure that audience."

"The dowager had her own notions," Jago said, "and did not permit it."

Did that mean as much as he thought it could mean?

"Why not?"

"She is the one Tatiseigi knows, and the one who should deal with him," Jago said. "Which is probably prudent, nadi-ji."

"But if I cannot persuade him—"

"Never, when the matter at issue is whether Ilisidi is on his side. That is personal, nandi, and your arguments can have no effect there."

An old liaison—one almost thought love affair, humanly speaking, but of course it wasn't that. Man'chi was tangled in it, who could trust whom, who would tell the truth, and who might be lying, and Ilisidi outranked the paidhi—his opinion could not break ranks with hers. Not in the way atevi nerves were wired.

"You mean I shall have no chance to convince him, nadiin-ji?"

"She will," Jago said. "She has done a great deal to convince him already. She is *here,* Bren-ji."

Blind human, that was to say. At times the ground he thought he knew developed deep chasms of atevi logic. Stay out of it, their nerves were telling them, don't try to intervene in this mine field. And back the boy to be aiji, in his father's place.

"If I back—" he began to say, the rest of the sentence being, Cajeiri as aiji—would it not betray Tabini? But he stopped there: the whole point of what they were saying was that the paidhi could *not* break ranks and set himself forward, ahead of the dowager, ahead of Tatiseigi, even ahead of Cajeiri, not in something that regarded the man'chi of atevi toward their leadership.

"I have records. I have brought images, in my computer, to support my argument. If I only send them and did not appear myself, nadiin-ji, people can say these images are only television. I can provide the images to the Atageini—if there is a computer in this house. But I should present them in Shejidan. I do not want to betray Tabini by supporting another aiji, even his son. I do not want to lose the argument in Shejidan, either. Most of all, I do not want to see the kyo show up here and find only humans to answer for this planet, when they have not done outstandingly well at communicating with them in the first place."

"There is a proverb in our Guild," Banichi said in his low voice. "One Assassin is enough. One assassin can overturn the vote and the good will of thousands. We are not speaking of the whole population. We are speaking of skilled attack. You should not go anywhere, until there is a request you go and an escort to make it likely you will arrive. Let them call you to speak. As they will. We have every confidence in them, if not in the higher powers of the government."

"Speed is critical in getting Tatiseigi to send any messengers he may send before the Guild," Tano said . . . always deferring to Banichi and Jago, but since his long stay in command of the stationside household, having an opinion of his own. "The longer the delay, the more likely the Kadigidi will get wind of our presence and attack us here."

"No question," Algini said.

"Then if the Atageini messengers should go, nadiin-ji," Bren said. The words had a hollow, ominous sound in his own ears. "If they do go, and if there is any stir about it, the Kadigidi will certainly know where we are, and they will blame Lord Tatiseigi publicly for sheltering us. Certainly they will know we are under this roof when Atageini messengers appear in Shejidan. And, forgive me, how long will Lord Tatiseigi remain well-disposed to our cause once Kadigidi assassins blow more holes in the lily frescoes?"

Laughter, from the grimmest of professions. It was a notorious event. "Such a move will not win the Kadigidi favor with him," Jago said.

"But can this house withstand a direct attack, nadiin-ji? This is not Malguri."

"It has a few more defenses than seems," Banichi said. Electronics, Banichi implied. Electronics. In this most *kabiu* of households. It would be a surprise to him. "More downstairs than up—the security in this room is alarmingly thin."

"Cenedi suggests we move out and spare us finding out the answers to these questions," Jago said. "It is not, he says, in our interests that the Kadigidi and the Atageini go at each others' throats yet. But the dowager strongly resists this notion and wishes to provoke Guild notice and to insist on a hearing. *She* assuredly wishes to get you before the Guild, nandi."

Forestalling him, at breakfast. Keeping the argument all on her terms.

"One would hesitate to question the dowager's grasp of politics," Bren said ruefully, which was the very truth, and his heart felt the chill of old experience with the dowager and her willingness to charge downhill. If Ilisidi was making her move, just in being here, and Cenedi was trying to advise against it, the fat was already in the fire, so to speak, and the Kadigidi would move. Fast.

"Perhaps I should prepare a convincing letter," he

said, "so we can offer it, at least, if this mission is in fact to go to the Guild."

"If the paidhi sees fit," Jago said, and Banichi said:

"A very good idea. A letter at least to confirm the dowager's assertions."

A letter which must be written by hand, not printed out from a computer: a computer-written message was not *kabiu* on so formal an occasion as a Guild hearing, even if the house had the requisite printer, and he would not offend this house by asking.

But writing it out first and copying it fair would save time, ink and paper . . . granted they could lay hands on paper. Granted only they could persuade the Atageini to carry it.

"I shall do it," he said, committing himself to the course of action. "I shall need pen, paper and the wax-jack. I shall provide Tatiseigi a copy, for his own reading. Might there be tea?"

They scattered on their various missions and he opened up his computer and stared at a blank screen.

Shut his eyes a moment, seeing steel corridors. Seeing forest paths where they had ridden. So many realities.

Then:

The paidhi-aiji to the honored members of the Assassins' Guild.

That much was easy. No reference to his lordly title in the heavens, just the ordinary one, the one he lived by, and hoped to continue to live by.

One is privileged to report to this august body that the aiji-dowager's mission to the distant station succeeded in every point. This mission prevented a powerful space-borne nation, neither atevi nor human, from advancing against this world with deadly force in its mistaken notions of offense emanating from here. By the extreme effort and sacrifice of the aishidi'tat in organizing this mission, and also thanks to the foresight of Tabini-aiji in sending the aiji-dowager as a high emissary on this mis-

sion, all matters have carried well. These foreigners, grievously provoked by human exploration in their territory, have been considerably mollified by negotiation with the aiji's close relatives and now accept the explanation advanced by the aiji-dowager that the binding authority of the world is indisputably atevi, and that atevi will not permit further provocations against them. More, we have removed the human authority responsible for this provocation and placed them under the authority of the atevi space station . . .

Atevi space station. *That* was a reach. But it was the situation Tabini insisted on, and had been fairly well on his way to having, before this catastrophe.

. . . making it absolutely essential that atevi shuttles maintain regular flights, to keep a firm hand on that situation, and to maintain atevi authority.

In the other matter, understanding that a wise and enlightened ruler sits in command of the situation here, namely Tabini-aiji, these new foreigners have settled a preliminary peace with the aishidi'tat, a situation which gives the aishidi'tat great advantage over other claimants to authority in the heavens, if the aishidi'tat will seize this opportunity and exert this new authority. The paidhi-aiji is ready to appear before the Guild to render a full account of these complex events, in the name of the aiji-dowager and the heir, and to present visual and documentary proofs of all events. Meanwhile, one urgently requests the Guild support the dowager, the heir, and the reputation of Tabini-aiji, by whose foresight peace was achieved, and on which peace now depends.

A rare moment of brilliance, if he did say so himself. Occasionally the words were just there, ready to spring out.

At such moments of overwhelming self-confidence— well to ask an impartial observer. He called Jago, who surveyed it both for felicity and persuasion.

"Excellent," she said, "excellently worded, nandi."

"I shall write it out," he said, and carefully did so, in

his most formal script, provided a reading copy for Lord Tatiseigi, a second one for the dowager, and affixed the paidhi's seal in wax to the actual missive. He weighed it in his hand, looked at the computer screen to assure himself that he had nowhere hinted the darker thoughts of his heart, such as the *damnable paralysis of your Guild* or *your general policy, which arises from willful ignorance, corruption, and scientific illiteracy of certain members*. He thought those thoughts. God, he thought them, with such force it seemed impossible they had not branded themselves on the paper in his own handwriting.

But he had been politic throughout. He had flattered. He had told the minimal truth. He had promised—literally—the sun, the moon, and the stars, if they would come to their senses and take authority. The alternatives were not pretty . . . three bands of humans trying to deal with the aliens they had thus far only antagonized.

He brought the letter and the copies to Jago, watched her take them out the door, and let go a deep breath, wishing every syllable had been perfect, which now he knew was not the case, wishing he had been brilliant, which he was completely dubious was the case, wishing he could miraculously transport himself to the dowager's vicinity to watch her reaction and answer questions; and to Tatiseigi's, after that.

And there was the question, the very good question, whether, even if the dowager wished it, the letter would ever get past Tatiseigi's grounds. The dowager would have to approve it before the next copy went to Tatiseigi, and Tatiseigi would have to approve it to get it out the door.

He walked to the open window, and gazed out on the cultivated fields, the broad expanses of grassland that lay behind the very ineffective walls of the estate.

Beyond those fields, barring the horizon, rose wooded hills; and beyond them the eye could find a faint haze where a range of snow-covered mountains would stand, if the mountains were being cooperative today. Today a stranger who didn't know such mountains existed would assume that haze was sky, the continent unbarriered. He would think there was no split between east and west.

Would history not have been different, if that were the case? Would history not have rolled over the human landing on this world, if that were the case? The western atevi were an inquisitive progressive lot, exceedingly prone to investigate, to take an oddity in the hand and look at it carefully. Humans had landed on Mospheira, and had ended up on the mainland, briefly. The mainland atevi, the westerners, had been astonishingly outgoing and accepting . . . until the war. A landing on the other end of the continent—just a little rotation of the world away—and there would have been no human presence left on the planet, in very short order. Ilisidi's people, Ilisidi's neighbors' forebears, would have obliterated any human landing, no great number of questions asked.

That would have kept humans in space, giving no alternative but the ship, and no leadership or authority but the captains who had insisted on going out and exploring further, ostensibly hunting some vantage from which they could figure out where they were—but in fact poking and prodding among likely near stars for further and further expansion of human presence, greater and easier resources.

They'd have touched off the kyo sooner or later, and sooner or later gotten the kyo here with blood in their eye . . . to the planet's detriment. And the planet would never have known what hit it or why—if those mountains had not existed, if those mountains had not divided eastern atevi from western and let humans get a safe foothold down here.

Curious thought, that humans might have endangered the world—but the humans down here were the ones who might prevent that danger from coming down on the world.

He had done his best, hadn't he? No matter it had done damage, it had not done the ultimate damage—had not let war come on the world unawares.

And not all the changes were harmful.

Thanks to his predecessor in the paidhi's office, and thanks to him, as well, planes had fairly recently rendered that divide much more crossable. Planes had united the two halves of the continent across that mountain divide that rail had found all but insurpassable, and brought the east into the politics of the west . . . which had brought benefits of peace, of cooperation, a flowering of art, a cross-pollination of atevi cultures. In her youth, Ilisidi had been an exotic foreigner herself, marrying the aiji of the west, arriving by train in what had been, half a century ago, an arduous and epic rail journey.

But darker politics had ridden those rails, too, before Ilisidi's day. Politics, and a rising resentment of the formation of the aishidi'tat in the west, eastern politics that had once seen that railroad as a means of war against the west, forging an alliance with a few conservative western powers like the Atageini and the Kadigidi, jealous of the aiji's authority, and most of all opposing a lingering human influence on the mainland, wanting even to take back Mospheira and obliterate human presence there. The east had missed the start of the War of the Landing—and the very knowledge the east might be coming in had led to the war-weary west and the human survivors entering negotiations before things flew out of control. The threat of eastern intervention had led to the ceding of Mospheira to humans and the relocation of the indigenous people of Mospheira to the coast, all before the east could get its chance to get in, and before it could find an excuse to ratchet up the war again.

So war and technology that sent trains across the mountains made peace among atevi, unachievable before there were humans to detest and decry. And from that time there had been paidhiin, trying to comply with the Treaty, leaking technology off Mospheira ever so slowly. Eventually the rail link had led to Ilisidi, an eastern consort for a western aiji. And the modern aishidi'tat was born.

Ilisidi's Malguri lay beyond that deceptive haze, still a three hour flight away . . . but only a three hour flight away, which he had made, oh, under varied circumstances, never the train trip. The distance was still difficult—on today's scale.

And the plainest fact of atevi politics was that the continental divide was still a political watershed as well as a geological one. There were still two very different atevi opinions, and because there was advantage to be had in turmoil, the Kadigidi and the Atageini, sitting in the heart of the west, still played politics with Ilisidi, the eastern consort, who chaperoned a half-Atageini heir of her own bloodline. And lately the Kadigidi had played even stranger politics by allying with south-coastal atevi, namely the Taisigin. And now there was another move, and a Kadigidi claimed to be aiji.

Only over his own dead body . . . granted numerous people would happily arrange that.

God, there was so much water under the bridge. Planets were so complicated, compared to the steel worlds he'd lived in the last few years.

And why did he think of such things? When his mind went into involuntary fugue, there was, damn it all, something bubbling down in the depths of his consciousness that was trying to surface, something that might be urgent, something that had been bothering him ever since breakfast, and he had sent that letter out, to what fate he now had no way of dictating.

For one thing, that landscape out there drew his mind down to planetary scale, down to the distances riders and trucks and trains could cover in a day, and reminded him how ordinary folk thought, and why they thought that way.

That view reminded him of the resources Tabini had had when, leaving here, one supposed he had headed for deeper cover, taking his Atageini wife with him.

But without an airplane or extraordinary determination with the cross-continental train, he could not have gotten much beyond those hills—nor would he have had much motive to exit the west, where he had some allies. In the east, yes, as the grandson of the lady of Malguri, he did have some cachet—but feuds predominated in that district and no outsider could exert any authority. No. Tabini would not lean to Ilisidi's side of the family. Tabini—

Tabini was waiting. Tabini *expected* the ship to come back. Tabini, once he heard of their presence on the planet, would not sit idly by and wait . . .

Not Tabini. No. It wasn't in his character.

A little stir near the door drew his attention. Algini had come to sit near it, just waiting, perhaps resting, in those odd moments that his staff caught rest.

Or watching him. Wondering why the paidhi stood staring out the window.

Everything became part of the fugue. Even the least talkative member of his bodyguard. Even a room in which they still dared not speak too much truth.

"Tell me," he said, to Algini's golden, impassive gaze. "If the aiji were to hear of our presence and come in unexpectedly, could he arrive safely in this house, 'Gini-ji? And would there be prearranged signals between him and the staff that we also should learn—if they exist?"

Algini was as rare with his smiles as with his words, and this smile was rarer still, a gentle one. "Your staff has indeed asked this question of the household," Algini said, managing not to make the paidhi feel too much the fool. "This staff will not confide to us any such signals, if they exist. They ask us to allow them to deal with any untoward event."

So much for complete trust.

"Does Damiri-daja know them, and is there a possibility she knows them and has not told Tabini-aiji?"

"One can by no means say," Algini said. "But we have considered that possibility, too."

A small look at the ceiling, at the peripheries, thinking of bugs, and a sober look back at Algini. "And the message, 'Gini-ji? Have you a clue how the dowager has heard it?"

"We have given the paidhi's message to Cenedi, and it may by now have passed into Lord Tatiseigi's hands, possibly further, into the hands of his staff. The rest depends on whether the messengers will go, and whether they will go by rail, which will bring them to Shejidan very quickly, or whether they will go in stealth, nandi. We cannot say." It was Algini's habit to answer only the immediate question. But he added: "Cenedi has confidence in this household's skill, if not in their equipment being up to date."

The dowager had more credit with Tatiseigi than he did. That was for very certain.

But it was worth remembering that Cenedi himself would have visited this house when Ilisidi had been, for extended periods, a guest, perhaps a lover, of the Atageini lord . . . possibly even while her husband was alive, if certain nefarious whispers were true, in the days after the birth of her son and during the dark days when the whole nation had tottered in uncertainty and suspicion, as to whether the eastern consort, namely Ilisidi, would steal away the heir and go to her own stronghold in Malguri to attempt to raise a rival power. In those days, the legislature in Shejidan had seen it as, yes, extremely possible that Ilisidi herself had come to the Atageini, gathering support among the more conservative central lords to seize power in Shejidan.

Instead, her son Valasi had grown up as a Ragi lord, had ruled with a hard hand. Valasi had died, not as an old man—some blamed Ilisidi herself, or Tabini—and the legislature had pointedly skipped over Ilisidi's suggestion that her election as aiji of the *aishidi'tat* might 'stabilize' the association. The legislature had appointed Tabini as aiji at a very young age, to the frustration of certain conservative lords—notably Tatiseigi, notably the Kadigidi.

By all he had heard, it had been a battle royal in the legislature. Tabini had been young, full of ideas, combative with Wilson-paidhi, who had resigned in distress. So Tabini had gotten a new paidhi-aiji. Him. A paidhi considered too young for his job, too. They'd had that in common from the start.

They'd taken too much to each other, perhaps.

They'd gotten too much done too fast, debatably so, in the opinion of very many people these days. Lucky or not—they'd been able to respond when humans arrived in space and reopened the abandoned space station. If they hadn't been ready, having pushed their technology past airplanes, to the brink of a space program—another loop of the fugue—they'd have watched the space station and possibly Mospheira itself run by a very problematic human authority. Those were the facts, but they weren't facts with which the conservatives could be at peace. Ever.

They certainly weren't facts the legislature loved, when the old men of the tashrid, the house of lords, got together to bemoan the younger generation.

Now, failing response from Tabini, with a Kadigidi upstart calling himself aiji, but not highly regarded in the central regions, in the very heart of his power, the Guild, which had sat paralyzed, might well move to install Ilisidi as regent for Cajeiri—and some few easterners might even hope to lose Cajeiri in some convenient accident. A move to install Ilisidi as a strong regent might gain support from Tabini's followers as well as from old-line conservatives like Tatiseigi. Various factions, united in their dislike of a Kadigidi aiji, might logically reconsider their support of the usurper and line up temporarily behind Ilisidi.

But politics—politics—politics. It would be bloody.

" 'Gini-ji?" A sudden thought. "Does one suppose this house might already have sent some secret message to Tabini?"

"Again, we have inquired, and gotten no answer. But we all think it far more likely Taiben has, nandi."

Of course. Taiben certainly would have contacted Tabini, if that district knew where to reach him. By mecheita, or even by phone—granted a phone line was still uncut or untapped in the district of Taiben, most notably the phone lines that followed the railroad . . . they might have just phoned him and said, The dowager is back.

While the Atageini staff kept refusing questions. Interesting. Disturbing.

And Algini sat watch, when he was in the apartment, and there was really no need. Reality came crashing in.

"Why are you standing guard, 'Gini-ji? Is something afoot?"

Algini shrugged. "The Atageini staff has gone on alert, nandi. One believes, in dispute between the Atageini and the Kadigidi, the staff foresees action. Possibly tonight. Possibly earlier. They have resources of information we do not."

"So will a message go to the Guild, 'Gini-ji?"

"Uncertain. One has no idea." Algini only cast a warning look at the ceiling. Not another word, that look said. God knew why.

Disturbing. A move underway, likely tentative, perhaps some forewarning. He envisioned the dowager, perhaps, being better able to politic without him. He could leave his files with her. He could withdraw to a more remote place, out of range. *She* had witnessed everything that needed swearing to, out in remote space. She and Cajeiri could tell everything that he could tell.

Certainly if he wanted to lessen the pressure on the situation here, there was Taiben for a retreat—and the foothills, on the other side, the forested skirts of those mist-hidden mountains. The mountain villages were, unlike the lowlands, not highly associated with the capital. The web of associations there looked more like a tangle, this village allied to one over the ridge, but not to the one nearest. In the old days, back when the Atageini house had had reason to be a fortress, those hills out the window had been a region of feuding chiefs and not a little outright banditry. As a refuge, it had its advantages. But it took a reference book to figure out the man'chiin involved between the villages, some of which territory neighbored Kadigidi land, for good or for ill.

Third loop of the fugue. What in hell was he thinking? Run from here? Retreat? Look for safety, where he could only endanger the Taibeni, or those villages, less prepared than the Atageini to hold trouble at bay?

A railroad linked the principal villages, and ran up to the highlands University, the apex of civilization in the district, itself lying outside man'chi and as neutral to all parties as it was possible to be, give or take minor allegiances to those lords and powers who endowed it—hoping an institution of learning would bring greater prosperity and less banditry to the region.

They had taken that route once, when they went up to visit the observatory. He remembered game running beside the antiquated train. Remembered a long climb up and down.

A lightning stroke. The hills.

The university.

The Astronomer Emeritus, Grigiji. The observatory, remote in the hills. A revered old man all but worshipped by his students, beloved by the court—but a man not likely in great favor with the new regime, his work having abetted Tabini's efforts to reach into space. Another likely to be threatened by the upheaval.

Up in those hills, toward the mountains. Grigiji.

Where *better* to keep an eye to the sky, to know when the ship had returned, even when the shuttle launched?

He felt a chill. He decided he didn't want to know Tabini's whereabouts. He didn't want to have that supposition in his head, remembering another time, early in his association with Ilisidi, when he'd been caught and questioned, very unpleasantly.

He wished he could talk freely with his staff, a free and open conference. But this wasn't the place. Bad enough risk they'd run, discussing the letter and the Guild. But Tatiseigi had to find out they were up to something, or he'd only listen the harder.

Fugue done. Threads knit. Wide awake. He looked uneasily at the sky—momentary flash of steel and plastics, close corridors. Jase. What are you up to? he wondered, feeling a little forlorn. Can't say I wish you were here at the moment. Not a good situation.

Flash of open sea and heaving deck underfoot. Hope you made it home, brother. And maybe got some fishing done. Stay out there, if you get the choice. Don't be answering questions from the press. That game's no good for a relationship. Good luck to you and Barb.

From brain-wearying fugue to a last few flashes of distance-spanning longing, pieces of him stretched thin. He'd never moved from the window. But he'd been on a long, scattered journey. Likely the tea was cold. He'd had only a single cup, and he'd learned it was precious, in the economy of the universe. He went and poured himself a tepid cup, drank it anyway, sitting in the well-padded chair. He was mentally tired, even physically tired after the mind-trip he'd taken. Curious how the brain wore the body out, and how it didn't work the other way around.

He shut his eyes, wishing he didn't know what he suspected he knew, but what—he reassured himself—Tatiseigi and his whole staff and the Kadigidi likely knew. He waited, cradling his lukewarm teacup. He thought about marauding Kadigidi creeping through the topiary hedges.

Over near the door Algini, clearly bored, stripped

and oiled his gun, waiting. Bren smelled the oil. He didn't need to look. He smelled the thousand scents that wafted through the open window. Curious, how many, many different scents a planet had, each freighted with significance.

Hadn't taken him long at all to acclimate to negatively-curved horizons. He wondered if Jase would get queasy again, after being back in his element so long.

Deep sigh. A state near sleep, hindbrain running autopilot. The teacup was still safe in his hands. He probably should ask Algini to do the same maintenance for his gun, which, with Shawn's computer attachment, was tucked into his gear.

Steps outside, ordinarily beneath his hearing, audible in the general hush. Algini got up.

Heavy steps. Several. Algini opened the door. Banichi and Jago were back.

"Bren-ji," Banichi said, and came and sat down in the opposite chair, Jago standing behind him. Banichi set arms on his knees and leaned very close. "Tano has been out by the stables. He reports there have been numerous mecheiti here before the rain, for what that may mean, and now there are only five, besides ours. Cenedi is aware. Possibly it is as mundane as the movement of an Atageini herd to the hills, after use in the hunt. On the other hand, there might have been visitors here in the last few days that the lord has simply not mentioned."

Tatiseigi, the old fox, had made a career of holding everyone's secrets, and moving very suddenly in the direction that gained him most. A patrol sent out, and never mentioned? Visitors, from one faction or the other, a diplomatic mission from the Kadigidi?

And not a word yet about his carefully crafted letter to the Guild. His brain threatened to enter fog-state again, having ten new things to process, none of them pleasant.

"Dare we speak, nadiin-ji?"

Banichi moved his eyes to the left, a slight warning. Bren bit his lip, increasingly uneasy in this luxurious, secretive house, and needing, dammit, more information.

"Lord Tatiseigi has read your letter, nandi, and is considering the matter."

So Ilisidi had sent it on, implying she thought it should be sent. Tatiseigi was considering. And Algini indicated they were fast running out of time.

Things absolutely had to be said. "Come," he said to them, and went to the writing desk.

He enlivened the computer screen. Wrote:

I have a wild guess, nadiin-ji, where Tabini is: with Grigiji.

Leaning over his shoulder, they read it, absorbed that with a little gratifying expression of surprise and a glance exchanged between them.

He wrote further: *Algini says that the Kadigidi may make a move tonight. What Tano found at the stables may mean there has been diplomatic traffic from the Kadigidi—or from Tabini-aiji—or simply that there are more Atageini patrols out that his staff has never mentioned. One hopes for either of the last two.*

Banichi signaled that he would answer. He dropped to one knee, took the computer, balancing it while he entered, hunt and peck with his much larger hand, and a telegraphic brevity:

The dowager says if Tatiseigi acts against her interests her staff will act against him, but that situation remains uncertain. She has considered Cenedi's plan to move against the Kadigidi, which would seize the initiative and make it more sure that Tatiseigi cannot waver in his alliance with her. He has also proposed to her that the paidhi take the heir and withdraw to some unknown place, maybe Taiben. If the heir were not here, it would complicate the Kadigidi's situation and divide their attention. Should something befall Cenedi and the dowager come to odds with our host, the boy would not be in Lord Tatiseigi's hands.

My God, he thought, and reached for the computer. *Does she think she is in danger from Tatiseigi? I cannot believe Cenedi would give up Ilisidi as lost in that event. Whose interest is he protecting?*

Banichi took the computer. *We are not confident in Cenedi's plan. Cenedi may not survive a mission against the Kadigidi, with or without our assistance, and he will rely only on us, not on the Atageini staff. He strongly believes there are spies in the house. He mentions the primitive nature of much of the monitoring equipment and communication here, which will be penetrated by the Kadigidi in any determined attack, and may give them access to our transmissions. Tano and Algini might go with him, and their help would at least raise the odds of his success, but Murini is much more likely resident in Shejidan, which means a very difficult operation, whether to draw him out to his province, or go after him in the capital. Your staff is not willing to throw all resources into this mission. If Cenedi should fail and we were all with him, no one but Tatiseigi's staff would protect you, Cajeiri, the dowager, and the resistance to Murini. This is not acceptable, and we will not take that course. We do not support Cenedi's proposal.*

He seized the computer, then hardly knew what to say. *It is absolutely not useful that the Guild see the heir as under my influence. I am the worst possible guardian for him. This is not feasible, nadiin-ji.*

Jago reached for the machine. Typed: *If you are correct that the aiji is at the observatory, putting Cajeiri into his father's hands would be one answer to criticism.*

He wrote, in his turn, rapid fire: *I am by no means certain the aiji is there, nor do I have great hopes of reaching him with the boy in tow. And if I deliver him to his father—forgive me, nadiin-ji, but right now the dowager can attract the more conservative elements of the aishidi'tat, but Tabini-aiji is at disadvantage in that regard, and to have me and the boy join him does not answer the criticism of human influence in the situation.*

Does this house staff believe it can withstand an incursion tonight, granted Tatiseigi is being forthright with the dowager about his man'chi?

Banichi shrugged. "Baji-naji, Bren-ji."

Dice-throw, that was to say. In Cenedi's best plan, they were down to attempting to assassinate Murini, an aiji with a following, and all-out clan warfare, regional warfare, was likely as a consequence. This was where the Assassins' Guild in Shejidan was supposed to step in, to declare which claimant to supreme power it supported. It should eliminate the loser and restore peace and balance.

But Cenedi would have the fat in the fire before the Guild could get into action, if Cenedi proceeded against Murini's clan, Tatiseigi's neighbors.

Unless his letter to the Guild could persuade Tatiseigi there was substance enough to throw his prestige behind it and affix his seal as a lord in support of his appeal, it would never reach the Guild at all.

Phoning that appeal in—was possible, if they could hijack a line; but a phone message was only informative. Legally, paper needed to be there, with house seals: the Guild operated by rules, with paper, with seals, with incontrovertible Filed evidence. A phone call had no legal standing.

But even if the physical letter did get there under seal, past all obstacles including Tatiseigi and Kadigidi interception, it was unlikely to produce immediate action. Unless the Guild had been waiting for some excuse to support Tabini, and fell upon his letter of appeal to the Guild as exactly the small legality they needed to have on record, they would not move fast enough.

Stalemate in the Guild. At best outcome, he was going to get a summons to a Guild hearing that would produce his safe conduct in a few days, but that did nothing to defend them tonight. Their immediate defense was in their own hands. The dowager's young men, though decorative, were certainly not ornament.

Neither, above all else, was Cenedi—who, yes, stood a marginal chance of doing exactly what he proposed: he was that good.

But the moment he left, then what did they get? Tatiseigi with the dowager under his roof and Cenedi off in Kadigidi territory? The heir here with her, in Tatiseigi's hands?

It was a line of thought that he really, truly didn't like.

He wrote: *The moment Cenedi separates himself from the dowager, we would have far less means under this roof to resist whatever Tatiseigi might decide to do.*

Banichi replied: *Tatiseigi is ambitious. This has never changed. One doubts he would harm the dowager, but he would seize the upper hand if he could get it. Moving the heir out of his reach would mean the boy would not return to Tatiseigi unless the dowager sent for him.*

His turn. *Has she agreed with Cenedi? Has she asked this of us?*

Banichi nodded.

He wrote: *And it has to be done now, if it is to be done.*

Another nod.

He wrote: *If my letter is to go out, it must go within the hour, it seems, or risk falling afoul of her plans. Is there no way to persuade the lord and the dowager to work together?*

Banichi and Jago exchanged a look, and then Jago took the computer.

We have argued strongly with Cenedi to defend this house and not to make this assault into Kadigidi territory. Cenedi believes this house is ultimately indefensible and that it is safer to carry the attack to the Kadigidi rather than to rely on the lord's antiquated equipment. We believe that his making this attack will be a fatal error, but we expect the dowager will allow it. She generally yields to Cenedi in such affairs. The security deficits are demonstrable, a surprise even to Cenedi, and we have no standing to dispute him.

He wrote: *Can I persuade her?*

Banichi took the computer back this time, and thought a moment. *Find her another course.*

Twice damn. As easy to move a river in spate than divert the dowager from her intentions, especially when she failed to trust her former lover and Cenedi's was the only advice.

And they all sat and acted under a roof where they could not talk freely, not only for fear of Tatiseigi overhearing, but for fear of Kadigidi spies.

He took the computer back. "I shall write another letter, nadiin-ji. This one to her. Thank you."

They understood. They left him to it, for what little time they might have. And he sat in front of the computer and buried his face in his hands, shutting out the light, trying to think.

Then he wrote:

> *Bren-paidhi to the esteemed aiji-dowager. Aiji-ma, if my continued presence in this household is in any wise a hindrance to negotiations you may see fit to conduct, I am prepared to withdraw and seek safety elsewhere. You might view a changed situation if you did not also bear the burden of protecting and defending me. I believe strongly that I can guess where Tabini is, and will undertake to reach him, since it seems little likely that I can reach Shejidan. I would also undertake to bring your grandson safely to his father if it seems wise or politic to you to entrust him to me. You might go with me, too, aiji-ma, but these are matters in which I can only offer alternatives, by no means advice to one wise and clever. The paidhi urges in the strongest terms that you spend no force agressively, but defend this house, allying yourself with Tatiseigi in that enterprise, with which he will much better agree. This close alliance between you and the Atageini, the paidhi believes, will not be what the*

opposition hopes to see, and the Kadigidi may be provoked into a succession of rash and expensive attacks which may wear down their forces and diminish their respect and their stature. One failure to penetrate your defenses will make them seem weaker than many have thought. Two failures will begin to make them look like fools. Three would cut deeply into their resources. And in the defense of Atageini land against the Kadigidi, one strongly suspects even Taiben would render assistance.

Most urgently I urge you to persuade Tatiseigi to send my letter to the Guild, as intervention by that body, if it could be moved, could save very many lives and preserve the peace.

Be assured I will abide by your wise decision.

I ask you to destroy this message utterly and send a message back with the bearer, with the confidence that I shall likewise destroy the message beyond recovery.

He wrote it out by hand, set his seal on it, and went and gave it to Banichi. "She will reply," he said, and settled down to an intolerable wait, staring out the window, with nothing to think about but disasters, and routes, and defenses.

It took much longer than he hoped. Perhaps Ilisidi had taken offense at his advice. Perhaps she and Banichi and Cenedi were down the hall having a bitter argument, which might bar Banichi from further consultations.

Worst thought—Tatiseigi might have gotten curious, or tried to intercept his message or her reply.

Sit and wait. Sit and wait.

Steps approached the door. Banichi came in and brought him a sealed message.

"Stay," Bren said. "Nadiin-ji, all of you."

Everyone took chairs near him as he pried loose the wax seal and unrolled the tight curl of the message.

The aiji-dowager to the paidhi-aiji. When has the paidhi joined the Assassins? Your arguments have already made several trips here wearing Banichi's face.

Damn, he thought. He'd failed.

In advance of any move against the Kadigidi, we have decided to consult our host regarding your interesting notion, and if he is amenable, to send one of our great-grandson's attendants back to Taiben to test their willingness to join in defense.

Taiben. For God's sake, it was not the point of his letter. It was a side argument.

If the Atageini will consent and if Taiben will respond to defend the Atageini, this would be unprecedented. But yours is an excellent proposal. There has never been such heredity as my great-grandson's. He has always been one of my best ideas.

Tatiseigi has sent your letter by courier.

Come to the library for tea within the hour.

He felt a little light-headed as he passed the note to Banichi, who read it impassively, and then with a little lift of the brows Banichi passed it to Jago. It went from her to Algini, and to Tano, and Tano read it and proffered it back.

"Destroy it, nadi-ji," he said, and Tano went to the desk and lit the wax-jack, then burned the message, and crumpled the incriminating ash to an irrecoverable smear across his hand.

11

Afternoon tea meant well and away a higher-dress event than breakfast. There was no Narani to see to a proper coat and lace cuffs—there was no truly proper coat, for that matter, and no source for him to find one ... Cajeiri's might almost have done, if Cajeiri had had a spare, which he did not. So Banichi and Jago brushed his morning coat, steamed the wrinkles from it and his shirt in the bath, and had him at least presentable.

All the same he felt ill at ease, going downstairs, and with Banichi and Jago having to ask their way of dimly cooperative servants, who said, guardedly, yes, m'lord was expecting him in the library for tea.

No security stood outside. He might be early. He slipped through the ornate, lily-carved doors and, seeing Lord Tatiseigi sitting by the fire, made as unobtrusive a bow as possible, wondering if there was any graceful way to slip out again and await the dowager. But no, there was no way to retreat now. Banichi and Jago had stayed at the door. The lord was here unprotected—ostensibly. But there was, at the far end of the room, another door.

It might be a test. An incredibly important test. "Nandi." A second small bow as he approached a chair. The old lord was resplendent in dark gold brocade, in a flood of pointed lace down the front of his shirt. He—was shabby, to say the least. "One regrets ever so much the inability to honor your hospitality with appropriate dress. This is so elegant a house, and my baggage was packed for rough living."

"You did not foresee a welcome here?"

"One extravagantly hoped to be received for an interview, perhaps gain permission to cross your lands, nandi." He still stood. Tatiseigi had not invited him to sit. "But one would not have presumed to take a welcome for granted."

"Ha." Tatiseigi looked not to believe it of him. He was a handsome old man, extremely jealous of his proprieties in a world that had changed far too fast for him. He was going some even to receive a human alone, in this inner sanctum, though they had talked before . . . in the Bujavid, principally, where social interaction was compelled and carefully choreographed—well, where such was supposed to be the case. There had been a most unfortunate evening . . .

"And does this gracious solicitude," Tatiseigi asked, "extend to gunfire under my roof?"

"One hopes not to endanger this household in any particular, nandi." There was the unfortunate affair of the lilies, besides the first one. Tatiseigi would never let that go. "I am particularly sensible of the passions which confront my return from this mission, nandi, a quite reasonable demand for an accounting, which I am prepared to give. One would never wish to bring political difficulty on this house, or to provoke the Kadigidi. I understand there is an imminent threat."

Tatiseigi simply gave him a fish-stare and kept staring, and had not yet invited him to sit down. The old lord had sent his letter, Ilisidi had said. He had dispatched a courier from his staff at considerable risk. But clearly it was not done for his sake.

The jaw moved. Briefly. "We will not contenance Kadigidi intrusion."

"One is informed, nandi, that the Atageini are very formidable in that regard."

"Ha. Spies, is it? Your Taibeni brats?"

At that point Ilisidi arrived, a rescue, a decided rescue. Tatiseigi rose to hand the dowager to a favored and comfortable chair.

"We see elegance, despite the circumstances of travel, Sidi-ji," Tatiseigi said, quite pointedly regarding the paidhi's less than splendid appearance, Bren was sure; and in fact the dowager with her black garments and blood-red lace made a very brave show, in a dark color in which packing wrinkles, if they were possibly allowed to exist, would not show. Much more practical, that, than his pale coat.

Ilisidi sat down with her hands on her walking-stick, ramrod straight. Bren took hers as a blanket permission to sit down, and he took the lefthand chair.

"Flatterer," Ilisidi said primly. "But we accept it. One notes there has not been complete warfare between you and the paidhi in my absence."

A small silence in which Tatiseigi, who might have protested that the paidhi had been perfectly gracious and polite in conversation, did not.

"Lord Tatiseigi has been very patient," Bren said dutifully, and Ilisidi's right eyebrow arched.

"Well?" she asked. "Patient, is it? A good thing, considering. And the letter has gone. Ah," she said, deliberately diverting her attention and deflecting argument as Cajeiri came trailing in. "Great-grandson."

"Mani-ma. Nandiin." A stiff little bow, and Cajeiri walked to the one of the chairs—there were five—next Ilisidi's right hand, and sat down, hands gripping the cushion edge. Late arrival, and very tight-lipped. One wondered what had occasioned the tardiness.

At that point, however, tea arrived through the main doors, a huge porcelain service in the hands of a very strong servant in green, followed by three young maidservants in soft gold and lily white coats.

No business was possibly appropriate while formal tea service went on in such a hall, nor, again, was it possible while the tea was being drunk. There were, at Ilisidi's request, two rounds of service . . . and then a third. Tatiseigi had been impatient. Now he became edgy and frustrated, raising an eyebrow at Ilisidi. Cajeiri looked at his great-uncle, then at his great-grandmother, and back again in increasing frustration.

The paidhi kept focused on his tea cup and kept quiet, trying to avoid being spoken to or looked at for the interim.

"So," Tatiseigi said, just that, after a mortal long time of waiting.

Ilisidi took a lingering sip of tea, and the lineaments of her face rearranged themselves subtly in what might be amusement. Or not. She made as if to set the tea cup down. And did not. She held it in her hands, carefully. "We have a proposition for our host."

"And what would this be?"

A long inhalation, a slight stretch of frail shoulders, and she held out the tea cup for the servant to pour another. In the background, servant desperately signaled servant: the tea had run out. There needed to be more. "One has a notion," Ilisidi said serenely, while servants scurried, "that the Kadigidi are bound to move against this house—I have even had the likelihood reported to me, as happens, through your own staff. One would be extremely distressed to see hostile forces move here to the detriment of the Atageini."

A slight move of Tatiseigi's shoulder. A shrug. "They would not be wise to do so."

"Oh, doubtless, but then the Kadigidi know the lay of the land as well as the premises, since you hosted that ingrate Murini during the last upheaval."

A muscle jumped in Tatiseigi's jaw. "A mistake."

"One we might ourselves have made, to be sure. But one is also very sure he was taking notes. Nor would such a slinking creature care for the odds as they might exist in a simple dispute between Atageini and Kadigidi, no, not this scoundrel. The Guild will not act. But Murini will gather reinforcement, and hire others, perhaps southerners."

"He is in Shejidan."

"Ah, but are all his servants, Tati-ji? Surely servants came with him, when he was a guest here."

"One believes," Tatiseigi muttered.

"They might easily advance onto Atageini land—in great numbers. And against such odds, and with their having observed the defenses at close hand, there might well be damage, even extensive damage to this house. We would ever so greatly deplore that. We had ever so much rather advance the quarrel to their territory and let it damage *their* crops and paintwork."

Paintwork was a very touchy topic with the Atageini, and Ilisidi had neither shame nor remorse.

"Cease your campaign, woman," Tatiseigi said with a wave of his hand. "We have sent this cursed letter, for all the good that may come of it, on your recommendation. The mission took away three of my staff, who might have defended this house."

"Ah, but now, now, Tati-ji, I know where we can gain three back, and thirty more."

"From what hidden source, pray?"

"My great-grandson, your grand-nephew, has acquired the man'chi of Taiben."

Two heads moved, Cajeiri's for a short sharp look at his great-grandmother, and Tatiseigi's as if someone had just thrown something cold and wet right in his face.

It was, however, Ilisidi sitting there, and Tatiseigi did not explode outright.

"By no means," he cried indignantly. "By no means, Sidi-ji, do we countenance these ragtag foresters who chase game into Atageini fields and refuse us any tithe of it! We have allowed two under this roof, but only on tolerance, and as a situation with our grand-nephew we earnestly counsel should never have happened, and should be dealt with at the first opportunity! Let them serve him at Taiben!"

"But look on it from a better vantage, Tati-ji. Your grand-nephew can mediate these ancient quarrels, which were quite justified . . . a hundred years ago, but a hundred years, nadi! Certainly you were wise, seeing how a grand-nephew's connections in Shejidan would be advantageous to the Atageini. You have always known that. But only consider his connections across your closest border, Tati-ji, just consider it, and forbear to waste this advantage. When a lord sits as high as you now sit, at the highest level of the aishidi'tat, the perspective necessarily becomes quite different."

"Abominable woman!"

The paidhi paid devout attention to his teacup. Few people argued with the aiji-dowager. Fewer engaged in a shouting match with her once, let alone twice in one day, and he could only add to the tension.

"Do not shout at my great-grandmother!" Cajeiri certainly had no such prudence.

"I shall shout as I please under my roof! And these ragamuffin adherents of yours—"

"Who are outside the door, nandi," Ilisidi muttered, "at least one of them."

"While the other steals the silver," Tatiseigi snarled, regardless of warnings, but at least in a lower voice. "Or lays plans to."

"They plan with us to save your precious silver from the Kadigidi, Tati-ji!"

"You bring Taibeni thieves under my roof, you ask me send three men to Shejidan in peril of their lives, and now you counsel me send more to Taiben, to rely on Taiben, of all possible allies, for our defense?"

"When you begin to prefer old quarrels to new opportunities, you have begun to die, Tati-ji! You have begun to sink, forgotten, into the slough of history. We, *we*, on the other hand, fully intend to live forever!"

"Great-grandmother. Grand-uncle."

"Hush!"

A small moment of silence, even Cajeiri not daring move a muscle.

"Make peace with Taiben," Tatiseigi muttered in disgust, shaking his head. "Ask them across our borders. How in all reason can we do this?"

"Courteously," Ilisidi said, in a voice dripping with triumph.

"Abominable woman!" But this came quietly. Tatiseigi took up his refilled cup and gulped.

"Do we then sit and wait for an attack, Lord of the Atageini?"

"Well, well, you send for them! Send your own staff, none of mine, on this foolish venture! Plague take the necessity—which is altogether your fault, woman, and say nothing more to me about foolishness and sinking into sloughs! Who was it went traipsing off to the stars to settle quarrels among a pack of renegade humans while the association fell apart?"

"Ah, there is the brave Tatiseigi we knew in our youth. Young again. An inspiration. Confusion to the Kadigidi."

"Ha!" Disgust. Defeat. "You make up your message to Taiben, woman. I shall add to it."

"Courteously."

"Courteously, always courteously. When are we anything but courteous?" The teacup, fragile as eggshell, clicked down on the table with considerable force. "So write this cursed message. And we shall see how to send it."

"Our young kinsman can compose the request, in his own words, in his own hand, and attach our appropriate sentiments. Can you not, great-grandson?"

"Mani-ma?" Wide, alarmed eyes.

"The boy is not yet nine!" From Tatiseigi.

"If he wishes to see nine, he knows what must be done, and how to do it. A force from Taiben must arrive here, as soon as possible, to counter Kadigidi mischief. We shall add our bit to this missive, Tati-ji, and it may go out under our seal, but we have taught this boy to write, and to express himself with appropriate courtesy. Let us see this letter your grand-nephew will write. There is a desk, boy. There must be pen and paper in this elegant house."

Cajeiri was uncharacteristically subdued as, at an insistent wave of Ilisidi's hand, he rose, bowed correctly to his elders collectively, and went to the desk.

Not yet nine. Not yet nine going on a hundred, he was. Bren was humanly appalled, watching that stiff carriage, that proper straight back as the boy sat down, opened the desk, and located pen and suitable paper with the same dignity his father might have shown. The paidhi simply kept his mouth shut while the boy wrote. Ilisidi and Tatiseigi calmly discussed the harvest, and whether the invading Kadigidi would be so barbaric as to threaten the fields and towns to the east, or whether they properly ought to bring the populace into this. There was at least a need to advise the people in that quarter to melt aside from any incursion. Brave local folk, underinformed, might undertake to hold off a rapidly moving force which might otherwise ignore them, and there was no hope of their resisting the skilled, well-equipped agents of the Kadigidi, who were just as likely to employ southerners as homegrown agents. The Guild might not budge, officially, but the Guild's inaction did not restrain Guild members in service to various houses from specific actions, directed by their lords. Among atevi, Guild actions, however desperate, were Guild actions, and farmers and tradesmen had no reasonable place taking up arms so long as their towns and fields stayed sacrosanct. Taiben, many of whose people were Guild, and who had long been attached to the aiji in their peculiar service, were somewhat another matter ... and involving Taiben inside Atageini territory escalated the potential for general, bloody war far, far above the usual measured sniping of Guild of one house for advantage against Guild members employed by another.

Bren took another cup of tea. It was the only use for himself he could possibly conceive under present circumstances, to sit and absorb facts as they floated past, to listen to the surmises of these two ancient and knowledgeable atevi until the immediate issues resolved themselves or, if only, if only, some brilliant notion occurred to him. He by no means liked the disposition of his last such inspiration. He wished he had never said the word Taiben.

Pen scratched audibly on paper for several minutes intermittently. Perhaps five minutes. Seven. Flurry of scratches at the end. The desk shut. The chair scraped softly on the marble floor.

Cajeiri walked back to face his elders with a second proper bow, paper in hand.

"A letter," he announced, like a schoolchild reciting, and squared it in both hands to read.

"Cajeiri son and heir of Tabini-aiji to nand' Keimi of Taiben. We are guests of Lord Tatiseigi. The Kadigidi are planning to send assassins to kill us and our great-grandmother, also Bren-paidhi and Lord Tatiseigi, perhaps tonight. We need help very badly. Great-grandmother thinks it is a good idea if you will come. Lord Tatiseigi says he will be courteous. I shall always remember your help and hope for you to send help here as soon as possible. The aiji-dowager and Lord Tatiseigi both asked me to write to you."

"Hmmph," from Tatiseigi.

"Perfectly fine," Ilisidi said, and asked Tatiseigi, "Does it suit?"

A scowl. "Well enough."

She drew her ring from her finger. "Seal it without comment. Tati-ji, he will do the same for you."

Tatiseigi drew off his own seal ring, and gave it into Cajeiri's hand with a scowl.

The boy walked back to the table, lit the wax-jack, and in very short order produced a properly furled missive, liberally done up with heavy wax and two ancient personal seals.

He returned each ring, his great-grandmother's first, then Tatiseigi's, and both rings went back onto fingers.

"So. Which of your staff will you spare for this errand?" Tatiseigi asked. "I will not subject my staff to Taiben's insolent behavior."

"My great-grandson himself has the means, and the best messengers we could send." Ilisidi waved a hand at Cajeiri. "Dispatch your message, great-grandson. Your grand-uncle will clear the way for them. He will take the western defenses down for an hour and give them free passage."

Cajeiri's face had a rigid look as he looked at the old man. Go tell his young followers to undertake what might be an extremely dangerous ride, if Kadigidi had gotten into Atageini territory? Cajeiri surely realized what Ilisidi was asking, and Ilisidi herself had not volunteered a protective escort. Nawari, who had watched over the young folk, was nowhere mentioned in the equation.

"Go, go, boy." Tatiseigi waved a dismissive hand. "All these things. Granted. Enough!"

Cajeiri bowed stiffly, took the message and left the room.

"A damnable situation you put us in, nand' Sidi," Tatiseigi said.

"Is it not?" Ilisidi said. "But in the meanwhile, our three staffs need to consult closely together, Tati-ji, with perfect accord and frankness. And who knows? The Taibeni may even respond favorably to the approach. They know I am here. They know we are your allies and that we may secure your benevolent cooperation . . ."

"And thereby open our defenses to illicit incursions, people who will likely make holes in our fences. You let them scout us out, and lay us wide open to their own mischief, to exercise what they call their hunting rights, damn them, which will be more trouble to us in future than the Kadigidi ever have been! You will not, I say, not give them our access codes."

"Your secrets are absolutely your secrets, quite firmly so, Tati-ji. We are certain the paidhi will agree, too, that what you tell us in confidence will remain as secret as within your own staff."

Bren gave a deep nod to that proposition. "With utmost appreciation of the sensitivity of such information, nandi, we have no hesitation to issue reassurances. My staff would not breach such a confidence, and they are no minor members of their Guild. I assure you, nandi. I have been a target no few times, and I am still here."

That chanced, unaccountably, to amuse the old lord. "So have we all, paidhi-aiji. And we are all still here."

"And Murini's predecessor is not," Ilisidi observed dryly. "But Murini, alas, is no improvement. Some work must be done until we have gotten it right. So! We are entirely surfeited with tea, Tati-ji. We shall go to the solarium. We have always esteemed your solarium."

"An honor." The scowl persisted. "Do make free of it at your leisure, Sidi-ji. We, meanwhile, have detailed instructions to give, to permit this doubtless useless message to go through. We shall lower defenses in the west, altogether, to have no possible misunderstandings. We shall instruct the gatekeepers to let this message pass and let in any Taibeni that arrive, there or at the hunting-gate. Nand' paidhi, if you will brief your own people and ask them to consult, to join a meeting of all our staffs—except these damned Taibeni teenagers, who will be told what they need when they need it, hear? I shall send three of my men with them, to see them pass the gate and get to the limit of our province. Immediately."

"Immediately, nandi." Bren rose, understanding a dismissal, and bowed. "With utmost attention."

He left. He gathered Banichi and Jago to him outside. Of Cajeiri or his young followers there was no sign.

"The heir has written a letter to Taiben, nadiin-ji," he said to them as they climbed the stairs.

"Antaro expressed her great desire to be the one to carry it, nandi," Jago said in a low voice.

"There might be Kadigidi out, even in that direction," he said. "Lord Tatiseigi says he will advise his security to let her pass, but we can by no means guarantee what else is out there that she might meet, the worse as hours pass."

"We did soberly caution her, Bren-ji," Banichi said. "And we advised going overland, by mecheita."

"The young gentleman is deeply concerned," Jago said, "and expressed a wish to send Jegari with her, but Antaro said he should not go. Jegari will likely not leave the young gentleman."

Will not, would not. Emotional decisions, man'chi, newly-attached young instincts at war with basic common sense, none of them Guild, none of them with adult comprehension of what they were up against, and Ilisidi encouraging this move, all because he had said one critical word: *Taiben.*

"They are attempting too much, Bren-ji," Banichi said. "Tano and Algini took these youngsters in hand last evening for brief instruction, but that only concerned house security. Jago requested the house staff give the girl a firearm: there is considerable resistence to this request."

"The lord has ordered thorough cooperation." They were in the upper hall. "Go back, Jago-ji, and inform them of that. She should have a gun, if she knows how to use it."

"Yes," Jago said, and dived back down the stairs, pigtail flying.

He was far from happy with the arrangement—with consulting the Taibeni, yes, that was a possibility with some value, if Ilisidi had sent Nawari. But he did not agree with sending a teenaged kid through a potential ambush, however remote from the expected line of combat, even if Tatiseigi had relented and sent an escort. He least of all agreed with the pressure the dowager had put on the boy, newly possessed of—

Damn it, *friends* was not the appropriate concept.

But whatever it was, the boy had just picked up longed-for companionship in a damned lonely world, a satisfaction of atevi instincts they had worried would never wake, and now Ilisidi used him and the two Taibeni youngsters without detectible compassion. Twice damn it. And damn the whole situation. He might have succeeded in diverting Cenedi from his notion of a hopeless foray into Kadigidi territory by making that suggestion of his, but it could be at terrible cost.

And now what did he do? He and his guard were committed to stay here—he couldn't pull his staff out of the defense of Tirnamardi after he'd backed this alternative plan to stop Cenedi from what his staff called a mistake. He couldn't urge the Taibeni to come in here, where they historically weren't welcome, and not be here to meet them, to iron out any misunderstandings. And he couldn't have sent an appeal to the Guild, asking permission to appear before them and then vanish into the hills, unfindable if things went wrong, or if that Guild safe-conduct turned up.

And he couldn't now take Cajeiri out of here, and pursue the chance of finding his father, not when Cajeiri was the principle reason the Taibeni might consent to come in to defend their historic adversary.

Jago rejoined them before they reached his door. "The Atageini staff agrees," she said, "and has gotten their lord's word on it. They will instruct her such as they can, providing both communications and a sidearm, and escorting her as far as the edge of the Taiben woods."

Much better. Damned much better, and Tatiseigi had come to his senses, not hampering any chance of success. Bren let go a deep breath. There was a chance they would survive this.

"Good," he said as Banichi opened the door and let them in. Tano and Algini were waiting inside, on their feet.

"We are staying here, nadiin-ji," Jago said. "One believes it may be an interesting night ahead of us. The Atageini have requested Cajeiri send Antaro-nadi to Taiben, to bring reinforcement."

Eyebrows lifted. That was all. But Banichi said soberly, "Measures will be taken all about the grounds, once the girl has cleared the perimeter. Likely we will see eastern defenses activated in very short order, if they are not now. But the Kadigidi will expect that, and go around, if they are not already in the province. House defenses are generally adequate on the first floor, Bren-ji, far less so on the upper floors. There exist some few very modern surprises. And we do not know if the house staff has told Cenedi all its secrets, either of deficiencies or of capabilities. Soft target, hard target. One earnestly begs you recall your precautions at all points, particularly if there is an alarm, Bren-ji."

Wires. Nasty devices that could slice a foot off. Electronic barriers. He hadn't had to live with such hazards since the worst days in the Bujavid, and coping with them now meant setting a series of checkpoints and alarms in his head, not to cross narrow places without extreme precaution, not to leave his bodyguard for an instant and never to precede them through a door, insert a key in a lock, or expose his head in a window.

And soft-target/hard-target. Which meant the upstairs was certainly not where they wanted to be tonight. The upstairs was where an attack was meant to enter—and descend at disadvantage, into much more modern devices, and defenders ready and waiting, likely in the dark. Soft-target, hard-target was a fairly transparent mode of defense, but one still hard to deal with, even if the enemy had reliable spies to inform them, because the line at which the defense would go from soft to hard was not going to be apparent and might change quickly.

Antiquated equipment, but maybe the sort to lull an attacker into thinking it was all going to be easy. He didn't utterly trust Tatiseigi to tell them everything.

But he didn't look forward to tonight at all. He didn't look forward to the rest of the day, which held a diminishing few hours of tedium and tension before twilight brought a rising likelihood of trouble. He had drunk tea enough to float, and his nerves were jangled—always were, after one of those breakneck logical downhills with Ilisidi, not to mention Tatiseigi in the mix.

Not to mention, either, a human urge to go down the hall and offer the poor kid some sort of reassurance or at least moral support, considering an order far too hard for children. Damn the situation. Damn the Kadigidi. He passionately hated gunfire. It always meant someone like him hadn't done his job. And there was far too much evidence of that all around him.

His staff settled down near the fireplace for some quick close consultation of their own, and he found there was one thing constructive he could do in that regard. He unfolded his computer and produced a detailed map of the terrain. He had no way, in the upstairs of this traditional and *kabiu* household, to print it out for them, but they clustered around him, viewing the situation down to the hummocks and small streams. There was a discussion of the stables, where their riding gear was stowed, which Tano had checked and located—it was the pile of stable sweepings, curiously enough, which had told Tano the story of recent visitations: one lived and learned. They discussed the dowager's rooms, which Jago had observed were similar in layout to their own, and they even considered the topiary hedges, where devices or automatic traps might be located, if such sensors had survived the mecheiti's foraging.

"There will be electronic sweeps," Banichi said, and pointed to a stream that ran from the Kadigidi heights down toward Kadigidi territory. "That low spot, Bren-ji, is as good as a highway for intruders, except one can be reasonably certain the Atageini will have detection installed there and at other such places. And the Kadigidi will know it. So there should be devices set at other alternatives. We could not pry details out of this staff. Unfortunately, we are far less sure the Kadigidi have not done so."

He had not considered such things in years. He studied the map, tried to recall how the pitch of the land had seemed as they had ridden in during the rain—a deceptive pitch. He remembered how cleverly the rolling hills concealed things one would never have expected—the whole length of the fence and the perimeter had vanished at certain times—which meant attackers might likewise be below electronic sweeps, moving as they pleased. His staff pointed out the probable course of a large, late incursion from the Kadigidi, and then the route the Kadigidi were likeliest to use because that first one was too probable.

A knock came at the door. The household staff came to beg his staff's attendance at a general meeting. Jago opted to be the one to stay with him and stand watch.

They went on calling up maps, he and Jago, Jago taking mental notes, absorbing what might be useful to the team tonight. The meeting elsewhere went on a considerable time, more than an hour, until finally Banichi, Tano, and Algini came back, very sober of countenance.

"One has asked the staff quite bluntly, nandi, about the activity at the stables," Tano said. "They maintain they shifted the lord's herd in eight days ago for a seasonal hunt and out again, in favor of a small group used for ordinary purposes, and that this was all done by staff. One detected no lie, and this activity predated any action the Kadigidi may have taken against us. The lord generally keeps only seven mecheiti here against personal need. That also agrees what what I saw."

An autumn hunt. Plausible. Plausible, because one did not move part of an established mecheita herd out of its territory—or one had the remnant trying to join the others cross-country and tearing up fences and crops in the process. Even if it had been a small hunt, the lord would have brought an established herd in for the use of his guests, and then moved back a small herd, following the hunt. One did not believe Lord Tatiseigi himself still rode. But his staff would. Out of such events came the meat for table, the meat for market, meat for all the people of the province, the cull of game before the coming winter. Hunters from every Atageini village and town would have participated.

"They may or may not have been completely forthcoming about the deficiencies or the strength of the defenses," Banichi said. "They had already activated the southeastern perimeter defenses last night, when we arrived." That would be, precisely, the Kadigidi boundary. "They say there had been nuisance activity, spies, that sort of thing—likely because of the ship in the heavens. The Atageini raised defenses on the others today, repaired the one we blew, and have privately called on the various town-aijiin to take other precautions, asking them to avoid conflict with outsiders and to avoid the boundaries, the usual sort of thing. The Taibeni girl left some time ago, with two men in escort. She will likely have passed the gates by now."

Things were moving.

Moving in the hall, too. Footsteps passed their door at a high rate of speed, drawing a look from his staff.

Jago got up and went to stand near the door, not opening it, but listening. She shot back an anxious look.

"There is some little disturbance," she said, from that auditory vantage, and her hand was on her sidearm, unconsciously or not. She made the hand sign for man, and run.

The staff got up from their chairs. Bren shut his computer, rising, listening, his heart beating a little faster. The dowager's rooms were in the direction toward which those steps had run. The boy's were in the direction from which they had come. But the steps were heavy, a man's.

Second set of hand-signals, Banichi to Jago, and she

unlocked the door, opened it a crack, then looked out, and went outside.

Banichi followed, hand on his sidearm, not quite going so far as to draw a weapon in an allied house, but a heartbeat away from that move. The door stayed ajar. Bren stood still, not retreating as he ought to the neighboring room, but again, it was an allied house, in which they had basic confidence. Tano and Algini were on either side of him, Tano a little to the fore, protective position relative to the door. They signalled a move out of line with the window. Algini moved instantly to check that, and evidently saw nothing alarming.

More running steps, these audible. Jago, Bren thought, headed for the stairs. He stood still, then remembered his gun and went and retrieved it, still within Tano's protective screen. He slipped it into his pocket, along with an extra clip.

Jago came back, running, and came inside. Banichi headed down the hall in the direction from which the first runner had come.

"Nandi," she said. "Cajeiri is not in his apartment. The window is open, the alarm is disabled, and no one is in the apartment."

"Damn." The thought was instant and ominous.

Tano and Algini headed for the door, going out the way Banichi had gone, doubtless to have a firsthand look for how and why.

But it was foreseeable. They'd gone, they'd gotten out of the house. Banichi reported Antaro had left on her mission, and now the boy and Jegari had vanished? Enemy action?

No. They were all three of them going, fortunate three, sticking together, while the house staff had been in a meeting and nobody had been expecting it—a human could at least hope that was the case, and not that some Kadigidi assassin had gotten in.

"The outlying defenses are still down," Bren recalled.

Had not this boy grown up on human novels, human stories, human notions of heroes and desperate adventures? "I know exactly what they have done, Jago-ji. They have gone with Antaro. We should check the stables."

Jago's brows lifted. She exited to the hall, and was gone for a moment.

An interminable moment. He shed his formal coat, hung it on a chair and picked the warmer, bulkier short jacket out of his baggage. He transferred the handgun and the clip, took his pocket com, a knife, and his pill bottle, then stuffed them into a zipped pocket, lace shirt warring with bulky, resistant jacket. He half fastened it, from the waist.

Jago came back.

"They have taken mecheiti," Jago reported, and by now Banichi and Tano and Algini had come in. "Nand' Cajeiri and Jegari have taken mecheiti, and the house has made a dangerous amount of inquiry on its antiquated com system. Bren-ji, what are you doing?"

"Going after them, nadiin-ji."

"By no means!"

"To appeal to Taiben was my idea, nadiin. It was my suggestion in passing that provided the notion, and the dowager forced the boy to write the letter himself." Personal distress overset coherent arguments, but in his mind, certain things had leapt up in crystal clarity, a boy's sense of honor, a new-made obligation, a shiny new man'chi, and a detestable letter he had been forced to write. "This job I can possibly do, since negotiations with the Kadigidi are highly unlikely tonight. The boy knows me; the Taibeni know me, if we have to chase them that far."

"They know us as well," Banichi said, clearly about to propose the paidhi stay put and his staff take the trip in his stead.

"And if they take you for Atageini staff riding across that line after them, there is every likelihood of misunderstanding, and of utter disaster if they take you for Kadigidi. Me, there is no mistaking, and the boys will less likely run from me. Go say so to the house staff. Say it to Cenedi. Get us mecheiti to overtake them." A car might have a certain advantage getting to the gate if there was one available that could go above a walking pace, but not on the estate's winding roads and certainly not overland, and least of all that ornate antique Lord Tatiseigi had used to meet them. The youngsters had had a long head start, and might well go overland. "Quickly, nadiin!"

He rarely ordered details of a security response. His staff habitually made all the operational decisions. But this was not a defensive situation, even Banichi knew it, and they took orders and left in haste, all but Jago, who stayed for his protection and made his staff's preparations, lightweight for her Guild, but involving plenty of ammunition, long and short, two rifles, a handful of other ring-clipped small bags, not a light load for any two humans.

"The computer," he recalled in alarm, and went and flung it open, dithered over the keys until he had it up, and input a personal code, then shut down and shoved it and Shawn's unit into the back of the linen closet, breathless with haste. "I have put it under lock, Jago. I'll tell you the code once we go outside. It will be safer left here, hidden. One fears it will be people that the Kadigidi will be looking for."

"Yes," she said brusquely, in working-mode, no nonsense and no courtesies. She held the door for him and they both exited into the hall.

So, it developed, had Ilisidi exited her rooms, between them and the stairs. Ilisidi was standing in the hall near the steps, appearing in no mood to trifle, and house staff was attempting explanations.

"Damned fools!" she shouted, or approximately that. "Nand' paidhi?"

"Aiji-ma, one hears the window alarm was disconnected. One supposes the young gentleman has undertaken the mission himself. I shall find him. Atageini might be shot trying it."

"So might he, the young idiot. We have emphasized that the western defenses must be let down for him no matter what happens here, which one trusts this household has the basic skills to accomplish. We have asked for an accounting of every person in this household, and we intend to have it! We only hope he has gone by his own will! Why are you standing there, nandi?"

"Aiji-ma." He hurried for the stairs, Jago right with him, hastened down them, and met Cenedi on his way up. "Cenedi-ji, we are going after the boy ourselves, at all speed. Can the gatekeeper possibly be queried and advised to prevent them without betraying the nature of the problem?"

One rarely saw Cenedi so distressed—not since the boy had pulled his cursed tricks on the ship. A houseful of Guild on high alert—but occupied in general conference—and the boy, who had heard all the complaints about lax security, had gotten out of his quarters and followed Antaro. One hoped that was the whole story.

"The window was open, nadi-ji," Jago said to Cenedi. "The window contact was pried loose inside and stuck against its receiver, this while the system was armed. We are headed for the stables. The young gentleman and his companion have taken mecheiti."

"Clever lad," Cenedi said, tightlipped. "Nandi." And with that parting courtesy and fire in his eye Cenedi went up to inform the dowager of whatever detail of the situation he had been going to report. Some of Ilisidi's young men were with her in the upstairs—one could hear Cenedi deliver instructions, sending his own men to manage a discreet phone call to the gate, and to check windows up and down the hall. By the time they reached the downstairs Lord Tatiseigi himself was out of his study in a cluster of his own men, looking entirely discommoded.

"Our precautions are adequate," Tatiseigi shouted at the commotion above, "unless sabotaged!"

Bren wanted no part of that dispute. He headed out through the lily foyer, out the front doors of the house, with Jago, and found Tano headed up the broad steps.

"The boys told the grooms that the dowager had sent them with a further message," Tano said. "They took the last two of lord Tatiseigi's mecheiti and rode out to overtake the girl."

"The scoundrels," Bren muttered, heading down the steps.

"Come, Tano-ji," Jago said, "all of us are going." Tano, whom Banichi might have sent back to watch the gear, changed course and immediately headed down the steps again, overtaking them on the cobbled drive and taking part of the load of ammunition and one of the rifles as they walked.

The path to the stables lay at the side of the house, beyond a well-trimmed, doubtless security-rife hedge, devices that would not likely have been activated, not with household staff coming and going to the stables on emergency missions.

Clever, damnable young scoundrels. Lying was not Cajeiri's usual recourse, but it was within his arsenal. It was in those novels he had been reading and those entertainments he had been viewing on the ship.

At least—at least, Bren said to himself, the boys were only loyal and stupid, not kidnapped.

Breathlessly, down the well-trimmed path to the stables. Mecheiti were complaining. Loudly. Banichi, Algini and the grooms were in the process of saddling up.

"You should not go, Bren-ji," Banichi said, heaving on a girth. "Our numbers are more fortunate without you."

Seven without and eight and ten with, counting the expected recovery of three fugitives and two Atageini escorts.

"But less fortunate numbers toward finding them in

the first place," Bren shot back. Two could do that kind of math, and his staff was by no means superstitious. "The defenses are confirmed down in the west, Banichi-ji."

Jago muttered: "One doubts the boy will join the escort. He will follow them. And we know what tale he will tell the gatekeeper."

"Someone is calling the gate to forestall that." But not someone with knowledge of how the boys had gotten the mecheiti. "Go advise them the boy is using the dowager's name, 'Gini-ji. Run."

"Yes," Algini said, and sprinted.

"They took the two remaining of the local herd," Banichi said, "prize stock, and were gone at high speed."

"One assumes you will take our own herd leader."

"I intend to," Banichi said. Another saddle had gone on, the last. "Up, Bren-ji."

Bren accepted the boost up, took up the quirt, kept quiet, under the overhang of the stable roof. Banichi accepted a rifle and an ammunition kit from Jago, slung it over his shoulder and mounted up. The rest of them did.

"We offer apologies," the head groom said, "profound apologies for this sorry affair, nandi."

"You were lied to, nadiin," Bren said, as good a grace as he could muster, and the stable revolved in his vision as Banichi took the leader out and the mecheita under him followed as if on an invisible lead.

The rest of them had mounted up, and moved out, Algini's moving with them. Behind them, wood splintered. A barrier shattered.

"Damn," Bren said, looking over his shoulder.

"We have mistaken one of our matriarchs," Tano said. And no question, in unfamiliarity with the herd, they had not recognized the mecheita in question, ranking matriarch. The gate was broken and the mecheita that had broken it surged past the grooms with a rip of her dangerous head. The grooms scrambled back. Three more mecheiti, exiting behind the other, took out a porch-post on their way to daylight, and with a thunder and a squeal of nails and wood, the porch sagged. The whole unsaddled herd broke out, following them along the path to the cobbled drive.

Algini met them on the drive, at the bottom, hard-breathing. "They passed the gate, nandi. But not the boys. Two loose mecheiti showed up with the party before they reached the gate, saddled, and joined the others. The boys have taken off afoot, likely to scale the fence."

Oh, two years of conning ship's personnel, building little electric cars and playing hob with ship's security had created a boy far, far too clever for his own good. It was not the Taibeni teenagers that had accomplished this entire escape. He had no such notion. It was an eight-year-old Ragi prince with far too much confidence in his own cleverness, a deft touch with electrical gadgets he had gained from building toy cars with Mospheiran engineers and Guild Assassins, and a way of assuming such conviction, such lordly force, that he often got past adults' wiser instincts. Not to mention other things he had gained from Guild company: speed to get near the gate, and never rely on the same trick twice.

Algini mounted up, the whole herd in motion. They rode clear of the despised cobbles, the mecheiti stepping on eggshells all the way. On the first edge of the roadway Banichi took out at a loping run, not a comfortable pace, not something they had done in a long while, and Bren took a moment to find his balance, already finding the saddle a renewed misery.

Too late already, too damned late to prevent a commotion. The defenses were down, the boys had had better than an hour to be across the fence, and, damn it all, the escort would be riding along beyond the estate fence with two extra mecheiti they could by no means drive off—instinct would not allow it; and with two boys hellbent on overtaking them.

"Nadiin," the young scoundrel would say to them when they met, his golden eyes clear and as pure as glass, "the dowager my great-grandmother has added a message, which we are to carry ourselves."

And what could two Atageini say to the contrary?

"Maybe," Bren said to his companions, foreknowing if there was any good hope someone would have seen to it, "maybe the gate can call ahead to the escort and have them bring the boys back."

"Not optimum, Bren-ji," Banichi said. "These cursed units of theirs make every transmission a risk. And that is not information to spread abroad."

Tatiseigi was known to be as tight-fisted about technology as he was liberal with artists, conservative, reputedly not replacing the house gas lights with electricity until, oh, about ten years ago. But—good God, to short his security. . . .

If the Kadigidi had monitored the house transmissions, everyone listening might get the idea that young gentlemen were roaming about the neighborhood virtually unprotected.

And would not the Kadigidi already be bending every effort to get there, while, thanks to the breakout, *they* had every last mecheita in the stable following after the young rascal, so that Cenedi and the dowager had no recourse but to stay and defend the house, or escape in Lord Tatiseigi's antiquated motorcar.

The girl's escort would not necessarily suspect the boys of lying to them. Prudence dictated they not load the airwaves with inquiries to confirm the story. The boys would simply get their mounts back, with only moderately suspicious looks from Tatiseigi's men—"We got down to fix a girth and they ran from us, nadiin. . . .we knew they would go to you. We ran to catch up."

Such a common mishap: mecheiti with two of their number having disappeared over the horizon were inclined to present a problem in control, once they got the scent on the trail, and only two very foolish boys would both get down out of the saddle at the same time.

Those boys were now, at all good odds, themselves on their way to Taiben with Antaro . . . and if that were all the trouble they were facing at this point, Bren said to himself, he would cease his pursuit and let the youngsters reach the Taibeni, and, granted the Taibeni's better sense, believe they would stay there.

But given all the fuss on the com system had made it likely the Kidigidi had wind of confusion on the northwestern side of Atageini land, he could not leave it at that. The Taibeni, on their side, would not have a clue to what was happening, and the two Atageini guards, while reasonably cautious, might not have any apprehension what a commotion had arisen around their mission.

Not good, Bren said to himself. It was not at all good.

12

Bren held on, clamped the leading leg against the saddle and kept a grip on the leather. Any random glance back showed the whole damned mecheiti herd crowding the narrow roadway, shoving against the low hedges, outright trampling them down as they went, where slight gaps in the shrubbery made spreading out attractive. Banichi stayed in the lead, and Banichi delayed for no second thoughts—in the hope—Bren nursed it, too—that Antaro and her escort would ride at a saner pace, perhaps stopping to talk at the gate, perhaps stopping to talk or argue where they met the boys—not long, but every moment gave them a chance.

The gate and the tall outer fence appeared as they crested a particular hill. The gatekeeper left his little weather-shelter amongst the vines and, clearly forewarned, opened the gates for them, to let them straight on through.

Banichi reined in, however, and all the other mecheiti halted, blowing and snorting, jammed up close.

"Nadi," Banichi said. "If the girl's escort comes back and we do not, send them back out to us. We may need help out there. We fear the Kadigidi may be on to the messenger."

"Nadi," the man said—not, perhaps, the same watcher they had antagonized the night before—"nadi, one had no prior advisement there was any possible difficulty—"

"Indeed," Bren said. "We know. They took the extra mecheiti with them?"

"Yes, nandi. They said the strays had overtaken them, and they were puzzled. I had no means to keep them, and one feared they would stray along inside the fence, if . . ."

"We shall find them. No fault to you. Be warned: we may come back very soon, or we may come back much later, at any hour, in company with Taibeni. Or maybe even Taibeni without us. That is the young woman's mission, under your lord's seal. They will be allies."

"Most of all watch out for yourself, nadi," Banichi said. "There has been far too much com traffic."

"We have asked the house to send out reinforcement. They are sending it."

"Good," Banichi said, and with a pop of the quirt set the leader in motion, which put all of them to a traveling pace uphill beyond the gate.

Tracks of the girl and the escort were plain on the road, tracks that by now involved five mecheiti—and now their own mecheiti, catching the notion of what they were tracking, entered hunting-mode, the leader lowering his snaky neck to snuff above the ground as they went. It was an unsettling move at a run. Bren's mecheita followed suit, an instant in which he feared the beast would take a tumble under him. He knew exactly what it was doing, and dared not jerk the rein.

Up came the head with a rude snort and a lurch forward of the beast's own accord, and it loped ahead, coming nearly stride for stride with Banichi's beast, which drew a surly head-toss . . . mecheiti were not averse to hunting others of their kind, with malice aforethought, and this sudden taking of a scent was not a happy situation, not safe, and not good for the ones being tracked.

And, my God, Bren thought, recalling where they had borrowed these creatures . . . these were hunters of more than game. Mecheiti were stubborn creatures, and these with uncapped tusks, that they had gotten from Taiben, from the rangers peculiarly charged with

Tabini's security—what would this band do, he wondered, when they overtook their Atageini-bred quarry?

"One fears they are hunting," he said to Banichi.

"That they are, Bren-ji," Banichi said, "and they will need a hard hand once we come in range."

Last night's rain had left a lingering moisture in the grass, particularly on the shaded side of hills, where the track showed clear even to human eyes. Mecheiti snatched mouthfuls of grass on the run, rocked along at that rolling gait they could adopt on the hunt, trailing grassy bits. They clumped up together, the herd-leader foremost, along with the young female Bren rode, and the unridden retired matriarch who had been their trouble back at the stables, all bunched in the lead. Low brush stood not a chance where the herd wanted to pass. When the leader moved, hell itself could not stop the rest . . . willingly headed, Bren began to add it up from the mecheiti's point of view, for their own territory, for Taiben itself, now on the trail of the others that their dim mecheita brains might reasonably think of as interlopers in that territory.

Trouble, he had no doubt. Trouble, and Lord Tatiseigi's prize stock, those likely with tusks capped . . . and what can I do to hold this creature?

Banichi reined back as they reached a trampled spot, a space where a handful of mecheiti had waited and milled about, grass flattened. Algini pointed to the side, and sure enough, even to a less skilled eye, a small track came in there, a line coming across the hill as one track, then diverging into two, and coming right up on their location.

"The boys joined them here," Tano said, but even the paidhi had figured that out—knowing the boy in question, if not how to read a trail.

"And got their mecheiti back," Jago said.

Their own mecheiti, milling about and getting the scent from the ground, had obliterated any finer tracks. Banichi started them moving again, and by now the

whole herd had the scent clear, and moved with una-
nimity . . . willing to run, willing to spend energy they
had not used on their way toward Atageini land.

A pop of Banichi's quirt and the leader lurched into
a flat-out run, a pace the Atageini would not reasonably
have adopted on their way. They were using up their
own mecheiti's strength, and even considering the
beasts were willing now, that would fade quickly.

We have a slim chance of finding them before dark,
Bren reasoned to himself, yielding to the rock and snap
of the gait, less sore now: numbness had cut in, and
nothing mattered at the moment but the hope of seeing
five mecheiti somewhere in the distant rolls of the pas-
tureland.

The sun sank, and sank toward the horizon. The
Atageini and the youngsters would almost certainly
stop for the night. They entered dusk, and the trail grew
dim, but the scent would not.

"Nadiin." Algini rode to the fore and pointed toward
the hill. Bren saw nothing. He hoped it was the youngsters and their escort, but their mecheiti gave no sign of
having spotted their quarry.

"Converging with their trail," Algini said ominously.

"What?" Bren was constrained to ask.

"Another track, Bren-ji," Banichi said. "Game,
maybe, but one fears not."

Something had moved along that hill and veered
toward the party they were tracking. Either it was an
older game track, that the youngsters' party had
crossed, or something was following them . . . and no
four-legged predator in its right senses would stalk several mecheiti.

Only other mecheiti would come in like that. And
none that they knew would be here just running loose
around the landscape.

Not good, Bren thought, and said nothing. His bodyguard knew the score better than he did. Banichi used
the quirt and took them up the hillside, veered over

onto the intersecting trail and there reined to a slower pace and to a stop, letting the herd leader get *that* scent clear before it joined the other trail.

Tusked head came up, nostrils flared, head swinging to that new trail like a needle to the magnetic pole.

And they started to move again, fast, with several pops of the quirt.

We could just as well run into ambush at this pace, Bren thought, but he no longer led this expedition: Banichi did, and the paidhi dropped way, way back in the hierarchy of decision-making. Jago had moved up beside Banichi, in front of him, pressing her mount to defy the ordinary order of proceeding, and Tano and Algini moved up on either side to keep the paidhi in their close company, leaving Banichi and Jago free to make more aggressive decisions.

Up and over the ridge, Tano riding athwart Bren's path to prevent his mecheita following Banichi's too closely at this point . . . they pressed along the trail that now was merged with the youngsters, or overlay that track, moving as hard as they could go, across a brook and up the other bank. The incoming riders had taken no pains to disguise their track.

Dark was falling fast now. And Banichi reined in just short of the next rise of the land, slid down and handed the herd-leader's rein across to Jago, but the creature pulled at the restraint, wanting to be let loose, eyes rolling, nostrils flared, and the rest of the herd trembled with eagerness, not that even the unridden matriarch would go past the leader. Banichi said something to Jago too low for Bren's ears, passed her his mecheita's rein and suddenly moved, slipping off along the top of the ridge with eye-tricking speed. He didn't crest the hill—he melted over it, and was gone. And Jago had clambered down and up to the other saddle, taking the herd leader for herself, her own left riderless with the rein looped up for safety.

Bren sat still and kept the rein wrapped desperately

around his fist, giving up no slack. He felt a skin-twitch shake the mecheita's shoulder under his foot, as it gave a soft, explosive snort of sheer lust for combat.

He dared ask nothing. He guessed too much already. The herd leader was trying to break Jago's control, and she hauled back with all her strength, pulling its head away from the direction it wanted to go, forcing it in a circle. It stopped, stood rock-steady.

Not a sound, except the small movements and breathing of the mecheiti under them and around them, the whole herd held with Jago's grip on the leader.

A gunshot, a single, horrendous pop and echo.

"Head down, Bren-ji!" Jago drove the leader forward and the whole herd lunged after her, up over the hill, down the other side in the dusk.

Bren ducked as low to the saddle as possible, tried to see where he was going. More shots echoed off the hills. Jago and two unsaddled mecheiti ran in the lead, one on each side of her, and suddenly they veered, plunged into a ravine. Mecheiti stood in the dusk ahead of them, whose mecheiti or how situated he had no time to reckon. The mecheita he was on gave a squalling challenge and charged through prickly brush, raking his leg, catching his jacket, breaking off bits against his trousers on its way to murder. They hit, another mecheita ripped a head-butt at his, and he plied the quirt desperately, getting it away. Two surges of the body under him and they were in the clear again, charging uphill after mecheiti in retreat.

He reined aside, to bring the beast slightly across the hill face without pulling it over. The heart of the fight was no place for him, whatever was going on. He had no idea whether they had just scattered the escort's mecheiti and driven off animals they needed. But his mecheita paid no attention, just ran blindly, crashed through other brush and kept going, defying his pull on the rein.

Someone rode near him, headed his mecheita off

from pursuit. Tano. Again. Behind him, a volley of gunfire exploded in the dark.

"Hold here, Bren-ji," Tano said. "Hold!"

He had no breath to object that he was trying to do
just that. He hauled, the mecheita hauled back and he
thought the rein might snap or the cantankerous creature, lunging ahead crosswise of the slope, would break
both their necks before he could get it to stop at the bottom. He risked one hand to reach back and lay in hard
with the quirt on the rump, which caused the rump end
to shy off, and the whole beast finally to turn in the direction he wanted.

But now the rest of the herd was coming back toward
them, Jago in the saddle, and the whole lot, riderless and
ridden, shouldered past him and Tano. Their two
mecheiti swung about, fell into the herd, and they
charged back down the draw, toward the origin of the
gunfire.

A whistle, a very welcome whistle, came out of the
brushy dark, and Bren drew a whole breath. Banichi
was all right.

Their mecheiti meanwhile settled to a determined
walk, and broke brush as they went. "Keep down," Tano
said, reining back near him.

Then Banichi's voice, out in the dark: "We are the
paidhi-aiji's guard. Identify yourselves."

"Banichi?" asked a very shaky young voice. "Where
are you?"

A gunshot. A whisper of brush. And from Banichi,
distant, "Stay where you are."

A long, long wait, then. Jago reined in and all the
mecheiti slowed to a stop, waiting, with occasionally a
snort at the information wafted on the air.

"They are moving!" The same high young voice.

"Damn," Jago hissed. "Tano!"

Tano and Algini both leapt off, instantly vanishing
into the brush and the dark, in silence.

"Bren-ji," Jago said. "If things go wrong, use the quirt and use it so hard it can't think."

Ride away, she meant. Get back to the gate. Get to Taiben. Go anywhere else. A young gentleman calling out instructions to his bodyguard had made himself a target and now his protectors had no choice but to go after his attackers.

Gunshot, flash in the dark. A brief scuffle somewhere, followed by a thump.

"Keep your head down." Banichi's voice came softly, ever so welcome, out in the distance. Meanwhile, Bren thought, he and Jago sat on mecheiti, silhouettes against the dark, he because he was helpless afoot, endangered by the mecheiti themselves, and Jago because if the herd leader slipped control they would all be afoot and trapped out here. That made them targets, no question, and all he could do was press as flat to his own knees as he could get, trying not to be shot by some ateva who could see far, far better than he could in this murk.

Gunfire. Gunfire responded, and something skidded on gravel.

"I shot him." A quavering young voice piped up in the darkness the other side of the brush. "I think I shot him, Banichi."

"You may well have, young aiji. Are you injured?"

Banichi had used the indefinite-number in that address, baji-naji, the whole future of the planet on a knife's edge. Bren held his breath, lifted his head, trying to hear, and hearing nothing but his mecheita's movements and the creak of the saddle.

"I am not. But they killed our escort." That same young voice, a young gentleman who, at least was still alive. And so was Banichi. But they had heard nothing from Tano and Algini.

Then a different whistle from out of the dark.

"Come ahead," Banichi said, and suddenly Jago shot ahead, and Bren's mecheita went with her and all the rest, down a gravelly draw, across a little brook, up another bank. A breeze caught them there, a chill little breeze, bringing a shiver.

"There were three," Tano said quietly out of the dark, "that we have accounted for. One may have escaped afoot. Keep low."

Bad position. One Guildsman unseen represented a major problem.

"Bren-ji," Jago said, "get down."

"Yes," he said, moved his leg from across the mecheita's shoulder, secured the rein, gripped the saddle and slid down, wary of the creature's tusks, expecting its head would swing toward him, and it did. He was ready for it. He popped it gently on the nose with the quirt and it swung that massive head back up, veered off indignantly and stood, as fixed by its leader's staying as if it had been tethered there.

Shadows, meanwhile, moved on the slope, softly disturbing the gravel of a little eroded outcrop.

"Nadiin," he heard a young female voice say: Antaro. "Nadiin, one regrets, the two Atageini are dead, down there."

More movement. "Dead, indeed," Algini said from their vicinity.

"The mecheiti ran away," Cajeiri's voice said.

"As they would, young sir."

"Did nand' Bren send you?"

"Nand' Bren is with us, young sir, and by no means pleased with your actions, no more than your great-grandmother."

"We have to go on, Banichi!"

"How do you propose to ride, young sir, with no tack?"

"We have our tack, nadi." That, from Jegari. "We had unsaddled for the night."

"We told them we should not stop." From Cajeiri.

The boy happened to be right. Even the paidhi knew that. They could well have kept going. They should have kept going to the border, given the urgency of the message, and without the escort's adult advice, the youngsters, schooled in a more desperate experience, would have.

"The tack and the supplies are right here." Antaro's young voice. A slide on gravel. "We were down here, nadi."

Atevi could see clearly in this darkness. It was all shadows to human eyes.

But suddenly: "Down!" Tano yelled.

Bren dropped to his haunches, behind the thin cover of the brush, and reached to his pocket, seeking his gun.

"Keep low!" Banichi's voice.

Someone must be moving nearby, sounds too faint for human ears. Bren sat holding his pistol, virtually blind, knowing his vision posed a hazard to his own people, and declined even to have his finger on the trigger until he could confirm a target. Somewhere out there, Guild were stalking each other. Some Kadigidi Assassin had let his mecheita go after its fellows, staying to carry out his mission, and the best the paidhi could do was stay very, very quiet, as wary of keen atevi hearing as of atevi nightsight.

Small movements within his hearing. He could not tell the distance. His heart was in his throat. And for a long, long time, there was no sound at all.

Scrape of brush from down the ravine.

More furtive movements, barely discernible. Their mecheiti shifted about. Jago had never gotten down, as he recalled. He feared she remained dangerously exposed. One of the most classic moves was to get the one rider holding the leader, encouraging the herd to bolt. But Jago was a good rider. She might be over on the mecheita's shoulder, shielded between two beasts.

Brush broke. Splash in the little brook, crack of a quirt, and all of a sudden the whole herd moved, crashed past Bren on two sides, rushed past like a living wall, down the stream-course, up the slope, and all he could do was duck. Gunfire broke out. Two shots. Then silence.

Bren sat still, blind in the dark, sure that his was the only piece of brush on the slope that had not been crushed flat. They might have taken him for a rock, dodged around him. They had no compunction at all about running over a man.

A calf muscle began to twitch uncomfortably. A thigh muscle followed. It became a shiver. He settled his finger onto the trigger of his gun. It was all he had, if any enemy circled back trying to get to the young people. He thought that Jago had ridden that charge, deliberately sent the whole herd down the throat of the ravine and up the slope, likely in pursuit of someone, or to flush a man out.

Not a sound from the young people, not a question from Cajeiri, not a twitch.

Then a rustle of someone moving along the bank. "Nandi."

Tano.

"Tano-ji?"

"We have gotten one of them, nandi, who may well be the last."

"Are you all right?"

"No injury, nandi. Put the weapons down, nadiin." This, to the children tucked down in the dark. "Come down, but keep low."

A pale glimmer. The two Taibeni wore dark clothing. Cajeiri had come out on this venture in light trousers, his beige human-style jacket that was the warmest thing he had—and an absolute liability in the dark.

"Nadiin." From Algini, whose approach Bren had not heard, a realization that set his heart pounding. "Gather the tack and supplies."

Mecheiti were coming back down, brush crackling under that shadow-flood of bodies. Bren judged it safe to stand up, and did, on legs strained from the unnatural position and just a little inclined to shiver, whether from the cold of the earth or the reckoning of their situation. He put the safety back on his pistol and slipped it back into his pocket as Cajeiri and Jegari came skidding down the gravelly slope together to join Antaro.

Then:

"Gunfire," Jago said from somewhere above him.

Bren could hear nothing at all. It must be distant.

"Tirnamardi?" he asked, a leaden chill settling about his heart.

"Yes," Jago said. "Whether at the gate or further east, I cannot tell."

"Saddle our spares," Banichi said. "We have no time to sit here."

General movement. It took perhaps a quarter-hour more to pick out three mecheiti from the herd and saddle them.

"Antaro-nadi," Banichi said.

"Nadi." Antaro's young voice, in the dark.

"Have you that gun, young woman?"

"Yes, nadi, I have one, and nand' Cajeiri has the other. And I have the com unit."

"Put them all away. They betray your position. Rely on your guard. Ride at all times to the paidhi's left, never otherwise. He knows where to ride relative to our weapons. Do not make a mistake in that regard, any of you. Someone could die for it."

"I shall try, Banichi-nadi." From Cajeiri, with a certain dignity.

"Never mind trying," Banichi said sternly. "Do, young sir. *Do.* Get up. Do you need help getting up?"

"I shall do it myself," Cajeiri said. "I *have* done it."

Bren worked his own way close to the herd, located Jago's shadow against the sky and located a mecheita with an empty saddle. He thought it was his, and by the scrollwork on the saddle, it seemed to be. He got it to extend a leg and bow down, and he heaved himself, stiff and sore, belly down across the saddle, then straightened around, got his left foot in position at the curve of the neck and unsecured the guiding rein. Everyone else was up, by then, and without another word, they started moving, climbing the other slope, passing through the greatest likelihood of further ambush. Bren's heart beat like a hammer while they passed that zone.

"Are we going to Taiben?" Cajeiri asked.

"Hush!" Jago's voice, sharply, to a boy, who, if he was not shot in the next hour, might be aiji.

And who, having spent so much time away from geographic referents, away from any subtle sense of the land, or the clues of the heavens, had trouble telling what direction they were riding. Cajeiri was lost. Terrible things had happened to so much bright enthusiasm. The maneuver the boys had believed would be a grand adventure and a great success had turned very dark indeed, and there was no mending it, only staying alive.

But after they had passed that region, after Banichi and Jago had exchanged a few quiet words, Bren found Cajeiri and the Taibeni riding next to him.

"Young gentleman?"

"Nand' Bren?"

"We are riding toward Taiben. The Kadigidi have attacked your great-uncle's house, and those of us who might help defend it are out here."

"Finding help!"

"Finding help, yes. But you should know it is well possible, young gentleman, that your encounter was not chance. Your enemies found you by means of your great-uncle's unsecured com system. Messages flew back and forth, unsecured, trying to prevent your going out here. It was not well done, young gentleman."

"And they might have ambushed Antaro and the escort all the same, nandi!"

Oh, the heir was not as beaten down as one might expect. He was his father's son. And his mother's. And that burgeoning arrogance, if unchecked, could get others killed.

"Consult. Consult Banichi and Cenedi, young sir.

Consult me. If your young staff had reason for misgivings about the mission, you should have told us, not gone off, stealing mecheiti, lying to the stable staff—"

"Grandmother would never have let me go."

"And do you think there was no reason for us to refuse such a request, nadi? And was there an excuse for lying to us?"

"When asking does no good!"

"Except that Antaro is Taibeni and might have accomplished this mission with a certain finesse which one does not see evident in our current circumstance, young sir."

"Except if Antaro was ambushed. And she was. And the escort would never listen to her opinions, or take her as important. And Cenedi thinks there are spies in the house. If I tell Banichi, Banichi tells you, you tell grandmother, grandmother tells Lord Tatiseigi and he tells his staff, and then the Kadigidi know everything you do, nandi. Maybe they *can* overhear the com units, but maybe, too, someone just told them."

It was a very sharp young wit, and a certain command of language. One saw his father.

"That may be, young sir, but there are always ways to consult in secret."

"No one uses them with me! No one takes us seriously! The Atageini would not listen even to me when I said we should keep going. They said we would sleep til dawn and I said they were fools! Now the Kadigidi are at the house attacking my grandmother, and it will be another day before we can even get to Taiben, let alone back again!"

"You are certainly right in that," he had to admit. "But mecheiti are not machines. They have to rest, and sooner or later, we will have to."

"One does regret very much that the guards are dead," Cajeiri said after a moment—a boy who had just shot at a man, killed him, and seen two decent men go down protecting him . . . never mind they had not done wisely.

"As one should always regret such an event," Bren said, and let it go. The boy had passed from deep shock to a reasonable, shaken outrage at the situation. Only eight. Only eight, with physical strength exceeding an adult human's and with two followers who had served only as a slight anchor on his high and wide decisions— an especially slight restraint in an Atageini hall whose lord radiated detestation of his Taibeni escort, and Ilisidi herself had maneuvered for advantage with that very powerful lord's opinions.

Had that been Cajeiri's inner conclusion as to why Ilisidi had sent Antaro away from him?

Not an accurate assessment of his great-grandmother, if that was the case, and Tatiseigi himself knew his old feuds with the Taibeni counted for nothing with Ilisidi. But he kept his mouth shut on further argument with the boy on that score.

"Well put, with the boy, Bren-ji," Jago found the opportunity to say when they did dismount and take a breather. They were shifting saddles about, his bodyguard trading their gear to others of the herd, except only the herd leader, who constantly carried, at least, Jago's lighter weight. She slid down to stretch her legs, keeping the herd leader at very short rein.

"One never knows, Jago-ji, what to say to him."

"Someone should listen to these young people," Jago said, uncommon criticism of, Bren thought, the dowager's dealings with her grandson. "Tano has tried."

"How should I advise them?"

"Exactly as you have."

"I gave them no advice at all, nadi."

"You listened to him as if he were a man, Bren-ji. That, in itself, makes a point."

It did, perhaps. Perhaps he had done that. His acquaintance with children in his whole adult life had been, precisely, Cajeiri, whose developing mind was rapidly turning in unpredictible directions, and he worried. The boy had killed—a child who had been very far from his own kind, in a situation rife with violence, a child far too exposed to human culture, a child who, given present circumstances, might soon *be* aiji over three quarters of the world, and who had not been on his own planet long enough to know instinctively which was east and which was west.

"I hardly know that a human has any business at all advising him. He may have read far too many of our books."

"He learned from the kyo as well, Bren-ji."

Odd to think that, in instincts if not experience, he might be as alien to the boy's hardwiring as were the kyo. Scary, to think that. They at least had shared a planet.

"Bren-ji." Tano walked up in the dark and pressed a paper-wrapped object into his hand, one of those concentrate bars they had gotten from the escort, as it proved. He realized he had not eaten since breakfast, and the slight definition he began to see in figures and shapes advised him that dawn was not far off, a new day coming.

They had gone straight through till morning. A morning in which, if the defense of Tirnamardi had failed, every power in the world he knew might have changed, and everything he relied on might have gone down in defeat.

In that cheerful thought, he wasn't sure he could get the food down, but he soberly unwrapped it and tried, a mostly dry mouthful. For the mecheiti's sake, they had stopped by a stream—perhaps the same one they had crossed before. He walked over past the herd, to drink upstream of the mecheiti's wading and drinking.

He squatted down on the soft margin, cupped up water in his hands.

Mecheiti moved, heads lifting. He froze, looked up, and saw a man standing on the slight rise across the brook.

He let fall the water, thrust his hand into his pocket

and settled his hand around the pistol grip. But a man bent on mischief would have lain flat on that rise and fired at them. It hardly seemed an attack.

"Papa!" Antaro exclaimed, a clear high voice in the night. But commendably from cover.

"Taro-ji." From the figure that was, indisputably, Deiso. "Is the dowager here?"

"No, nadi," Banichi said, from their side of the brook, and stepping into the clear. "But the paidhi's guard is."

"Banichi-nadi. We saw the fire in the east. Is that my son?"

"Papa," Jegari said from somewhere beyond the wall of alert mecheiti. "It is. With nand' Cajeiri and the paidhi-aiji."

"Your daughter was sent to find nand' Keimi," Banichi said, "with a message from the dowager. The fire in the dark is likely a Kadigidi attack on Tirna-mardi."

"Kadigidi Assassins killed the men with us," Antaro said. "And the paidhi and his guard came. And I have the message, papa, with Lord Tatiseigi's seal and the dowager's both. They need help."

"My great-grandmother," Cajeiri said in a clear, young voice that carried through the dark, "asked me to write the letter. And great-uncle signed it and put his seal on it with hers. He asks politely."

A small space of silence.

"One knew there would be inconvenient entanglements," Deiso said, "when the aiji took an Atageini consort."

"My mother!" Cajeiri declared in his father's tone. "And you are my cousin, once removed!"

"That I am," Deiso said.

"*I* will go back and rescue my great-grandmother," Cajeiri said. "And *we* will go back." That familiar we, that we-myself-and-my-house—including, now, the man's own son and daughter. "Come with us, nandi."

God. It *was* his father, top to bottom.

"The heir should not go back," Deiso said. "These young people should none of them go into a firefight."

"And where will the mecheiti go?" Cajeiri asked, standing his ground. "I am not a good rider, nandiin. I am sure he would break away and go with you."

"He is a Taiben mecheita," Jago said, "and going to his home range. Failing that, the young gentleman can safely walk to Taiben."

"No," Cajeiri said flatly. "We shall go with you, Jago-nadi. We will go back to my great-grandmother, and nand' Deiso will bring his people to rescue her and my great-uncle, and we cannot stand here wasting time and arguing the way the Atageini did!"

"Time," Banichi said, "is already running against us. Transmissions have fallen silent."

Had there been any? Banichi had not said.

"An appeal from the aiji-dowager," Deiso said, and gave a warbling whistle, which brought a number of others over the rise in the gray hint of a dawn. "We have mecheiti."

None were in evidence at the moment. The rangers had made a silent, careful approach. Very many things had turned up in their path that the paidhi's human ears had never caught. He felt a little lost, and exhausted, and they seemed to be losing the argument with Cajeiri. He didn't like that aspect of things, didn't know whether he could gain anything at all by objecting, or whether the boy would at all regard a protest from him.

"There are nine of us," Deiso said. "By no means all the force we can raise. Nand' Cajeiri, here is one job well suited to young people. Get to a relay and advise Keimi we need help, and that we need it soon."

"Nandi," Cajeiri protested.

"Young sir," Banichi said, "do it. This is necessary."

"Yes," Cajeiri said. "But when they come, we are coming with them!"

"As may be," Deiso conceded, and walked among them, touching his son and his daughter, a brief contact, a bow from the young people, a goodbye. "You know the situation. Nand' Keimi will ask your authority. Say the wind has shifted. Remember it. Go."

"Go, indeed." Banichi lost no time in escorting Cajeiri to his mount and boosting him up to the saddle. The Taibeni youngsters hurried to reach their own mecheiti, and with their agile skill, were up before Cajeiri had gotten the quirt and the rein straightened away.

The youngsters departed at a run, headed back to this herd's home territory, under strong persuasion and use of the quirts—the three would part with the others. It was the herd leader who had to be fought back and held—Jago had scrambled up beforehand and gotten him under restraint, and while two of the unsaddled mecheiti decided to go with the departing youngsters, Tano and Algini showed up between them and the three outbound, turning them with mere broken branches, moving them back to the herd, remounts, Bren said to himself, that they were going to need to make any speed at all.

And in that moment of argument, his own mecheita relatively still, if weaving in confusion, Bren thought he should get its attention and get up while he had his chance. He grabbed the saddle leather, hauled himself up as the beast turned in place, the best and chanciest mount he had ever executed in his life. He snatched the rein unsecured, got the quirt properly back against the hindquarters, to steer it straight—damned proud of himself, that he was not lying in the dirt being rescued. Tano and Algini, who had come to rescue him, went to their own mecheiti.

Other mecheiti were arriving over the low rise, the two herd-leaders squalling at each other, and more rangers, some mounted, some afoot like Deiso, brought them. The youngsters' mother was likely with them, Bren thought, not to mention cousins and uncles and aunts, all keeping a weather-eye toward Atageini territory and not hesitating to ride well into it, when they'd caught wind of trouble . . . *without* that message, they might have come in, a whole lineage set at risk for the sake of a son and daughter involved in this chancy business, and never, so far as he had observed, had a word to that effect passed between father and children, nor had their mother come in to wish them on their way. But they were headed in a safe direction, the best and safest direction Cajeiri could take. In Taiben there were unquestioned allies, people to support and protect the heir if the worst happened and the paidhi and his great-grandmother and all the rest perished in this foolishness. Worry was wasted in that direction, he decided.

But he had no choice. If Taibeni were going to the heart of Atageini territory at his urging, he had to go with them, he had no question of that at all—no way out of this, no real desire for one—only an urge to get back to Tirnamardi as fast as this weary beast could carry his aching bones. He was ever so sorry to have involved his bodyguard in this mess, and ever to have mentioned the word *Taiben* in that message, and wished he and they had better choices, or that he had made better ones years ago, when there had been a chance to dissuade Tatiseigi from his flirtation with Kadigidi rebels.

Power-seeking. Political games. The old, old reason.

Hell of a mess, was what it was.

He held his mecheita still beside Tano's. The rangers sorted themselves onto their mecheiti, with few words exchanged in the process. The two bands had stayed somewhat apart, the herd-leaders having come to a tusk-brandishing statement of dominance, so that there was a primary and a secondary leader—even possible that the mecheiti had been one herd before this . . . such thoughts drifted through a dazed human brain. He only knew this batch wanted to clump together, and that put him with his own bodyguard, and meant they would react that way in a fracas, which he much preferred. And now that they moved, they headed cross-country, as directly toward Tirnamardi's distant fence as they could dead-reckon it, by what he could tell. He settled himself to the even gait, trying not to wonder what might have happened back at the estate, but he could not help it. The Kadigidi might have gotten in. The dowager might have perished. He detected Banichi at least trying to get information by tuning in the pocket-com, but only briefly. "Can you tell anything?" he heard Jago ask him, and Banichi:

"No transmissions."

It did nothing to comfort any of them. He would have gone all out. But mecheiti who had been run all night had self-protection enough not to kill themselves, and as the day dawned, clouded and dim, the mecheiti of their party slowed, and slowed further. The rangers, in the lead, dropped the pace, until finally they stopped for water at one of the loops of their meandering brook.

"Rest an hour," Deiso decreed. "Keep under saddle, nadiin, nandi."

An hour. An hour of delay. He wanted to be there. He wanted that hour to be past, but there was no choice. He slid down his mecheita's rock-hard side, the creature so bone-weary it was already in the process of sitting down. It folded its legs and settled and his feet hit the ground. He sank down to sit leaning against its sweaty warmth, rested there, propped up, eyes shut, deliberately, concentratedly relaxing muscles that had been tense for hours, one at a time, starting with the toes and fingers.

Bodies gathered around him, one and the other, atevi, warm and as bent as he on rest, no talk, not a word out of any of them, a mortal comfort. Safety, in an unsafe world.

Silence for a space and inner dark. A mecheita snorted: that was the wake-up. His companions moved at once, and the mecheita Bren was leaning on suddenly decided to get up. Hands reached. Jago pulled him to his feet.

All the mecheiti were getting up. Time to be under

way, Bren thought, and wordlessly turned to grab the saddle, but Jago's hand fell on his shoulder and caught his attention. Mecheiti had gone on the alert.

Riders were coming in, riders in dark green and brown, more rangers—and bringing in a sizeable herd of mecheiti with them. Bren gazed at them with rising hope that they could now make speed—and indeed, with hardly a dozen words of discussion with Deiso, the rangers started shifting saddles about, theirs and everyone's, in an economy of motion and fuss that argued this must have been the order that had gone back to Taiben, and that the youngsters had gotten there safely, or somehow delivered their message and reached another band of Keimi's men. He counted. They were no longer fourteen; they were thirty-three, a sizeable force, and armed, and Jago saddled him a mecheita that had not carried weight all night, a creature herd-bound to the rangers' mounts.

He stood there with his legs shivering under him, exhausted, and knowing his own staff, including Jago, who handled that saddle as if it were a feather, must be feeling it in their bones. She secured the girth. He reached and touched Jago's arm, that human-primate move, and she set a hand on his shoulder, that atevi instinct, bunching closer, group-made-solid.

"Can you do it, Bren-ji?"

"No question," he said, and she took hold of him and lifted him up to the saddle, while Deiso and his people saw to the details, and exchanged rapidfire briefings the gist of which he caught in a half-sleeping haze. Yes, the youngsters had met up with them, yes, Cajeiri and his young bodyguard were safely on their way to Taiben— did he dream that? He fought mental drifting, brought his head up sharply and caught his balance as a strange mecheita moved under him. Stupid, he chided himself, to be falling off to sleep—he was apt to fall right out of the saddle; but he had been roused up out of a dark spot and handed information none of which was fitting together, not all of which made clear sense. The children were safe. This party was the aggregate of Deiso's party, that had been out probing Atageini land for trouble since the gunfire. The other had been hunting trouble that might try to come around the Atageini flank—defending an old curmudgeon who didn't want to be defended by Taibeni, but doing it all unasked, as their own best defense, only common sense, he heard Tano say.

Yes, they had seen the fire last night, and they had come across the children, heard the story, and sent them on to Keimi.

Thank God, Bren thought, in his private darkness, behind closed lids. Thank God. He could let go his worry for the youngsters.

"They will be safe, nandi," he heard from Tano, and from Banichi himself:

"Keimi thinks the Atageini will be only a first step, that the Kadigidi will probe into Taiben as far as they can. They intend to stop that."

"Wise of him." More than wise. Necessary. He rubbed his eyes, making them stay open . . . his mind spiraled off into one of those fugues, those desperate quests after disconnected information, looking for hooks to tie things together. Woodland and meadow. The long stretch of Atageini hunting land, long in dispute, rolling away to Tirnamardi, the source of game for Atageini tables, a no-man's-land between two associations long in contention—

Contention in which the Taibeni, closely bound to Tabini-aiji, had looked suspiciously on the Atageini's dalliance with the Kadigidi, that old lowlander, central province association that had coveted Taiben's woods, cut down trees, intruded into the highlands in countless raids, before the modern age.

Now Taiben came onto land they historically, before the clearing of these meadows, regarded as their own— bitter, bitter pill, the dowager's insistence on Tatiseigi's putting his seal to that letter. Tatiseigi would have an apoplexy if he knew the Taibeni had come in without it.

But Tatiseigi could pitch his fit. It was another thought he was chasing through the underbrush, beyond the Kadigidi-Atageini affair: another old, old association: the woodlands, the highlands, the long sweep of surviving woodland that swept right around the flank of the Kadigidi, woodland toward the west, outflanking the lowland association, serving as a barrier against lowland expansion. Come into that forest, and die.

Richness of game. Cover for movement . . . Atageini towns, historically, more afraid of those woods than they were of the plains-based Kadigidi. They would not go into the north. Would not intrude there. Would not poach that land, only appealed to their lord in Tirnamardi when game herds spilled over and damaged their crops . . .

Dusty papers, books, research in his cramped little office, the week he had succeeded Wilson-paidhi, all those years ago. Sunlight slanting through the window of the single room, its shelves piled high with books, facts obscuring truth in sheer abundance of paper . . .

Blink. Hindbrain made conclusions. Realized they had traveled northwest, away from the road. Were going due east from their meeting-spot, aimed at that long, long hedge and fence. They weren't going in the gate.

Blink, again. Tabini had stopped on Atageini land, paid his visit, played his politics; and the Atageini had stayed firmly bound to the aishidi'tat, not falling in with the Kadigidi, not trusting, so long as Lady Damiri stayed bound to Tabini-aiji, any blandishments of the Kadigidi—because the Kadigidi would never rely on the Atageini lord, not with Damiri mothering Tabini's heir, Tatiseigi's kinsman . . .

Taiben had reason to think the Kadigidi would push the Atageini and that the old man ruling at Tirnamardi would have no choice but to play politics, having no force, no great establishment of security and weaponry such as Taiben had built during Tabini-aiji's rule.

That mathematics went on in the dowager's head, no question. No question his staff had understood it in all its permutations, with no word said among them. He began to have his own gut feeling that maybe his suggesting Taiben had never been a bad idea, that the dowager had been inclining in that direction and hadn't seen quite how to do it ... until she pounced on Cajeiri as the key part of the equation, necessary to tip the old man into compliance. Atevi, he had long suspected, didn't always logic their way through such calculations at etherial distance: they felt the pull of clan and house and influence, they moved, they acted in a peculiar symmetry, and, cold and logical as the dowager could be—she might have had a piece snapped into place for her, thanks to him. Or had she, damn her, forced a move?

Gut-sense said their little band was going in the right direction now, if not before. Safety was behind them. Chaos was swirling around Tirnamardi, trying to destroy the dowager, to suck the lord of the Atageini right down into it—damned right, the dowager had known the hazard, known that a very key player would be tottering, the more as their arrival onworld shoved hard at the situation—what was Tatiseigi going to think when they came back, if they didn't come to him and expect his help?

And what, conversely, were the Kadigidi going to assume as fact, when he hosted the dowager? Every atevi involved in this mess had to feel the swing of that internal compass: man'chi. Man'chi applied even to him, as clearly as he had ever had that sense, and the dowager pushing every button she could reach ... setting herself right at the crux of the matter and demanding extravagant action. Come and save us—move, if you have any disposition to move, and the hell with waiting for it.

Atevi weren't given to fighting wars. Not often. But one was certainly shaping up here. Not just the usual skirmish, the usual Guild action, the fall of critical leaders: this was in one sense a small skirmish, but it happened on the dividing line between two forces, and the Guild, such as it was, had begun to engage—his staff, on this side. Kadigidi, on the other . . . and the only thing Ilisidi hadn't foreseen was the boy, of all her resources, kiting off to Taiben, following his *own* developing instincts. Cajeiri had forced every power in play to readjust position . . . the boy had been under intolerable pressure, seen the situation, and, being his father's son, he'd *moved*, damn his young hide, seized power of his own, without consulting his great-grandmother.

Atevi mathematics. Calculations he had to logic his way through. And now the fool human was riding the wave back again, having gathered force enough, he hoped to God—force that looked, by cold daylight, a little less precise, a little more weather-worn, Jago's hair for once straying a few wisps out of her braid, their uniforms, even their faces smudged with pale trail-dust, frown-lines appearing that did not exist, otherwise. Exhausted. All of them, Deiso and the rangers as well, not to mention the beasts that carried them. It was a dangerous condition, and logic had nothing to do with what they were doing now, except evolutionary logic—mass movement of the forces across the continent, politics on its grandest scale.

They rode, leaving the mecheiti that had carried them outward to graze, rest, and wander on their own logic back to Taibeni territory, or to trail after them if they were so inclined. The sun rose. The landscape passed in a haze of autumn grass, low scrub, the rolling hills. No one explained or talked or wondered. They all knew. Even the human did, now. Bren shut his eyes, locked his leg across the beast's neck, trapped under his other knee, wrapping his arms as close to his center of gravity as he could, and for a few moments at a time he found he could rest, waking in a kind of daze, with no coherent thought beyond a realization that, yes, check of the internal compass, they were still headed east, to Tirnamardi, and, no, he hadn't fallen off. No one spoke, which suited him, and the thunderous quiet began to seem the whole universe, closer and closer to an armageddon that wasn't going to involve humans—except this one. There was some solace in that.

Eyes shut again.

Opened. The world had hushed. Stopped moving. He was still in the saddle.

"Nandi." A ranger was standing beside his right leg, offering him up a canteen and a stick of concentrate. He discovered hunger he hadn't known he had, wolfed the small bar down, barely a bite for an ateva, and drank deeply before he gave the canteen back.

Awake, this time, fugue-state never having produced specific information, only a general centering where he was, in what course he was taking. He had no interest at all in dismounting and having to climb up again. He was settled. He might die on mecheita-back, somewhere across that intervening distance. At least he wouldn't have to walk there to do it.

Banichi rode alongside for a moment, inquired how he fared.

"Well enough," he said. "Well enough, Banichi-ji." He asked no opinions. In the headlong rush of elements in this chaos, there was nothing orderly at all. Jago was near him. Tano and Algini were behind him. That was what he needed. That was what they all needed. It was an atevi sorting-out, as necessary to them as the mecheiti moving with their leader. He was the one with the illusion of absolute choice. And where was he? Where his heart led him. Going to get the dowager out of a mess. End of all questions.

And having discovered that, shortly after they set to moving again, he let his head droop and honestly fell asleep—waked, suddenly, as balance changed, his heart skipping a beat. They had hit a long downward slope. A dark bar crossed the meadow ahead, and, bewildering him for the instant, the sun had somehow sunk well down the sky—

God, how had they gotten this far, this late? He both wanted to be closer, and was appalled that they were this close, choices, if there ever had been, steadily diminishing. Was there a better political answer? The paidhi was supposed to find them, if they existed, and he was bereft of other ideas. Was there better than going along that fence, or finding the hunting gate Lord Tatiseigi had said existed? His staff had that expertise, if there was a way.

A smell wafted on the wind, faint scent of disaster, urging they had no time for alternatives, that maybe they were already out of time.

"Smoke, nadiin," he said. It was not a strong smell. It was wind-scattered, but he was very sure of it, and he was sure they had caught it, too, and drawn their own unhappy conclusions.

"There will have been plenty of it, one fears," Banichi said. "But there has been no more sound such as last night. Scattered gunfire."

"They are still shooting?" He took that for hope.

"Sporadically so, nadi," Banichi informed him, and he cherished that thought as they rode the long slow roll to the crest of the next hill.

From there they had that view they had had on a prior evening, with Atageini farmland to the north, in the distance, and their bar, mostly arrow-straight, resolved as one part of the considerable hedges and fence of Tirnamardi's grounds.

They rode closer. There was no visible smoke rising, but the smell persisted. Banichi listened, with the com unit, and shook his head, riding ahead to confer briefly with Deiso and his wife.

There was no view of the house at this distance. It lay behind a roll of the land. The hedge grew more distinct in their view, with no variance. He wished he had binoculars.

The conference between Banichi and the rangers

continued. Their pace slowed, and came to a halt just off the crest of the hill, down in a low spot where they wouldn't present a hilltop silhouette to observers near the hedge. The whole group bunched up, mecheiti sorting into a lazy order, dipping their heads to catch a mouthful of volunteer grain that had strayed from farmer's fields into the the meadow grass.

A glance westward showed color. The sun had begun to stain the sky at their backs.

And the conference continued.

Shots, Banichi had said. Sniping. They were coming in to overset whatever balance had been struck.

Towns existed north and south of here, and some further east. There was no sign yet, of a wider conflict, of farmers and craftsmen drawn into what still remained, thus far, a matter for lords and Guild. That might yet happen. If passions were too far stirred, it could well happen, common clansmen against common clansmen of the neighboring province—that was what they had to avert. It was the lords' job to prevent it.

And that—the scattered bits from his musings began to try to gel—the lords had to get provocations away from the people. If they had not lost the dowager already, their own last and best chance—with Cajeiri safely committed to Taiben—was to snatch up Ilisidi and veer around Tirnamardi *and* the Kadigidi, northeastward, through those forestland corridors and toward the mountains, where his best guess said he might find Tabini, or at least find help. Those mountains, hazed in twilight, floated above the landscape where they waited, a vision distant as the moon in the sky, and seeming downright as difficult to attain, bone-weary as they were.

He could, if he were a coward, draw off his staff, even yet, pick up Cajeiri, get back to the coast and try to raise support in the north, maybe even back off to Mospheira and make another try from there. His mind was awake.

Alternatives were spinning through the attic of his thoughts, none viable.

Folly, riding in there, blind and possibly much too late. He contained so much knowledge—but, ironically, it was knowledge an eight-year-old boy had, that Jase had, the star that was the station and the ship not yet apparent, but he knew it was there, and that thought held like an anchor. For once in his life he had backup, of sorts, and he could afford a risk. He could be a total fool, charging into the situation, as if he could rescue the two oldest, canniest connivers in all the aishidi'tat . . .

Ilisidi wouldn't call him a fool. *She'd* bet on him showing up. Probably so would Cenedi, who wouldn't have gone throwing his life away on an attack against the Kadigidi. *She* would be thinking about those mountains, too, and yet still stood by a pivotal old politicking fool, to be sure he didn't collapse and cave in the belly of the aishidi'tat—

Forcing the issue, damn her. Forcing all of them. Forcing the Guild itself, from its perch in Shejidan, to have a look at the escalating chaos . . . and to face a new fact: that Murini-aiji didn't control the middle lands or the north.

Banichi rode back to them, swinging his mecheita in close. Jago moved near, companionably. And a movement in the tail of Bren's eye advised him one of the rangers had gotten down, and now left afoot, running.

"Toward the hunting gate?" he asked his staff.

"Not that far, nandi," Banichi said. "Get down. We shall, to rest here and wait. He should make the fence about twilight."

Half an hour or so. Banichi himself dismounted, while his mecheita resumed interest in the scattered heads of grain. Bren experimentally slung both legs over the side, his mecheita likewise occupied, and slid down. Banichi caught him under the arms and set him down gently as if he were Cajeiri.

"There," Banichi said gently. "Go sit down, Bren-ji. Your staff has business with the Taibeni."

"If I have a regret, nadiin-ji, it is ever bringing you into this situation."

"The paidhi-aiji's company is usually interesting." A wry smile from Banichi. He couldn't help but laugh, however thin and soundless it came out, and however upset it left him.

"Go," Jago said, laying a hand on his shoulder. "Rest, Bren-ji. Your company may be interesting. But our talk will be dry detail."

A stray civil servant, indeed, wasn't highly useful to Guild at this point, particularly Guild trying to think of all possible eventualities. He took Banichi's advice, walked over to a spot where it seemed little likely that mecheiti would step on him. There he sat down, knees drawn up, head on hands for a moment. He seemed to have filled his quota of sleep, such as it had been. Rest seemed unlikely. Clear thought was not producing any comfort. Seeking some occupation for his hands, then, he unloaded his gun, checked its condition and blew out a little lint before he reloaded, all the while trying not to think more than five minutes ahead of him.

He never had mastered that knack.

13

Wind blew the grass, clouds moved with incredible slowness, the mecheiti grazed, one of them always head-up, watching the surrounds. And a close band of atevi sat laying plans while the sun went down.

Bren wished he could sleep. He couldn't. He sat, rested his knees together in front of him, feet apart, and his arms against him, not a graceful position, but one that kept him mostly off the cold ground, and kept the wind at his back—since wind there had begun to be, now, a brisk wind that equaled the chill of the ground, against which his jacket was no defense at all.

The sun slipped past the edge of the world, and he rested his head down, aware that his bodyguard had come back to him and settled down to rest. He wouldn't make them go through it all again for his information— he wouldn't rob them of the sleep they'd won, and pursued, while strangers watched over them.

He did drift, waked in total disorientation, still sitting up, conscious of complete night, of movement around him, and for a single panicked moment not knowing what mecheiti were doing in his cabin.

Atageini land, a hellish mess, the dowager somewhere beyond that ridge, and Banichi and Jago up talking to people who were, yes, Taiben rangers. Tano and Algini were with him, one on a side, and everything was, considering the presence of a couple of dozen mecheiti, very quiet, very hushed. He didn't want to chatter questions. But he tried to get his legs to move. It took a couple of efforts and finally Algini's help to get up. He stood, a little embarrassed, rubbed numb spots, not an elegant process.

"Our spy is back," Algini told him.

"What do we know?"

"The house remains protected, and inner defenses are still live, nandi,"

Supremely good news, and it represented a great risk on the part of the ranger that had gone in to find out.

"The estate perimeter fence is inactive," Tano said. "One believes they have taken the house as the sole point of resistence, and the stable burned, which was likely the light we saw, but overall the house is still a point of resistence, and one believes now the neighboring towns may feel it necessary to intervene."

Not good news. Townsmen who elected to get involved in a Guild action were as likely to create confusion for their own side, and the Guild on the other side would not spare them.

"We are moving in, nadiin?"

"One believes so," Algini said.

Time he did talk to Banichi and Jago. He walked, still massaging a stiff leg, over to the conference.

"Likely we can get inside, nandi," Deiso said as he joined them. "Getting out again—if they add forces—may be a very great difficulty. One advises your lordship retreat at this point."

"No," Bren said without even thinking on it. "No. If my staff goes in, I go. And we know the inside."

Outrageous, in atevi terms. He only dimly reckoned that, after it came out of his mouth.

"Reason with him, nadi," Deiso said.

"He is capable, no matter his size," Banichi said, entirely unexpected, and the statement sent a little quiver of adrenaline through his nerves. *Capable*, he was. It was better than Lord of the Heavens.

And he had no wish, after Banichi saying that, to act the fool. He folded his arms and listened to Banichi lay out the plan, attempting dignity, and silently absorbing the simple outline, which was to go in the way the scout had: he had gotten through without problems at the fence. The rangers had wire-cutters in their collective kit, and meant to go in without need of going the long way round.

Crosscountry, from the fence to the house, trusting other defenses would be down, since their scout had met none.

After that . . .

After that, they approached the house—in the fervent hope they were not too late.

"A wonder they withstood the first attack," Banichi said, "except the first incursion was a probe. Maodi is the chief of Guild that serves the Kadigidi. A ruthless sort, but not reckless, and if Murini is in Shejidan, as we have reported, that means Maodi will be there, not here—he will not want to stain his hands or his lord's with this unneighborly move. That means secondary force is involved, and one perceives they were tentative, not committing great force."

" Tonight," Deiso said, "tonight they will bring force in. We have other bands coming, and they may be here before daylight. But we ought not to wait for an outcome, nandi."

"Whatever Banichi says," Bren stated, "I accept."

More Taibeni forces coming in behind them was good news; but the chance of the Kadigidi getting in and slaughtering the household—not considering the Kadigidi might have agents on the inside . . . he was very ready to go without them. He would be dismayed if Banichi counseled waiting any longer.

"The paidhi is with us," Banichi said.

"No question," Bren said, and Deiso:

"Then we should move, should we not?"

Ten thousand questions, a whole world he wanted to know—but certainties were not available. He went back to his mecheita. The rangers mounted up, and he did, and fell in with his own staff. The band started to move eastward, in the deepening dark, up the low rise and down again. Clouds had moved across the stars, taking away even the starlight, and a breeze-borne chill swept down at their faces, numbed his hands and made him wish, not for the first time on this trek, that he had at least remembered his gloves, and put on a sweater under his coat. No Narani, that was what it was. He had gotten used to such items turning up in his pockets. Now all he had was his gun, his useless pocket com, his pill bottle, and a spare clip.

He ought to be terrified. He actually wasn't sure about that, then decided what he felt wasn't quite fear, rather a sense of fatalism, of foreboding—that he really, truly couldn't envision their success in this operation, or more to the point, envision exactly what they were going to do once they had gotten onto the grounds and rescued the dowager, even granted their success. He doubted Ilisidi was up to a long, breakneck ride—she'd surprised him before, but she'd been out of the saddle for two years herself. And even if she could surprise him, he knew of a certainty that Lord Tatiseigi wasn't up to it—and what were they to do to prevent consequences from overwhelming the one key lord in the middle provinces?

Over all, he feared they were going to have to stand and fight to keep Tatiseigi and the dowager alive, hoping for their own numbers to increase, as surely the Kadigidi were going to bring in reinforcements. Which would be very bad for the Atageini house, and its fragile lilies . . . worse for its surrounding towns, and their peaceful existence. The farmers—the locals—could have their whole structure blown to bits . . . vulnerable as the porcelain lilies.

His own affairs—he had wrapped up, leaving the next tries to Jase and Yolanda. He had delivered Cajeiri into the hands of his Taibeni relatives, to get to his father if they could. He trusted Toby was back on the island, likely hovering near the shortwave and hoping for news . . .

God, this was morbid, cataloging and disposing of all his ties to the world. But the ruler he served seemed less and less likely to get back to power, the more blood they poured on the matter, and if it didn't happen, the world didn't need a paidhi whose advice had led to civil war and bodies lying in windrows. . . .

That was the underlying thought, wasn't it? There was a certain justice in his being here, and he had run out of remedies. If he sent his staff off to take up service with Cajeiri, in the first place, they wouldn't go, and if he went, himself, it would bring Cajeiri association with him. Everything seemed circular reasoning. Everything led where he was . . . which left him unable to see the outcome. He couldn't even see how it mattered, except he might kill some Guildsman who adhered to the Kadigidi, and they might kill him, and nothing, in the long run, would get fixed, not by him, would it?

Maybe by Jase. Maybe by Lord Geigi, who could sit up in the heavens and say, you idiots, I told you so. Are you ready to stop killing each other?

Because the kyo would show up. And somebody had to be in charge. He was sure of that, as sure as he was that the whole current enterprise was unlikely to succeed.

Once he analyzed it that way, he began to have a roadmap of what they had to do, and what constituted a win—if only raising enough hell on the planet that Geigi and Jase got wind of his failure early, before the Kadigidi could capitalize on their win.

At best, getting Ilisidi back to Taiben and making the Kadigidi look a little less powerful than they claimed. That would put egg on their faces . . . start one hell of a war, but it wouldn't leave the world to Murini's nonexistent common sense. Get Ilisidi to Taiben. That prospect might even budge Tatiseigi to go, be it in that antique roadster, not to mention the Kadigidi would never be able to claim the man'chi of the Atageini populace . . . who would rally to their oldest enemies, the Taibeni, and create a very hard kernel of resistence right next to the Kadigidi.

Damn, he was starting to think again, not on a cosmic scale, not of the politics of species, but in the dirt and sweat world of detailed politics and the knack of leaving an enemy looking less successful, while one's own tattered cause emerged looking as if it had won something. Atevi, like humans, dearly loved a neatly carried action, an outrageous enterprise.

He became downright foolishly cheerful, as cheerful, at least, as contemplating the necessary obverse of that coin could let him be. The wind altogether seemed a little warmer, the dark a great deal friendlier to them.

Give the Kadigidi a surprise? Maybe. His backside had passed the tingling point, far past pain, where the jouncing and jolting of the mecheita's gait was concerned; he could ignore discomfort, now. The darkened landscape passed in a shadow-play of his own staff riding near and then past him and back again, the rangers tending to the lead, in a territory they seemed to know much better than Lord Tatiseigi might like—down one long slope and another, and finally toward a dark line of shadow that his eyes began to resolve as artificial, the hedge that would conceal a fence, the estate boundary.

It came closer and closer until it barred off their forward progress, an ancient hedge more than head high to a mecheita, thick and tangled and stubborn—and how they could possibly pass it, he had no idea . . . but their scout had.

They drew up to a hard-breathing halt in front of that barrier, and a number of the rangers slid down and took equipment from their saddle-packs. Some of them bodily forced the hedge aside, one attaching a rope to his saddle and urging his mecheita to turn and pull, which bent two ancient parts of the hedge aside. Then men set to work with hand-axes, others spelling the effort in quick succession, so that the rhythm and strength of the blows never flagged for a moment. The center of each bush began to give way, and once they gave, another ranger pressed into the gap and set to work on the chain link fence, sharp, quick snaps of a wire-cutter: Lord Tatiseigi's fences and the Taiben rangers seemed, by what he saw, an old, old matter. Bren sat his saddle, shivering alike from anticipation and from the chill breeze that ruffled the grass even in the hedge-shadow. Thunder rumbled out of the west. Lightning was not their friend, not in terms of being the tallest items in the landscape, and not in terms of secrecy in this invasion.

But the fence, thank God, was no longer carrying a charge ... the house had ordered defenses lowered. But had they ever gone up again? He thought of the Atageini gatekeeper, alone out there. The man might not have survived the night.

Not to mention the destruction that might have fallen on the house itself. He saw Banichi check the pocket com for information, detected nothing unexpected in Banichi's demeanor—it had told them nothing it had not told them before.

The wire-cutter meanwhile did its work. Rangers forced their way into the gap and pulled, and the fence, gleaming faintly metallic in the dark, peeled back on either side of the missing bush, and now Deiso quirted the herd-leader through the gap, breaking brush and probably losing a little hide off him and the mecheita in the process.

Bren grabbed for a hold on the saddle as the whole herd decided to go through that atevi-sized gap at once, his own fighting to get ahead of others. Brush broke. Bren had a chaotic view of chain-link bent aside and flattened, and then his mecheita scraped through, dragging his right knee painfully past an unyielding broken branch and ripping his trousers in the process.

They were onto the estate grounds, then, with a single mecheita's wounded protest. The rangers still afoot had scrambled to the saddle and come through, joining the moving mass. Bren found Banichi on one side of him and Tano on the other, with, he was sure, Algini and Jago just off to their respective sides, in a breathless confusion of mecheiti sorting out their traveling order and broadening their front. A peevish toss of a head, tusks gleaming in the dark, an answering snort and head-toss, riders maneuvering as they picked up the pace.

They were on Lord Tatiseigi's land, now, concealed by a clouded dark, and coming in at a thirty-degree angle to the front door of the house, the opposite side from the stables . . . Bren had at least the glimmering of an idea where they were, a kilometer or so yet to go; and a remarkably clear notion of what they were going to do once they got there, which was to get as close as they could, dismount, and conduct a Guild-against-Guild operation around the house hedges, a sort of conflict in which one human with a sidearm was not outstandingly much help.

Deep breath. The mecheiti hit their traveling pace. Too late for second thoughts. His gun was safe in a fastened pocket, so it wouldn't fall out. Extra clip in his inside pocket. He hoped against all instinct that the core of Tatiseigi's questionable staff was loyal; he hoped the dowager was still safe, and that Cenedi was.

Over another low rise, and now the house itself showed on the opposing ridge, a dark lump amid dark hedges, not a glimmer of light.

Then a sullen glow, like an illusion. "A light," he said to those nearest, and Banichi:

"Clearly, nandi."

Not clear to his eyes. But the house was not deserted. Something was going on in an upper window.

The land pitched. They lost sight of the house on the downslope.

Then gunshots racketed through the dark, four, five, a volley so rapid there was no separating them.

Up again, into full view of the house, that looked no different than before.

"Bren-ji," Banichi said, "this sort of action will be no good place for you. Pick deep cover and get into it. And get back to the hedge and out before daylight, if we fail."

"One hears, Banichi-ji." It was not advice to ignore, no matter how it stung his pride.

An explosion and a gout of orange fire shattered the night. Two explosions, three. More fires started.

"Near the stable," Banichi said, which Bren desperately took for hope that that light in the house window had not been an invader, that there was still force holding out, deliberately provoking enemy action to get a bead on them. A spatter of gunfire racketed out, echoing.

And suddenly the leader hit an all-out pace and every mecheita followed. Bren grabbed for the saddle and recovered his balance, held rein and saddle with one hand, letting the quirt dangle as he unfastened his pocket and pulled out his pistol.

Safety off. He didn't make that elementary mistake. The landscape, the blazing fire with its rising smoke, the figures around him were all a jolted blur in the dark,. The gait was that breakneck, ground-devouring run that humped the mecheita's back and knocked the rider against the rear of the saddle—flung him all the way off, if the rider didn't keep his center of gravity forward and his leading leg locked around the mecheita's heaving shoulders. The back had to give, thus, to the sway inherent in the motion. He wasn't a novice, just a long time out of practice, and this beast had a scary habit of crashing around obstacles at the very last moment—nearsighted, he swore; but it was more than following its leader. The damned creature had suddenly taken ambition into its brain, and wanted further forward, carrying lighter weight and being suddenly full of charge-ahead enthusiasm.

Up the final rise onto a mown lawn, and the rattle of gunfire ahead seemed to have nothing to do with them. He hadn't enough hands for the quirt, the gun, the rein, and a good grip on the saddle: he had to pick the gun and the rein and trust his balance.

The house hedge showed ahead, a black wall against a red-tinged haze of smoke, and the herd leaders were undaunted—vying with one another, jostling for position, they plowed through the low obstruction like so much scrub, flattening it as they poured onto the drive and the whole herd hit the cobbles, a footing they loathed, and scrambled to get away from. The leaders dived into the stable-lane, beside the house, but a rider rode athwart his beast's head—Tano, heading him off from that charge. Then Banichi himself rode across his path, jostling his mecheita, forcing it to a complete stop on the drive.

"Get down!" Banichi yelled at him, and he questioned not an instant. His mecheita was stamping and head-tossing at Tano's beast, trying to get to the lane, and he simply flung a leg off, kept hold of his gun and slid down next to the house hedge, controlling his fall with a grip on the mounting-strap until his feet hit uneven cobbles and exhausted legs tried to buckle under him.

An atevi arm grabbed him around the ribs and one of his staff hurried him against the building, down into the hedge, an atevi hand pressed his head down—and then was gone, his staff—all of them, having left afoot, armed, and with definite intent.

Damn, he thought. They'd gotten down primarily to get him to cover. Now they were dismounted, the mecheiti having followed all the others around the corner toward the stables, and he was stuck here beneath a hedge, behind a stone corner and a second, facing hedge that didn't let him see what was going on.

He ought to stay put. He knew that. But he didn't like being near the house, which could be a target of explosives and grenades. He was in possession of one gun, of their few. He was in concealment and the hedge was as good as a highway. He wriggled behind the thick central growth of the hedge, crawled, assassin-fashion, on his elbows and belly. Gunfire rang off the stonework, and the ruined arch above the stable hedge lit with fire and smoke. His staff was doubtless in the thick of it.

More gunfire. The hedge across the stable path offered better advantage, a short crawl in the open, and he scrambled for it, forcing his way in. He came up against a metal stake that must be some of the surveillance equipment—which, God knew, might be telling the house at this very moment that there was an intruder in the brush. He felt for wires, found a conduit, wondered exactly what it led to, but there was no cut-off point, no switch available.

Not a place to linger, in any case. From his new vantage, wriggling further, he saw the stable yard, its rails down, mecheiti milling about against the skeletal ruin that had been the stable itself.

And he saw atevi moving down the drive, coming from that direction—not his staff, he feared.

Then he saw half a dozen atevi running in his direction, down the drive, toward his former hiding-spot at the corner of the house.

Not his staff, a dim judgement said, and he whipped up his gun and pasted a single shot at the house corner.

The movement halted, spun about, flattened, and now fire flew in earnest, shots chipping the stonework, ricocheting off the ruined arch over his head. He'd been right—he hoped he'd been right, that his shot had warned Banichi, that he hadn't aimed at some of Deiso's men by accident. Or—a sober second thought—Tatiseigi's.

A shot whisked through the branches above him, clipping evergreen, giving off a strange vegetative pungency in a night air choked with fire and gunpowder. He flattened himself all the way against the dirt, and heard the men who'd taken cover at his one shot now attempt to move. He sent a second shot toward the brickwork, and then, remembering what Banichi and Jago had taught him, slithered as silently as possible back along the hedge to a changed perspective, down among the roots, a much smaller target than atevi would generally be aiming at, and he had possible hiding-places an ateva wouldn't fit into.

Electric shock jolted his arm, right to the roots of his teeth. He jumped—he couldn't help it. But he didn't cry out.

He'd found the only damned live wire in the hedge.

He eased back, nursing a numb arm, and tried to figure out where that loose wire was, and what it was connnected to, which seemed to be a junction box, a little down from his position, not particularly well-protected, and cut, at this end. Deliberately disabled, and not by someone inside the house, who controlled the master cutoff.

What had been cut could be rejoined. He wondered what would happen if he did. Wondered whether it was sensors or lights connected to this line. Lights could expose his own people, as well as the other.

But there was a buildup of hostile force in his area, which was exposed, and likely nervous, hesitating to move into chancier cover where Banichi and his crew waited. He reached through the brush another few meters and located what he'd crawled over. Pulled it gently, rolled on his shoulder while shots continued to go off and uselessly chip the pale stonework near the corner.

Hell, he thought. Whatever was going on around the house, if Cenedi and the dowager were still holding out inside, they couldn't know what was going on. One thing would tell them, encourage them, give them the notion things weren't all to the attackers' liking. He dragged the wire back. Touched it to the live one.

Snap! The lights popped on and a siren blared for about a second before he jerked the wire away.

Gunfire spattered through the hedge. He hoped to God he'd not gotten anyone on his side killed. But Banichi wasn't easy to surprise. Neither, he hoped, were the Taibeni.

Then he heard a whistle he knew. Once, twice. Fortunate three.

He reconnected the wires. And all hell broke loose above his head, shots going every which way. Mecheiti squalled, and all of a sudden one broke through the hedge, catching the wire, jerking it right out of his hand.

He didn't know where it had gone. He couldn't find it. He didn't know which way his own side was. The firing kept up, and a concussion went off against the corner of the house, sending a shockwave right over him, deafening him for the moment, in a small fall of leaves.

Not a good position, he decided, and decided, too, knowing the lay of the hedges, that he'd better go back past the live wire and back toward the drive, toward that hedge that ran along the driveway cobbles—it was low, too low to conceal an ateva, and as good a cover as he could get. It was certain he'd been too active in the last few minutes to remain safe where he was.

He moved in that direction, wriggling along, finding and following the live wire, and trying not to make noise, never mind the volleys of shots that were going off on every hand.

He heard whistles. That was Banichi or Jago. He thought so. Hoped it was. He didn't want to distract them with his problems. He had the gun in hand, had counted the shots he'd made, being sure where he was in the clip. At the same time he asked himself what else there was for a weapon around the stableyard, and he tried to see what might be left of the stable wall, beyond the moving shapes of mecheiti. The herd had occupied the yard and now defended it, so far as he could tell— there was a great deal of milling about, a great bluster of snorts and head-shaking, none of which he wanted to challenge—anyone, ateva or human, who attempted the herd in that mood was taking a real chance.

A moment to regroup, lying concealed along the driveway hedge. He remembered he had the pocket com. No one had tried that mode of communication ... he'd gotten no signal from it. He didn't know but what a signal just from turning it on might be picked up, if not understood, and he decided not to try it. Just staying still and undiscovered was a contribution to their side. He could do Banichi the most good just by not getting in—

A shadow moved near him, hunkered down and creeping along the hedge. He could see the face, at least in profile, and it wasn't one of his. He was relatively sure it wasn't one of Deiso's men. Someone—one, no, two of them, attempting to maneuver along the hedge, going right past him.

Stay still? Let them pass? Let someone else handle it?

He fired, fired once and twice more, and the two men went down, one atop the other. He scrambled among the brushy growth, further down the hedge, weaving among the roots, as riflefire cracked and richocheted off the cobbles of the drive.

Pause to catch his breath. He didn't know but what there were more after him, but they wouldn't expect anyone could get underneath the spreading branches, in this small, earthy dark.

A lengthy period of quiet. A sprinkle of rain came down. He laid his head against the ground. Cold had spread through his trousers, and now through his coat, but that was only discomfort. He wasn't likely to be found if he just didn't move, didn't twitch. Except—

He caught a gleam of fire over by the stables.

Someone out there had lit a fire, spooking the mecheiti to move out. They squalled and bolted, trampling brush, some crossing the hedge. The fire blazed up and his skin shone like the moon through branches. He did all he could to keep his hands tucked and his face away from the light. He hated not looking. He heard movement outside his hiding-place. He heard a step come right beside him, and the urge to look was overwhelming.

A shot. A body hit the ground right beside him, and now he did look, and saw a man down right beside him—wounded, not dead. It wasn't one of his side; and sensible as it might be to do for him, for the safety of his own side—he scrupled to become an executioner. He scrambled to get out the other side of the hedge, eeled his way back, while, behind him, someone else tried to get to the man.

Full circle. He'd gotten back in view of the corner of the house, not well enough covered by the hedge, and by now not sure where his own side was. He wriggled underneath the branches and found himself back near the live wire.

Whistle. Banichi's. Or Jago's. He held his breath, tried to judge where it had come from, and he thought it was near him. He hunched down, face down, for a moment, to ease his position, arms under him, then looked up.

Straight at a pair of boots.

He didn't move. Scarcely breathed.

Eventually the owner of the boots crouched down and moved off. His own, or the other side, he had no idea at all. He stayed still, breathing in controlled ins and outs, listened to occasional shots, and finally, strange in the dark, heard whispers, someone discussing the situation, but faint and far. They were talking about Lord Tatiseigi, about his security arrangements.

"The old cheapskate will never afford a wire," one said, to his strained hearing. "And the power is down. Get in, take the dowager, take the heir and the paidhi, and what they do out here has no effect."

There was indeed a wire. Or two. They misjudged, and it could be messy, if the lights had been deliberately turned out and if the house still had power.

But letting them try it—was too great a risk. He

moved an elbow, eased his whole body over, and saw a knot of skulkers over beside the porch. He hated to let off a shot. He was running out of hiding places. They knew a human was in question. If they adjusted their concept of what to look for, they might suspect where he was. But he saw nothing else to do.

"Look out!" one yelled, looking his direction and moving, and he let off one shot and two and three and four at that knot of shadows, then ducked back among the roots, catching sight of a ground-floor window opening, but no one near it.

Then a couple of bodies dropped from the window down to the ground. Someone from inside the house.

He had the pocket com. He was in a position to see something. He drew a deep breath and risked turning it on for a second, adjusting it with his thumb in complete dark.

"Banichi," he whispered. "Banichi. Someone has exited the house."

Tatiseigi's men had mixed themselves into the affair.

"Stay down," the answer came to him. *"Shut it off."*

He turned the unit off, stuck it back into his pocket, hoped not to hear from it again until there was reason for Banichi to want to find him. He stayed there, face buried, listening, listening. A twitch started in his shoulder muscles.

It was quiet for very, very long after that.

He changed position, half-numb, muscles shivering from strain. He moved very, very carefully. He wiped a little mud over his face and hands and ventured a look out.

A flurry of shots ensued, and a squall of mecheiti.

He ducked back. Stayed absolutely still, relaxed, finally, except for shivers from the cold. Minutes turned into half hours, and half hours to an hour, at least. He heard absolutely no sound from anything but the restless mecheiti and the crackle of the ebbing fire over in the stable area.

He moved enough, finally, to rest his cheek against his left hand, which warmed both. The Guild could be very patient. They could stay like this for hours, waiting for something to change, and what would change was the planet turning on its axis, and sunlight coming over the horizon.

Daylight would come. At dawn things might begin to move again.

White light flared, ran across the cobbled drive. He lifted his head, peered up through the branches, seeing a spotlight glaring from an upstairs window. It played over the hedges, and off over the lawn.

Then it went out.

More waiting. He relieved the stress on his neck by dropping his head to his hand again, and wondered what was going on in the house. It had gotten ungodly complicated. If Cenedi was inside, Cenedi couldn't just shoot at whatever moved out here.

But Cenedi could just toss pebbles into the pond, looking to raise a ripple, to force whoever hadn't taken good cover to do so. That light might represent such thinking.

Or possibly Cenedi did as he had done, and signalled his rescuers that they were still alive, still in control of the house upstairs and down. He hoped that was the case.

Long, long wait. Then the spotlight flared out of another window, playing on the hedges, and running along the ground—Bren saw it through a black lattice of branches—toward the regrouped mecheiti, who disliked it, and started milling about and creating noise of their own.

The com vibrated. Bren laid his pistol on the ground and dug the device out of his pocket, pressed it to his ear.

"We are on the grounds, on your trail," a voice said, and one he thought was Banichi's:

"One is advised, nadi."

The transmission cut off. If the enemy had intercepted it, that news could only make them more anxious. Day was coming. Help was coming in, from Taiben. The odds were beginning to shift.

Then a voice from somewhere far to the right, Banichi's, loud and clear.

"Kadigidi. Our allies are moving in. Atageini forces are coming in. Clear the grounds. Guild truce. Recover your wounded and go."

Bren moved his hand to his gun, slipped his fingers around it, lay there, expecting a volley of shots to pursue that voice.

"Guild truce," a clear voice came back.

And thereafter small movements began, one very, very close at hand. Bren lay hardly breathing as a shadow left the hedge, evergreen whispering, oh, so quietly. Small movements went on, increasing in the vicinity of the stables, and mecheiti took exception.

Further and further away, those sounds moved. He had heard of such things, that the Guild, being a professional brotherhood, would limit damages, that there were mechanisms to prevent the waste of lives, among those who, in the Guild hall, might share a pot of tea.

Then silence, long silence. If Banichi wanted to move out and trust it was safe, Banichi would move, but Banichi did not, nor was there any sound at all but the mecheiti milling about. Bren lay there, chilled through, his fingers no longer feeling the gun. He didn't know if anyone ever agreed to, then violated Guild truce. A very great deal was at stake, and if no one ever had done such a thing in the history of the Guild, it still might not mean safety. There were non-Guild who sometimes mixed into these affairs—like him. It had all been stealthy—thus far.

The next round . . . who knew? Airplanes. Bombs. He didn't like to think what the day might bring.

But if they went that far, if it got beyond Guild, then the farmers and the shopkeepers *would* take a hand.

And it would be bloody war, with farmers on this side attacking farmers on the other. Utter disaster. Everything they had done last night was one thing. They never wanted it to get to the utmost.

Long, long wait. He took up the com unit in his left hand, rested his chin on that wrist, waited.

It vibrated, and he had it to his ear in a heartbeat.

"Bren-ji?" Jago's whisper, blessed sound.

"I'm fine," he whispered back.

"Are you in a safe position?"

Amazing that Jago had to ask him. He'd learned a few things in his career. One of them was not to blurt out his position on a compromised communications system. "Are they gone?" He had heard no mecheiti leaving.

"We think so. But we shall not trust them. Work your way toward the stable path. Algini will meet you. Our allies will be here in moments."

He shut down, pocketed the com and wriggled forward, following the curve of the drive. He could only think of Taibeni allies inbound, and the fact that he didn't know the sort of signals the rangers passed, or the Guild, either, for that matter. He slithered among the roots, beside another wire, another connection, and up where the stable path left. A shape crouched there, watching, the slight gleam of starlight on a rifle-barrel.

He stopped, frozen, the instant he realized that shape.

"Bren-ji?" it asked.

Algini. He moved again, as far as the path that divided them.

"Stay still, nandi," Algini said. "Stay as you are."

He was no longer alone, at least. And in a moment more, another figure turned up, crouching low along the hedges. Tano, he was relatively sure.

There was quiet, a lengthy quiet. He put the safety on the gun, at least, feeling that secure, and put it into his pocket, so as not to get dirt in it. But beyond that, he didn't move.

The mecheiti began to stir. One called out.

They're coming, he said to himself. Their help was coming in.

He lowered his forehead against his hand and drew several even breaths, listening, listening as the mecheiti decided, unrestrained, to go wandering out along the stableyard walk, one passing right by them, but, disliking the cobbles of the drive, not going further. His position was becoming untenable not because of enemy action, but because of mecheiti.

He eeled forward and got up as far as his knees, when Tano seized his elbow and hauled him back, as all of a sudden mecheiti poured past onto the hated cobbles, and other mecheiti came crashing through the ruined hedge on the other side of the drive.

"Taiben!" someone called out, and from further down the path, another recognition.

"Cajeiri got there," Bren ventured.

"One believes a message did," Banichi said, appearing near them. "One hopes that he got there."

He was numb. He watched the mecheiti milling about, and then a tall rider drew up in front of them and slid down to the cobbled drive.

"Bren-ji," that man said, in a resonant voice that, once heard, was never forgotten.

"Aiji-ma!" Bren said, with no doubt at all. One never hugged atevi, least of all one's lord, but it was, it very much was Tabini-aiji.

"One somehow knew Bren-nandi was at the heart of all this fire and smoke," Tabini said. "Where is my grandmother?"

"In the house, aiji-ma, at least one hopes she is."

No hesitation, no explanations. A tall figure, wide-shouldered and clad in Assassin's black, Tabini strode off toward the house steps. A woman in ranger's green joined him, and two other Assassins in black—Damiri and Tabini's guard, Bren had no doubt, though he was still stunned. He watched the bodyguard stride to the fore and heard them hail the house.

"Open to Tabini-aiji, nadiin!"

Bren felt Banichi's hand on his shoulder, and flinched as lights went on in the house, porch lights and all, throwing the milling, squalling crowd of mecheiti and riders on the driveway into relief.

And lighting the several figures on the steps.

Jago had come up beside. Bren found his legs a little uncertain. He was cold, he was filthy, but when his bodyguard moved toward the lighted porch, he walked with them, toward the handful of figures that had gone inside, into the battered hallway.

The lilies in that foyer had, unhappily, suffered in the assault. Bits of porcelain facade lay as white and green rubble on the floor where Tabini and his lady walked. Bren came in behind them, with his guard, and Nawari came into view at the top of the steps, while a few of the Atageini guard appeared behind him in the dimly-lit upper landing hall.

"Lord Tatiseigi?" Tabini's voice rang out in that vacancy. "Grandmother?"

"Grandson." The dowager's voice from the hall above. The fierce stamp of her cane echoed up and down in the stone stairways and shocked nerves lately acclimated to gunshots. "About damned time you showed up, young man! Have you seen your rascal of a son lately?"

Tea, incredibly, hot tea, served to Lord Tatiseigi's guests in the damaged sitting-room . . . while a great deal of confusion went on outside, noise of men, and, over all, the squalling complaints of irate mecheiti.

A Taiben ranger, Keimi himself, sat taking tea in the Atageini hall with Lord Tatiseigi, not to mention Tabini-aiji, Lady Damiri, the aiji-dowager, and the just-arrived mayor of Hegian, who had rallied three other local lords and their very minor bodyguards in a brave and enterprising move to cut off the Kadigidi's second advance without involving their towns, a little light, a little noise, well-placed rifles. The amount of racket alone, one might judge, had persuaded the intruders they had tripped a wider alarm than they had looked for.

The driveway, meanwhile, was full of the Atageini home guard, who had arrived in several noisy farm trucks, and, precariously situated near them, a sizeable contingent of Taibeni rangers, arrived in advance of that guard, and camped with their mecheiti on what had been a manicured lawn.

"Outlaws," Tatiseigi complained, not, in this instance, meaning the Taiben lord sipping tea at his elbow. "Outlaws! Renegades! And employed on my own staff! There were traitors!"

"We will see to that matter," Tabini said. "We have names." He had grown thinner, and grimly sober. He wore Assassins' leather, black, with only a thin red scarf about the right arm to betoken his house colors. The sight and sound of him was still incredibly good to have. "But we have a long way to go, nandiin, to remove Murini from Shejidan."

No hint of blame, Bren thought, no indication Tabini blamed the source of his advice. It by no means absolved him.

"We shall send letters," Tatiseigi said, "strong letters, to the Guild and to the legislature."

"Letters," Ilisidi scoffed. "We shall do better than letters, this round, Tati-ji."

"You," Tabini said, "should take yourself to Taiben, mani-ma, and take care of your great-grandson."

"Advice from my grandson, who spent his time skulking in the woods, with never a message to us when we were there!"

"Grandmother," Tabini interjected, reasonably. "I was in the hills, somewhat further on. You came here, doubtless to raise a furor that I would hear, and I heard, and our hosts' foyer is, unhappily, a ruin, by no fault of his."

The paidhi sipped his tea, aware, at the bottom of everything, that some commotion had arrived outside, and that staff had moved, even security moving from their posts to have a look at the door.

"I swear I would sacrifice the lilies," Tatiseigi said, to whom that was a very bitter sacrifice indeed, "for my hands on the scoundrels that dared sit on my staff and plot against their own comrades. You believe the downstairs is a shambles, aiji-ma. You should see the upper hall! You will see it, unhappily, in your lodgings."

"We are by no means sure we should stay the night," Tabini said. "We should take ourselves back to the hills."

"And leave us to deal with the Kadigidi?" This from Ilisidi. "No! We have every right to advance over their border and settle accounts. This is no time for retreat!"

"We are by no means sure of success," Tatiseigi objected.

"We have help from Taiben, we have my elusive grandson and doubtless resources from the Guild . . ."

"The Guild remains a problem," Tabini said gravely, "and one that we cannot force."

"We have written to them," Tatiseigi said. "We have posed one complaint. We have gathered reason enough for another letter."

"Letters," Ilisidi scoffed.

There was a stir at the door, and two travelworn, dusty young Taibeni came in past the guards, and a third, not Taibeni, and not as tall—a ragamuffin of a prince, an exhausted young gentleman who had no trouble at all getting past the guards.

"Father." A hoarse, strained voice. "Mother."

Tabini got to his feet. Damiri did. And did the young gentleman do what a human would do and fling himself into a parental embrace?

No. Bren watched as the boy walked up and gave a

grave, deep bow, which father and mother returned with equal solemnity.

"You have grown," Tabini observed, and reached and laid a hand on the boy's shoulder.

"I have tried to. And I came against orders. I heard you were coming here to rescue mani-ma."

"And how did you hear that?"

"That would betray a confidence," Cajeiri said, "from someone who thought I would follow orders."

"We taught him better manners," Ilisidi said.

"You did, mani-ma. But we had to."

"Had to," Damiri said, and came and turned the boy about to face her, for a long, long look, a little touch at his cheek, which brushed away pale dust. "You *had* to."

"Yes, mother." A strange mix of regal contrition in that high, young voice. "Nand' Bren was coming back. And we had sent reinforcements ahead of us."

"Coming back," Tabini said, "from where?"

"That takes some telling," Ilisidi said, from her seat, her hands braced on her cane. "Some of which *we* are interested to hear, nandiin."

"Might there be hot tea?" Cajeiri asked, and added: "For my bodyguard, too?"

"Oh, indeed, your bodyguard?" from his father.

A great deal to tell. A great deal yet to learn, on all sides. Bren held out his tea cup for a second service and drew a deep, long breath as he took the cup back into his hands, a warm and civilized act, no matter the dusty ruin outside.

CJ Cherryh
Classic Series in New Omnibus Editions

THE DREAMING TREE
Contains the complete duology *The Dreamstone* and *The Tree of Swords and Jewels.*   0-88677-782-8

THE FADED SUN TRILOGY
Contains the complete novels *Kesrith*, *Shon'jir*, and *Kutath.*   0-88677-836-0

THE MORGAINE SAGA
Contains the complete novels *Gate of Ivrel*, *Well of Shiuan*, and *Fires of Azeroth.*   0-88677-877-8

THE CHANUR SAGA
Contains the complete novels *The Pride of Chanur*, *Chanur's Venture* and *The Kif Strike Back.*
    0-88677-930-8

ALTERNATE REALITIES
Contains the complete novels *Port Eterntiy*, *Voyager in Night*, and *Wave Without a Shore*   0-88677-946-4

AT THE EDGE OF SPACE
Contains the complete novels *Brothers of Earth* and *Hunter of Worlds.*   0-7564-0160-7

To Order Call: 1-800-788-6262

DAW 9

C.S. Friedman

The Best in Science Fiction

DAW 17

Julie E. Czerneda

THE TRADE PACT UNIVERSE

"Space adventure mixes with romance...a heck of a lot of fun." —*Locus*

Sira holds the answer to the survival of her species, the Clan, within the multi-species Trade Pact. But it will take a Human's courage to show her the way.

A THOUSAND WORDS FOR
STRANGER
0- 88677-769-0

TIES OF POWER
0-88677-850-6

TO TRADE THE STARS
0-7564-0075-9

To Order Call: 1-800-788-6262